# Black Rigg

## Mary Easson

2nd edition (revised)

First edition published in 2014 by Ringwood Publishing
Second (revised) edition published by the author 2021
Cockleroy Books, Scotland

ISBN 978-1-8383530-2-5

Typesetting and cover design by
Raspberry Creative Type

# Acknowledgements

This tale of life in a fictitious mining community is based on the social history of the Scottish coalfield before the onset of the Great War. Starting out as the introduction to a story inspired by my grandfather's wartime experiences, it developed into a novel in its own right, set in 1910.

Whilst researching family and local history, I was struck by the resilience of the mining communities in the face of harsh living and working conditions. I hoped that in writing Black Rigg, I would encourage an interest in the people who have gone before us and engender a greater appreciation of their struggle and their legacy. Much has changed since 1910 but much remains the same. We would do well to find out more.

Thank you to my family for their love, support, and encouragement when I first decided to write this book, and during the publication of this new edition. A sequel titled, The Cold Blast, covering the years 1914 – 1918, is also available from 2021.

Thank you to the West Lothian Local History Library, The National Library of Scotland, and the historians of Scotland for their hard work in keeping the story of Scotland alive.

This book is dedicated to the generations of my family who worked hard and made the best of it.

"It is not down on any map,
true places never are."

*Moby Dick, Herman Melville*

# Prelude

People hadn't lived long in this place, not long in the scheme of things. It had been a place just for passing through, en route to somewhere else; a wild place to be endured for a short time, full of imagined dangers, savage and unbroken. Monks held tightly to their wooden crosses, fearful of the menace of the black morass as they followed the bell of the lead horse to their lands in the west. A baron in his stronghold to the north strayed no further than the crag of ancient rock they called The Law. Then men from fertile lands came to cut peat and catch fish in the lochs, and someone thought to stay. Human habitation was carved into the bog, draining the water and removing the stone. Long rigs were dug with the spade and the soil was improved with lime and manure. The coming of the Old Great Road brought people and trade, and changes. A village they called Blackrigg appeared on the dry land above the burn, just a straggle of houses for the shopkeeper and the blacksmith, with an inn at one end. But it did not merit a church. It remained on the edge, a difficult place out in the wastes, out on the fringe of a small fiefdom. When they found the coal many fathoms down, and the railway came to take it away, workers came in their hundreds. It became the centre of things, a place of wealth creation and progress, a place to stay, put down roots and raise a family.

# List of Principal Characters

## Rashiepark Estate

David Melville – Laird of Rashiepark, lives at Parkgate House with his sisters

Isabelle Melville – elder sister of David

Phee (Euphemia) Melville – younger sister of David and Isabelle

Roger Stone – estate factor

Grant – Rashiepark's gamekeeper

Billy Dodds – stable lad and chauffeur to the Melvilles

## Blackrigg and beyond

Neil Tennant – local blacksmith

Murdo Maclean – farmer and chairman of the school board

Rev Richard Fraser – minister at Blackrigg Church

Elizabeth Fraser – younger sister of Richard, lives at the manse

Dr Matheson – local doctor

Rose Matheson – doctor's daughter, friend of Phee and Elizabeth

Ernest Black – village schoolmaster

Miss Foulkes – lady schoolteacher

Charles Imrie – owner of the Coal Company, the main employer in the area

Catherine Imrie – only daughter of Charles

Mr Brownlee – pit manager

Andrew Brownlee – son of pit manager, at school

Constable Mackay – policeman stationed at Blackrigg police station

Mrs Gow and the Widow MacAuley – village women

Old Morton – tenant farmer at Back o' Moss

Daisy Gowans – tenant farmer's daughter, at school

## Stoneyrigg

Alex Birse – miner

Mary Birse – wife of Alex, nurse and midwife to the mining community

Jim and John Birse – adopted twin sons of Alex and Mary, at school

Jimmy Broadley – miner

Ellen Broadley – wife of Jimmy

Bert Broadley – middle son of Jimmy and Ellen, at school

Geordie Broadley – younger son, at school

Robert Duncan – miner

Peggy Duncan – wife of Robert, friend of Mary and Ellen

Rob Duncan – elder son of Robert and Peggy, at school

Sandy Duncan – younger son, at school

Davy Potts – miner

Dan Potts – son of Davy, at school

Tom Graham – builder employed by Coal Company

Meg Graham – eldest daughter of Tom

Nell Graham – daughter of Tom, domestic servant at Parkgate House

Minn Graham – fourth daughter, at school

Sarah Graham – fifth and youngest daughter, at school

# The Linlithgowshire County Courant

TRIBUTES At the close of the year, generous tributes were paid to Major and Mrs Arnott Melville of Rashiepark who died within a very short time of each other. All sections of the community have sent their sincere condolences to the family. The Melvilles have not been strangers to personal tragedy in very recent times. The future of the estate has passed into the capable hands of youngest son, Mr David Melville, who has left his university studies to take up the reins at Rashiepark in the best traditions of duty, devotion and self-sacrifice.

BUILDING WORK The Public Hall is nearing completion and the project has been praised for the benefits it will bring to the community where meeting places for the many groups and associations have, hitherto, been in short supply. The cost of the hall has been met by the ratepayers and by generous donations from Lady Moffat of Blairhill and Mr Imrie of the Coal Company.

MINING The Coal Company has announced the acquisition of the pits owned by Thomas Gibb & Sons. This brings the number of local pits owned by the company to twelve. Under the ownership of Mr Imrie CONTD the Coal Company has embarked upon a period of vigorous expansion across the county.

HOUSING SHORTAGE The registrar reports a significant increase in the population over the year past, due to the many employment opportunities made possible by continued expansion in the mines and manufactories. A shortage of housing has resulted from the large numbers of people moving into local villages.

LOW OUTPUT In the southern district of the county, the Coal Company reports that there was a poor turn-out at the pits after the New Year holiday, with only one in four men reporting for work. It is hoped that there will soon be a return to full strength and output will achieve the high levels set at the end of last year, before the stoppage.

ELECTION Candidates selected by their respective associations for election to Westminster in the upcoming Parliamentary election met with voters as part of a busy schedule of visits to local communities. The election has been called by the Prime Minister, Mr Asquith following the rejection of Mr Lloyd George's budget by the House of Lords. It is Mr Asquith's stated belief that the will of the people must be made effective within the CONTD lifetime of a single parliament. The Lord Advocate, Liberal Party candidate and sitting MP, Mr Alex Ure KC, addressed a packed schoolroom. He explained that the taxing of income and land, and luxuries such as tobacco and liquor, would pay for much needed social reforms as well as the programme of battleship building to which the government is committed. In the church hall, Mr Will Smith KC of the Unionists spoke vociferously against the Liberal Government's Budget Bill, particularly its plans to tax landowners to pay for very costly social reforms.

MEETING A speaker from the Anti-Socialist Union of Great Britain spoke to a packed church hall on Wednesday last on the topic of 'Socialism and Christianity'. Robust opinions were expressed and he was left with a clear impression of how deeply our menfolk feel about such issues.

ALLOTMENTS The society has announced that a number of new allotments has been made available on adjacent land, following an approach to the Coal Company. These will be allocated on a first come first served basis.

TEMPERANCE The speaker at the first meeting of the year will be Mr France from the Broxburn branch. Donations welcome. 7pm Wednesday, Church Hall.

# Part One
# Spring 1910

# Chapter 1

## THE START OF IT ALL

The geese had left. They'd headed north with the sunrise, lifting up from the Black Loch all at once, splashing across the surface on pink feet. Two small flights of them, calling out in the clear air, had passed over The Law before disappearing out of sight. The skeins were smaller than before, on account of the guns. It had gone on all winter: the loud report of strangers at play or farmers coveting fields of sweet grass, hard won from the peat in a hostile land. But the peewit had returned with their familiar call and their companions, the golden plover, fresh from muddy estuaries and farms on lower ground. They'd joined the hawk and the short-eared owl that had stayed through the worst of it, and the small brown meadow pipit now rising and falling in drifts, marked their territory in song.

The schoolroom was packed with children at the end of another day of toil. Desk lids snapped shut then everyone stood to attention. A hushed silence fell on the ranks and all eyes followed the teacher's imperious form as she paced slowly and deliberately across the floor, surveying her young charges and revelling in her position at the head of this small society. Movement in the corner and a stool clattering to the floor brought quick rebuke.

'John Birse.' She spat his name as if she could hardly bear it. John looked up into her cold eyes and contempt pierced his heart. She stared down on his bare feet then moved on, leaving him in no doubt of his worth. Like many of his fellows, he did not feel good about himself in school. It seemed that was not its purpose. The clank of the school bell in another room signalled escape but the tension remained as she waited, watching. She liked to keep them guessing. The order to leave finally came when, with careful timing, she said quietly, 'Not you, Birse.' His heart sank and his eyes closed with a silent sigh.

The rest of the children departed quietly leaving John to his fate. The walls enveloped him like a tomb and the brightness of the sky in the windows high above his head only confirmed his confinement. He made to pick up the fallen stool, not to mitigate his punishment but to restore order. This was a mistake. In this place, thinking for oneself was insolence and such a challenge to authority had to be met with the full force of the law.

He saw her commanding form towering above him, her hair scraped back severely into a small neat knot, and rows of pin-tucks rigidly ironed into place down the front of her starched, white blouse. She was everything he was not, big and imposing, ordered and precise. He took comfort from the worn, tweed cap held tightly in his hands, fingering the familiar weft and weave of the woollen threads.

'I beg yer pardon, Miss,' he said, a lump in his throat.

Her narrowed eyes told him the utterance, offered without permission, was another error but he knew that not to apologise would have been equally culpable. She was judge and jury and not given to benevolence. He truly was sorry and was glad he'd said it, sorry for being such a fidget in the first place and sorry for being here with this witch of a woman who had the power to inflict pain on a whim, while his friends were free to go. He followed her menacing glide towards the desk drawer that held the leather belt. Nothing would save him now so he held out his hands in the usual manner.

John emerged into the bright light of the spring day, liberated with throbbing hands tucked into his oxters to relieve the sting. He blinked back his tears and fought the need to pee, relieved no one had waited to witness his undoing. He needed to find Jim and his friends, to make the most of what remained of that precious, unconstrained interval between school and going home. Eagerly, he looked back and forth but Main Street was deserted except for a staring cat and Jimmy White, the grocer, on his delivery bike. Jimmy gave a cheery wave as he wobbled forth, then his outstretched hand pointed down the Doctor's Brae and John knew where they were. His spirits suddenly lifted, he set off at full pelt in the manner of all boys in search of freedom, companionship and adventure, the trials of a good Scotch education left far behind.

John ran down the rutted track past the last of the thatched cottages towards the old mill yard, jumping the worst of the mud but making good work of the deepest puddles, landing with a heavy splash and a whoop of joy. The mild southerly wind lifted his fair hair and brushed his face with gentle warmth. Rowans and elders were bursting into life and yellow primroses and bluebells carpeted the roadside between Spittal Cottage and the pond. He inhaled the earthiness of wet soil and the powerful smell of ramsons as he stretched out his arms, careering instinctively onwards, like a swallow newly arrived from Africa.

He was heading for the Meadie, a swath of bright green grass beside a stony beach on the north side of the Red Burn. Upstream, a ford led to the southern edge of the parish and the farming and mining communities of the county of Lanarkshire beyond. In an upland landscape of bog, peat and moor the Meadie was an unusual and special place for the children of the village. In days past, horse drawn carts full of corn from nearby farms would have drawn up there for unloading into the Clattering Mill, now roofless and abandoned behind a screen of scrub. These days it was occasional grazing ground and a place to play.

John heard the pals before he saw them. Laughter and derision by turns and the calling of each other's names told him a game of football was already in full flow. His arrival on the scene was greeted with a hearty cheer and quick instructions about the teams and direction of play. He located the other members of 'the blues' and called for the ball. Wriggling out of his jacket, he threw it onto one of the heaps of discarded garments marking the goals and defining the field of play. Barely ten minutes into the game and the blues were one goal down so there was work to be done. The boys ran and kicked and called out, engulfed and invigorated by the joy of competition among friends. Disputes were settled, and frustrations and disappointments instantly forgotten in a closely fought game. The teams were evenly matched, mixing big and small, weak and strong, fast and slow and the skilful from the less so, with brothers deliberately kept apart to avoid dynastic rivalries. As the number of goals for each team mounted, the players battled on, hoping that the end wouldn't come until their team had the upper hand.

As with all good things, the end did come. Billy Tennant's little sister appeared at the bottom of the brae shouting that it was time for his dinner, that he better hurry up or his ma would be furious. Hunger and exhaustion might not end a game quickly but the call that it was dinnertime and a mother was waiting always brought things to an abrupt conclusion. Billy collected his jacket to a chorus of cheerios before heading swiftly in the direction of the Smiddy, leaving the others prostrate on the grass.

Geordie Broadley was the first to remember that John had been kept back at school. 'Are yer hauns sair?' he asked.

'No noo. But they were,' replied John, remembering the pain as he examined the palms of his hands.

'Whit wis yer crime, then? Did she tell ye? Or does she jist no like ye cause yer sae wee?' questioned Dan Potts, raising his spent body onto an elbow.

'He was belted for fidgetin'. He's a fidget an' she disnae like fidgets,' interjected Jim Birse who took umbrage on behalf of himself and his twin brother at Dan's reference to their small physical stature.

'Yin things for sure,' said Rob Duncan. 'When she looks at ye, she's a face that would curdle milk.'

'She's a face like a burst ba' when she looks at ye,' added Sandy Duncan, Rob's younger brother, holding up the home-made ball to peals of laughter. 'Here. Catch it, ye wee fidget!' He threw the ball forcefully in John's direction.

Everyone laughed and the injustice done to their friend was forgotten as they watched the ball soar over his head then fall straight into the burn. They were up on their feet in a flash. The ball of straw, weighted in the middle and covered in a scrap of crudely stitched hessian, floated long enough for the assembled group to note its position in the middle of the deepest pool along that stretch of the river. A variety of stones and sticks were hurled in its direction in the hope of propelling it back towards them but the small waves returned the ball back to its original position. Ripples bounced off nearby rocks and repeated efforts only served to sink it further below the surface.

Geordie saw a rare opportunity to gain favour with the group and advanced into the flowing stream armed with a long branch to retrieve the precious commodity. He was a wide, flat platform of rock and several boulders out from the bank, when he remembered that he was wearing boots. These he removed and placed carefully beside him to the encouragement of the excited onlookers. He reached out tentatively with his stick but could only prod the ball further away. He watched and waited for it to return on the next small wave, then struck.

His brother's call to take care came too late. He slid from his perch, sweeping his boots with him in a flash. Geordie was in! The wool of his outer clothing, made heavy with river water, dragged him into the peaty depths.

Then the call went up. 'He cannae swim!'

Excitement soon turned to anguish as Geordie's head resurfaced, his mouth gasping for air, eyes wide, and his arms flailing the water in terror. Bert Broadley was the first to his brother's aid. He scrambled out to the middle of the stream then draped himself over the boulder that Geordie had slipped from. He held out a stout stick to no avail. Geordie disappeared into the water once more. Two of the bigger boys waded in, held Bert's ankles as he shuffled head first as close as possible to the water without actually disappearing into the depths himself. Despite stretching out his hand to its furthest extent, his brother was unable to reach back. Cries of advice and encouragement from the bank soon turned to silence.

Bert's fear for his brother's life turned to icy dread as a huge dark shadow loomed over them and a deafening roar, like the cry of a warrior going into battle, came from behind. The figure of a man came from nowhere, plunged into the cold, watery darkness and emerged with Geordie, limp in his arms. As he waded ashore, the pals crowded round hoping for good news but the small, pale figure seemed lifeless as his rescuer placed him carefully on the ground and knelt down beside him checking for vital signs. He pressed on his back, first with gentle resignation, then vigorously with both hands, adjusting his own position for maximum effect. River water spewed from the unconscious boy's mouth. The man turned the boy over, worked his arms up and down. Then the assembled crowd watched in amazement whilst wee Geordie Broadley was brought back from the dead before their eyes by Neil Tennant breathing life into his deflated lungs.

Amid his coughing and spluttering, and the cheers and congratulations of the others, Geordie was soon able to thank Neil for saving his life and turn his attention to more pressing matters.

'Did ye fetch ma boots, Mister?'

Neil laughed and ruffled the small boy's wet hair. With big, heroic strides he went to the deep pool and retrieved the pair of sodden boots bobbing in the current. He knew the difficulty families like the Broadleys had in keeping growing children in footwear. If a child outgrew his boots during the winter, he wore them anyway in spite of the corns and callouses they'd cause. As soon as the worst of the winter weather was over, he would go barefoot unless a pair discarded by an older sibling was available. So,

Geordie thanked Neil from the bottom of his heart for saving both his life and his boots, the loss of which would have been taken out of his hide by the strong arm of his mother's wrath. Neil told the boys to take their friend straight home, making them promise not to go near the Mill Pool again until they had learned to swim, and the boys watched with awe and grateful admiration as the tall, dark figure of their saviour strode off like a colossus.

Neil Tennant was a blacksmith like his father and had been returning home from a visit to Morton at Back o' Moss on the south side of the burn. Old Morton wanted his horses shoeing and had sought the smith's advice about the state of his carts and farm implements. The old man drove a hard bargain seeking the lowest price possible but Neil, now a young man of nearly twenty years, had become experienced at standing his ground where his elders and betters were concerned. Well satisfied that a date and a price for the work had been agreed, he had set off home by the ford, taking care to use the biggest stones and keep his feet dry. As he climbed the Doctor's Brae, leaving the commotion on the Meadie behind, he reflected on how life could change in an instant. Woven as he was into the fabric of other people's lives, an unforeseen event, the actions of others, could turn a quiet existence upside down for good or bad, changing the future irretrievably.

Lost in his thoughts, he was brought abruptly back to the present when he stepped into Main Street just as a motor vehicle careered past in a spray of thick mud, sounding danger with a horn akin to the honk of an angry goose. He watched the vehicle come to a stop outside the church and the daughter of the manse emerge from the car, waiting briefly to wave goodbye to the remaining passengers before hurrying out of sight. His gaze lingered a moment on the space where she had been, unaware of the nearby presence of Mrs Gow and the Widow MacAuley who were deep in conversation, the sight of him bringing their gab to a halt. They eyed him up and down like two hens in a farmyard in search of scraps, taking in the matted hair plastered over his forehead, the squelching feet and everything else in between, now sprayed with mud.

'Guid day to ye, ladies. Grand weather for a dip,' he said with his most engaging smile.

Neil manoeuvred delicately around them, out of reach of their formidable peck. He tipped his tweed cap and departed, leaving them gawping, open-mouthed and none the wiser.

He felt their eyes following him across the road. He knew they would make it their mission to find out what was what, their curiosity heightened by his calm composure. Neil plodded home, still dripping wet as he entered the yard behind Smiddy Cottage, aware that he would never be too old to get a right telling off from his mother for the state of his clothes.

Back at the Meadie, Bert comforted his brother who sat with his head between his knees, recuperating on the river bank. Geordie threatened to bubble as the reality of what had happened hit home. He could have died! Bert slapped his back when he coughed; made encouraging noises when he vomited air and river water onto the stony beach between his feet. The others watched with solemn faces, willing Geordie to a full recovery. Dan took each wet sock in turn and wrung them out. Rob did the same with his jacket, a ton weight on account of all the water. He twisted and squeezed the thread-worn fabric till the worst of the wet was removed. Bert emptied out his brother's boots with a sploosh before helping him to get dressed. He was starting to shiver and they had to get home. Sandy wrung out Geordie's cap then slapped it on the boy's head. He said it looked like a half-eaten bannock which made everyone laugh because nobody knew if he meant the cap or the head. Even the beleaguered Geordie laughed, chittering against the cold in his crumpled and creased attire, still dripping wet. Ever the comedian, Sandy kept Geordie's spirits up as he was chaperoned along the riverside path, reminding him that he was both a hero and a survivor, even if he did look like a tinker's wean.

As boys peeled off one or two at a time into their respective homes, the gaggle of excited figures escorting Geordie home up the Station Road soon became a straggle comprised only of Stoneyrigg boys. Stoneyrigg was only a short distance from the main part of the village but, in many respects, could have been another world. Some local inhabitants chose to think of it like that: a world apart. It comprised a few blocks and terraced rows of brick-built houses with slate roofs, single story 'but and bens', housing the many coal miners, pithead workers and quarrymen who swelled the population of the village. Stoneyrigg had been built to house a labour force for the working of the underlying geology by a succession of companies who had come and gone over the years. Surrounded on three sides by coal pits and quarries, coke ovens, brickworks and a network of rail and trackways, Stoneyrigg was the beating heart and soul of an island of ordered industrial chaos that belched smoke and fumes and noise amid a sea of sedate rural order and composure.

All was quiet, the streets deserted, as the boys approached *the raws*. The excitement of the adventure by the burn had dissipated. Instead of the adulation he had enjoyed, Geordie could feel only the discomfort of wet, woollen trousers rubbing between his legs, and a heaviness in his chest that no amount of coughing seemed to lift. Weighed down by feelings of responsibility towards his brother, Bert knew he was about to be judged and would be found wanting. How easily the unbridled pleasure of a game had almost turned to tragedy, avoided only by the intervention of Good Fortune or Providence. The experience of Bert's short life told him neither could be relied on when they were needed most but, on this occasion, a calamity had been prevented by a guardian angel in the form of a man.

Then suddenly, Ellen Broadley was there in the street, eyes agog at the sight of her youngest child, cold and bedraggled in his wet clothes.

'Ma wee lamb,' she cooed.

His brother got a cuff round the ear.

She put a protective arm around Geordie's shoulders, enfolding him in her long skirt to stop the shivering, before ushering his trembling form in through the door to the safety of their small home. Bert followed with the look of a guilty man heading for the gallows.

'See ye the morn, Bert,' said Rob supportively on behalf of the huddle of friends.

'Aye, see ye the morn,' he replied with some doubt.

'I hope Geordie'll be fine,' said Rob finally. The friends peered in through the doorway as Bert disappeared inside.

The door closed, shutting them out and they turned away with heads bowed, making for their respective homes.

Mary Birse was sitting by the fire in the end house of the Back Row, enjoying the peace and quiet and her own company when her adopted twin sons arrived home. The hiss and spit of the burning coal and the reassuring, rhythmic knock of the clock on the wall were lost in the familiar sounds of their return. She ladled broth into two plates waiting on the table; poured boiling water into the teapot. On the outside step, Jim removed his muddy boots with great relief whilst John wiped his bare feet as best he could on the cloth provided. The boys hesitated as they peered round the door into the small room.

'Whaur's faither?' they asked cautiously together.

'Come awa' in, he's no here,' she said sadly, sensing their apprehension. 'An' he's had his denner so he'll be a while yet.'

They relaxed into hard wooden chairs at the table by the window and supped the soup like they hadn't eaten for a week. White bread spread with dripping had never tasted so good and hot tea from the pot warming by the fire brought an inner glow. This was a time that John loved: when he came home tired or hungry or cold, or all of those things put together, and his mother was there by herself to give him his tea and a smile and listen to what he had been doing that day. John liked to stare into the small, bright nucleus of burning coal in the fireplace, the source of heat for the cooking of food, boiling water for washing people and dishes, and for warming the living space beyond. There was little furniture in the room, just the table and chairs where they ate their meal, two chairs by the hearth and a kist for spare bed covers and clothes, though these were few in number. In a corner, a simple plate rack, some shelves and a tin basin on a small stand formed the scullery. Most of the wall opposite the window was taken up by the curtained recess of a box bed with its hand-stitched quilt. Mary liked to arrange the curtains in swags. Pinning them back with strips of cloth revealed the bed and this made the room look much bigger than it actually was. The valance, concealing the space under the bed where the coal was kept in an old bath, was always closed. Everything was clean and in its place. From the small rug made from rags on the brick tile floor to the gleaming windows, pride and dignity shone out. This was her world and here she ruled the roost.

Jim and John would have told the story of the game of football and of how Geordie Broadley had nearly drowned in the burn fetching out the ball but, even though everything had turned out fine after Billy Tennant's big brother had happened by and saved the day, they decided it was best not to make her fret. Besides, they didn't want to risk being banned forever from going near ponds and rivers. John also decided not to tell her he had been belted by the teacher since it was customary for a parent to reinforce the discipline meted out at school by repeating the punishment at home, though he would have owned up had he been asked directly. The framed needlework on the wall caught his eye as usual and Mary saw him looking,

> 'Work Hard
> Be Honest
> Fear God'

She started to speak but the tone of her voice changed at the sound of men talking in the street and the door latch lifting.

'Richt, ben the room, the pair o' ye. Skedaddle! Yer faither's hame. I'll be through efter.'

They were gone in an instant.

# Chapter 2

## DINNER AT THE BIG HOUSE

David Melville and his younger sister sat in the drawing room of Parkgate House enjoying a rare moment of quiet conversation together. She listened attentively to her brother's account of his day in charge of Rashiepark, the family estate. He tried hard to follow the intricate details of the social encounters that made her such a font of knowledge about people, places and all that occurred in the district. David was the third and only surviving son of Rashiepark and, as such, the future of the family name, its properties, and estates lay with him. His eldest brother, Clive, was a hero of the South African campaigns. He had returned there briefly on a diplomatic mission but contracted a fever and died on the ship home, breaking his father's heart in the process. Andrew, the second son had grown up in Clive's shadow and, since he had never felt able to compete with his brother for his parents' affections, had chosen to spend his time and their money doing all of the things he knew they would disapprove of most. Unlike the prodigal son, Andrew had not been welcomed back into the fold and he died a lonely death in a paupers' hospital in London. As the third son, David had been allowed to choose his own destiny, within the confines of propriety of course, although his father had made clear his preference that he should become a career soldier like his brother. David chose to study medicine at the university in Edinburgh, the thought of inheriting and managing Rashiepark never entering his head in all the years he had spent there as a child. As a young student he had been happy to live among the glittering spires of Auld Reekie, looking forward to life in a rapidly changing profession that offered so much hope for the future well-being of humanity. But Fate had other plans for him and he had come home to Rashiepark, leaving his studies and his dreams behind.

'You do like it here, don't you?' Euphemia Melville asked her brother, searching out his eyes.

'Of course I do. As long as you're here, Phee... to make it bearable.' He used the shortened form of her name which she much preferred.

'I hate to think of you unhappy,' she went on. 'First, we lose Andrew, then Clive and since Mummy and Daddy died you've had to take on everything... the house, the leases, all the legal stuff, meetings with Stone, trying to make Rashiepark pay and managing the men too. Sometimes I think Grant is a law unto himself.' She shuddered as the gamekeeper came to mind.

'It's all quite new but I'm learning fast. Isabelle looks after the house and you're here to keep me right. And cheer me up.' He gave her hand a squeeze then looked out into the faraway beyond the bright sunlight shining in through the drawing room windows.

Phee studied her brother, wanting to say more. She waited for him to continue but he remained silent, his lips pursed.

The drawing room door opened and a tall, elegant figure draped in ivory lace and satin entered. Isabelle Melville greeted her younger siblings with a nod of approval to their formal attire and timely arrival for dinner. Fresh from her tour of inspection of the kitchen and the dining room, she swept in from the hall, a finger trailing across successive pieces of highly polished furniture in search of dust. From the centre of the large room, she surveyed the carefully positioned assemblage of fine porcelain and glass, books and brassware that complemented the Georgian walnut and rosewood, and the rich reds of the carpets woven in the Persian style. The array of family portraiture culminated in the domineering figure of Sir Henry, scourge of the Jacobites, dressed in white breeches and scarlet coat, reproduced in oils and hanging above the fireplace. Isabelle perched on the edge of a leather armchair satisfied that the evening's dinner guests would encounter a true reflection of the status and authority of her family, the Melvilles of Rashiepark.

'Only ten for dinner tonight, including ourselves of course,' began Isabelle, bringing the others into the picture. 'Richard and Elizabeth Fraser from the church, Dr Matheson and Rose, Mr and Mrs Maclean from Whinbank, and I've invited the new schoolmaster, Mr Black, to make up the numbers. Thought we should have a good look at him and see if he's up to the mark. Don't you think?'

Phee stifled a giggle and was rewarded with a scowl.

'Wasn't Lady Moffat able to come after all?' enquired Phee of her sister, counting up the guest list on her fingers, thankful that the evening might be less of a trial than expected in the absence of Her Ladyship.

'Unfortunately not, such a shame. She had a prior engagement but we shall endeavour to bring her into our humble home in the very near future,' Isabelle explained in the clipped tones of disappointment.

'Must we?' replied David who remembered his relief when nurse had packed him off to bed as a small child after greeting the mammoth lady prior to his parents' own splendid dinner parties. In fact, he thought he would much rather be upstairs with a good book than receiving guests for polite conversation over beef and claret.

'Yes, we must make the effort,' shot Isabelle, seizing him with her dark brown eyes. 'David Erskine Cunningham Melville, you cannot hide away behind those stuffy books any longer. You must make connections around the county and establish yourself as the new head of the family, for all our sakes. Tonight can be your debut, albeit in less distinguished and,' she hesitated, 'for your sake, less intimidating company.' Isabelle looked at her reluctant younger brother and saw her vocation. David might be the heir to Rashiepark but she, Isabelle the eldest survivor, would be the guiding force, transforming him into a worthy successor to three centuries of Melville history.

'In the very near future, we will bring Mr Imrie of the Coal Company to our table,' she continued with the look of the spider about to invite the fly into her parlour. 'But you must be well prepared for that encounter, David. These adventurers take all of the risk and drive a hard bargain when negotiating for leases. With foreign coal fields opening up and driving coal prices down, we must do what we can to encourage further interest in the minerals on our land but, at the same time, make the best deal for the estate... and the family.'

A tall, grey-haired servant in waistcoat and tails appeared in the doorway. He gave a short bow. The guests had arrived.

'Mr and Mrs Maclean and Mr Black, if you please, sir, m'ladies.'

An elderly couple in old fashioned garb almost knocked the butler over as they rushed through the door to greet the Melvilles with out-stretched arms, kindly faces and a genuine warmth borne of long acquaintance.

'It's lovely to be back here again,' chirped Mrs Maclean like a mother bird fussing over her chicks. 'We miss your parents very much. They were such a rock of stability within the community, and we need that more than ever in these changing times.' She turned to the man of the house. 'I'm sure you'll carry on where they left off, David, and make your own mark too. With help from the girls of course, while they're still here at Parkgate,' she added, taking Isabelle and Phee each by the hand. She did not know where things stood in the marriage stakes for the two sisters but they were clearly eligible in both grace and status.

'Have you met Mr Black from the school?' interrupted Mr Maclean when he got the chance, indicating the small, well-dressed gentleman standing awkwardly behind him. 'I must say his Latin and Greek are very good. I was testing him all the way along the road in the carriage. Never faltered! Well done, young sir!' Mr Black blushed at the complement and coughed at the slap of Mr Maclean's heavy hand on his back.

'How kind and do please call me Ernest,' he said with a gracious bow to each lady, followed by a self-assured click of his heels and a firm shake of David Melville's hand.

'It's very nice to meet you, Ernest,' replied Phee. 'I've heard a lot about you – I hope you'll be very happy here in charge of our school.' Mr Black nodded his thanks for her good wishes.

'Good evening, Mr Black,' Isabelle said severely, looking reproachfully at her far too familiar younger sister. 'Do sit down, everyone. The Frasers and the Mathesons will be here soon, I hope.'

A conversation ensued about the mild weather so early in the year, the poor condition of the roads, and the advantages for the village of the new gas street lighting, soon to be extended to Stoneyrigg. Then just when it seemed that Mr Black was about to become a little too passionate about the importance of Latin in the curriculum for young boys, the door opened once again and four more dinner guests were led in.

'You all know Reverend Fraser from the church and his sister, Elizabeth. And Dr Matheson and his daughter, Rose,' said Isabelle beginning the introductions. 'David, perhaps you haven't met Mr Fraser's sister since you've been out of the county for a while. Elizabeth has joined him at the manse, following the tragically sudden passing of their parents.'

'I am delighted to meet you at last, Miss Fraser. I have heard so much about you from my sister.' David took her hand, his mood brightening in the presence of such pleasing company. 'Please accept my condolences.' Then remembering the death of his own parents and how much his life had changed as a result, he added, 'We have something in common it would seem.'

A pretty, fair-haired girl of eighteen years with a diffident smile gave a polite curtsey to the assembly, quietly acknowledging the sympathy extended for her bereavement.

The shared experience of a difficult winter past was not lost on Dr Matheson, a widower. 'My daughter Rose often accompanies me now, following the death of my dear wife at the turn of the year.' He held out Rose's slender hand to his host. David took her hand and brought it gently to his mouth.

'We truly are in gracious company tonight', he said to Rose, looking into her soft grey eyes for a moment longer than he should.

He was interrupted abruptly by Murdo Maclean who could always be relied upon for a philosophical interlude when the situation required, and more often when it did not.

'Aah, such is life, my friends,' he sighed with a reverential dip of the head. 'Full of meetings and partings, meetings and partings indeed.'

'The Lord giveth and the Lord taketh away', added the Rev Richard Fraser mournfully but glad of the opportunity to justify his presence.

Phee stifled a groan.

Isabelle shot her a look of annoyance from across the room.

'Your mother was a wonderful, kindly woman, Rose,' continued Maclean, now in full flow. 'Such a comfort and support to your father in his difficult and necessary profession. And you have the look of her, dear girl. Your future husband, whoever he may be, will indeed be blessed.'

Rose blushed visibly, embarrassed to have her eligibility referred to so openly, and in such company. She kept her eyes down, convinced that every man was looking at her.

Maclean continued, turning to the departed Mrs Fraser's offspring. 'I much admired Mrs Fraser too, a strong woman to have by one's side,' He looked Elizabeth in the eye as he took her hand. 'The church is not an easy vocation, as you will agree having been raised in the manse, my dear, and now when supporting your brother in his ministry. A minister needs a kind and gentle presence in the home to soothe and calm his enthusiasm for the spiritual, else he may be consumed by his own fiery passion.'

Elizabeth did her best to smile whilst she digested what had just been said. She uttered something inaudible, her eyes fixed on the floor in front of her, whilst she extricated her hand from Mr Maclean's grasp.

He paused, remembering the deceased Rev Fraser. 'I so enjoyed your father's sermons,' he continued with warmth in his voice. 'They were legendary in these parts, both for their fury and their poetry. He was truly mighty in the Scriptures.' Maclean raised a glass, looked eagerly at his host. 'If I may take the liberty and offer a toast, young David? Absent friends!'

'May we never deviate from the path of righteousness they have set us on', added the minister, his own enthusiasm for the spiritual reinvigorated at the mention of his father.

The butler offered glasses of sherry from a silver salver and the guests each murmured a sorrowful, *'absent friends'*.

Having looked on aghast as Maclean delivered his speech on women and marriage and the dearly departed, Phee took a mouthful of the dry liquid, swallowing hard. She'd had enough, deciding that any appeal to righteousness was best left to the Sunday morning sermon.

'Shall we have a walk in the grounds before dinner?' trilled the youngest Melville, rushing to open the French windows before Isabelle could disagree. A vista of lawns and borders, full of the bright colour of spring flowers bathed in late evening sunshine, was revealed. Arm in arm, Phee swept her friends, Rose and Elizabeth, out of the closed confines of the drawing room and onto the terrace.

The others were left speechless but not for long. David followed on, gravitating towards Dr Matheson, a kindred spirit, who asked to see the old sundial in the rose garden. The Rev Fraser wandered out after them, absent-mindedly looking at the daffodils, whilst Mrs Maclean held Isabelle's arm in a clutch of reminiscence about the old days at Rashiepark. Mr Black looked on forlornly as the group of young ladies dashed off ahead, leaving him firmly attached to Mr Maclean who threatened to test him once again on his Latin conjugations. They made their way across the terrace then down stone steps onto a wide lawn.

'Are you wondering how an old farmer like me can possibly know his imperative from his subjunctive, young fellow?' Maclean asked intently without waiting for an answer. 'Well, believe it or not, I was a scholar of the Classics, many years ago now. But I found myself here helping my mother to run the old coaching inn after my father died. You may have heard of it, along at Craigpark? In those days, it was a stopping off point on the old turnpike that ran between Baillieston and Newbridge: the Great Road they called it because it was such an improvement on what they'd had before, and took such time and effort to build, I suppose. Or perhaps it was such a boon to the economy, opening up markets and giving access to resources,' he mused to Mr Black's captive ear.

'The stagecoach passed through every day, each way, between the two great cities of our land. I loved working with the horses in the stables, and the ostlers, of course – far more than with the travellers themselves if truth be told. Though I met many interesting people, I have to say. Can you believe the inn was a popular hostelry for parties from the cities? And often visited by honeymooning couples, looking for a friendly retreat?'

Mr Black brought to mind the smoking chimneys and pitheads of the present, said that he had no idea Blackrigg had been a pleasure resort in the past. He declared himself altogether taken aback at the fact.

'The number of businesses in the village, dealing with leisure and provisions, still attracts a fair few visitors from near and far on a Saturday morn or on holidays.' Mr Maclean's enthusiasm for the area and its people was very evident. 'But times have changed,' he continued, taking the conversation back to the old days, and sounding sorrowful. 'The railway came and the coaches stopped soon after. My mother took it hard when the business changed. There were always plenty of residents at the inn, mind you, attracted by the riches of the area above and below ground. Men in trade from Glasgow came for shooting and fishing. As good as the Highlands but on their doorstep', he explained. 'And men surveying the land for coal and iron and stone, reporting back to masters with money to invest for a good return. But it was never the same without the horses. We missed them – with their quiet, steady ways, their constancy, even the smell of them. We all have to adapt to changes in life but sometimes there's that one thing you can't come to terms with, that helps you choose a different path in life. So, after my mother died, I sold up and became a farmer. Met and married Mrs Maclean late in life and here I am, never happier. I came to help my mother out for a summer and sixty years later, I'm still here and happy to be so.' Maclean gave the young schoolmaster a huge smile of contentment. 'Who knows where you will be in sixty years, young Ernest?'

Mr Maclean could see that the schoolmaster's attention had wandered to the ladies sitting by the perimeter wall. '*All things that happen, happen as they should, Mr Black. If you observe carefully, you will find this to be so,*' he offered wisely, nodding sagely.

'Ah ......is that ...Seneca. No, no... Zeno?' guessed Ernest, somewhat distracted, but sensing he was being tested again

25

by the wise old owl. 'It's not Shakespeare is it?' he added quickly, stabbing in the dark.

'No! Wrong, young sir!' the old man laughed, delighted that he had finally caught the younger man out. 'It's the Stoic, Marcus Aurelius, of course!'

David Melville's voice came from behind. '*Whatever may happen to you was prepared for you from all eternity; and the implication of causes was from eternity spinning the thread of your being.*' He sounded wistful, almost dejected.

Maclean and Black smiled kindly at the new laird of Rashiepark.

Then much more brightly David added, 'Shall we join the ladies, gentlemen?'

The grounds of Parkgate House were defined by a high stone wall that kept at bay the wilderness of an extensive area of raised bog known locally as the Black Moss. Earlier generations of Melvilles had used the same statute labour that built the Old Great Road, to transform a portion of the acidic wastes of the moss closest to the house, removing the peat whilst carefully managing the waters with a network of drainage ditches that led into the burn on the far side of the road. Inside the wall, patterns of lawns and flower beds visited by gravel paths were laid out with the changing fashions of garden design, a statement of the family's power over nature and their engagement with the contemporary world. Stands of trees, many of species native to distant shores, spoke of foreign travel for knowledge and empire. For the more ambitious members of the family, the vastness of the wasteland on the other side of the wall had symbolised the limited extent of their influence and fostered a yearning for expansion and greater power.

Overlooking the formal gardens, Parkgate House faced west, towards the empty moss beyond; three floors of sandstone bathed in the rosy glow of the setting sun. From the road, a long, sweeping drive lined with beech trees led the visitor to a grand entrance under a stone porch carved with coats of arms. The old house was hidden from visitors by this early nineteenth century facade, created by a great grandmother who had come over the border as a young bride to transplant a little bit of Surrey into mid Central Scotland. She had made sure the new house faced away from the village, insisting that the name of the house be changed to something more acceptable to her ears, *'Parkgate'*. Her husband's desire to please her stopped short of the complete removal of the old name from the map, so the estate remained as Rashiepark.

The original building was out of sight on the eastern side: white-washed; four storeys; a seventeenth century laird's house with a conical tower incorporating a spiral staircase; narrow windows on the ground floor for the safety of the occupants. The low wooden door was accessed through a tangle of ancient rowan planted to keep the witches away but always alive with sparrows and finches. The door sat in a weathered stone archway that led into a vaulted hallway lined with swords and shields from bloody battles proudly fought, a distant memory passed down to those who cared to listen. The narrow corridors and small rooms of the old house were now the preserve of a dozen servants who, by their dedication and hard labour, kept the family in the manner to which they were accustomed.

Phee, Elizabeth, and Rose sat talking quietly in an alcove of stone set into the garden's south-facing wall; three friends eagerly looking forward to what life had in store for them.

'I have some news for you both,' Rose said carefully. They looked at their friend, intrigued, wondering what was to come. 'I've been accepted for medical school. The term starts in the autumn and I can hardly wait! I didn't want to say anything until I was sure I had a place'. She hesitated. 'What do you think?'

'I can hardly believe it,' said Elizabeth. She sat back quite stunned. 'You, Rose! A doctor! A lady doctor! Gosh. Well, that's wonderful. Wonderful!'

Rose gave Elizabeth's hand a squeeze. 'I'll miss you both of course.' She waited for Phee to say something.

'I'm so happy for you, Rose,' said Phee at last, giving her a warm embrace. 'The prospect of making your way out into world must be, well, wonderfully exciting! What did your father have to say about it?'

'He was taken aback at first but then he encouraged me! He wasn't at all old-fashioned and stuffy about it,' replied Rose. 'When my mother was alive, he used to say she'd have made a brilliant doctor but it wasn't the way of things then. I know he'll miss me now that mother's gone but he's kept busy with his patients and all of the public health matters, and I'll be back often for his advice.'

Phee and Elizabeth agreed that they would miss her too, during her long absences, but they promised to write often. Perhaps they might visit her sometimes, and her visits home at Christmas and summer would be great fun: swapping stories and memories, visiting friends and family together. Rose did not realise just how deeply her news was felt by her friends, or that none of their lives would ever be the same because of it. The three lapsed into silence, each lost in their own thoughts.

Phee followed the progress of the men around the garden. She listened intently as the guests clung onto her brother's every word, their deep voices caught up in clever conversation about serious topics, peppered with laughter from time to time. Isabelle and Mrs Maclean, still wrapped in the glow of the good old days, appeared through a gap in the beech hedge. Phee looked around, surveying the house and the garden from the safety of the arbour where she liked to sit on dry days, reading a book or listening to the sounds of the bees in the roses and the owls hunting over the moss at dusk. Tonight, that wilderness beyond the garden wall beckoned her.

Elizabeth had never thought too deeply about her own future until then. The only daughter of a minister, she had always been a part of the Kirk and its great mission to bring Truth and salvation to the people. She had accepted without question that her future life was mapped out by God who would reveal His plan to her in His own time. Her horizons had never shifted beyond His church but was it up to her to look beyond those walls, to find out for herself what that plan was? Elizabeth felt a new uncertainty in the pit of her stomach and it frightened her. She looked at the sky above the garden wall, bright blue with the final remnants of the setting sun, changing quickly to deepest sapphire high above, pierced by the first and brightest of the stars to appear that evening. She pondered the vastness of the world from where she sat, so small, a tiny being in the middle of God's wonderful creation.

'Aren't you cold sitting there?' enquired Mr Black, peering through the silence and the shadows of the gathering night. 'It's early in the year to be sitting out so late without a coat. Ladies, you will catch your death of cold.'

'The female sex is more robust than you give us credit for, Ernest,' replied Phee, irritated by the man's concern though she knew it was kindly meant. 'Besides, it's warm over here, come and see for yourself. Our Victorian predecessors thought of every conceivable way of making life easier and more comfortable for themselves. Look, you can see the wall is made of brick. It's hollow, and heat from a coal-fired furnace on the other side warms the wall, providing the house with fruits of all kinds that otherwise could not be grown here.'

Everyone admired the line of fruit trees, tied and trained into a lattice along the entire length of the wall, and already covered in a profusion of buds and flowers. The party agreed it was a remarkably clever idea that had taken great Victorian ingenuity and planning to create.

'And heated by coal? How wonderful!' remarked Rev Fraser, seeing an opportunity to engage the flock. 'God's gifts are glorious indeed! And we are much-blessed here in Blackrigg. Thanks be to the Lord!'

Yes, coal had made all of their lives much more comfortable and God was generous in his bounty they all agreed, laughing and chattering as they made their way across the lawn back into the warmth of the house for dinner.

# Chapter 3

## SICKNESS AND HEALTH

Ellen Broadley sat on the edge of the box bed in the front room of the miner's cottage she shared with her husband and three sons. The fire was heaped up with coal that blazed furiously in the small grate, throwing patterns of shadow and light around the four walls, and making the room unbearably hot. She wiped the sweat from the back of her neck with her cotton apron, stained from a long day of domestic chores, then buried her face in the tired cloth to hide her tears. Her husband looked across from the table where he sat with Bert, their middle child.

'Is there nae change in him, Ellen?' he asked at last.

Ellen looked down at Geordie asleep, lying on his back with his arms stretched wide across the bed, the covers kicked off, and his legs splayed. Beads of sweat stood out on his forehead and ran down into the pillow. His cheeks were a fiery red. Tenderly, she placed the palm of her hand on his brow to feel his temperature.

'He's no onie better,' she said after a while. 'I think he's gettin' worse, he's burnin' up somethin' fierce.'

She reached across to a metal bowl, wrung the cloth of its mixture of vinegar and cold water. Carefully, she washed down his thin white limbs and his scrawny chest. With infinite gentleness, she brushed back the wet, black hair from the nape of his neck and around his face, from his temples and his brow. She watched the rise and fall of his chest as she listened to the sound of his breathing before turning to her husband. 'Can ye go an' fetch Mary Birse, Jimmy?' The tremble in her voice could not be hidden. She held him in her gaze long enough to let him know he was to hurry.

Jimmy Broadley got swiftly to his feet, took his cap from the nail by the door. 'Richt, ye're wi' me, Bert, come awa',' he ordered.

Father and son left the house, both relieved to be out of the suffocating air of the sickroom. Although he counted himself a caring, loving father, Jimmy was always astounded at the hours of devotion his wife could give to their children when they were ailing whilst he just wanted to get on with his own business after a very short while.

'Dae ye think he'll be a'richt, Faither?' asked Bert as they ran to the end of the terraced row. Going to fetch help with his father hardly assuaged the guilt Bert felt about his brother's illness since it had come on following Geordie's near drowning at the burn.

'I hope sae, Son,' came the reply. 'I dinnae ken an' I widnae lie tae ye. But mind whit I'm sayin', ye're tae stop blamin' yersel. Dae ye hear me?'

'Aye, I hear ye. Ta, Faither,' replied Bert though the awfulness of the guilt remained. 'I hope Highland Mary's in!' At which they ran even harder across the washing green to the Back Row.

Highland Mary was the nickname assigned Mary Birse by the children and adults of Stoneyrigg but it was never used in her hearing. She was Mary Campbell to her own name and still retained a little of that Highland lilt that she had brought with her as a girl of barely fourteen years when she had made the journey south to Edinburgh in search of work in the company of her sister. Within her community, Mary was much respected for her medical knowledge and opinion. Through her experience in domestic service, she had acquired skills in ambulance and in nursing the sick. The women of Blackrigg and Stoneyrigg called for her when they went into labour, as they seemed to do with regular frequency. As a nurse and midwife, she went unpaid but she would take a small fee for dressing the dead.

On that evening, as was their custom, Mary and her husband Alex sat at opposite sides of the fire without talking. She peered through the gloom of the dimly lit room at the sock she was darning, holding it into the firelight for a better view, as he tried to read the latest paper reporting the work of the Miners Federation. Their twin sons Jim and John, adopted by them at birth, had been banished to the back room earlier when their father found fault with something said or done by one or other or both. She was punishing Alex for his treatment of the boys with her silence. Meanwhile, Alex spat periodically into the fire because he knew she hated him doing it. The large black expectorations, hacked up from the depth of his lungs with dramatic effect, hissed when they landed on the hot coals, serving to remind her who put food on the table and at what cost. She had been his Highland Mary once upon a time, as dear to him as light and life, just like another Mary Campbell had been in another time for Robert Burns but somewhere along the way their loving had gone cold, stone cold like the icy Arctic wastes that had seen many winters.

When Jimmy Broadley's feverish knock came to the door, Alex answered it grudgingly. He found it hard to respect a man who had called his three children after royalty – Edward, Albert and George – but when he saw how worried Jimmy looked, he invited him in. Mary hardly waited for an explanation before putting on a clean apron, wrapping her shawl round her shoulders, and ushering him back out before her into the night. They made swiftly for the small dark room where Ellen Broadley sat silently praying for her youngest son.

'He hasnae been richt fae he fell in yon burn,' Ellen explained, relieved at the sight of Highland Mary. 'He's been coughin' up stuff thir last twa-three days an' wheezin' somethin' terrible. I've had him sittin' by the fire wi' the kettle belchin' steam, a mustard poultice on his wee chest. It a' seemed tae be helpin'. The mixture calmed his cough for a while,' she explained further, indicating a small bottle of cough medicine on the shelf. *Veno's Lightning Cough Cure, excellent for all diseases of lungs, chest and throat, 9½d.* 'But he wouldnae rest. I claucht him oot in the road when I cam in frae the wash hoose. By God, I gied him whit fur! An' noo he's burnin' up. He's no lang feenished tellin' me he was seein' sodgers comin' oot the fire, hunders and hunders o' them'.

Mary considered the sleeping child and his symptoms, the time scale of events, and didn't like what she saw.

'Whit colour wis his spit?' she asked.

'Greyish, mebbe yellae,' came the reply. 'There wis nae blood in it,' she added emphatically, mindful of the signs of pneumonia and the dreaded tuberculosis.

'Weel yon's a guid sign, is it no?' continued Mary reassuringly. 'But I'm thinkin' ye should fetch the doctor in, tae be on the safe side, Ellen. On accoont o' the high temperature,' she explained kindly.

Ellen breathed heavily at the mention of the doctor.

'You cool him doon again wi' the cloot an' I'll open the windae tae cool doon the room an' git some air in the place,' Mary continued calmly. 'It's stiflin' in here.'

'I dinnae want him gettin' a chill though, Mary,' said Ellen.

'Ye've got the room lik a furnace, Ellen. How's that gonnae get his temperature doon? He'll be fine in the bed there wi' the windae open jist a wee bit,' explained Mary. 'An' we'll no gie him onie mair o' thon cough mixture. He needs tae cough up the infection an' git it oot his lungs.'

Ellen saw the error of her ways. She looked at the older woman with gratitude for her common sense and practical advice. Ellen knew that her son was very ill, that the doctor was coming was proof of that, but she felt more hopeful now as she cooled Geordie's fevered brow with the cloth and watched Mary put the kettle on the fire for a cup of tea.

Jimmy and Bert split up in their search for the doctor. Jimmy took the road to the east where Dr Matheson had his home in the next village. Bert was sent west to the Post Office to ask Miss Shanks if she could telephone Dr Matheson's house. The only telephone in Blackrigg was located in the Post Office but there was no guarantee Miss Shanks would be there and, even if she was, there was no guarantee the doctor would be in at the other end. He knew that if Highland Mary was telling them to get the doctor then Geordie's illness was very bad indeed because his parents didn't have money for one. As he ran along the road he fell over his own feet, such was his haste to alert him to Geordie's plight. He picked himself up, out of the dirt, before running headlong into a man on a bicycle coming the other way.

'Whit's the hurry, ma mannie? Ye'll damage yersel' an' ma bike intae the bargain if ye dinnae tak tent. Whaur ye gaun?' came a familiar and kindly voice. 'Is there somethin' the matter?'

'Aw, its yersel, Neil', said Bert, relieved when he recognised Neil Tennant. 'It's ma wee brither, Geordie, again. He's gey bad wi' a lurgy. I'm gaun tae get Miss Shanks tae telephone for the doctor. He's got a terrible cough an' an awfy high temperature. Ma mither says he's hallucinatin'!' Bert stopped to draw breath, studying Neil with anguish in his eyes.

'Ye'll no get the doctor thon wey,' said Neil. 'The telephone isnae connectit up yet. It was jist the apparatus that was delivered this week past. It'll need a' manner o' cablin' afore it'll work.'

Bert gasped in despair. New fangled machinery could be pernickitie and fair perplexing, he realised.

'Are ye lookin' fur the doctor, laddie?' came a voice from the semi-darkness, beyond the gaslight on the other side of the street. Mrs Gow and the Widow MacAuley stood at their doors happed up in shawls, enjoying a pipe of tobacco in the mild night air. 'I'm thinkin' ye'll find him up at the Big Hoose, the nicht. He went by a while back in his motor car. Picked up the meenister an' Miss Fraser… he hasnae come back this wey yit.'

'Are ye sure?' asked Neil.

'Aye. Look, the manse's in darkness yet.'

Neil knew that little passed these two women by. He turned to Bert. 'Awa' hame, Bert. I'll gang tae Parkgate an' get the doctor. I'll bring him roond tae Geordie. A' richt?'

'Richt,' agreed Bert.

Neil started along the road on his bicycle. 'Whit number dae ye bide at again?' he called back as an afterthought.

'Twintie-fower,' shouted Bert. As he watched Neil go, he looked up at the night sky, bright with stars. 'Hurry, Neil,' he whispered. 'Please hurry.'

# Chapter 4

## AN INCONVENIENT INTERRUPTION

With their younger sister and guests relaxed and seated amid the splendour of the dining room at Parkgate House, David and Isabelle Melville looked at each other from opposite ends of the vast oak table. David was taken aback at the opulence of the preparations for dinner that recalled a golden age he had considered past but he said nothing. He had only been back in Rashiepark a few weeks. As the new master he had much to get used to, not least his changing relationship with his elder sister. A tall, angular woman of nearly thirty years, Isabelle sat proudly erect, her auburn hair swept back from her face, coiled and curled into a chignon, decorated with a large diamond encrusted clasp that held a curving ostrich feather in place at the back of her head. Since this was the first social occasion held at the house since the death of their parents the previous year, Isabelle had paid attention to every detail, aiming to stamp the authority of the new generation on the proceedings, leaving those stalwarts of the community in attendance with a good impression, though they ranked well below the family in social standing.

Painted Highland landscapes of mountain and flood in heavy gilt frames were ranged around the walls, expanding the enclosed space of the room out into the beautiful Scottish countryside with delight in the sublime and a heavy hint of national pride. Candlelight glimmered across the assembled company from silver candelabra and a central chandelier of Venetian glass. Isabelle delighted in the way the soft light shimmered and glinted in the family silver and crystal. Every piece was embellished with an extravagant capital '*M*' for *Melville*, set out on a snow-white linen cloth embroidered with an intricate pattern of intertwining thistles, shamrocks and roses.

At Isabelle's command, Richard Fraser started the proceedings with a polite version of the Selkirk Grace.

> '*Some have meat and cannot eat and some*
> *would eat that want it,*
> *But we have meat and we can eat and say the Lord*
> *be thankit. Amen.*'

The diners mouthed their approval. The humble words of thanks, handed down by the national poet, whetted their appetites and justified the indulgence to come.

A succession of platters and bowls laden with steaming hot food was carried in and carried out by the servants: a thin onion soup with croutons served from an ornate tureen, followed by poached trout caught that very day in the Black Loch; then the roast beef, an enormous cut of succulent meat to be carved by the male head of household, accompanied by horseradish sauce and onion gravy from a silver gravy boat; new Ayrshire potatoes smothered in butter, juliennes of carrots and petits pois flavoured with sprigs of mint from the garden.

Isabelle played the perfect hostess, encouraging her guests to eat heartily and making sure the butler kept the ruby red claret flowing. At the same time, she used the conviviality of the evening to grill her male guests for information about their individual specialisms, whilst conveying her own feelings and superior standards about each and every subject.

When Rev Fraser remarked that there was a disappointing attendance at church on the part of the miners, the most recent arrivals in the rapidly increasing population being particularly elusive, Isabelle proclaimed that this was easily explained by the widespread immorality of that particular class of people. It could be traced back to the parliamentary legislation which had absolved landowners of their responsibility towards these erstwhile serfs. Just another stepping stone to the unfortunate collapse of an older and more stable society, in her opinion: a society of tenants, cottars and labourers knitted together with the land, looked after by the landowners who exercised powers of patronage over the church, and saw to it that the Christian message was at the centre of daily life. The reverend nodded deferentially though his instincts told him he perhaps disagreed with some of what had been said. However, as he was unable to think quickly enough to make any sort of meaningful reply in the few seconds allotted to him before his hostess moved onto the next topic, he let the comments pass.

When Mr Black correlated the high levels of absenteeism from school with aspects of the farming year such as harvesting and sowing, childhood illness and lack of footwear, Isabelle countered with her own theory about a lack of moral fibre amongst the working classes, reminding Mr Black that it was his duty to fight dumb ignorance and instil discipline, respect for elders and betters, and the law of the land.

'If parents lack the knowledge and breeding to bring up their children according to fundamental Christian principles,' she continued in lecturing style, 'then, surely, the school has a moral duty to remedy that situation? And I cannot understand,' she went on in her most caustic of tones, 'why people who cannot afford to provide shoes for their children's feet have so many offspring in the first place. It really is beyond all comprehension,' she declared emphatically, staring each and everyone present into an uneasy submission, defying them to come up with an explanation that absolved the poor of any blame in bringing about their present predicament. Isabelle knew from experience that at her most formidable, few people would ever dare to disagree with her. She smiled proudly when a collective murmur of agreement was returned.

David glared at her from the other end of the table but continued to say nothing.

'The situation is quite complex,' began Dr Matheson, feeling uncomfortable at the way in which the company seemed to have turned on poor people less fortunate than themselves and who, after all, were not present to defend themselves. As he was about to challenge the simplicity of her remarks, Isabelle was approached by the butler in a state of agitation and the discussion came to an abrupt end. With obvious irritation, Isabelle asked for everyone's pardon before sweeping out of the room in high dudgeon to deal with 'a mundane but pressing matter of housekeeping'. The fawning servant followed closely.

'Well thank God for that!' said Phee. 'Perhaps they've burned the millefeuille,' she added with a giggle, successfully lightening the mood to everyone's relief.

'Oh, I do love a piece of pastry to finish off a splendid meal,' offered Mr Maclean. 'Don't we, my dear?' he asked, turning to his wife who agreed heartily. 'With a bit of cream and a raspberry or two in season,' he added with obvious longing, hoping the dessert wasn't far away.

'Do you remember Mrs MacGregor's Scotch Trifle, Richard?' said Elizabeth to her brother, laughing, reminding him of their old housekeeper and her substantial puddings.

'Divine,' came his reply, 'especially when she overdid the sherry!'

'My favourite's lemon soufflé, and cranachan a close second. What about you, brother dear?' continued Phee, instigating an enthusiastic conversation about pansy jelly and savarins, paté sables with almond cream and hazelnut meringues, strawberry vacherins on summer afternoons and chocolate mousse at any time of the year.

'I believe the French are hard to beat when it comes to such niceties,' interjected David, finally succumbing to the playful mood that had developed in the absence of his elder sister. 'Crêpes served in even the humblest of Parisian establishments are to die for! Don't you recall, Phee?' He waxed lyrical, caught up in memories of happy family vacations and beautiful food. 'Do you remember the delight of Tarte Tatin et café noir after a day on the Seine?' he asked her. 'It has to be the original recipe, of course, from the Demoiselles Tatin de Lamotte-Beuvron. Magnifique!' He kissed his finger tips in the exaggerated manner of the French, laughed heartily, catching Rose's eye with a wide smile.

'Mais oui, bien sur,' replied Phee, 'Ahhhh, les Français sont les meilleurs pour nourriture et l'amour,' she said in her most ridiculous French accent, looking directly at Rose and Elizabeth with wide eyes and a huge grin.

'Don't forget the Italians,' advised Dr Matheson, a little disconcerted by Phee's French recollections and insinuations but reminded happily of a climbing trip he had made to the Dolomites as a student. 'I find their meringues much superior to the French or the Swiss. The sugar is made into a syrup before adding to the egg-whites, I believe. Gives the meringue a delightfully chewy texture,' he explained.

Rose blushed at her father's expertise in the culinary arts. 'You think you know someone then find out they're an expert in the most unexpected of matters,' she said to the others, gently teasing her father, making everyone laugh.

David looked at Rose and thought her the prettiest girl he'd ever seen. Her dark hair swept up into a tumble of curls on the top of her head, her soft white skin and pale pink cheeks, her grey eyes and perfect mouth accentuated by a green silk dress. David's attraction to Rose wasn't lost on Phee who had noticed him watching her all evening. She smiled happily for her brother, catching the eye of Elizabeth who raised an eyebrow and smiled back knowingly.

The laughter and easy conversation ended sharply with Isabelle's return. They sat up straight with all the appearance of naughty schoolchildren caught out by a dreaded school ma'am.

'My apologies, everyone. It was a matter of no consequence,' she sang. She took care to arrange her skirts, patting her hair into place as she sat down. 'Do continue, don't stop on account of me,' she commanded, referring to the sudden silence that had descended on the party, then added quickly before anyone else had the chance, 'Now, where was I? Ah, Doctor,' she remembered, pinning him down with the eyes of a cat on the prowl. 'Now tell me, how are things on the health front? I hear you've advertised for another doctor – a fellow practitioner to take over the Blackrigg patients – such is the demand on your time and the magnitude of the difficulties facing you.'

'Yes indeed,' he agreed becoming serious again, 'With the population growth of the last few years, I cannot cover the villages and the farms by myself. I also have to make regular visits to the fever hospital at Allerhill to check on any of my patients admitted there. The vaccination scheme alone is quite laborious. It's difficult not to miss someone, especially when I go in at the front door and they go out of the back window, and I have to return later without warning to catch them!'

This elicited a loud tut of disapproval from Isabelle who felt vindicated in her earlier comments. 'What did I just say about dumb ignorance and immorality?' she reminded the gathering.

Phee stifled a giggle as she pictured some poor fellow desperately jumping out of an open window in order to avoid the doctor's needle.

Feeling a full report had been called for, Dr Matheson continued. 'Another doctor would also give an almost permanent presence at Spittal Cottage here in Blackrigg which I think you will all agree would be a good thing. We have two cases of scarlet fever in Stoneyrigg at the moment but the diphtheria outbreak of the winter seems to have abated, you'll be pleased to learn.'

'Thank you, thank you, Doctor,' Isabelle interrupted briskly having had quite enough of medical matters, deciding Dr Matheson had held the floor for long enough. 'How fortunate we are to have such a dedicated practitioner here in Blackrigg,' she said with every ounce of gratitude she could muster, bowing her head towards him in an exaggerated fashion.

Then turning quickly to the others as if about to share a wonderful secret she asked, 'Would you like to hear about my plans for a Harvest Home in the Autumn? Yes?'

She surveyed the clueless company, ready to burst into full flow.

'Shouldn't you discuss this with the family first, Isabelle?' David interrupted in alarm, trying to urge caution in announcing details of what might be an outlandish idea, best suited to past times. After contemplating all evening how the estate was going to pay for Isabelle's extravagant plans for the family and the house, he thought it better if the matter was fully discussed with himself and the factor first.

But she was having none of it. She launched into a vigorous description of her idea to revive the age-old celebration of 'Harvest Home', to bring back the good, old days which were so sorely missed by no one more than herself.

'The tenants will be invited and their servants. We'll hold it in the big barn at Home Farm, just like they used to in the past. We'll have speeches and supper, singing and dancing – perhaps Mr Simpson will come with his quintet – and you, Reverend Fraser, shall offer a prayer for the bounteous harvest gathered in.' Isabelle stopped, suddenly aware that no one was listening.

All eyes were focused on the doorway behind her.

She turned slowly in the silence to see what had taken their attention and there was Neil Tennant glaring back at them with a face like thunder.

'Dr Matheson,' Neil began.

Immediately, he was pulled backwards into the hall as the butler slung an arm around his neck then yanked hard, gagging Neil with his free hand. They fell together onto the floor. A small circle of servants, attracted by the fracas, watched open mouthed. Dishes of trifle and platters of sweetmeats held aloft in vain, clattered to the floor in the scuffle that followed, covering both men in a mess of cream and confection as they slithered in and out of each other's grasp. Finally, Neil twisted out of his adversary's slippery hold and got to his feet. He advanced towards the doorway to deliver his message again to the astonishment of the awestruck figures at the dinner table who sat riveted by the sudden turn of events.

Isabelle shouted for the butler, 'Jameson, take him away!'

Neil held onto the door frame with both hands as Jameson came for him once again from behind. He pushed back against the elder man with the full force of his body, catapulting himself forward into the room.

'Get out of here, you ruffian,' she said to the dishevelled intruder. 'It is not convenient, I told you to wait.' The diners looked at Isabelle as it dawned on them why she had been called away earlier by the servants. 'How dare he barge in like this and interrupt our gathering,' she said with indignation, as if to explain.

Neil took in the glass chandelier, the candelabra dripping with candle wax, the family silver on the snow-white tablecloth. He saw the florid complexions of the men in dinner suits and wing-collars, finely-etched glasses full of red wine set before them. He saw pretty ladies in silk dresses, their pale complexions warmed by cheerful conversation and merriment: the younger Melville sister who was often seen passing through the village; the dark-haired daughter of the doctor; and the shy, fair haired girl from the manse whom he'd spotted across the crowded church on Sunday mornings. They were staring back at him, their eyes wide in alarm.

'A young lad lies sick and in need of help, his family out of their minds with concern while you sit here in all your finery,' said Neil emboldened by anger, indicating the surroundings with his outstretched hands. 'For pity's sake,' he implored.

David looked at his elder sister, 'What is this, Isabelle? Jameson, leave him be,' he ordered as the butler appeared for another attempt at removing his quarry. 'Leave him be and let him say his piece.'

Dr Matheson introduced Neil as one of the blacksmith Tennants, 'You all know the family,' he told them. 'Now, young man, what is the matter?' he asked, standing up in preparation for a quick departure.

'You're needed urgently in Stoneyrigg, Doctor,' Neil explained. 'It's young George Broadley, sir. He was pulled from the burn barely two weeks ago and is now ill with a fever. The family ask that you attend.'

'And very brave you were to save him, Neil,' replied the doctor who knew of the incident at the burn. 'Skilful too. And here you come to his rescue once again.'

Neil wanted no complement for himself. 'It's a matter of great urgency, sir. I've been kept waiting for some time. They would not let me in,' he explained looking in Isabelle's direction, 'Or pass on the information it would seem.'

Dr Matheson turned in disbelief towards Isabelle then removed the napkin from his collar with a flourish. He could not hide his distaste at her behaviour in keeping him from his calling. He stood beside the young blacksmith, gave his sincere thanks for the evening to David and Phee.

'Come Rose. Come, my dear,' he said, holding out his hand to his daughter. 'It's high time you saw what was ahead of you in your chosen profession.' She gave Phee and Elizabeth a quick embrace; nodded a shy smile in David's direction.

The three figures hurried into the hall then out into the night, leaving the rest of the gathering with nowhere to look, their eyes downcast.

'But we haven't had dessert yet,' whined Isabelle after a while, 'Or toasted the King.' She raised her glass. 'God Save the King?' she offered weakly.

No one said a word. Red wine splashed onto the tablecloth when she returned the glass clumsily to the table. The gathering watched dumbstruck as the red colour spread quickly across a wide area, travelling outwards along the fibres of the pristine fabric like gossip on an ill-wind.

David stared at the blood red stain appearing before his eyes. He pictured the doctor with his beautiful daughter rushing through the night to the aid of a poor, ailing child. He could hardly imagine what they must be thinking of the Melville family and all they stood for. Was he, David Melville, tainted by his sister's vanity? Was the family forever reduced in their eyes as conceited and vacuous when compared with the noble actions of a humble blacksmith? He looked with contempt at his elder sister, dressed in expensive silks and lace, a ridiculous feather in her hair. He saw a gross caricature of the Victorian values and manners she espoused. Her cold heart was devoid of empathy; her youthful beauty aged and disfigured by ambition and self-interest. The glittering evening that had held such promise was suddenly tarnished and spent, like the candles guttering in the candelabra, now dripping with grease. David took his napkin, set it on the table before him, clearing his throat and doing his best to appear calm. He adjusted the wing collar which threatened to choke him.

'Shall we retire to the drawing room for coffee before we call it a day?' he asked, rising from his chair.

Led by their host and his younger sister, the guests rose from the table. They quietly left the room, leaving Isabelle all alone.

# Chapter 5

## THE DOCTOR AND HIS DAUGHTER

Dr Matheson and Rose sat immersed in their own thoughts as the small motor car sped through the darkness towards the village lights. A few people wrapped up in coats and hats against the cold night air of early spring could be seen leaving the various halls and venues in the village where Friday evening activities and assemblies were drawing to a close. Several times, the doctor had to employ his horn to warn pedestrians out of his way. Their destination lay waiting in a pall of smoke beyond the end of the line of gas lights marking the roadside. Rose could smell Stoneyrigg long before she was able to pick out the faint shapes of the dimly lit windows. Fumes from the coke ovens wafted in from the south, catching the back of her throat; the stench of the dry closets came and went as the car was driven slowly along the long line of the Bottom Row in search of house number twenty-four.

'You wait here, Rose,' said the doctor as he reached behind the seat for his leather medical bag. 'If the situation allows it, and the family agree, you can come in later.' He looked at her as he made to close the door. In the shadow of the unlit street, she resembled his late wife in so many ways and, despite all of his training in science and rational thinking, he briefly feared the illness present inside the house might take her away from him too.

'You'll be fine here. I won't be long,' he said as he hurried away to his patient.

Rose thought of the young boy inside and of what might ail him, of his poor family distraught with worry, and hoped her father would return soon with good news. She watched the empty street for a while with growing trepidation. A distant cough heightened her senses till the sound of silence was a loud rush in her ears. Occasionally people appeared from houses or behind her, from the direction of the village, then disappeared again into the darkness. Both the vehicle and its young lady passenger attracted enthusiastic comment from pairs of young men passing by but they moved on quickly when they realised it was the doctor's car.

Rose drew her coat up around her neck, slumped down into her seat, hoping to find warmth and invisibility. Her father seemed to have been away for ages and this wasn't the sort of place she wanted to spend any more time in than she had to. Miss Isabelle's insistence that Stoneyrigg was full of the intemperate, the feckless, and the debauched without Christian values preyed on her mind. She looked longingly at the door of number twenty-four as two men with caps pulled low over their eyes appeared from nowhere. They circled the vehicle, admiring the gleaming blue paintwork and the chrome finish. She watched them carefully as they inspected the radiator grill, the shiny spokes, the tyres, and the small running board on the driver's side, peering in through the back window for a glimpse of the leather seats and pronouncing themselves well impressed by the workmanship of the Airdrie manufactory where the vehicle had been produced. They did not seem to acknowledge Rose's presence at all but she became increasingly convinced that they were about to jump in and drive off with her. She grew gradually more and more agitated, her heart beating faster till it was almost a flutter. When one of the fellows put his hand on the handle of the driver's door, she'd had enough. She shot out of the passenger side like a frightened bird released from its cage then flew in through the door of the house her father had disappeared into earlier. Both lads looked after her in consternation, completely unaware that anyone had been in the vehicle, engrossed as they had been in the wonders of the latest engineering marvel and at what money could buy.

When Rose burst into the safety of the Broadley home, she apologised immediately for her intrusion, such was the warmth, calm and pathos of the scene that greeted her. She was given a chair by the father of the house who stood by the window as she was brought into the small company guarding the bed where the sick child lay. Rose could see how easily her own father fitted his role and why his patients held him in such high esteem. He sat composed beside the bed with his sleeves rolled up, his starched collar removed, his jacket draped casually over the back of his chair. The child's mother sat in the only other chair in the room as she watched over her sleeping child. An older woman perched on an upturned wooden box by the fire, quietly observing. The doctor introduced Rose to the three adults present, explaining that she was to begin her medical training soon. He patted her hand, giving it a squeeze to let her know that she was welcome.

'I think Geordie might be just about over the worst of the fever,' he explained to her, knowing that Rose was too sensitive to the feelings of the family to ask the question foremost in her head, in case the prognosis was very poor. 'He was pulled from the burn a couple of weeks ago; contracted bronchitis but it's been treated very well by his mother with steam and poultices,' he continued, smiling at Ellen Broadley and nodding encouragingly. 'The question is, why the fever now? His lungs sound fine, which is excellent news but he has a sore throat and a very flushed face.' He summarised the main symptoms for the benefit of Rose but mainly for the family even though there had already been a lengthy discussion. 'Perhaps some nausea and stomach pain earlier today too,' he continued, almost thinking aloud. 'Then the fever came on.'

'It could be the scarlet fever, Miss,' said Ellen softly, unable to hide the fear in her eyes.

'On top of bronchitis?' said Rose trying not to sound alarmed.

But Ellen Broadley articulated her thoughts. 'Aye, yin condition would be bad enough but twa the gither's faur worse than twice as bad as yin would be on its ain.'

Rose knew instinctively what Ellen had meant though she did not speak the same language.

'We'll know better in the next few hours,' replied the doctor, intent on keeping the mood positive. 'The important thing is that Geordie's temperature seems to be coming down. He's a strong lad and he has age on his side. He's not a wee tot anymore, nearly ten years old, in fact,' he explained, feeling the boy's brow with his hand before turning to the mother. 'I'll come back in the morning, Mrs Broadley. Try not to worry, get some sleep yourself. Remember, plenty of fluids when he wakes up and keep the room cool. Best leave out the vinegar when you're cooling him down. It's an antiseptic more than anything else and he'll have had enough of that. Just plain water will do.'

Rose looked at the much-loved child, tucked up in his parents' bed, his head resting on a pillow of chaff, his long dark eyelashes sweeping down onto an angelic face and she wondered what his future held. She said a silent prayer for him, blinking back tears that threatened to come. As she got up to go, Rose was struck by the modesty of her surroundings: a tiny room where three chairs, a wooden box and a small table were the only furniture. Rose thought of the grandeur of Parkgate House where she had spent the evening; looked down at her fine clothes and shoes, aware of her carefully pinned and decorated hair. She blushed, shamed by the stark contrast between her own comfortable life and what she saw around her. The woman called Mrs Birse, who had sat silently by the fire, saw her looking around the room and sensed her discomfort.

'So, ye're tae be a doctor lik yer faither, Miss Rose?' she said, fixing her with a beady eye. 'Thon's a fine profession, nae question. You mak sure ye're a guid yin. Some'll say ye shouldnae be a doctor, you bein' a wuman an' a'. But ne'er heed them. We had a lady doctor here a while back, an' a fine doctor she wis tae. Guid luck tae ye, Miss Matheson.' Mary Birse held Rose in her gaze then added, 'When ye're up at the medical school, mind whit ye seen here.'

'Aye, guid luck tae ye, Miss. Thanks for yer concern for the lad,' said Geordie's father as the pair made to go out the door.

'Thank you all very much,' Rose said finally, humbled by their good wishes for her at such a difficult time for them. 'I hope... I hope Geordie will recover soon.'

She made to follow behind her father only to find herself in a crush at the doorway. The two ruffians who had been looking over the motor car earlier were pushing their way into number twenty-four. Startled, she almost fell into the street. She pulled herself together, straightening her coat, before hurrying into the vehicle.

'What are they doing, going into a house where there's a sick child, at this time of night?' she asked her father. 'There's hardly room to swing a cat in there!'

'They live there, of course,' her father explained. 'One is Geordie's elder brother and the other is probably a boarder.'

'A boarder?!' she exclaimed as she settled into the front seat for the drive home. 'But where do they all sleep?'

'In the back room, of course. And there's another son too but that makes only four, in addition to the parents of course. There are families of twelve children in this village, living in two rooms. That's fourteen in total, and those families often have boarders living with them too, to make ends meet.'

'But it shouldn't be allowed,' she said. 'It can't be healthy... or dignified.'

'And would you have them starve, Rose?' her father asked. 'Poverty, good health and your definition of dignity do not go together, I'm afraid.'

'But why do they have so many children, Father? Surely that's at the root of the problem.'

'It's part of the problem. But Rose, I think you have a lot to learn about the human condition and the sooner you attend a few anatomy lessons the better,' he teased.

Rose squirmed in her seat. She closed her coat tightly around her, bright red with embarrassment that her father should think her so naive or allude to the subject of reproduction at all, even though she was about to enter medical school. For all her success at school in science, mathematics and the Classics, nothing had prepared her for her visit to Stoneyrigg that night. She knew then that she had a lot to learn and come to terms with. She looked ahead as the headlights picked out the journey home through the night, at the inky black mesh of the wind-hewn hedgerows against the dark sky, and the bright eyes of animals scurrying across the road on their nocturnal forays for food. She thought about Geordie Broadley and the likelihood of him having scarlet fever. Was there nothing that could be done for him beyond cooling him down and waiting for nature to take its course, watching him and praying for him? She thought of Beth March in 'Little Women', a favourite book of her childhood. Gentle, musical Beth had scarlet fever but all the family could do was watch her getting weaker, their prayers going unanswered. And her death affected them all – Meg, Amy and Jo – changing the way they thought about their own lives and how they acted. But that story was set more than fifty years ago. Had medical science done nothing to progress the fight against this condition in all of that time?

'He has a fight on his hands,' said the doctor, reading her thoughts. 'They've isolated the organism that causes the disease but there's no cure yet, or vaccination to prevent it in the future. We can only wait and see what happens, Rose. The next forty-eight hours will be crucial. If pneumonia sets in because of either condition,' he explained, reminding her of the bronchitis, 'there's little hope. It can spread to other parts of the body, including the brain.'

'Meningitis?' she offered. 'Shouldn't he be in the Fever Hospital away from that... that slum?'

'If it was smallpox, typhus or tuberculosis, yes. We'll see how he is in the morning,' he replied. 'It may not come to that. As a doctor, I have a duty to reduce the opportunities the scarlet fever has to spread, if that's what it is, and I'll have a word with the family tomorrow about people coming and going from the house whilst he's infectious. But Geordie's better where he is – with his family I mean. Believe it or not, I've seen worse living conditions. And there is something there that might make all the difference to him, Rose.'

Rose looked at her father and knew what he meant. She saw it in his eyes.

Love, she thought. Geordie is much loved. Where there is Love, there is always Hope. She smiled and looked ahead into the night as the small vehicle purred along the road home.

# Chapter 6

## LIFE IN THE RAW

The railway running through Blackrigg was double tracked, a linchpin within a dense network spread across Scotland from east to west like a huge web of iron, connecting many hundreds of small pits and quarries for the purpose of removing coal and other minerals to local and regional centres for manufacture and distribution. Sidings were constructed as the variety of freight destined for the area increased. The station in the village was created as an afterthought, when passenger travel was well established elsewhere and local demand sufficiently high for its potential profitability to be recognised by the railway company. The addition of a ticket office, two rest rooms and a second platform with an iron bridge to cross the line in safety, marked the beginning of the boom years for the area's economy and put Blackrigg on the railway map. Though not as Blackrigg exactly but as Craigpark, the former having been judged too harsh and unattractive a name.

Craigpark station was a favourite haunt of local boys with nothing better to do, much to the distress of the stationmaster. As they wandered down the Station Road from the village, the comings and goings of passenger trains and their smaller workhorse cousins, controlled from the big white signal box just beyond the railway bridge, held their gaze. The sight of the signalmen actually moving the long, shiny levers back and forth to change signals and points never disappointed because the impact of their actions was immediately apparent in sight and sound. The noise of steam puffing and chuffing out of blackened funnels and shrill whistles of warning incited excited lads to hurry down the hill to get a better view.

Discussions about engine sizes, classes of locomotives, and methods of operation were animated and often heated as was the case early one cold spring morning when John and Jim Birse stood at the best vantage point for viewing the shunting and pulling of coal wagons back and forward into serried ranks on the sidings by the pits. They marvelled at the power of the speedy little pugs and at the order they brought to the chaotic scene of coal heaps, stockpiles of bricks, and assorted stone mounds that punctuated a landscape black with coal dust. Several bings of waste rock in various stages of creation identified the area's numerous pits, near and far. They could pick out Broadrigg Collieries Nos. 1, 2 and 3 where their father and most of their friends' fathers worked and, in the distance, Netherrigg and Southrigg Pit bings rose out of a patchwork of sunny, green fields: two grey pyramids of spoil that testified to the sweat and toil of a hundred men working underground. They pointed out the brickworks that processed the reddings of the underground levels of the mines. Several brick-built chimneys belched thick, black smoke and heat that shimmered against the clear blue sky above. The power station, the washery, and the long row of coke ovens built in association with Stoneyrigg Pit, filled the space between the roadway just below the miners' rows where they lived, and the main railway line and the marshalling yard where the incessant activity of shunting and pulling held such fascination for them. In a couple of years, when they had left school, Jim and John would be in amongst it all, working boys in a world of men. It was their destiny. The thought of it thrilled and alarmed them at one and the same time.

Saturday morning had dawned bright and fair after a night of heavy rain and a brisk easterly wind blew cold through the hawthorn that grew beside the road. The brothers had been hounded out of bed by their mother who had given them a breakfast of white bread spread with syrup and a cup of tea before sending them out on their quest with a tin pail each and one shovel between them, ordering them to come back with full pails or they would catch it from their father.

'Awa' an earn yer keep,' she had called after them, shutting them out in the cold with a slam of the door.

Although the morning was bitter enough to bring a tear to the eye and a drip to the nose, they were glad to be out of the fetid air of the back room which they shared with Davy, also adopted by Mary and Alex, and two boarders. Davy and the lodgers worked down the pit. They made such a fuss and clatter when they got dressed in the morning that the twins were awake anyway and couldn't get back to sleep.

The sound of steam and mechanical activity from the general direction of the station reminded the brothers of their quest. They ran down the ramp into the station yard beside Platform One then peered along the track. In their hodden grey, peeking out from behind the painted white gates, they hoped to disappear into the stony background. The stationmaster stood in his smart uniform with a whistle in his mouth, his chest stuck out like a sergeant at arms, waiting for the 07.15 to Glasgow to build up enough steam to take its leave. A final slamming of doors, then he blew his whistle with a passion as he brought his flag down by his side, commanding departure. The twins watched him set about his business, careful not to distract him from his busy schedule. This was a man whose life was ruled by the clock, who timed his meal breaks and visits to the toilet by the railway timetable, and checked his watch at every hoot and toot. The local boys had learned to mimic these sounds, spending many a happy hour watching his frustration and confusion grow with each whistle they delivered from a hidden spy hole. Had no one told these scallywags that he was a very important person, he often wondered? He had the biggest house in Blackrigg to prove it and people from far and near measured their day by his whistle. He was responsible for the smooth running of the railway and for the safety of company property, responsibilities he took very seriously indeed.

John fidgeted behind his brother as they waited in their hiding place. Jim told him to stay still or the stationmaster would notice them. He would know what they were up to, lurking in the bushes with two pails and a shovel.

'I cannae help it, Jim. I'm deein on a pee,' explained John with his legs crossed, tormented by the cold which made his bare feet sting and throb.

'Whit did ye tak yer boots aff for? The cauld aye maks ye need tae gang,' replied Jim.

'Ma feet were sair. They rub ma heels an' ma taes somethin' terrible. The cauld's better than sair feet,' said John, defensively.

'Weel wheesht an' haud it in,' ordered his brother. 'Thon's whit ye get when yer feet come awa' sae fast,' as if indicating divine retribution for a growth spurt. 'Ye'll get a new pair o' boots in the summer an' no afore.' After a while, he pointed as the signal dropped. 'Here's the train, get ready.'

They peered through the gaps in the fence and saw a large locomotive advance slowly towards them from the Glasgow direction. The points on the line shifted sideways and the engine snaked off the mainline onto a siding followed by a line of large covered trucks. It slowed to a halt out of sight with a gradual grinding of the brakes and a long skoosh of steam.

The boys ran to the back of the waiting room building then crept along the wall to where a group of scrubby trees gave them cover. They watched two men with ruddy complexions and stout sticks move across the yard to engage the driver in conversation. A guard and three young boys, not much older than Jim and John themselves, joined the discussion. One of the men and two boys positioned themselves near the entrance to the station yard, perilously close to where the twins crouched down in the shadows, whilst the other men set about opening the first of the trucks, bringing the wooden side panel down onto the stony ground to form a ramp.

John hated this part of the proceedings but subterfuge was always tinged with excitement. If they succeeded in their quest and got off scot-free, the elation would be delicious. If they got caught by the stationmaster, the worst he would do was grab them by the ear and slap them round the head, yelling that they were worthless Staney lads, useful only as cannon fodder. Whatever happened, they had to go home with two full pails or they would feel their father's wrath and the back of his hand as they often did. His insults were much worse than the beatings, though. Words hurt more than blows. He would call them useless and feckless and good for nothing. He would shout that they were nothing but wee bastards that nobody else wanted and were they not grateful for the food and shelter he provided? Did they not know how hard he worked, down in the bowels of the earth every day to put siller in rich men's pockets?

The first of the cattle emerged from the truck, poised tentatively at the top of the ramp, noses down at their feet bracing themselves against the descent, and with fear in their eyes. The men and boys shouted and whacked their sticks to get them moving. Hooves sliding and skittering down the wooden ramp brought lowing from the animals still captive in the train. In the commotion, no one seemed to notice the two young interlopers in amongst the throng of legs, scooping up the excrement slopping out of the frightened beasts. As each truck was opened and emptied, the yard filled further with moaning animals that seemed to sense they were about to make their last journey. Jim and John stooped low between the barrel-shaped cattle, ducking beneath the heaving forms in search of another splat of wet defecation, avoiding the hefty kicks when they came, holding their noses tight against the stench while breathing through their mouths.

Their plan was to follow the animals out of the yard and onto the road where further cow pats could be retrieved but the boys had learned that the station yard was always more productive. Besides, they could only follow the herd a couple of hundred yards up the road before they entered the territory of the Netherrigg clan who would be out in force to gather cow pats for their own use. Some people said that folk in Netherrigg were so poor they had dirt floors and burned cow dung on their fires. Neither boy relished a fight over a pail of cow pats.

The twins thought they were doing well, none of the cattle herds had seen them, the stationmaster hadn't appeared, and their pails were filling up fast. Then their luck ran out.

'Hey You! You boys! What do yous think you're doing?' came an authoritative voice from the pedestrian bridge across the railway. Then, at the sight of the pails of steaming dung, 'Thon's railway company property. Stop thieves!' But as his temper rose, he reverted fully to his own tongue. 'Stoap, ye maukit wee scunners!'

'It's the stationmaister,' said John, 'Run for it!' The boys ducked and wove between the cattle, clutching their precious booty firmly in one hand.

'Easy lads,' said one of the men, 'Dinnae fleg the beasts.'

But no one had warned the stationmaster about frightening the beasts and his whistle's piercing sound filled the air. The bigger animals started to bellow loudly; heads went up as they jostled for position and in one seething mass they moved towards the track onto the road, slowly at first then faster and faster in time to the whistle which continued relentlessly.

'Stop that, ye daftie!' called one of the men, adding to the pandemonium. 'Staun back, lads!' he shouted to everyone in the vicinity as the stampede took off. The terrified animals veered onto the Station Road, careering headlong in the direction of Blackrigg with the minders following them at full pelt.

Jim and John shadowed the chaos as far as the road then sloped off in the opposite direction, realising they wouldd have to escape through the fields, go the long way round, back through the village to evade the long arm of the stationmaster's law. They ran up the road to the gate of the nearest field, climbed over into the mud : two brothers in arms who'd survived another of life's battles together. The twins laughed at the sight of the ragged children of Netherrigg waiting patiently with their pails at the bottom of the hill in the cold. They would have a long wait.

'It's no railway property at a',' said John when he'd caught his breath. 'He wants it for his ain gairden, tae put oan his roses. He wants tae win the prize at the horticultural show again.'

The Horticultural Society had flourished since the miners had been rented land for allotments by the Coal Company. Prizes at the show were much sought after and keenly fought over.

'Weel too bad,' said Jim. 'This lot's for faither's leeks an' oor soup.' They laughed heartily at the thought of dung soup and with relief that they had enough in their pails to fertilise their father's allotment, or at least to keep him quiet till the next consignment of cattle for the Cooperative Society slaughterhouse came in by train.

The brothers made their way slowly along the side of the field, heading for a suitable place to cross the railway line which formed an impenetrable barrier between where they were and where they wanted to go. The pails of cow dung proved to be exceedingly heavy when carried so far. To make matters worse, the fields were sodden after the long, wet winter and full of potholes that sucked their feet down threatening to hold them fast. More than once, Jim had to retrieve a boot plucked by the mud from his feet which were now as cold and wet as his brother's. John felt vindicated for having taken his boots off then leaving them in the hedge at the top of Station Road before the start of their adventure. He intended to retrieve them as they passed their hiding place on his way to Stoneyrigg, and he wouldn't have to spend ages cleaning off the mud and polishing them like his brother.

Eventually, with tired legs and sore arms, they came to the bridge from Back o' Moss Farm that gave access to Blackrigg. They followed the old cart track to the ford on the Red Burn that led to the Meadie.

In the sheltered places by the burn, where the willows kept the cold, easterly wind at bay and the morning sun shone through the branches, the brothers dallied in the warmth, looking for small fish like minnows and sticklebacks. They sought out the best stones for skimming, arguing about who could bounce them the furthest across the mill pool. They watched a dipper balance on a rock, its dark brown plumage black against the pale stone. A flash of white and he was gone, plunging deep into the clear water, only to reappear with an empty beak ready to try again. To the clink of the hungry dipper and the song of the snipe courting in the fields, Jim sat down to wash his muddy feet and boots in the river water. It felt perishing to his hands but warmed his feet, leaving them tingling as the blood started flowing again.

They were alerted from their reverie by the noise of the 08.35 from Glasgow chugging along the railway line on the other side of the burn and into the station further up the line. The sun was higher in the sky and they hadn't meant to be so long. They could hear the sounds of people calling to cats and neighbours, doors slamming, a motor vehicle passing on Main Street. Rather than take the path that followed the burn where it was overlooked by the new houses at Burnside, they headed up the Doctor's Brae, hoping that people wouldn't notice two boys walking along the road carrying pails of fresh manure; hoping also, that the chaos of the stampeding cattle was a thing of the past and had gone unnoticed, before most people were out and about.

The boys made their way along the kerbside, unseen by adults going about their business. They were just another couple of lads sent out for a message by a mother busy at home. Even Mrs Gow and the Widow MacAulay were too intent on their own concerns to notice anyone else. Their conversation focused on the lateness of the bread delivery at the Co-op, delayed by some commotion or other along at Craigpark, which neither woman could inform the other about at that particular moment. Each promised to let the other know if they were appraised of any information in due course. Jim and John looked at each other knowingly and hurried on. They would soon be home.

A horse and cart making its way in their direction looked familiar: Old Fletcher with a delivery of eggs from Mosside with Dan Potts up beside him, earning a few bob as an errand boy. The horse clopped passed in the direction of the grocer's further along Main Street as Dan waved cheerfully, proud to be out and about earning some money, proving his worth to the world. The brothers waved back as they went on their way.

Less welcome was the sight of the Graham sisters approaching from Stoneyrigg but, thankfully, on the other side of the road. At least the girls wouldn't smell the terrible stench of dung the brothers were leaving in their wake. The girls looked across wavingly happily. The middle one was called Minn and she sat behind them in class. She had lovely, long, black hair, a beautiful smile and a temperament to match. The twins smiled back wanly, not wanting to encourage a closer encounter. They were glad she remained on the other side of the road, on her way to the Co-op with two of her sisters.

John ran ahead when they neared the junction of Station Road and Main Street at the Craigpark Inn. He made for the spot where he had left his boots, expecting to find them where they had been stashed in a gap in the hedge, just out of sight of passers-by on the road.

As Jim approached, John turned as white as a sheet. 'They're awa'!' he said, a sinking feeling in his stomach.

'Whit dae ye mean, they're awa'? Are ye sure ye left them richt here?' replied Jim, joining John's frantic search. 'Ye've had it when we git hame, if ye cannae find them,' he added, stating the obvious. 'Ma could sell them oan tae somebody when she gits ye a new pair in the summer.'

'It's even worse than that, Jim,' said John with rising alarm in his voice. 'They werenae ma boots! They were Davy's!'

He saw the look of horror on Jim's face.

'I took them aff cause they were ower big an' were rubbin' ma heels. I think somebody's stolen them.'

'Ye daft bat! A brand new pair o' boots left in the hedge? Ye micht as weel have put a sign oan them sayin "Steal Me".' Jim couldn't believe his brother's stupidity and carelessness with somebody else's boots. Especially Davy's boots.

'Whit are you twa up tae?' came a voice from up the road. It was Rob Duncan and his brother, Sandy.

Just whit we need, thought John when he saw the boys. They were friends but great rivals at the same time. He knew they wouldn't miss a chance to extract the maximum pain from their situation. 'Oh, nothin',' replied John. 'Jist lookin' in the hedge. Ye never ken whit ye micht come across.'

'What's thon smell?' said Sandy, the younger Duncan brother. 'You twa been sent for the messages again?'

Rob laughed loudly, appreciating Sandy's humour.

'Awfy funny,' said Jim. 'It's the day o' the cattle delivery for the slaughter hoose. Ye ken how it is.'

'Aye, we ken,' replied Rob, feeling some sympathy for his friends and glad his mother insisted he wouldn't be doing such things. She wanted a better life for him, better than grovelling about in the muck from the back end of an animal.

'Somebody's taen a pair o' boots he sat here,' said Jim. 'They're Davy's boots. If ye hear oniethin aboot their whauraboots, let us ken, will ye? He'll get a hammerin' fae ma faither AND fae Davy when they find oot he's lost them,' explained Jim, pointing at his dejected brother.

The Duncans looked at John with growing empathy. Davy Birse was known as a hard man down the pit and Alex wasn't unknown for letting fly with his fists, especially in his younger days, though it was said that his bark was worse than his bite. *Birse by name and birse by nature*, a man whose face had borne a frown since the dawn of time.

'We best get hame an' face the music,' said Jim.

'Aye, cheerio,' said Sandy. 'We'll let ye ken if we hear oniethin.'

The twins made their way wearily along the road, weighed down by their burden of guilt and a pail of dung each. Maybe they would get a warm cup of tea before they had to tell their mother the story about the boots. She would be happy with the two pails of manure. She would laugh at the story of the stampede and at how upset the stationmaster had been at the sight of them. She would say that when some folk are given a uniform, it goes to their heads and they need to remember where they came from. After all, the stationmaster was just plain Wullie Johnstone whose father had been a poacher a while back. She would say that some people needed to learn how to share. If people learned how to share then the world would be a much better place, she would say.

# Chapter 7

## THE REQUEST

On warm summer evenings, when the hours of daylight stretched on into the late hours or at other times of the year when the weather was in the least clement, Blackrigg people were out and about in search of conversation, leisure and fresh air. Leaving behind the confines and cramped conditions of the workplace and the home, they had their own definition of fair weather suitable for outdoor gatherings and activities. It was forged by their experience of life in a place not well-blessed by sunshine. At a relatively high altitude in the very middle of the country, winds from any direction could bring precipitation. Temperatures were always lower than those experienced by their fellow countrymen living in more temperate, sheltered valleys and coastal plains, not far distant, but a world away from Blackrigg itself.

It was common for the working men of the community to be seen standing in the street talking, sometimes in twos and threes and sometimes in much bigger gatherings. The newly opened Public Hall, built by the ratepayers with generous contributions from both the Coal Company and Lady Moffat, offered plenty of space for discourse and assembly but the men inclined towards the open spaces and natural meeting points of the street. A favourite rendezvous was Craigpark where Blackrigg's Main Street led onto the road that ran east towards the Rows and met with the hill road that contoured The Law to the north, and the Station Road leading south into Lanarkshire. The Craigpark Inn had gone out of use long ago. It stood empty and forlorn but the steading, once occupied by the horses for the stagecoach, was used by the farm of the same name for the storage of hay and equipment. On the village side of the hill road was the Smiddy that had served the stagecoach company. It remained a working blacksmith's but covered a wider range of business over a bigger area than before.

On the afternoon of the day of the cattle delivery, the east wind had not abated and the air felt cold and fresh. The blue sky was punctuated by high cumulus and a blast of chilling rain or hail later in the day seemed possible. Several Stoneyrigg men, hands in pockets, stood blethering at Craigpark, scarves knotted and collars turned up against the breeze. Their spirits were high, as they always were on a Saturday afternoon, after the short morning shift and at the prospect of a day and a half of relaxation and recuperation from the heavy work of the rest of the week. Some would head up the hill road towards their allotments where the ground needed to be prepared for cultivation. Others would walk to the nearest football match, either as spectators or participants, and the rest would head to the bowling green, the cricket pitch or to the back of the Village Inn for a game of quoits. Conversation often revolved around the football league, angling and other pursuits, and the comedy of ordinary life, usually involving the hapless and the errant. There had already been much laughter at the tale of the stationmaster terrifying the cattle with his whistle, sending them galloping up the road through the village, to east and west, hotly pursued by angry minders.

When Alex Birse arrived at Craigpark, a debate about Walter Shiels having been fined ten shillings for poaching rabbits and pigeon on estate lands, his second such offence, had divided the camp into two. Those who saw life in black and white argued that poaching was wrong because it was theft. Davy Potts asserted that Walter should never have been on estate lands in the first place far less stealing the birds and the beasts thereof, invoking the words of the Ten Commandments to back up his case. Those men who saw the situation more in shades of grey pointed out that Walter had been unemployed for some time due to ill-health and was reliant on the Parish to pay his rent and put food in his children's mouths. Wasn't he to be given some credit for trying to overcome his illness and find a source of income to make things a little better for his family? *There but for the Grace of God go I,* many agreed, unwilling to condemn a man for such a trivial offence when they all lived with the fear of poverty through lack of work or health. Surely, he could only be criticised for being stupid enough for getting caught?

Alex looked at his friends and neighbours and despaired at the simplicity of their thinking and the shallowness of their analysis.

'Whit herm does it dae the Melvilles if a puir man taks a rabbit or a fish noo an' again tae feed his faimily?' said Alex.

'They have their business tae run like onie ither.' replied Davy Potts. 'The law shouldnae be broke. It's been haundit doon tae us fae the Bible, tae keep us a' safe.'

'Havers,' said Alex ready for a good argument. 'The Melvilles mak the law, or at least their ancestors and them's like them mak it. For their ain benefit, tae look efter their ain interests and keep a'yin else, like you and me, in their place ablow the Melvilles' thumb.'

'We should a' ken oor place. Anarchy benefits naebody but the anarchist,' said Davy. He had no time for Alex and his revolutionary talk.

'It's no anarchy I'm arguin' for,' continued Alex. 'Jist ither laws that suit us a' and no jist the rich. Why should Walter Shiels an' his faimily live in poverty, gaun cap in haun tae the Parish for haun oots when the land that he bides in hauds sic riches?' He gestured to the evidence behind him: a productive and busy landscape of pitheads, brickworks and farms. 'His weans gang hungry while landowners and coal maisters grow fat on the profits fae whit lies ablow oor feet. Aye, an' profits made by oor sweat, oor labour.'

'Thou shalt not steal,' Davy reminded Alex.

'Sin ye insist on bringin' God an' His Commandments intae it,' Alex countered, 'Why did God gie a' these riches tae jist yin faimily? Thon doesnae seem awfy fair tae me.'

'Ye've got a point there, Alex,' called out Robert Duncan from the back of the small crowd. Several of the men nodded in agreement.

'Tae ma mind, a lovin' God would be a fair God. Ye couldnae disagree, Davy lad?' continued Alex, increasingly thrilled by the tambour of the debate and the positive murmurings of the crowd in his favour.

'Aye, weel,' but Davy was lost for words. In truth, when he thought about such things, he could never reconcile the inequities of life with a fair, loving God. You just have to have faith in the Lord, he decided, but there was no point in talking to a man like Alex Birse, firmly rooted in the here and now, about the importance of having faith in a God who would reveal His plan in His own good time.

'But here's a possibility,' Alex continued, pointing his finger like a teacher lecturing a class of ignorant children. 'Mebbe yon fair and lovin' God did gie the treasures o' the Earth to us a', equally. But the Melvilles an' their like stole them! Or acquired them b' hook or b' crook. Mebbe the Melvilles telt a'body they would look efter them on oor behalf. Then efter a while we, an' they, jist forgot they were oors in the first place, fegs! So they were the yins that broke the Commandment lang afore puir Walter Shiels cam on the scene!'

'Aye, whaur's the justice in thon?' voiced several of the men as they savoured the argument, tut-tutting and shaking their heads. Conversations erupted about the luxury of life in the Big House, and expressing resentment about the influence the Melvilles had over everything that happened in the area.

'How's puir Walter tae pey a fine o' ten bob an' a'?' someone asked. 'Is thon justice?'

Alex enjoyed these spontaneous debates with his comrades, unfettered by the four walls of a hall or a conference room or the agenda of a union meeting. The environment of Craigpark suited him, held great meaning for him. He looked at the hard-working men before him and, in the background, their places of work, where they wrought a living from the earth by the sweat of their brow and the skill of their hands.

In amongst the chimneys, the glaur, and the dirt lay Stoneyrigg Pit. It had been idle now for more than eighteenth months, closed by an intransigent Coal Company that had to have the last word in its dispute with a labour force that refused to accept a cut in wages below what had already been agreed. The men and their families had stood together resisting the evictions threatened by the managers. Without doubt it had been a long and difficult time for those affected but most had stuck together, and stuck it out. For Alex, Stoneyrigg Pit stood as a monument to the conflict between master and worker and to the power of working men and what they could achieve when they stood together, united against the tyranny of capitalism. Here was proof that capital was impotent without labour. Here also was proof of the brutality and bloody-mindedness of the coal owners. It was a sad fact that the other pits in the immediate vicinity, Broadrigg Numbers 1, 2 and 3, were owned and operated by the same company that had closed Stoneyrigg Pit. Most of the local men worked in those pits and the brick workers, the coke oven operators and the power station workers all depended on their output. That same company continued to mine the very same coal seam that lay below Stoneyrigg, devouring it from all around like a glutton with an insatiable appetite for money and power.

The thought of it made Alex boil inside with fury. He frowned when he thought of the speed at which the minerals of the area were being consumed, the considerable wealth from rock and stone leaking away into the pockets of landowners, bankers and capitalists. Had the great Keir Hardie not said, *'Our day will come?'* But what would be left for the Scottish working man and his children when that day finally came? It could not come soon enough for Alex Birse.

For some of the workers, Alex's socialist harangues were too depressing to take in large quantity, especially on a Saturday afternoon. The group of men threatened to break up as they bid their leave to attend various sporting activities and pursuits of choice. Meanwhile, Neil Tennant had been busy at the forge when he spotted Jimmy Broadley in the middle of the gathering. Still dressed in his leather apron, he crossed the road to enquire after Jimmy's son, Geordie.

'Thank ye kindly for askin',' said Jimmy, touched by Neil's concern. 'An' thanks yince again for comin' tae his rescue. Then fetchin' Dr Matheson for him yestreen.'

Neil nodded, humbled by the man's gratitude.

Jimmy continued. 'The doctor cam by this mornin' again. It's the scarlet fever he's got, for sure. He's got the rash noo but we'll jist have tae see how he progresses. On tap o' the bronchitis frae thon dookin he got in the burn, he's in a gey sorry state.'

A murmur went round the men, summarising the history of Geordie's illness and its origins. Praise started to come Neil's way.

'Ye'd a' hae done the same in ma position,' replied Neil modestly, 'I kent whit tae dae efter gaun tae the ambulance class up at the school. An' ma faither taught me how tae swim when I was a boy. If the lads learn tae swim, this'll no happen again.'

'Yer right, Neil,' agreed Robert Duncan. 'Whit we need is a place at the burn where the weans can learn tae swim wi' supervision frae the adults. No at the Meadie though, thon deep pool's ower dangerous. We need some place aboot twa – three feet deep whaur the watter's no gaun ower fast.'

'Some place whaur hail faimilies could pitch up wid be ideal,' suggested Davy Potts, eager to say something without recourse to religion. 'A place whaur the wee yins can paddle an' the big yins can have a seat an' sit back in the sun.'

'Thon'll be the Sooth 'o France yer meanin',' chipped in Alex, showing his lighter side, and eliciting some laughter from a serious debate.

'There's a streek o' the burn on Morton's ground that would be guid,' remembered Neil. 'Jist up frae the ford.'

'Aye, guid choice,' said several men together.

'We could approach the Parish Cooncil wi' a plan,' one man continued.

'Naw, thon'll take forever,' interjected another. 'A hail class o' weans could've droont b' the time they get roon tae tellin' us we're no allowed.'

'Hoo aboot Neil writes a letter tae Mister Melville at the Big Hoose?' said Robert Duncan. 'Askin' for a meetin' aboot oor proposal, emphasisin' the urgency o' the situation, bairns lives bein' at stake an' that. Whit dae ye say, Neil? Ye'll ken whit tae write an' a sma' number o' us can gang up tae state oor case.'

Everyone to a man voiced their approval of Robert's suggestion on how to take the matter forward. Neil agreed to write a letter asking that local people be granted access to the Red Burn where it crossed Old Morton's land. He also agreed to lead the deputation of workmen at any future meeting with the laird. It seemed a straightforward proposal that wouldn't do any harm but doubt crept into Neil's mind immediately. Something told him that the idea might not be so well received at Parkgate House.

# Chapter 8

## THE BEST DAYS OF THEIR LIVES

Over four hundred children were enrolled at Blackrigg School, almost double the number recorded a decade earlier when the school was held in a damp building with only two rooms. This population increase had brought about the construction of a new building on Main Street, with five classrooms, two further rooms for cookery and science, and a hall for physical education, representing a considerable investment by the ratepayers. For once, everyone on the School Board had been in agreement. A water-tight and commodious environment was essential for the efficient delivery of the curriculum but, even so, it had taken many hours of committee meetings and debate before plans for a new school had been pushed through. Board meetings were often fraught. Murdo Maclean for one, lamented the belligerence and prejudice that some members brought to the discussions. They imported the petty squabbles and jealousies of day-to-day life, looking to apportion blame and exact punishment for life's failure to satisfy their personal vanity and ambition. Like Miss Silver who could only speak of Stoneyrigg children with spite and animosity in her voice, even though she professed great concern for the education of young minds. Did she really think they were to blame for the transformation of Blackrigg from the rural idyll of her childhood years, Murdo wondered? Perhaps that was the nature of committees though, every member brought his or her own agenda to the meetings and it was up to him, as chairman, to ensure that discussion and planning were carried out in the best interests of the school.

He was saddened by the lack of progress made by some children, had to content himself with the knowledge that every pupil had at least some instruction in the 3Rs. A small number of the poorest children, with the support and determination of their families, did progress to more advanced schooling where their knowledge and intellect would be honed. A career beyond the pithead or the farm steading, or even a university place, was possible. It proved to him that Blackrigg was a good school, fulfilling its role within the community. He was particularly proud of his part in the expansion of Continuation Classes under the auspices of the Bathgate Landward Schools. A range of subjects was offered in the evening to those who, for one reason or another, had missed out in their early years and who chose self-improvement through the acquisition of knowledge. The recent saving of a child's life from drowning vindicated the inclusion of the ambulance class. Other classes covered arithmetic, English composition, physiography, domestic economy and sewing. They were very popular even though attendees had to pay. Those who attended regularly had their fees reimbursed as a reward. In Mr Maclean's experience, people valued what they had to pay for. Education was very like health, he had decided. It impinged on every area of experience and a person's likelihood of success relied on the diverse conditions and priorities of the individual and his family. *You can take a horse to water but you cannot make it drink,* as the proverb said. The underlying ethos of a good school like Blackrigg, he asserted, had opportunity for self-improvement at its heart, encouraged self-respect and respect for the community, for the greater good of all, defending society from discontent and non-conformity.

Blackrigg School's defence of society started anew at the beginning of every school day when the bell was rung by Mr Black at nine o' clock precisely, the signal for pupils to form orderly lines outside the entrance doors marked *Boys* and *Girls.* Stragglers on the road or coming across the fields, ran like the wind at the sound of the school bell then joined the back of the queue, hoping they had made it on time. The female teachers stood at the top of the steps, making sure that their lines were straight and even, with no fidgeting, pushing or talking. Lines could not be allowed to enter the building until Mr Black, with the experience and superior status of the male schoolmaster, had given his consent. He strutted back and forth in front of the lines like a sleek, young crow in its prime. Slightly stooped, his hands behind his back, he walked with his black academic gown billowing in the breeze, and his spectacles balanced on the end of his nose so that he had to peer over them, emphasising his scholarship and his vigilance. Although he had only recently taken up his position at the school, pupils already knew his mantra. *Beware the all-seeing eye!* It put the fear of God into both the younger and the more conscientious pupils, and induced laughter and some excellent mimicry in the wayward.

On Monday morning, the boys in the fourth class noticed that Bert Broadley was absent from the line and the word went round that Geordie had the scarlet fever so Bert would be kept off school for at least a week to reduce the likelihood of the infection spreading through the school population. A question went up and down the boys' line. In the absence of Bert, did anyone else have a ball for the football at playtime? No one was forthcoming and the mood was despondent.

There was a final call for quiet then the command came from Mr Black that the class could enter the school building. Two perfect lines of children marched in through their respective doors, boys to the right and girls to the left, only to meet in the corridor inside and squash through the classroom door together. It was a daily ritual that went unquestioned.

When all seventy pupils had settled themselves down and the clatter of desk lids had ceased, the register was taken. With so many names on the list this was a protracted affair, especially on a Monday. Miss Foulkes demanded details of Bert's situation and of others absent due to ill health, duty bound to assist in the compilation of statistics for the use of the medical authorities in their fight against the infectious diseases of childhood. Then several pupils backed up the assertion that Tibby Stein wouldn't be coming back to school because the family had done a midnight flit on Friday night, being so far behind with the rent, and no one knew where they'd gone. Also, Jeannie Shiels had gone to live with her granny in Perthshire but then somebody said she wasn't at her granny's at all. She was in service in a big house near Edinburgh because her father was unemployed and had a fine to pay for poaching.

Miss Foulkes was just getting to grips with the details of her pupils' lives when a knock came to the door. Mr Black appeared, ushering in a new boy who was introduced as Andrew Brownlee. He clutched his cap in terror at the sight of seventy unknown faces peering back at him then nearly jumped out of his skin when Miss Foulkes told him where to sit, beside Minn Graham who, in the absence of Tibby Stein, had an empty desk next to hers. The boys in particular watched Andrew as he made his way to his desk. They absorbed every detail of the new boy: his smart tweed jacket and matching short trousers (possibly new), the long brown socks (no holes) and the highly polished black leather boots (cost a bob or two). Many questions went through their minds. They would find out the answers in good time.

Morning lessons started with the class chanting their times tables en masse, followed by mental arithmetic to exercise the brain and perk up those not long out of their beds. Miss Foulkes was always on top form during mental arithmetic but started softly, asking questions and taking the answers from volunteers with their hands up. Then she made the class stand up while she went round the class, asking each person a question in turn. Those who answered correctly could sit down. Nobody was allowed to sit until he or she answered a question correctly. The same pupils were left standing day after day – it could take some of them ten questions or more before they were given permission to sit down.

Next was slate arithmetic. Miss Foulkes put the questions on the blackboard and gave her pupils ten carefully timed minutes to write the answers. She asked pupils to swap slates then mark each other's work according to her direction. When the totals had been added up and slates returned to their rightful owners, pupils had to indicate how many correct answers they had achieved by putting up their hand. She always started at twenty out of twenty, working her way down to the lower numbers. Day after day, the same pupils had to wait till the end before they could put their hands up. Sometimes she varied the method of degradation by asking everyone to stand up and pupils couldn't sit down until their score had been read out. Day after day, the same pupils had the lowest scores and were left standing longest. The poor soul who never got anything right stood in the middle of the class all alone, all eyes trained on his pathetic figure, an example to the rest of the class of what they didn't want to be and why they had to work hard.

After arithmetic came reading. Miss Foulkes praised herself for the high standards she expected in reading. She came down heavily on any pupil who hesitated, insisting on accuracy, and on what the government inspectors would call '*expressive modulation*'. Every day she would encourage pupils to read at home to improve their fluency and every day she would say, '*What do you mean you've no books at home?*' She made pupils read in turn and had usually just reached the end of that day's quota of readers when the bell rang for the start of playtime. After another morning of ritual humiliation, some children left the room, their spirits crushed, knowing that they would never ever amount to anything worthwhile in life.

John Birse had had such a morning, though he was by no means the worst performer in the class when it came to reading and arithmetic. He had come to school already dispirited by the consequences of taking boots that didn't belong to him and then losing them. He'd had to own up to his actions when Davy had come home from work early on Saturday afternoon, ready to spruce himself up for a visit to the football, Thistle against Bluebells. After a wash in the tin bath by the fire, Davy had turned the house upside down, saying that he couldn't understand how a pair of boots could get lost in such a small house.

'It was me,' said John.

Davy Birse looked at the boy, quizzically.

'I taen yer boots this mornin',' he admitted, 'I put them in the hedge cause they were hurtin' ma feet an' when I cam back for them, they were awa',' he explained. 'Disappeared. Stealt.'

Davy stared at his brother in disbelief while John quivered.

'John's richt,' said Jim, supporting John the best way he could. 'We raked a' place for them. Somebody's taen them.'

'Awa' ye gang, Jim,' said Mary. 'This is naethin tae dae wi' you. Awa' an' mind yer ain business.'

Jim glanced across at John. He left the house reluctantly, unhappy at what he knew was about to occur.

John looked at Davy then at his mother, afraid at what was coming. It was how disputes were sorted out in the Birse household and how people were repaid for crossing Davy and Alex. He backed into a corner with his hands up protectively but there was no avoiding it.

'I said I was sorry, I cannae say onie mair than that,' he offered finally.

The first of Davy's blows landed weakly until he got the measure of things. Then he let fly with the full force of a manual worker used to shifting tons of rock every day, grunting his fury with each punch.

'Stoap him, Mither! Please! I'm sorry,' called John, pleading for Mother Birse to intervene but she let a few more blows land before reacting.

'Richt thon's enough, Davy. He's had whit he deserves,' she said firmly.

Davy landed another couple of punches before standing back, fury still palpable in his scarlet face and his heavy breathing.

'I said *enough*!' said Mary.

'I'm no sae sure aboot that,' came Alex's voice from the doorway. 'Staun back, Davy,' he ordered, removing his belt with a flourish.

'The lad's had enough, Alex,' intervened Mary. 'He didnae mean tae lose the boots.'

'Staun aside, Wuman,' said Alex to his wife who was standing in his way. Then pointing at John, 'Richt, you, ben the hoose.'

John stared at Mary, a pleading look in his eye. She shook her head, said nothing more. He looked at Davy who stared back, a smirk on his face. He'd had the same treatment often enough as a lad, was revelling in John's fear.

In the back room the sting of leather on the bared flesh of his backside made John's eyes water. He closed his eyes, built a wall around himself, a wall of defiance inside his head and around his heart. He tried to blink back the tears, took his punishment without a sound. Alex stopped once he had drawn blood. Then he rolled his belt round his hand with a degree of ceremony, savouring the moment.

'Ye'll stey in this room till the morn, nae supper, nae nuthin,' he said through dritted teeth as he made to leave the room. 'That'll teach ye tae interfere wi' ither folk's stuff, ye stupid wee bastard. Dae ye think pairs o' boots grow on trees?' He twisted the knife of abasement a further turn. 'Yer worth less than the shite ye broucht hame in thon pail. Even yer ma didnae want ye when ye were born, think on that.'

Only when the door had closed and he was left alone with his pain, did John cry. The wall inside him crumbled. Silent tears ran down his face as he searched out the bright sky through the small window. Any mention of his birth mother brought a sadness that was hard to shift but on top of the pasting he had just received from Davy and Alex Birse, it started a fit of sobbing that was impossible to control. He wondered what she had been like and where she was in the world. He asked himself whether she would defend him against these brutes or stand back and watch like Mother Birse did, doing little, it seemed, to help him. He was sure his real mother wouldn't let anyone hurt him, that she must have had a good reason for giving her twins up for adoption. Perhaps she had died, thought John. Though Alex had said she hadn't wanted him so she had given him away. The seed of doubt about his worth had been planted early by Alex Birse. John had to fight hard to contain it – like a gardener in an endless battle against bindweed that seemed to grow from nowhere, long choking tendrils creeping through the undergrowth, strangling the flowers and blocking out the sunlight.

Gradually the tears stopped. John lay in the cold room without moving from the bed, watching the light in the window dim and darken as the hours passed into night. No one came near him until Jim appeared at bedtime and the two got ready for bed without any mention of what had taken place. They lay side by side and John fell into a deep sleep, warmed by the presence of his brother, already asleep beside him.

When they were released into the playground for interval, John gave an almost imperceptible nod to Minn Graham. Sitting behind him in class, she had noticed his visible bruises earlier that Monday morning, sensing his discomfort from the hidden marks on his backside when he sat down after mental arithmetic. When he had stood up later, she had folded up her jacket before putting it onto his seat. In relieving the physical pain, it hadn't helped much but her kindness touched him to the very centre of his being. It had sustained him through the worst reading he had ever done in class.

Minn said nothing, just smiled back at John then watched him limp over to join the other lads milling around in the boys' playground. She felt sorry for John. He looked downtrodden at times, much more so than his elder brother ever did. She wondered why he had been given such a beating from his father and the thought of it made her shudder. No one had ever done that to her.

When she noticed that Rob Duncan was looking over, she blushed and quickly looked away. Rob was a good scholar who was often top of the class, especially in arithmetic and geography. He was taller and more confident than the other boys. All of the girls thought he was very good looking and she thought the same. As she waited for her friends to join her, she stood alone and conspicuous in the middle of the girls' area. it took all of her determination not to look back in Rob's direction. Her face gradually flushed and she wished the ground would swallow her up. Then she saw that Andrew Brownlee was standing beside her for safety and protection from the new situation he found himself in. A quick look in Rob's direction then she realised that he wasn't looking at her at all. He was looking at Andrew and so were the others. No wonder the boy was terrified, she thought to herself. Andrew, in his fine clothes with his plummy voice, being glowered at by that bunch who couldn't just say *hello*, and make the boy feel welcome.

'Hello, Andrew,' said Minn, turning her back on the motley crew. 'The first day at a new place must be hard.'

'Aye it is,' he replied, overcoming the lump in his throat whilst looking over at the boys.

'Mebbe this'll help,' she said, reaching discretely into the pocket of her pinafore.

'Thank you, Minn,' said Andrew with a smile.

She watched him walk away from her towards Rob, Jim, John, Dan Potts and the others.

He held out the ball she had given him. They clapped him on the back and cheered, shouted, *'Guid man, Andra!'* then divided into two teams straight away with Andrew in goals for Rob's team. Andrew smiled over at her and she smiled back. Then she turned to join the girls who were already cawing the rope for some skipping games.

# Chapter 9

## THE SISTERS

Minn Graham lived in Stoneyrigg with four sisters and their father, Thomas Graham, master bricklayer. The family had lived in a number of different places across the county as Brickie Graham moved around in search of work. With the growth of mining and manufacturing, there was always plenty of employment for builders, constructing works and homes for the expanding population. The booming economy of Blackrigg had attracted Tom Graham and he had helped build the new rows and the houses at Burnside for the Coal Company. Tom had been a widower for some eight years, his wife finally defeated in a long battle with consumption soon after the death of their infant son, James. Left to bring up five daughters on his own, Tom had no choice but to continue working as before and leave the domestic side of life to the girls who ranged in age from fourteen to two years at the time of their mother's death.

The eldest girl, Meg, had stepped up to the plate, taking on the role of mother and domestic servant with aplomb. She was already experienced in the skills of housekeeping and in nurturing her younger sisters, especially in those final months when her mother was bedridden. She had been allowed to leave school before the statutory leaving age because the needs of the family dictated it. Meg had a happy disposition and didn't grumble about having to leave school. That was what life had in store for her, the die was cast. You just had to get on with it, was how she looked at it. The younger sisters had helped Meg when they could, bringing water in from the well, scrubbing floors, going to the shop for bread and meal, preparing food at weekends to let her rest. So, the Graham sisters were very close. They helped each other, talked, laughed and cried together, making sure that their father was well fed, that he had a clean bed to sleep in and clean clothes that were darned and patched where necessary.

Tom Graham thought about his wife every day as he went about his work in all weathers. On some days, when the icy blast of the wind brought a drip to the end of his nose and it was hard to see what he was building for the tears in his eyes, or when the rain lashed down incessantly, chilling him to the bone, he felt the anger at her passing rising in his throat. He wanted to curse God to Hell for taking her. He would ask her, silently, why had she left him to struggle all alone in this world? Then he would remember Meg and Marion, Nell and Minn, and the youngest one, Sarah and he would thank her for the daughters she had given him. They were his joy. He smiled to himself at the end of each working day, knowing that he was going home to their chattering and fussing, and a plate of Meg's broth, hot from the pot on the fire.

Minn and Sarah arrived home from school to find the house draped with washing, bed linen, and items of clothing rescued from the washing line before the onset of rain that had threatened to soak everything. A mattress, taken outside for airing, had been dragged back into the house just in time. It was lying in a formless heap so the girls helped their sister pull it back into place on the recessed bed in the back room. Sarah was delighted to be given the job of evening out the lumps and bumps of straw and chaff that filled the tyke. She immediately started to jump up and down on all fours, while her sisters pretended to grab her, bringing on a fit of the giggles followed by hiccups and a plea for surrender.

'Whit can I smell?' said Sarah as she lay gasping.

'Dae ye mean the paraffin?' asked Meg. 'I've been spring cleanin' the day.' The house did smell vaguely of the paraffin that Meg regularly daubed on the cracks in the walls in her ongoing battle with bed bugs.

'Naw! It's soup! I'm starvin'!' replied Sarah. But the delicious aroma of broth, cooking on the fire, threatened to invade the freshness of the washing which couldn't be allowed.

'Tak that pot up tae Ellen Broadley, would ye?' said Meg to Minn. 'She's got a lot on her plate wi' Geordie bein' poorly. I've got a bone and the vegetables cut up for anither potfu'.'

Minn agreed, to Sarah's disappointment, quickly removing the cooking pot with great care using a wet cloth to protect her hands from the hot, metal handle. She made her way gingerly out of the door, mindful of the scalding steam, through the drizzle to the Broadley home. She chapped the door and waited. Ellen's face lit up when she saw Minn with the soup.

'Thank ye kindly, Minn. An' thank yer sister tae, will ye?' said Ellen, taking the pot but keeping Minn at the door while she transferred the soup to a pot of her own. 'She happened by this mornin' askin' efter the lad and promised me some broth. Sic a kind lass, your Meg, an' hard workin',' she called from inside the house. 'She'll be missin' Marion and Nell noo they're in service'.

'Aye, its no the same withoot them in the hoose. I'll pass on yer regards, Mrs Broadley.' said Minn, looking past her into the room, hoping for a glimpse of the patient. 'How's Geordie gettin' on? Is he onie better?'

'Have ye had the scarlet fever, Minn? If ye have ye can come in an' say hello tae him,' said Ellen.

'I had it mild when I was a bairn,' replied Minn, stepping in through the door at Ellen's request, in the knowledge that she was unlikely to catch the fever again.

Geordie was lying in bed and gave Minn a weak smile. He liked her very much.

'The fever's doon but he's awfy poorly an' just lies there. But he hasnae been hallucinatin' since the ither nicht, thank the Lord,' Ellen added, trying to look on the bright side.

Minn sat in a chair by the bed. 'Are ye feelin' better, Geordie?' she asked. 'Would ye like a drink?' 'Will ye tak some soup in a while?' 'Is thon rash awfu' itchy?' 'Is the calamine lotion helpin' at a'?' 'Did ye miss gaun tae the school the day?'

Her questions went unanswered. Geordie just looked at her with his big brown eyes and smiled serenely.

'I hope the fever hasnae affected his brain,' said Ellen, 'I havenae kent a word he's said for days. No that he's had ower muckle tae say.' She looked fearfully at her son then busied herself at the fire, using the poker to make a place for the soup pot. As she turned over the hot coals, the prolonged squeal of burning gas escaping from the coals got Geordie's attention.

He looked from the fire to Minn's kind face. 'Thon's the coal fairies,' he said with a smile.

Ellen looked at her son, her mouth open in disbelief.

'Thanks be!' said Ellen, hugging Minn. 'Thon's the first thing he's said that's made onie sense for ages. It's you bein' here, Minn Graham. Thank ye, thank ye kindly for bein' here, lass.'

# Chapter 10

## THE INTERESTS OF RASHIEPARK

David Melville sat at his desk in the study of Parkgate House. For the convenience of receiving guests on official business, it had been located in the south-facing corner of the new wing, just inside the main door, with large, floor-length windows that looked onto the beech-lined avenue and the wide sweep of improved pastureland beyond the Old Great Road. David sat with his arms folded looking at the grey rain clouds boiling up across the sky, threatening to block out the sun. The letter received two weeks earlier from Neil Tennant, requesting a place for recreation on the Red Burn, lay on his ink-blotter awaiting attention. David knew that he would have to make a decision about it soon but had delayed discussing the matter with the factor, Roger Stone, though he wasn't sure why. Perhaps it was because he knew that the request was perfectly reasonable, indeed laudable, but that his instincts told him Stone would not agree it was in the best interests of Rashiepark.

The house had been quiet for a few days. David was alone with the servants. Phee was staying with an old school friend in the north whilst Isabelle had taken herself off to a cousin in London for a period of rejuvenation.

She had tried to shrug off her behaviour at the dinner with Dr Matheson but a rock, thrown through the window of the motor car as she was being driven to visit Lady Moffat the following day, had let her know that news travels fast and bad news travels fastest of all. When she had returned from church this Sunday past with a large mass of spit on the back of her coat, she had found it hard to hide her distress. She hadn't known the perpetrator but, through her tears, said that the lower classes certainly knew how to communicate their feelings. Not normally one to be told what to do by a family member, far less be intimidated by a ruffian from the village, her bags were packed the next day and she left for London, hoping that the reputation of the Melville family as a whole had not been tarnished by the gossip emanating from *a minor faux pas*.

David missed Phee's presence in the house rather more. She was cheerful, always bright and sunny with an interesting take on things. She was outward looking and challenging, never stuffy. And, of course, she had attractive friends. Elizabeth Fraser seemed to be a good influence on his sister, encouraging her to help at the Sabbath School, bringing out Phee's more serious side, and giving her a channel for her love of life and love of people. Rose Matheson, too, was a purposeful young woman. David couldn't imagine his sister frittering away her time and her talents when she kept company with the beautiful and intelligent Rose. He recalled the evening when Rose had hurriedly left the dinner table with her father. It had taken David a few moments to realise what Dr Matheson had meant when he'd said to his daughter that it was time for her to see what her chosen profession involved. Her chosen profession? When Phee had confirmed later that Rose was to start her medical training in the autumn, she had noticed the disappointment in her brother's eyes.

'You wouldn't deny her the same opportunity that you had, would you?' she had asked him. 'Just because she's a woman.'

'Of course not,' he had replied though unsure of his true feelings. There had been a woman in his year at medical school so it was nothing new, but uncommon. Women were asking for the vote and showing skill in business, he had admitted to himself. But how would Rose's education affect the possibilities for the future? His future, their future together, though they hardly knew each other at all.

A wave of despondency and loneliness washed over him as he returned to the beauty of the view, of the huge grey turbulent sky, and the pouring rain that gushed from the gutters and dripped from the beech trees, drowning out the sounds of the silent, empty house.

A knock at the door irritated him momentarily then he turned back to the business of the day. Jameson announced the arrival of Mr Stone and Mr Grant for the weekly meeting. Nell Graham followed them in, carrying a tray set for morning tea.

When the servants had left the room, the usual pleasantries were exchanged between the three men as tea was poured. The factor, Roger Stone, explained that Grant had joined the meeting for a few minutes to give details about matters relating to poachers and other pests, and about the management of the fisheries. When David had arrived back to take over Rashiepark on the death of his father, he had taken a dislike to the gamekeeper. As he looked at him again, he decided that he hadn't changed his mind. There was something about the man that he couldn't quite put his finger on. He hadn't liked the way

Grant had watched the servant girl when she had brought in the tea, for example, a girl of barely sixteen and him a married man with a child of his own. He always had a surly look about him but he was well balanced, give him that. As they said in these parts, Grant had a chip on both shoulders.

David started the meeting with a note from the county hunt thanking him for his cooperation with the March outing at Rashiepark, and praising the gamekeeper for his help in locating dens and flushing out their quarry on the day. Grant solemnly nodded in appreciation. Stone reported that bookings by anglers for the remainder of the season were satisfactory at around fifty per cent but that he hoped more would be received in due course. He suggested that advertisements in the Glasgow newspapers might be useful in attracting further enquiries. Grant reported that some good catches of trout were to be had on the Black Loch since the fishing season had begun and visitors seemed well satisfied. The winter repairs to the fishing station had made a big difference to the comfort of the anglers – it was a much more pleasing refuge when the weather was particularly stormy as it had been during April. The smaller lochs and the top of the Red Burn were not so productive of large specimens but a few good catches of the smaller fish were satisfying the anglers. Grant stated forcefully that the lack of larger fish was probably due to poaching by the miners. He made it clear that he did not like their presence in the area, blaming them for every ill, including two recent break-ins across the estate.

'Do you have evidence to back up this assertion?' asked David.

'I keep ma een open as best I can, sir, but they're a wily bunch an' I've but a few men to help me. It's a gey big area tae cover, ye ken,' replied Grant, taking the opportunity to gripe about his workload. 'Cannae be a' place at the yin time.'

'You'll be aware that one of the miners, Shiels, was convicted and fined at the Sheriff Court last week, Mr Melville,' interjected the factor. 'For poaching.'

'But that wasn't for taking fish was it?' asked David. 'Do we have to come down so hard on an unemployed man who takes a pigeon here and a rabbit there? It wouldn't affect the income of the estate, would it? Might even reduce the farmers' losses, taking out a few of the pests!' he suggested, almost laughing.

'It's always been the estate's policy to convict when someone is caught,' replied Stone, ignoring what David took to be a reasonable argument in favour of culling pigeons and rabbits. 'Gives a clear message that the estate does not tolerate theft in any shape or form.'

'Mr Stone's right, Mr Melville,' agreed Grant. 'They scavengers need firm boundaries. They cannae cope wi' grey areas,' he stated, referring to the miners. 'Need things tae be spelt oot in black 'n white, if ye ask me, sir.'

'Well, we need to find a way of getting along with them,' said David making his feelings clear. 'They live right next door to us and they're here to stay.' He thanked Grant for his contribution to the meeting and bid him good day, asking the gamekeeper to keep him posted should any further indications of the extent of the poaching and other criminal activity come to light.

The gamekeeper rose laboriously from his seat. He walked slowly and deliberately towards the door. There was something approaching insolence in his lumbering, slothful gait. A feeling of unease crept over David as he watched.

When the door had closed on Grant, David turned to his factor, 'They're not even on our land any more, Roger. Stoneyrigg and the other pits, the quarries and so on, I mean. So, we haven't the same influence on the mining community, not like in the past. More's the pity. Father sold those three farms outright to the coal companies and the quarriers, rather than take the royalties from the minerals produced.'

'In retrospect, sir, that was a mistake,' said Stone. 'The advice he was given grossly underestimated the wealth underground. The estate should take this into account in any future negotiations regarding the development of mineral extraction.'

'I'm worried about this new land tax, Stone, as if our financial position wasn't bad enough, the government wants to hit us for higher taxes. The Lords are passing the Budget Bill after all of the prevarication of the last year. *"Increment value duty on land"*. Sounds like we might be hard hit if and when we transfer any leases from the present tenants to mining concerns.'

'I'm not sure how the new tax will work, sir, but developing the minerals seems to be the way forward for Rashiepark. We're a sitting target when it comes to raising revenue, Mr Melville. It's assumed landowners have pots of money stashed all over the place.'

'And we know that's not always the case, don't we? See if you can throw any light on things, will you?'

It was agreed that Stone find out about the potential impact of the new tax; that he prepare a paper outlining a strategy for the future development of Rashiepark's mineral wealth for the next meeting. It was a matter of some urgency that the income of the estate be increased since expenditure was presently far greater, putting Rashiepark in the red.

'Of course, a review of expenditure would also be prudent, Mr Melville,' suggested Stone. 'Perhaps staffing costs could be looked at? And a rolling programme of maintenance following an audit and survey of the farms and the cottages, and Parkgate House itself, would be beneficial. At the moment it's a case of crisis management, I'm afraid. We're reacting to the worst situations as they're brought to our notice.'

'I agree totally,' said David.' I want to take a long-term view of the estate, determine what the future holds for Rashiepark.'

As Stone made to take his leave, David asked him to remain seated then handed him the letter from Neil Tennant. He watched his factor read and digest the simple request.

'Well written letter for a common workman,' the privately educated Stone stated as he returned the piece of paper to his superior. 'Completely out of the question, in my opinion, we owe these people nothing. They're the responsibility of the Coal Company and the other employers.'

'Wouldn't it be an opportunity to improve relations?' David asked, swayed by his impression of Neil Tenant as a decent man and bringing to mind the ill-treatment of Isabelle by persons unknown that had led to her recent retreat to London.

'You heard what Grant said about them, Mr Melville. They need everything in black and white. Give an inch and they take a mile,' said Stone, emphatically adding yet another cliché. 'Old Morton's the tenant at Back o' Moss. He wouldn't be too pleased at a bunch of ragamuffins tramping over his ground at will. Would they remain in a small area by the burn?' he asked, having already decided what the answer was. 'It could affect our income from the tenancy, in fact. That's not exactly what we're trying to achieve at all. Is it, sir?'

David Melville had to agree that it wasn't what they were trying to achieve in relation to increasing the estate's income. 'Let's mull it over and we'll have a deputation along for a meeting,' he said. 'Whatever we decide it's got to be in the best interests of the estate. Agreed?'

Agreed,' said Roger Stone and he left his employer to ponder the advantages and disadvantages of the request. And to look out of the window at the beautiful vista, wondering how the responsibility for all of what he saw had come to him, and him alone.

# Chapter 11

## THE DEPUTATION VISITS
## THE BIG HOUSE

It had been a full four weeks since the informal assembly of workmen had appointed Neil to write to the Big House. Nothing had been received in the meantime so the mood was pessimistic that any word would be received at all. This was grist to Alex Birse's mill of negativity and he was never happier. On a warm, sunny day in May, he broadcast his contempt for the Melvilles and their kind to whosoever would listen, as his neighbours and fellow workers happened by Craigpark on their way to Saturday afternoon leisure activities.

'Have we heard nothin'?' said Davy Potts, disappointment in his voice. 'Mind when the wee fella fae the Back Row droont in a big hole in the road?' he reminded everyone. 'We got the roads fixed, quick as a wink by the cooncil. I'm surprised Mr Melville wasnae persuaded by the argument for a swimmin' place, 'specially when the wee laddie Broadley near droont at the Big Pool.'

'Aye, it maks for a helluva convincin' argument, when a bairn near deed for want o' learnin' tae swim,' said Robert Duncan, shaking his head in disbelief.

'Yer surprised?' asked Alex Birse. 'Yer surprised? He's jist like the rest o' his class. We're an inconvenience lest we're makin' money for them tae squander oan there big hooses an' la-di-da weys. They think they owe us nuthin. We're no on Melville's land an' we're no workin' for him. So, I widnae be too surprised if I was you.' Alex finished with a petulant grunt and folded his arms.

'Even the rich have a conscience, Alex,' continued Davy Potts. 'It would be the Christian thing tae at least meet wi' us an' hear oor point o' view.'

'Christian?' laughed Alex. 'Their kind jist use the scriptures tae their ain benefit, ye ken. When was the last time ye heard thon stuffed shirt up at the manse say oniethin in oor favour? Eh? Last I heard he was cavortin' wi that lot up at the Big Hoose when they widnae let Neil in tae fetch the doctor for wee Geordie.'

A grumble of disapproval and contempt went round the assembly like a rumble of thunder on a far horizon.

'They gie tae the poor, the landowners I mean. A while back it wis a' channelled through the Kirk tae,' Davy reminded Alex.

'Weel, that's big o' them, aint it? Giein a wee bit o' whit belongs us back tae us,' he moaned, singing his usual song. 'The kirk used tae dae a lot o' things. Like condemin' usury. Noo its a wey o' life. The bankers are fechtin for the best pews on the Sabbath.'

'Is this no gaun aff the point a wee bit?' said a voice from the back. 'The point bein' we want a place for oor weans tae learn hoo tae swim an' there's nuthin suitable on Coal Company land.'

'Aye, whit dae we dae next?' called another. 'Whau's country is this oniewey?'

Alex started to get excited. This was revolutionary talk.

'I got a letter from Mr Melville this very morn,' interrupted Neil Tennant from behind.

Alex spun round, looking daggers at the younger man. 'Tellin' us whit?' he asked, hopeful that their proposal was dead in the water and the revolution could begin soon, here in Blackrigg.

'He's offerin' us a meetin',' said Neil. 'Tae discuss the matter. There's nae indication o' whit he thinks either wey.'

Disappointed, Alex withered visibly at the news that the laird was offering talks. 'Weel he taen his time,' he said intent on being critical, doing his best to ensure that the mood wouldn't become too optimistic. He turned to the assembly and called out, 'Whau wants tae gang wi' Neil tae state oor case for permission tae gang oantae Auld Morton's ground then?'

A heated discussion ensued to find the best speakers. Names were put forward; excuses were made by those who were not so keen. Nobody suggested Alex's name. He was secretly glad but felt hurt at the same time. Many of those who were unwilling to join the deputation sited lack of fluency in the English language as their main reason though some were extremely articulate in their native tongue. With this perceived ineloquence came lack of confidence and a refusal to join the delegation even if they weren't required to speak. In the end Neil Tennant, Robert Duncan and Davy Potts agreed to attend on everyone's behalf. The other men were satisfied that the three would be able to put the case forward in a reasoned and non-threatening manner. Neil would do most of the talking, backed up by Robert when necessary, with Davy adding a deferential edge to the trio.

On a fine evening several days later, the small delegation arrived at the gates of Parkgate House in plenty of time for the meeting but the men were faced with a dilemma straight away. Which door should they approach? Through the rowans to the ancient door of the old house or along the beech-lined avenue to the new door of the grand Victorian extension? For Robert and Davy, the old door seemed the natural choice but they reasoned this was because they had never seen the new one. It was hidden from the road by trees and they had never had occasion to visit Parkgate before. Neil reminded them about his experience of trying to gain admission through the old part of the house when he had gone to fetch the doctor so they agreed that it would do their case no good at all to sneak in by the *back door*. They duly made their way along the wide avenue to the front of the house, walking three abreast. The trio felt diminished by the huge dimensions of the beech trees towering above them as they walked towards the imposing edifice of the house by an avenue that had not been designed for negotiation on foot. They cut a forlorn sight as they approached the *front door*, silenced by grandeur, glad of each other's company. Robert reminded his companions that a community of hundreds of people was right behind them so they stuck their chests out and walked a little taller. Under the portico, in the cold shadow of the great house, Neil looked each of his comrades in the eye. He gave a cough to clear his throat then reached out his hand and delivered a confident knock at the large oak door.

Jameson opened the door a crack and sneered at the sight of Neil, mindful of their last encounter. He led the deputation into the vestibule, told them to wait whilst he informed the young master of their arrival. The men took off their caps then nervously brushed their hair back into place. In Davy's case this did not require much effort as he was almost as bald as a coot and Robert was happy to tell him so. When Jameson reappeared, he led them into the study.

David Melville left his stance by the fire, greeting them warmly with a firm handshake. He introduced his factor. Roger Stone rose from his seat on the far side of a huge, walnut desk and shook each man's hand cordially. In unison, the visitors turned down the offer of tea, unable to cope with the comedy of manners that such an activity might create, preferring to get down to the business that had brought them there.

David Melville took his seat beside Stone. He indicated three chairs on the other side of his desk. 'Sit down,' he ordered. 'Please,' he added more cordially. He waited whilst the men organised themselves. The sight of Robert and Davy attempting to sit in the same chair elicited a smile which he quickly hid. Then he summarised the reason for the meeting and took the upper hand by making his decision clear from the beginning.

'Gentlemen, it is only fair to tell you from the outset what our decision is on this matter. We are unable to agree that it would be in the interests of the Rashiepark estate to allow local people to trespass on our land,' he stated firmly, looking each man in the eye in turn.

All three visitors were taken aback, having expected an opportunity to argue their case before any decision was made. They had been caught most decidedly on the back foot. Neil knew he had to think quickly in order to retrieve anything from the situation but it was Davy Potts who spoke first.

'I am surprised that ye should invite us here only to tell us that yer mind is already made up on the matter, Mr

Melville,' he said, taking great care over his diction. 'As ye'll appreciate, sir, this is a matter of some importance whaur we're concerned. Whit we request would dae little harm tae an estate o' this magnitude, I'm sure.'

'Surely you will take the opportunity to hear our reasons and our point of view, Mr Melville? We speak for the entire community,' continued Neil. 'We ask that you hear us out at least.'

'Go ahead then,' replied the landowner, folding his arms against the discussion to come. He did not give any lead that might have made it easier for the men to know how to proceed. Stone had briefed him well.

'The local people request access to a stretch of the Red Burn that would give them the opportunity to teach their children how to swim, a skill that is shown to be useful by the near drowning of a young lad in recent weeks. Of which you will be aware, Mr Melville,' said Neil, hoping to invoke memories of the elder Melville sister's callous behaviour and, thereby, engender some compassion. 'The opportunity provided by such a place of recreation would avoid a possible tragedy in the future. I'm sure a man of your conscience would not want such an event to recur,' he suggested.

'I cannot see that it is the responsibility of this estate to provide the facility you request,' explained Melville. 'Surely it is up to your employer, on whose land you live and work, to consider it. If there is any responsibility towards you in this regard then it lies with him and his company, though it is doubtful that such an obligation lies with him as landowner and employer in any case.'

'The folk of Allerbank have sic a place called "*The Glen*",' interjected Robert Duncan, referring to the mining community downstream from Stoneyrigg. 'It's a very popular resort for bathing and relaxing but the burn at Blackrigg isnae suitable except at the place we've described, upstream frae the ford.'

'As we've explained the burn is unsuitable in both depth and speed of flow elsewhere,' reiterated Neil. 'And the land by the river upstream of the ford is flat and suitable for simple recreation,' he continued.

'So, you are asking for land for football and other games as well as access to the river for swimming practice?' asked Stone, exploiting Neil's indication that the miners might stray onto the surrounding farmland. 'How do you expect the tenant farmer to respond to such a request?'

'The land there is commonly used as grazing, and very productive it is too. Trespassers would not be welcome,' stated Melville, building on the factor's line of thinking.

'We are well aware of the law of trespass and do not wish to be trespassers,' explained Neil categorically. 'That's why we're asking for permission for access from you as landowner. A simple extension upstream from the present right of way across Back o' Moss Farm is what we request, with conditions of use laid down to ensure responsible usage that wouldn't interfere with the farmer's business of rearing livestock.'

'It is our experience that miners do not understand the ways of the farmer,' stated Stone, giving away some of the prejudice he felt towards them and their ilk.

'We can learn,' replied Robert, stung by the criticism which he couldn't help but take personally. 'Mebbe we could have a trial period an' we could meet ye again an' discuss onie problems that micht have arisen in the meantime.'

But the factor and the landowner were keen not to have any sort of trial period in case the use of the burn at Back o' Moss proved to be without difficulty. Give an inch and take a mile was foremost in their minds.

'It's quite out of the question,' said Melville firmly. 'The estate does not want to be responsible for having people on the land for recreation,' he continued.

'But the estate is visited by anglers and sportsmen for just that purpose,' Neil reminded him quickly. 'And the hunt goes across the tenant farmers' land at will,' he ventured, aware of the many complaints farmers made afterwards about damage to hedgerows and ploughed fields by riders on galloping horses.

Both Melville and Stone were taken aback by the blacksmith's challenge.

'It would take away from the normal business of the estate and would require time to monitor, probably by our gamekeeper who's hard pressed as it is,' retorted the young landowner off the top of his head, annoyed that he was being taken to task by a mere workman, especially one who made sensible points that could not be refuted. 'You people do not live on estate land and we are under no obligation to you in this regard.' He stood up to indicate that the meeting had come to an end, that his decision had been reached.

The deputation rose from their chairs reluctantly.

'And where does our obligation to our fellow man begin and end, Mr Melville?' Davy Potts asked as he shook the younger man's hand. He held the laird in his grip, maintaining eye contact for a few uncomfortable seconds. 'It's been maist interestin' tae meet ye, sir, very enlightenin' indeed.'

The laird and the factor remained silent.

It was clear to the visitors that no further discussion of the matter was going to take place, not at that particular meeting at least. Davy, in particular, was taken aback at their sudden dismissal, sorely disappointed at the new laird's intransigence. Neil and Robert politely took their leave and manoeuvred Davy out of the room.

With great satisfaction, Jameson led them out of the house before vigorously closing the enormous wooden door, shutting them out in the cold. In the shade of the stone portico, they looked despondently at each other. The optimism they had shared barely five minutes beforehand had been dashed. They had failed in their task.

'Mebbe the laird'll have second thouchts efter we're awa',' ventured Davy. He always tried to see the best in people.

'It's no likely wi' yon flunky, Mr Stoneyface, tellin' 'im whit tae dae,' replied Robert, finding his voice now that he was free of the restriction of a foreign tongue. 'Money aye wins oot ower Christian principles, in ma experience. Whaur they kind are concerned,' he added. 'They'd mak' ye pey for the pleasure o' the birdsong if they could.'

A flurry of starlings lifted up from a small copse growing by the roadside, leaving a waft of wings and whistles in their wake. The companions smiled at each other.

'Money isnae uppermaist in their minds here, though it's a consideration in the wider scheme o' things,' said Neil enigmatically.

Robert and Davy looked at him but he would say nothing more. They stepped out briskly along the road to the village, their backs warmed by the evening sunshine that cast long shadows on the road ahead of them.

All the way home to the Smiddy, Neil thought about their proposal, about how the meeting had gone, and about the principles at stake for the community and for the estate. He surveyed the parks and the hedgerows, the hills and the mosses of Rashiepark, all brightly lit by the sun. There was far more at stake for the Melvilles than the loss of a small amount of income from a farm tenancy agreement, he decided; something much bigger and worth hanging on to, from their point of view. Neil had known it all along.

'That'll be all, Roger. We'll speak in the morning,' said David Melville, dismissing his factor after the deputation had left.

He was upset at how the meeting had gone and was glad to see the back of Stone. David was glad to be alone. He poured himself a stiff drink, stood staring into the flickering flames of the fire that brought a welcome glow to the chilly gloom he had let engulf him. He hadn't handled the matter at all well, he thought to himself. The question posed by one of the older men had stung him into silence. *Where does our obligation to our fellow man begin and end, Mr Melville?* He had been unable to answer the truthful points made by Neil Tennant. His own petulant response had been to invoke his power as landowner and close down the discussion immediately. He had to admit that the three workmen, in spite of their inferior education and breeding, had acquitted themselves with humility and immense dignity. In trying to defend the estate's position, he had gone against his own instincts as to what was just. He was nothing but a hypocrite and in one of the first challenges of his new status as the Laird of Rashiepark he had been found wanting. All he'd succeeded in doing was to follow Stone's commercial instincts like a puppet.

David rolled the fine malt whisky round his tongue and swallowed hard. He savoured the peaty taste and the warm glow it brought, rising up from his stomach and his throat, reaching his ears and easing the muscles at the back of his head. He leaned against the mantelpiece, stared down into the red hot coals, asking himself how the outcome of the meeting would be received by the rest of the community.

Bright yellow flames, sometimes red, sometimes blue, licked upwards through the smoke. Pieces of coal turned into grey ash, settling and sinking into the inferno beneath. He felt the heat through his thick tweeds as he watched, deep in thought. He saw the half empty glass in his hand then hurled it into the fire where it shattered into a thousand pieces. He saw the flames leap up towards him and felt the heat of the blaze colour his face.

# Part Two
# Summer

# Chapter 12

## A WOMAN'S LOT – SOWING

The principal role of the women of the time was to look after matters relating to the home and the family, and to present an image of respectability to the community, regardless of family income. Inevitably, some women achieved this more than others. The setting up of a branch of the Cooperative Society at the beginning of the year had been a red-letter day for the village. Until then, female members of the community would stand in all weathers to buy their provisions from one of the Co-op vans that visited from the nearby town or they could shop at Jimmy White's grocery in Main Street. The Cooperative Movement was an antidote to the inability of private enterprise to provide goods at a price and standard acceptable to those on a low income, the majority of the population in those days. It operated on the basis of bulk-buying good quality goods to be sold at reasonable prices and it gave members a share of the profits, called the dividend or *divi*. Gone was the monopoly of private enterprise, selling highly priced, often poor quality provisions. Worst of all had been the dreaded truck system, operated by employers across the country before it was outlawed. The older industrial workers could still remember how some companies had either paid employees in tokens, accepted only at the company shop, or trapped workers into a cycle of indebtedness, tying families into a system of extended credit for over-priced goods.

The Co-op was hugely popular with the women of Blackrigg. They had a stake in it after all. It was also a place to meet other women, hear the latest news and enquire after each other's families far and wide. After six months in the village, gratitude for the wonders of *the store* was still an opening line in any encounter with friends and neighbours. Mary Birse and Peggy Duncan met in the shop doorway on a cool, rainy weekday in early June. They began discussing the price of kitting out their children for the Gala Day parade to take place at the end of the month, agreeing that the prices at the Co-op were very reasonable, and that the *divi* helped to cushion the family finances from some of the expense. They were soon joined by Ellen Broadley who had rarely ventured outside the house since Geordie had taken ill, several weeks before.

'It's thanks to thon lovely lass Meg Graham I'm here. Offerin' tae look efter Geordie for a bit,' she explained to her friends. 'I was gaun roond the bend in thon hoose a' the time,' she declared, grateful to be out and about again.

'Aye, thon's a lang while since yer lad first taen ill, Ellen,' said Peggy. 'How's he daen, the wee soul?'

'Weel, the doctor's dumfoonert hoo he's made it as lang,' said Ellen in a whisper, mindful of how unpredictable illness could be and as if speaking out loud might tempt Fate. 'He's no makin' onie promises but he thinks the signs are guid that Geordie'll mak a recovery. We'll jist have tae wait an' see, an' keep prayin'.'

'That's guid news, Ellen, yin day at a time, eh?' said Mary. 'We're a' prayin' for him, lass.'

'Ta, Mary. Jimmy an' me are gratfu' for a'body's concern. I cannae help thinkin' the lad should never have fell intae the burn in the first place, though. Should there no be a sign up at the Meadie warnin' folk aboot the dangers?'

Her companions looked at Ellen, both silently questioning whether a danger sign would make any difference to a scamp of a boy like Geordie.

'Some o' the men were talkin' aboot that very thing,' said Peggy who was married to Robert Duncan. 'Somebody thocht the landowner could be tae blame for whit happened tae Geordie. Ye ken, if there had been a fence, the lad micht no have gang intae the watter at a'.'

'An' did they tak advice aboot that?' enquired Mary. 'Whit was the outcome?'

Peggy explained. 'Weel, Neil Tennant looked intae it an' found oot there was a case a couple o' years back when somebody taen the Glesgae Corporation tae court efter a wean droont in the Clyde. The beak said there were places a' ower the country that could mak for injury, an' naebody could be expectit tae protect folk a' place. The beak said it was uptae folk tae use their common sense. Thon's whit the common law's built oan, so he said.'

'But, whit aboot folk like Geordie wha've nae bloody common sense?' said Ellen in her very matter of fact way.

The women laughed wholeheartedly but kindly at Geordie's expense.

Suddenly serious again, Peggy said, 'Aye weel, the Glesgae Corporation wasnae found guilty o' negligence in thon case. That's a' I ken aboot it.'

'The best wey furrit is tae learn the weans hoo tae swim,' said Mary, 'An' we a' ken hoo helpfu' the estate's been oan the matter. No yin bit!' After a pause she added, 'Alex was fair mad when he heard aboot the meetin', Peg.

He said the big wigs up at the Big Hoose'll be taen doon a peg or twa, yin o' thur days. They'll get whits comin', mark ma words,' she said, her hand shielding her words from eavesdroppers although there was no one else in the vicinity.

It sounded as if trouble was brewing. Ellen and Peggy stared back, unable to hide their concern, so Mary quickly changed the subject. 'Are ye feelin' a'richt Peggy? Yer lookin' a bit peaky the day?'

Ellen agreed after appraising her friend closely.

Peggy swept a loose lock of greying hair from her face, anchoring it firmly behind an ear. 'Aye well, I micht as well tell ye. Ye'll find oot sooner or later,' she said, causing the others to give a start.

'No?!' said Ellen, bringing her hands to her face in horror. Then in a low voice, 'No another bairn, Peg? When's it due?'

'Anither five month yet, November time I reckon,' she said with a sigh, stretching out her tired back, hands on hips. 'At ma age tae, ye'd think I'd ken better!'

'Och, hen,' said Mary with a look that suggested the end of the world was nigh. 'There's weys o' avoidin' it ye ken.'

'I widnae get rid o' it,' said Peggy, affronted. She crossed her knitted shawl across her breast, held it shut with folded arms.

'That's no whit I mean,' explained Mary. 'There's aye abstinence, ye ken. Ye've got tae watch, haen a bairn at yer age. Ye've been on the road mair times than Queen Victoria an' only got three weans tae show for it. Get that man o' yours telt tae leave ye alane.'

'Weel that widnae be ower great,' said Peggy blushing. 'It taks twa ye ken,' she continued loyally, and with a twinkle in her eye, refusing to let Robert take all of the blame.

'Ye can tak... weel ye ken, measures,' ventured Ellen, raising her eyebrows.

'Whit dae ye mean, Ellen? Explain yersel, hen. Yer lookin' gey red in the face,' observed Peggy.

'There's things ye can dae,' continued Ellen in a loud whisper, 'Tae kep a bairn in the first place.'

Peggy flushed. It was too late this time round but there could be useful information to be had for the future. She bent her ear close to Ellen who whispered something into her ear. Peggy recoiled.

'Whit's the guid o' thon?' she asked. 'It'd be like eatin' a sweetie wi' the paper oan!'

The women laughed till the tears ran down their faces.

'It's whit the gentry dae,' said Mary. 'I was in service lang enough tae ken!'

'Or some folk dae this.' Ellen beckoned her companions to come closer.

Peggy looked at Ellen. 'Git aff at Haymarket? I'm no gettin' yer meanin'?' she said with a frown, looking at Mary for help.

'When ye git oan the Edinburgh train,' explained Mary, 'Ye dinnae have tae gang a' the way tae Waverley, dae ye? Ye can git aff at Haymarket.'

Peggy looked from Ellen to Mary then back again. When the penny finally dropped, she opened her mouth wide. 'Weel,' she declared, 'I havenae ever been on the train tae the toun, an' I'll certainly no be gaun oan it noo!'

Her friends studied her, bemused, unsure if she had fully understood the advice she'd just been given but unwilling to go into such a taboo subject in any further detail. Instead, all three burst out laughing again, continuing until interrupted by an elderly customer who wanted to enter the shop. They blushed and coughed as they stood aside for her to pass.

'Mind an' look oot for yersel, Peg,' said Mary, wiping tears from her face as she made to take her leave. 'Let me ken if I can dae oniethin for ye nearer the time,' she added, reminding Peggy of her role as midwife and nurse. 'You tae, Ellen, if ye need a wee spell awa' frae, Geordie, I'll come an' sit wi' him.' She turned to go. 'Mebbe we can get the lad alang tae watch the parade on the Gala Day, if it's a nice day.' She burst into another fit of the giggles. 'Cheeri-bye, hens, cheeri-bye.'

# Chapter 13

## THE CHILDREN'S GALA

The last Saturday in June dawned fresh and fair, flying in the face of all of the predictions that it would be cold and rainy as usual. The Gala Day, as it had come to be known, was a celebration of life and hope for the future, placing children at the heart of a day of speeches and other more pleasurable activities.

Every community across Scotland had a special day such as this with similar elements of pageantry and entertainment but each was unique according to the landscape and the history of the place. In Blackrigg, there was no checking of ancient boundaries as in the Border towns or at the Linlithgow Marches; no elevation of a young girl to the status of queen, unconsciously evoking the pagan fertility rituals of the past or mimicking Victoria on her throne as in Lanark; no carrying of trades' banners as in the mining towns of Midlothian and Fife. Blackrigg folk assembled along each side of Main Street late in the morning, whilst the children lined up to be piped to the top of The Law for the hill walk. With the glories of Nature spread out below, prayers were said by the minister thanking God for His bounty and asking for His continued blessing. The walk returned to the village for a picnic, games and sports held in the field behind the manse. In the evening, the adults could choose to attend one of two activities, a dance in the public hall for the more vigorous or a recital in the church hall, suiting the more genteel and sedate.

The children of Blackrigg looked forward to the Gala Day for weeks beforehand, partly because it was their special day, and partly because it came straight after the end of the school term and marked the beginning of a long summer holiday in relative freedom. They anticipated a day of friendship, enjoyment and exhilaration, even if the reality of the previous year's experience hadn't quite lived up to their expectations. It was an occasion when they found themselves at the heart of the community, were the centre of attraction, on show in their Sunday best. It was a day when children could enjoy the innocent pleasures of childhood, leaving behind the worries and problems of the dark corners of their lives.

Mr Black and Rev Fraser waited patiently at the front of the parade observed by a growing crowd of onlookers. The children assembled in pairs, girls in front, boys behind, shortest to tallest, except where an older sibling was forced to take the hand of a recalcitrant five-year-old who refused to cooperate otherwise. The two men, pillars of the community, stood looking at their pocket watches whilst the schoolteachers and the teachers from the Sabbath School, all female and adorned in their best and most flamboyant bonnets, organised the children into a long orderly line behind them. The ladies strutted and fretted like mother hens as children threatened to undo the newly established order by seeking out a position closer to their friends. The girls wore white pinafores over dark clothes and had bright ribbons in their hair. The boys wore their best tweed with starched collars, long black socks and highly polished boots. Each had their hair plastered into shape by a mother's firm hand.

The band struck up the first tune, 'The Rowan Tree', then led the way along the street to the cheers of proud parents and grandparents. They held babies and toddlers aloft and were accompanied by elder offspring, ineligible for the parade now that they were working. The children smiled brightly as they waved their flags: the yellow and red of the Scottish Lion Rampant for the land of their birth and the red, white and blue of the Union Flag for the King and the Empire.

Tom Graham and his eldest daughter, Meg, waved at Minn and Sarah as they passed by hand in hand. With a tear, his love reached out to them, like the spreading shade of the rowan tree described so sweetly in notes and phrases by the pipes. He sang the words of the song softly to himself. His girls were the pride of the summer, like the flowers of the rowan, and its bark would be forever carved with their mother's name.

Robert and Peggy Duncan stood together, accompanied by Lizzie, their eldest child, and her husband Archie. They waited patiently for Rob and Sandy to pass, gave them a huge cheer when they did. Peggy shouted out their names to make sure her boys could see where their mother was standing. It brought a wide smile to Sandy's face and a glower from Rob who thought he might be too old to be singled out so vocally in front of his friends. Peggy was proud of her sons. They were fine strong lads, good looking and clever at school and they held such promise for the future. Didn't they look grand in their new jackets and boots?

Mary Birse waved at the twins who marched side by side in front of Bert Broadley and Dan Potts. Jim waved back shyly, uncomfortable in his starched collar and hating the way she had clapped his hair flat onto his head with grease. John gave her a beaming smile when he saw her, almost falling over his new, shiny boots, anxious to show them off with an exaggerated gait. He had been over the moon the day she had appeared with them from the store, and had hugged her hard until she had to tell him to stop.

The walk passed the church and the top of the Doctor's Brae, then White's Grocery, the Cooperative Store and all the other small shops and businesses in between. Shop workers were out on the street in their aprons. Two of the shopkeepers stood on either side of the line of children with a pail filled with caramels for the walkers. Eager hands delved in and no one thought to take more than one. What a treat! This was a great day!

They marched on towards the turn at the Smiddy and Craigpark where the hill road climbed steeply away from the village and up to The Law. There seemed to be a lot of cheering and commotion up ahead. The children craned their necks to see if they could determine the source of the excitement. The boys could see and hear a wave of cheering and flag-raising coming their way down the girls' line, and it wasn't long before they caught sight of the culprit. Geordie Broadley, happed up in a tartan shawl, sat in a wooden chair held aloft on the broad shoulders of his father, Jimmy and big brother, Eddie. Ellen Broadley stood beside them with tears rolling down her cheeks as the children passed giving her youngest son three cheers, time after time. Geordie sat speechless, hanging onto the arms of the chair for dear life, smiling widely despite his weakened condition. He would show them. He would get better, would be up and running very soon, back at school before you could say *Jack Frost*. As the boys' part of the parade started to pass, Jimmy and Eddie manoeuvred themselves and Geordie, like an Indian prince on a litter, into the line behind Bert and joined the walk. That got the biggest cheer of all.

As the parade wound its way up the hill and the gradient became steeper, the cheers died out and the crowds thinned. The pipe band did its best to keep up the tempo until the corner at Kaim Farm. There the band marched off along the footpath to Mansefield to await the return of the children after the ceremony up on the hill.

When small children rebelled, they had to be picked up by older siblings whilst the teachers made encouraging noises to keep everyone moving. The minister marched on, his eyes on the summit far ahead, blithely unaware of the long trail of children behind him and the difficulties they faced on the climb. When Elizabeth Fraser looked round to make sure the stragglers were making good progress, she laughed at the sight of a smiling and elegant Phee Melville taking up the rear with a small group of urchins, a tiny bedraggled child in each white-gloved hand.

'I don't think they're part of the walk,' said Elizabeth as Phee and her entourage came within earshot. 'They're not dressed for it,' she continued, eyeing the children's dirty clothing and bare feet that looked as if they hadn't seen a bar of soap for a month.

'Well, they should be part of it!' exclaimed Phee. 'They were sitting by the roadside watching, with everyone gaily marching past not even noticing them. Didn't you see them?'

Elizabeth had to admit that she hadn't and felt chastised. 'It looks like their parents didn't want them to join the procession,' she said, thinking they might not want to be with the others who were all spruced up. 'They look like gipsies. There's an encampment over at Crawhill... they keep themselves apart,' she stated, trying to explain why the ragged group should be left alone.

'Well, the children seem happy to join in,' retorted Phee. She squeezed the hands of her two ragged companions and giggled reassuringly at them whilst they smiled back with watery eyes and snot in their noses. 'Come along, everyone,' she called out, 'Let's hear Mr Fraser pray for our souls then we can have some cake and milk at the field.'

As the road wound round the back of the hill, the walk took the footpath to the summit. Rev Fraser led the way clutching his bible to his chest, whilst Mr Black blocked the road with arms outstretched to make sure no one escaped the sermon by running on to Allerbank or along the back road to Woodhill. He stared in disbelief as the elegant Miss Melville led her foundlings onto the hill to join the others. She spotted Mr Black's distaste at the children's poor state.

'Suffer the children to come unto Me,' she said, sweeping past him before he could say anything in reply.

'Indeed, just what I was thinking,' he called after her, inventively but a second or two too late to impress her.

The natural bowl of ice-carved rock around the summit formed a perfect amphitheatre into which the younger children crowded with the older ones spilling down the south-facing slope. Phee and Elizabeth made sure there was space for the new additions much to the displeasure of Daisy Gowans and Pansy Morton who had to sit beside them. When Daisy sat holding her nose against the stench of the small, unwashed creature beside her, she was given a dunt by Miss Melville.

'Manners, Daisy, dear,' she commanded. 'Manners and sit up straight.' Daisy was close to tears. She wasn't used to chastisement of any kind. Besides, her mother would be furious if she went home with nits in her hair.

The minister stood on the summit in the middle of his flock with his arms raised, elevated heavenwards so that all eyes were trained on his dark form, shaped like a cross against the blue sky.

After thanking God on behalf of the assembly for the beautiful day and for the many earthly blessings He had bestowed upon them, Rev Fraser beseeched the children to be perfect just as the Heavenly Father is perfect. By following the path to perfection, he told them, they would find the Kingdom of God.

Daisy Gowans compared her beautiful starched-white smock with the dirty rags of the tinker beside her, convinced that she must already be much closer to perfection and the Kingdom of God than the filthy urchin could ever be. John Birse, who knew just how imperfect he was, felt renewed guilt for being careless with Davy's boots. His toes curled inside his brand new shiny leather boots, lately purchased by his mother from the Co-op for this special day. *Unworthy* did not describe how bad he felt. Bert Broadley prayed that Geordie would recover fully from his illness and become perfect again so that his mother could stop worrying. He waved across at his little brother who sat near the summit in his chair. Minn Graham lifted her face to the warm sun, promising God that she would try to be a better person, deserving of His Love, and Rob Duncan looked across at the girls, asking himself who was the most perfect girl on the hill?

The minister moved onto the eight blessings of the Sermon on the Mount.

'Matthew Chapter five, Verses three to twelve,' he called out in a deep, commanding voice.

Many of the younger children simply stared in awe at him, his moral teaching about love, compassion and humility going straight over their heads. They might not have much of a clue about the meanings of the words but they did know they had to listen to every last one. So why did the minister always tell you chapter and verse where he was quoting from the Bible, they wondered? Nobody had a Bible to look up and a few were so busy trying to remember the numbers, they'd lost the gist of things right from the start. Some of the older children started to think about the picnic and the games to come and became restless, the list of the Blessed a lecture more suited to another day.

'I dinnae ken aboot hungerin' an' thirstin' for righteousness an' bein' filled but I'm starvin',' said a voice from the middle of the boys.

'I'm hungerin' for a bun an' thirstin' for a cup o' milk. I want ma belly filled!' whispered another, setting up a ripple of sniggering.

Mr Black delivered a slap round the back of the miscreant's head. The boy recoiled in horror, his arms raised, bracing himself against further punishment.

'Woe unto you that laugh now! For ye shall mourn and weep,' threatened Mr Black with exaggerated menace, pointing a long finger. His arm swept around like a wizard casting a spell. 'Luke Chapter six, Verses twenty-four to twenty-six.' A gasp went round as every child within hearing distance trembled.

'Beware the all-seeing eye,' whispered a lad who was further away and felt safe.

Mr Black glowered and the culprit cowered, his eyes wide.

When the Sermon on the Mount was finally over, the children perked up. They sang *All Things Bright and*

*Beautiful* in voices unsurpassed in sweetness and innocence. A prayer followed in which the late King and his successor featured highly, bringing about an impromptu rendition of *God Save the King* and much waving of flags. The benediction calmed things down again but even the adults began to wonder if it was ever going to end.

When the word *Amen* finally came, it might just as well have opened the sluice gates in a dam. Boys and girls got to their feet, ignoring the pleadings of the adults to line up in pairs. Every year the grown-ups seemed to forget that the race to Mansefield had become something of a tradition. With a collective scream, the girls ran along the footpath to the top of the road then a river of white smocks and coloured hair ribbons surged down the hill road towards Kaim Farm. The boys yelled as they took the old route in the opposite direction, straight downhill slipping and sliding across the grassy hillside, like a tidal wave of pent up energy and desire, suddenly released. They cut to the right where the pipes and the filter tanks for the new water supply blocked their paths, made straight for the footpath beside Kaim Farm steading, intent on beating the girls to the sports field where food and entertainment awaited. A tall, athletic girl called Mavis Wood won the first leg to the farm for the girls. She continued along the path to the field followed by an assorted straggle of puffed-out children. As they arrived to applause from their waiting parents and a tune on the pipes, the boys made it clear that they were not happy to be beaten by Mavis. Beaten by a girl? All sorts of excuses were made for their defeat, from the slipperiness of the grassy path on the hill to the unequal distance covered, ignoring the fact that the hill road taken by Mavis was clearly much longer.

As the children arrived from the hillwalk, some with skinned knees and grass marks on their clothes, they joined the long queue for food. Tables by the gate from Manse Lane were piled high with bags of sandwiches and cakes, guarded by a number of local worthies charged with distributing the bags on production of a ticket.

Phee watched the urchins she had befriended earlier join the back of the queue. Eventually, they approached the table. When two of the men in charge ushered them away like stray dogs, she marched over, demanding that the children be given a bag.

'They haven't got a ticket', said one of the men indignantly. 'No ticket, no bag was what we were told.' He looked defiantly at this confident lady in her fine clothes. She was clearly an upstart.

'Clearly there's been a mistake, in that case,' said Phee, 'You have plenty of bags left and six children are here without tickets.'

The men looked at each other and remained reluctant to oblige.

'Who paid for the purvey?' she demanded, 'Not you, I'll wager,' looking each man in the eye.

'The ratepayers and the Coal Company paid for it,' one man admitted.

Each child was given a bag, grudgingly, as if the men had paid for the entire contents out of their own pockets. Glumly, they watched the tinkers steal away, devouring the fare like ravenous beasts.

Elizabeth looked on, admiring her friend's audacity. Phee had immense confidence and didn't mind challenging accepted norms. Elizabeth often cringed when Phee stood up for common sense or followed her instincts rather than sit back. She was no shrinking violet and Elizabeth wished she could be more like her at times. They strolled across the field acknowledging admiring glances with a nod of the head to this one and that, then joined the other teachers and the minister in the tea tent out of the warm sun, leaving the ordinary folk to their simple sporting pleasures.

As the afternoon wore on, competitions in athletics, cricket and football were rolled out. Fathers came and went from the field as it suited them, taking part in the games or the races, meeting in groups or escaping altogether to their allotments or the Village Inn. Unlike other Saturdays, it was a full day off at the pits and the other works so they were out to make the most of it. Mothers were thankful to be able to relax and chat to friends, collectively keeping watch over discarded clothing, bags and prizes. They soothed skinned knees, supplied water for thirsty offspring, whilst keeping an eye on toddlers bent on making a break for freedom.

Eventually, as the afternoon's entertainments wound to a close, mothers were the first to leave, trailing their children behind them in various states of tiredness and mood. There was no evening recital or dance to look forward to for women with families. Even on this day of celebration, their duties would be prolonged until after the last child had gone to bed and preparations for the following day had been completed. Some would lie awake for a long time waiting for the return of their men folk, hoping they had resisted the temptation of the demon drink, wondering what their mood would be, and fearful that a week's pay had just gone down the drain.

# Chapter 14

## THE MINISTER AND HIS SISTER

Richard Fraser was having a wonderful day. Due to the good weather, he had been able to give the children the extended version of his sermon and was convinced that they were all the better for it. He loved walking out in front of the parade of children with parents looking on admiringly. The spiritual development of their issue was a heavy responsibility but he was convinced he was up to the mark. Arriving back at the field was another special moment. He made a grand entrance with his helpers in tow – the shepherd who'd brought his flock down from the hill. Mr Black was proving to be a man of intellect and dedication, he had decided, and very helpful in taking the Lord's message into the school. They seemed to share many opinions, got on very well together even when they disagreed about matters of scripture. And Richard had to admit he enjoyed the company of the lady teachers and the other eligible spinsters of the congregation who buzzed around him, keen to please and support him in his mission. Although he wasn't actively looking for a wife, he was sure that the right lady would come along in time.

The Reverend was glad to get into the shade of the tea tent after a morning out in the sun. Too much brightness disagreed with his fair complexion and blond hair, and left his cheeks and scalp a fiery red. He almost regretted the decision to leave his sunhat behind but he had to be careful with the image he projected for the sake of the church he represented. Nothing could be allowed to affect his authority, even if it meant a sunburnt scalp. It was just one of many sacrifices he had to make for his calling. He was thankful for the cool of the tent which had been erected against the rain that usually afflicted outdoor events in these parts. On this particular day, it provided a welcome retreat from the sun. The mood was quieter in here, calmer too. It was a relief to leave the common rabble behind for a while, he thought, and enjoy the more refined company attracted by the shade. He chose a seat in the middle of the tent, knowing that a cup of tea would come his way without having to ask.

'Can I bring you a cup of tea, Reverend?' asked the infant mistress kindly.

'That would be lovely, Miss Gibson,' he replied. 'Perhaps a sandwich and a piece of cake too? I was just about to offer, of course. It is better to give than to receive,' he said recalling an old sermon. 'But if I am not prepared to receive then you cannot have the pleasure of giving!' He gave a chortle completely devoid of shame, impressed by his own cleverness.

Mr Black followed the gentle Miss Gibson to the counter where he paid the cost of a selection of sandwiches and cakes whilst she paid for the tea. Thrift was an admirable quality but he could not allow one of his lady teachers, on such a small stipend, to be taken advantage of by Mr Fraser who should know better. They returned to find a gaggle of admirers camped beside the minister, making it difficult to reach him through the throng. Miss Gibson placed the tea in front of him then reluctantly retreated to the next table and the only available seat, barely within shouting distance of the great man.

Richard Fraser was the centre of attention. He fielded the compliments and questions that came his way with all of his professional experience and learning. Engaging with his flock was a central part of his work. He had to cultivate good relations, taking every opportunity to spread the gospel and encourage the willingness of others to work for the good of his church. It was sometime before the company around him began to thin and he noticed the presence of his sister at the next table. She was talking with Mr Black and a number of the teachers who had officiated on the walk. The younger Miss Melville was also present. He was glad to see her friendship with Elizabeth continue. Coming from a family of influence, she would lead his sister into society that could be advantageous to her. Elizabeth was such a meek and mild young lady, he felt. She needed some assistance when it came to social considerations.

'Good afternoon, Miss Melville,' he called. 'Did you enjoy the parade?'

Phee did not respond but continued her discussion with the schoolteachers about the small group of outcasts who hadn't been included in the preparations for the walk.

Richard was taken aback when a second enquiry fell on stony ground. Surely, she had heard his polite intervention, he asked himself, feeling the blush of his embarrassment add fire to his sunburnt face. Phee continued in conversation with her back to him. She was a cool one, he had to admit, and rather rude, sitting there so ostentatiously in her bonnet with its ribbons and bows. None of the other women would have ignored him like that. She was attractive too and she knew it, he fancied, preening her femininity like a swan in her first season, waiting for a mate. Feigning disinterest in him, he was sure. He had seen the way she'd brought those tinker children into the proceedings on the hill. As a Sabbath School teacher, that had not been her place. It showed a level of initiative that was unattractive in a woman. He determined he would have to tread carefully around the younger Miss Melville, make sure her influence over his sister did not go too far. At the same time, he would maintain good relations for everyone's benefit. He made his way to the next table where he sat beside his friend, Mr Black, making sure to enjoy a hearty conversation that did not include Euphemia Melville. Two could play her game, he decided.

'Goodbye, all,' Phee said suddenly to the company grouped around her table, getting up and straightening her dress. 'I'll see you all at the recital this evening, I hope.' As she turned to leave, she saw him. 'Mr Fraser! You're there. I wanted to tell you how much I enjoyed the parade. The children were delightful and I am so looking forward to this evening's entertainment. Goodbye, Elizabeth,' she said brightly, kissing her friend warmly on the cheek before leaving.

Richard followed Phee's elegant form as she made her way into the brilliance of the afternoon outside of the tent. So charming, he thought, but how rude not even to congratulate him on his sermon. He felt deeply slighted.

'I did enjoy your Sermon on the Mount!' said gentle Miss Gibson with excellent timing, pleased to have a chance to speak with Mr Fraser at last.

'Thank you, Miss Gibson,' he replied. 'I do not look for compliments, of course, it is all part of my mission after all. But I thank you, most humbly, for your kind words.'

The evening recital at the church on the last Saturday in June had been Richard Fraser's idea. There seemed to be a lack of entertainment for those members of the community who did not want to dance the night away and who enjoyed more quiet recreations. He realised that filling that void could take his mission forward. When he had first come to the parish barely two years before, he could see that there was a job to be done in filling the pews and in communicating God's Word across the locality, though the two were not necessarily the same thing. He had come to Blackrigg at a time of population growth, when many people were attracted from elsewhere in search of work in the expanding industrial sector. This did not, he noticed, result in an automatic increase in his congregation as many incomers chose to stay away. He sensed that this was not down solely to their rejection of the spiritual side of life, as someone like Isabelle Melville might have it. He felt that the church had to find new ways of reaching out to people, in an age when the church's own interpretation of the Gospels had moved from hell-fire and damnation to the idea of a loving and forgiving God. The choice that this gave people, in taking or leaving the church, was a challenge that he had to rise to. Also, the competition from the various churches that had taken root in the village was an added and irritating trial. The Free Church, the United Presbyterians, the Church of Christ and the Plymouth Brethren all had premises now, grand and not so grand, and there was Roman Catholicism that took the Irish out of the community altogether, to the chapel in the next village.

Along one side of the kirk hall, the ladies of the Women's Guild had laid out a fine spread for supper, to be taken after the recital. The elders stood at the doors welcoming the audience. Although, the evening's entertainment had been planned to reach out further than the normal congregation, the same faces that filled the pews on a Sunday morning seemed to be occupying the seats. Richard had noticed, with irritation, that two of the other churches were also putting on alternative evening entertainments this year. How deeply annoying he felt the competition for people's souls. But he was heartened to see that the Melvilles had put in an appearance in response to his personal invitation. At least he was ahead in the race to attract the most prestigious souls, he thought wryly.

David Melville attracted the stares and admiration of many of the younger ladies in attendance. They craned their heads round, watched him negotiate his way to the seats reserved at the front for his party, passing many who wanted to engage him in conversation and introduce their daughters. Whispers of approval about his dark good looks and his handsome attire travelled across the rows. There was general agreement that he was a big improvement on his crusty old father who'd had little time for anyone in the village. The presence of the much-respected Dr Matheson in the Melville party, gave the new laird added credibility but the beautiful dark-haired woman who accompanied them caused a stir of a different kind. David Melville seemed to be fussing around her, making sure she was seated close to him. Some asked, 'Who could she be?'

'Naw, surely no the doctor's daughter, young Rose?' said a woman's voice.

'My, how she's grown,' remarked an elderly lady in black.

'And a beauty, make no mistake, very like her late mother,' said Miss Millar, reminding everyone that the good doctor was a widower and, perhaps, *available*.

'Dae ye think there's an engagement in the offing?' someone asked, returning their attention to the question of a possible relationship between David and Rose.

'What a pity for the rest of us!' came a disappointed reply that spoke for many, including some in fairly advanced years.

The Melville sisters appeared rather late in the hall, mainly because Isabelle insisted on talking with as many people as possible to prove how gracious and interested in everyone's affairs she was. Phee smiled politely but longed to sit down more anonymously. Their attire was much admired. The younger sister had developed a good eye for what suited her, aware that simple lines and expensive fabrics were shown off to perfection by her slim figure. Also, Isabelle had ditched the out-dated styles she had craved for so long. She had returned from her recent trip to London with a trunk full of the latest fashions, chosen with the help of a cousin who knew her way around the fashion houses of the capital.

'Look at thon pair,' said a whispered voice in the middle of a group of ladies. 'Think they're the bees' knees, so they do.'

'Their dresses are beautiful,' said a younger voice. 'She fair suits thon shade of lilac wi' her auburn hair.'

'They must have cost a small fortune,' said another.

'They're jist like you and me under a' that silk and tulle,' stated a large matronly type.

'Well not exactly like you, I'd wager,' said her husband without tact and even less forethought, surveying his wife's ample proportions. She looked askance, would make him pay for his remark later but it provoked a snigger or two across the company.

'Isabelle and Euphemia, is it?' came a curmudgeonly

138

voice. 'They're jist plain Isa and Effie when it comes doon tae it.'

Elizabeth Fraser sat in the back row of the audience catching a little of the tittle-tattle and it saddened her immensely. After the praise and admiration heaped on David Melville for his good looks and status, his sisters were being torn to shreds for the very same reasons. Why were women so hard on other women? She caught Phee looking over, gave a small wave. The Melville sisters had only made it half way down the hall but it looked as if proceedings could start at any moment. Phee took her chance. She promptly advanced towards the empty chair beside her friend.

'Is anyone sitting here, Miss Fraser?' she asked brightly. 'May I join you?'

'Delighted if you would, Miss Melville,' replied Elizabeth, allowing Phee to squeeze past her knees into the spare seat. 'Not sure the view will be the best from here. You'll see much more at the front,' she advised.

'This has a better escape route, however,' explained Phee in a whisper, smiling broadly. 'Have you heard Miss Shanks before?' she asked with exaggerated innocence from behind her hand.

The minister appeared on stage to start proceedings, unaware that his face was a bright, shiny red. The skin on his nose was already peeling from a day in the sun. He gave a short summary of the programme, mainly to let the audience know that tea and a light supper would be served at the end. In his experience, an audience was much more amenable if they knew exactly when food and drink was to be available. He gave a quick prayer asking for God's thanks for the glorious day: a prayer that was short and sweet, to everyone's great relief. His congregation had come to accept that the Reverend could make a substantial meal out of every occasion. But those members who relished his harangues were not in attendance on that particular evening. Frippery such as arias and old Scotch sangs, no matter how old, were not their cup of tea.

The minister gave a mild, affected cough as he introduced the first act but found it hard to be enthusiastic since the original supporting act had cancelled at the last minute. He blushed nervously though no one noticed, his face having turned a shade of scarlet early in the proceedings. He hoped that the replacement act would be met with a degree of tolerance, praying that the man would be bearable. Though the Reverend was not convinced. The act had turned up only ten minutes beforehand with a fiddle, proclaiming that he couldn't sing a note and that a piano accompaniment would be advantageous, thank you very much. When he'd said that his act was called 'Archie Syme, the Highland Laddie from Shotts,' the Reverend had almost swooned.

'I'm sorry to have to inform you, Ladies and Gentlemen, that Mr Gordon, baritone, has had to cancel at the last minute due to ill-health,' he explained in his most honeyed tones, 'And I'm sure you will join with me in wishing him a speedy recovery. However, we owe a great debt of gratitude to Mr Syme, violinist, for agreeing to step in at the last minute. I am sure you will not be disappointed,' he continued.

A collective murmur of discontent went round the audience. A mass folding of arms suggested they were ready for disappointment.

'Please give a warm welcome, everyone, for Mr Archibald Syme with a medley of Scottish tunes on his violin, accompanied by our very own Miss Foulkes on the piano!'

Polite applause welcomed this hitherto unknown talent, as a sturdy young man with a huge bright smile that complemented his kilt, appeared on the stage. Miss Foulkes sat down at the piano with a face like thunder. She had been drafted in at the last minute, persuaded only by a distraught Rev Fraser. There hadn't even been time for a brief practice to make sure they could play in harmony and Miss Foulkes always liked to be in control.

Half an hour later, the Highland Laddie was still going strong, egged on by the enthusiastic singing and foot tapping that had started up after the first tune. Miss Foulkes too, not one to show her lighter side in public, had become quite enthusiastic. She lapped up the adulation and participation of the crowd as she hammered out the tunes on the piano keys.

'Isabelle, will be hating this!' whispered Phee, hardly able to contain a fit of giggles, 'But I'm enjoying it! How about you?'

'It's good! Cheerful!' replied Elizabeth, clapping in time to *Comin' through the rye*. 'Maybe Miss Shanks should've been on first!' She joined Phee in fanning herself with her programme. The hall was heating up quickly with so much enthusiastic singing on such a warm summer evening.

After an encore of mammoth proportions during which *Comin' through the rye* had featured more than once, Archie was persuaded to leave the stage and give Miss Shanks a turn. The audience were generous in their praise for his version of the old Scotch sangs so it took some time for the applause to die down. The Rev Fraser gave a short speech about God working in mysterious ways before Miss Shanks appeared with her own pianist and violinist.

As soon as the first few bars were trilled, Phee Melville knew that she would not be able to take any more. The horrified looks on the faces of the audience who had taken Archie Syme and his fiddle to their bosom was a sight to behold. Phee was soon stifling a fit of giggles. Elizabeth squirmed in her seat, suddenly wishing her friend could show a bit more deference at times.

'Come on, Elizabeth. Let's go!' whispered Phee. 'Let's go outside and sit in the sun,' she suggested.

Elizabeth was reticent about leaving. She didn't want to be rude.

'No one will notice,' Phee continued persuasively. 'Besides you can hear that noise half way to Glasgow. We can nip back in at the interval – dear Richard will never know. What do you say?'

Phee pushed open the double doors at the back of the hall, closely followed by Elizabeth who helped her wedge them open, each pretending to be thinking of the overheating audience when, in fact, they were planning their escape. They held their breath until well out in the sunshine and round the corner of the building, before exploding with laughter.

'You are so bad, Euphemia Melville,' said Elizabeth. 'You will get me into so much trouble, one of these days!'

At that moment, Miss Shanks missed a top note. The escapees fell giggling onto a bench, mightily relieved to be out in the evening air.

# Chapter 15

## THE DANCE

The Gala Day dance was being held in the public hall for the first time and the organisers anticipated a full house. The old country dances of Scotland had been waning in popularity in favour of waltzes and polkas but a band that could turn their hand to all types had been booked. Walter Heggie and his Band duly arrived on the train from Airdrie and Sandy Scott, ploughman at Craigpark Farm, had been despatched to meet them with a flat cart. The five musicians piled onto the cart alongside their instruments then Charlie, a fine brown Clydesdale, hauled them up the Station Road and along Main Street in the late afternoon. It wasn't a long journey but they attracted a great deal of interest and hand waving from passers-by. Walter decided to do a bit of advertising for future business, since there was plenty of time to spare before the dance was due to begin. With Sandy's agreement and five chairs, the band set up their instruments on the cart, merrily playing a few tunes as the unflappable Charlie, with a swish of his black tail and a shake of his long mane, pulled them back and forward through the village. Astonishment soon turned to appreciation as a fair-sized crowd clapped them back and forward along the street. Even Mrs Gow, not known for merriment, was seen tapping her feet and clapping in time to the music, and a gaping smile formed in the toothless hollow that was the Widow MacAuley's mouth. Some reckoned that such a thing had not been seen since the day her husband had passed away in 1869.

The dancers arrived in anticipation of a wonderful evening, expectations heightened by the break from the routine of continuous toil and the arrival of unusually warm, sunny weather with the long, endless evenings of midsummer. A predominantly young age group gathered early, the youthful and the eligible, keen to appraise the attractiveness of the opposite sex and stake their claim to a mate, even if just for an evening. Those in established relationships arrived slightly later along with the newly-weds who were still in the throes of romantic love, without the trials and tribulations of family responsibilities. Last of all came a small number of older married couples who were rekindling the flame of their youth now that their children had flown the nest. An assortment of aging bachelors and widowers, still romantically inclined and hopeful of an end to the loneliness of a single life, propped up the doorways and littered the entrance hall, forcing women arriving without male accompaniment to run the gauntlet of close appraisal. The dearth of young, single women was evident from the start. Many worked in service, far and wide, and they wouldn't be given time off for their own entertainment.

The Temperance Movement was strong in the village with a good following across all sections of society so no alcoholic beverages would be made available at the dance. A cup of tea was to be served part way through the evening to quench the thirst of the merrymakers. However, as the evening wore on and the hall became stiflingly hot, the exit door that emptied onto a lane would be opened to reveal a circle of men of all ages, passing round one or two bottles of spirits for immediate consumption. On the ground would be the bottle tops, squashed underfoot to indicate that the contents were to be consumed there and then, and nothing would be taken home.

'We'll just have a look for a minute or two,' said Phee. 'Elizabeth, what harm can it do?'

Elizabeth stood under the huge yew tree by the church, listening to the muted sounds of the dance band drifting up from the public hall. She wasn't able to explain to Phee what harm it could do to look in on the dance but every instinct told her that she shouldn't go, not even for a very short time.

'It's a beautiful summer evening, Beth, and most of the people our age are enjoying themselves at the dance,' stated Phee in frustration. 'Yes, it's different for us. Convention says it's different because you're the sister of the minister and I'm the sister of the laird and we don't go to village dances. But why should it be so? Can't we make up our own minds?' she implored.

'No, we can't. Make up our own minds, I mean,' said Elizabeth, quite resigned to the fact. 'Richard would be furious. It would reflect on his work.'

'Uhh,' Phee gasped. 'Why should you be ruled by Richard's work?'

'You know why! Because it's all about morality in this life and saving souls for the next,' Elizabeth explained.

'So what happened to forgiveness?' asked Phee, intent on changing Elizabeth's mind.

'I think God would forgive me before the ladies of the Tea Committee would,' replied Elizabeth, in a droll way that hinted at a latent sense of humour.

Phee found it hard not to laugh. Her friend could be so funny without realising it. 'David wouldn't be too upset, 'too' being the operative word, but Isabelle would be furious if she found out I'd gone to the local dance! Soooooooo vulgar!' She laughed. 'That's a good enough reason for me to take a peek.'

They stood for a long time listening to the distant ebb and flow of fiddles and accordions playing waltzes and polkas, interrupted occasionally by applause and laughter.

'You're right,' said Elizabeth looking directly at her friend. 'We're old enough to make up our own minds. Why shouldn't we go along? Just for a look.'

'Well, we haven't got a chaperone,' Phee pointed out with a wry smile, giving Elizabeth a chance to change her mind. 'It would never do to go unaccompanied.'

'No problem,' replied Elizabeth, boldly, straightening her back. 'I shall accompany you and you shall accompany me.' She held out her arm for Phee to take. 'Just for a look remember,' she said.

Phee giggled. They made their way down the steps of the church onto Main Street like two singers in a Music Hall act, and strode confidently towards the sound of the dance.

When it came to actually entering the public hall building, they did so with some trepidation – even in Phee's case for all her outward bravado. They hadn't expected to attract so much attention but people generally stopped staring, carrying on with their own enjoyment after a while. The two did their best to blend into the background by standing in a corner. Phee told Elizabeth not to stare back when people looked, to keep her head up and exude confidence no matter how weak her knees felt. They watched a waltz and a reel, enjoying the music, smiling with the dancers as they moved around the floor. The crowd represented a fair cross-section of the working community: tenant farmers, agricultural labourers and woodsmen, business people, shop workers, miners and seamstresses. Elizabeth thought it was wonderful to see everyone enjoying themselves. Where was the harm in such a happy gathering?

As a waltz came to an end, the band leader announced the next dance. 'Take your partners for a barn dance, ladies and gentlemen. I'll talk ye through the first set till ye get the hang o' it, if ye dinna ken how it goes.' The musicians gave a few bars of the music as an encouragement whilst men eagerly sought out ladies with the stamina for the last dance before the interval.

'Miss Fraser, would you dae me the honour o' dancin' wi' me?' Elizabeth almost leapt out of her skin at the sight of Mr MacCullough, the tenant at Mosside, standing before her, his florid complexion and sweating brow a consequence of both his large size and his enthusiasm for dancing.

'An' would you dae me the honour, Miss Melville?' said Mr Brogan, the cycle agent in the village.

Both girls looked at each other, unsure, then spotted Mrs MacCullough and Mrs Brogan waving manically at them, telling them to get on with it. Clearly, the menfolk had been put up to it by their wives.

Well one dance couldn't do any harm, could it?

They were led onto the floor where they lined up in long rows with the other couples. The band leader organised the sets, then the music started at a steady pace. Elizabeth and Phee were last in their set of eight so they had a chance to observe the steps before they were birled by their partners and led up and down, turning with each man one at a time. After a few rounds, the music livened and the dancers quickened their pace, throwing their partners around with great delight. As Elizabeth stepped across to lead off with Mr MacCullough for the fifth time, she held out her hands. To her great astonishment, they were taken by Neil Tennant. He saw her puzzled expression and shouted above the music, 'His wife says he's had enough. He'll kill himself if he doesnae rest. Dae ye mind, Miss Fraser?'

'Not at all,' she said blushing and nervous. 'Not at all, no, not at all.'

Instead of holding her by the hands at arm's length as Mr MacCullough had done, Neil took her right hand and placed it beneath his upper arm whilst he did the same in return. He held her left hand firmly with his then drew her close to him. She gasped, briefly closing her eyes in disbelief at being pinned so closely and unexpectedly to a young man's chest. The phrasing of the music marked the beginning of their dance together and they took off in a whirl. When Neil let her go to each of the other men in turn, she longed to be back with him, holding his arm, feeling the energy from his body. As he danced back up the row, leaving her briefly for each of the other women, she waited for him, smiling, ready for his return.

When their dance together was over, they stood opposite each other, clapping whilst the other dancers birled and turned. She looked into his deep, dark eyes across the chasm between them, smiling at his broad, white smile with a happiness she had never felt before. She was entranced. Several times her thoughts were abruptly interrupted as the other men in the set came to swing her round.

Too soon, the music stopped. The dancers gave a collective sigh of relief, a round of applause for the energetic playing of the band, and for their own energy and stamina.

Neil led Elizabeth by the hand back to the corner of the room.

Don't go, she thought.

He gave a short bow to both ladies. 'Would ye like tae tak some air, Miss Fraser, Miss Melville? It's very stuffy in here. I could bring ye a cup of tea.'

'That would be very kind of you, Mr Tennant,' said Phee, sensing that her friend might be far too overcome to reply.

Elizabeth smiled, nodding shyly.

'We'll wait outside for you, Mr Tennant, thank you,' Phee called out as she led Elizabeth away from the melee.

'Lucky old you,' she said when they were out in the air. 'I get the overly athletic and married Mr Brogan whilst you strike lucky with tall, dark and handsome... and young... Mr Tennant. Gosh he scrubs up well!' she added, referring to his smart attire.

'He seems rather a nice young man,' said Elizabeth, completely understating Mr Tennant's obvious charms.

'I'll say! Those broad shoulders and strong arms...... holding you close! And what a lovely smile. Mmm. Ssssh, here he comes... and he can balance three cups of tea at once! Could make a good husband,' she joked.

'Really, Phee!' said Elizabeth blushing, a smile as wide as the Clyde on her face.

As they sipped tea, pleasantries were exchanged: about the parade earlier in the day, the weather, the dancing, and the colour of the sky, now a glowing pink in the west and a pale turquoise merging with the deep blue above them. A number of people, enjoying the evening air, either in pairs or in small groups, took great interest in the unusual group of three. Neil ignored several calls and whistles for his attention, smiling broadly all the while.

'The band will be startin' up again in a bit. Are ye gaun back inside?' asked Neil.

'We shouldn't really,' said Elizabeth, but ready to be persuaded. 'We only came along for a little while.'

'We were at the recital, you see,' explained Phee. 'We really should get back before we're missed.'

'Ahh, ye escaped then,' said Neil knowingly. 'An' ye dinnae want to be found oot.'

'Certainly not,' said Elizabeth with feigned indignation. 'I was feeling rather hot, faint I mean, and we came out for some air. We heard the music and... and...'

'An' ye thocht a jig would mak you feel better!' laughed Neil.

Phee and Elizabeth were somewhat dumbfounded at this forthright and much too honest young man. Didn't he realise he should be sparing their blushes?

'Well, they're callin' a reel. Just whit the doctor ordered,' he said quickly to them both. 'Would you do me the honour an' join me in anither dance afore ye go back to the recital?'

'Oh, all right then. If you insist,' said Phee quickly, in case something occurred to stop them.

They took his hand, allowed him to lead the way back into the dance where they lined up, Neil in the middle with Elizabeth on one side and Phee on the other. They faced a handsome girl with a boy on either side and bowed as the first chord was played.

Neil was an excellent teacher, neither of his partners having much idea of the steps. He set to the left and right with a pas de basque then turned each partner on his arm, one after the other. They held hands, danced backwards and forwards, dipping under the arms of their opposite numbers, ready for a repeat of the dance with a new threesome. The young women laughed heartily as they stumbled, making mistakes, but they soon got the hang of the steps. Then the six danced around in a circle then back again, fast till their heads were spinning.

Elizabeth loved the exhilaration of the reel and the sheer joy of being that it brought. She loved to hold this young man's hand, seeing his wide smile when he turned her on his arm. She loved sharing this moment with her friend Phee who so often rebelled against the stuffiness of life in the Big House, looking as free as a bird in the wild, whirled around in time to the music by Neil Tennant. As each section of the dance started anew, she felt that she would die of exhaustion but, in truth, she never wanted it to end. She thought she could have danced with him till the end of time.

As the poem goes, *pleasures are like poppies spread* and it all ended too soon. The music stopped then Neil led his partners, laughing and catching their breath, to the side of the hall. He bowed graciously, thanking them for their company. He was just about to offer to walk them back to the recital when he was interrupted by another man, concerned and flapping. It was Mr Black.

'Good evening, ladies,' he said, 'Good evening, Mr Tennant. Thank you for keeping the ladies safe.' He gave a short bow of acknowledgement to the younger man then turned his back, deliberately cutting Neil off from his dancing partners by moving into the space between them.

'We've been perfectly safe, Ernest,' replied Phee, irritated by his insinuation that she couldn't look after herself and annoyed at his rudeness towards Neil. 'We can look after ourselves.'

'Your presence has been missed at the recital,' explained Mr Black with hugely exaggerated concern. 'It finished early and you were expected to help serve supper, Miss

Elizabeth. Your brother went to look for you at the manse thinking you were unwell but couldn't find you.'

'And here I am safe and sound, as you can see,' said Elizabeth. She held out her hands to show that she was indeed hale and hearty. 'There can hardly be a dearth of ladies willing and able to serve supper,' she continued glumly, looking at her friend with resignation and disappointment in her face. 'I suppose we should be getting back, Phee.'

'Yes, you really should,' said Mr Black looking around the hall just as a fracas was developing at the far end by the exit onto the lane. 'Not the sort of place for you to be spending the evening,' he said with distaste, examining the clientele. A large, lump of a man was attempting to pull two reluctant women onto the dance floor, only to be dispatched out of the door by a couple of younger men.

As a small crowd grew around the commotion, Mr Black ushered Phee and Elizabeth off in the other direction. 'I'll manage, Mr Tennant,' he said as Neil made to follow them. 'I'll escort the ladies to safety, if you don't mind.'

Elizabeth and Phee looked back at Neil as they departed the hall.

'Thank you, Mr Tennant, we enjoyed our dance very much indeed,' called Phee.

'Goodnight, Mr Tennant!' Elizabeth searched for Neil, but the schoolmaster had already hurried her out of view.

'Hurry, ladies,' he urged. 'You don't want to be caught up in any trouble. It's bad enough to be seen in such a den in the first place.'

As the women disappeared into the dusk, they heard Neil call after them. 'Goodnight, Miss Melville. Goodnight, Miss Fraser.'

'Goodnight, Neil,' said Elizabeth again, this time quietly to herself.

As Mr Black chaperoned them along the road, the sounds from the dancehall grew faint. Distant laughter and conversation overlapped the rise and fall of the music.

'A waltz,' thought Elizabeth. How she longed to be held at that moment in the strong arms of Neil Tennant, to look up into his dark eyes, inhaling the smell of him. He would smile his broad, white smile for her, a smile that lit up his entire face with gentleness and sincerity, a smile only for her.

'A waltz,' thought Phee sadly, as the gentle melody reached out to her through the evening air. She wondered who Neil Tennant was dancing with now.

They picked their way along the gravel pathway but had to stop several times to remove gravel from Phee's satin shoes. Elizabeth did her best to help whilst delaying their return to the church hall as much as possible.

Mr Black was not the most patient of chaperones. He was doing his utmost to hurry them through the shadows of the graveyard surrounding the church when a scream rent the air. It was a young woman's scream. Then came another, followed by a deep voice, brutish and threatening. Was it coming from the public hall? No, much further away to the right, down by the burn perhaps or out beyond the village towards Parkgate.

'We should help,' said both women at once, looking plaintively at Mr Black.

'It's none of our business,' said the schoolmaster in spite of another scream in the distance. 'Someone else will see to it.' He put out his arms barring the way, to stop them from retracing their steps. He made his charges walk in the direction of the church hall, ignoring their protests. 'Come along, ladies. People will be worried about you. And you don't want to miss supper entirely. Do you now?'

# Chapter 16

## FORBIDDEN PLEASURES

Nell Graham and Maggie Lennox had been in service at
Parkgate House since 1908 when they had left school at
the age of fourteen. Although their families lived barely a
mile away in Stoneyrigg, it had been a wrench to leave
home for life as a domestic servant. They shared a room
in the attic of the old house and their friendship soothed
the loneliness of living apart from close-knit families. Once
a month, the girls were allowed off on a Sunday afternoon
to visit their parents but had to return in good time to
help with the supper. Parkgate House seemed cavernous
at first, a maze of corridors and hidden stairs linking a
warren of rooms, each with a specific purpose, very unlike
the cramped conditions of a workman's cottage. Largely
invisible to the Melville family, the girls worked from dawn
till late evening in uniforms of grey dresses and white
aprons. A starched, white mutch hid their hair, removing
any remaining hint of individuality. The family seemed
polite but remote, though only Miss Isabelle radiated the
stern bearing and presumptions of her class that warned
*tread carefully*. Gossip about the family was not encouraged.
Nell and Maggie had learned early that it paid to keep
their eyes and ears open and their mouths shut.

As the lowest members of Parkgate's servant hierarchy, Nell and Maggie worked under the direction of the housekeeper and the cook, fulfilling a range of tasks as required. They ate meals in the servants' quarters beside the kitchen, at a long table presided over by the butler, Jameson. From time to time, estate workers appeared for a meal, bringing their cheerful chat and news from the farms and nearby villages. Maggie and Nell looked forward to new faces at the table, except in the case of the gamekeeper, Grant. In common with the other female servants, Maggie and Nell disliked his presence, keeping their heads bowed when he was around.

On the evening of the Gala Day dance, they had finished their work by nine, slightly earlier than usual because the family and their guests had left at seven thirty after a light repast, heading for the evening recital at the church. Jameson would remain on duty should anything be required on their return. The girls said goodnight to the cook who grumbled a complaint about the state of the roasting tins but conceded that they would suffice on this occasion.

'Grumpy auld nag,' said Maggie as she climbed up the back stairs to the attic rooms ahead of Nell. 'Nuthin pleases her so why dae we bother daein guid work at a'. Micht as well be slap dash, we'll get snash either wey.'

'Shhh,' urged Nell as if walls had ears. 'Somebody'll hear ye an' we'll get whit for.'

In the privacy of their room, uniforms were discarded; their long hair was brushed then pinned up in a more fashionable style. Black stockings and plain work shoes would have to do. It was all they had. They lifted their mattresses and removed the patterned garments they had secreted there. Nell put hers on, whirled around, delighted with the transformation brought about by the green dress. She was a petite girl, barely five foot tall with blonde hair and baby blue eyes that made her look younger than her sixteen years. She longed to be taller and more grown up.

'Weel done, Meg, ma first ever frock,' she said to her sister in her absence. 'Whit dae ye think, Maggie? Oor Meg made it frae an auld curtain an' a bit satin she boucht fae the pack wuman on her last visit,' she explained, referring to Jinty Auld who did the rounds of the villages with an enormous pack of second hand clothing on her back. The pack woman was a welcome source of garments and fabrics at affordable prices, to be made into a range of clothes by nimble fingers.

'The material's braw an' it's a nice style. I like the rim o' satin roon the neck,' replied Maggie. 'Dae ye like ma new blouse? I got it frae Jinty tae. Ma mither nipped it in the waist an' let oot the seams.' She smoothed down her tired old skirt, put her hands on her waist to show off her blouse to good effect. 'It's a bit auld-fashioned but, whit the hell, it's a' I could afford.'

'The blue colour suits yer dark hair an' yer blue een,' said Nell in admiration. 'Ye look ready for a dance!'

'Aye, nearly. A' we need noo is a wee bit poother an' paint.' She produced a small pot of rouge.

'Whaur did ye git thon?' exclaimed Nell staring at a small glass crucible of creamy red paste.

'Haud yer wheesht, Nell,' said Maggie reassuringly, 'Dinnae fash yersel, I didnae steal it. Miss Euphemia was chuckin' it oot. Shame tae waste it, daen't ye think?' She put some of the red colour onto her finger then applied it to her cheeks.

'If oniebody finds it here, they'll think we nabbed it!' Nell was unhappy that contraband was being kept in their room. She looked at Maggie's pale face, a circle of red on each cheek like one of the dolls in the nursery. 'Thon's ower muckle,' observed Nell after a delay. 'Ye look like yer awa' tae the Waverley Steps tae mak a bob or twa,' she added, quoting a commonly heard insult for shameless women who paid too much attention to their appearance. The Waverley Steps, leading to Edinburgh's main railway station, was notorious as a haunt for ladies of the night.

'Quick, then. Help me tak it aff,' said Maggie horrified. 'A wee touch is a' ye need.' Nell took her friend's advice when applying the rouge to her own cheeks. They added the lightest of touches to their lips, well satisfied with the effect.

Stifling a giggle, they opened the door of their attic room, charily, then waited a few seconds to ensure Bertha, the ladies' maid, hadn't heard them. The sounds of blissful snoring from the next room let them know that Bertha would not be a problem. They did not have permission to leave the house, sure they would be sacked on the spot if they were found out.

Every one of the back stairs creaked as they descended slowly. The girls could hardly breathe. The ground floor corridor was dark so they felt their way along the wall to the door next to the stairwell that led down to the servants' quarters. A faint light shone upwards; movement could be heard. Jameson was down there, reading no doubt, and helping himself to the cooking sherry. They edged passed the light then found the door out to the laundry block and the drying green. A look to the right and the left, a quick scurry across to the rowans, over the stile and they were safely away from the house. As long as they kept away from the road and stayed behind the hedgerows, no one would see them making their way towards the music and the dance.

As they approached the hall, the girls were careful to stand back from the small crowd that had been cooling down and drinking tea in the shade of the large, spreading chestnut trees that lined the street there. They had to be careful not to be seen by other staff from the estate who might recognise them and spill the beans to the cook, next time they paid a visit to the kitchen. As the music started up, Nell and Maggie followed the last of the dancers in through the front door as if they were part of the group and had been at the dance from the beginning. They picked their way through the crowd to the far corner of the hall where they stood against the wall, trying to feel inconspicuous behind a group of young women who were engrossed in conversation. The girls still had a good view: they had only come for a short while after all, long enough to have a look and to hear the music. They had heard so many tales about the dance: at sixteen, their curiosity was spiked. They watched a reel, feeling they'd love to have taken part: to be whirled around the floor by a nice lad then walked home perhaps, hand in hand. Maggie was in the middle of pointing out the pretty dresses worn by the women when she recognised a handsome threesome making their way around the hall in their direction, Miss Melville included!

'Look whau's here, Nell. It's Miss Euphemia! Whit'll we dae if she sees us?' asked Maggie, fearing immediate dismissal without references and the prospect of facing unemployment as well as her mother's wrath in an instant.

'If we stay here, we'll be fine,' answered Nell hopefully but still concerned. 'She's no used tae seein' us dressed up like this. Jist keep talkin'. Dinnae look in her direction.'

A few sets passed before the girls thought they were out of danger. The dance had been going for ages and some of the heavier built participants looked as if they might peg out at any moment. It couldn't go on much longer before Miss Melville and her friends would leave the floor. If she walked over towards them, the girls would slip out the back door to safety. Their employer and her partners were now dancing with their back to them so they felt more relaxed again. Nell turned to Maggie, exchanged a look that said '*all clear*'. Until a large, leering figure smelling of strong drink leaned over them and placed one hand on the wall above where they stood.

'Well, jist look whit we've got here,' said the gamekeeper, recognising the two young servants through a haze of alcohol. Both girls were rooted to the spot and stared up at him. They hated Grant when he was sober in the relative safety of Parkgate House, when he came in from the parks and looked them up and down, ogling them, making them blush with embarrassment without having to say so much as a word to them. Here in the dance hall, drunk as a newt, he was a bigger threat. The girls sidled along the wall together in an attempt at escape but he was having none of it.

'I think we could hae a dance thegither,' he slurred, attempting to grab each girl by the wrist. 'Come on, the band's still playin'. Dae as Mister Grant tells ye.'

The girls tried to make their way towards the back door of the hall but he put out an arm to block their passage. Ducking down would have made them vulnerable. They felt trapped like wild animals in one of his snares.

'We have tae go, Mr Grant,' said Maggie.

Grant was having none of it; he stepped closer.

'Please, Mr Grant, let us past.' Fortunately, the music was still playing and Miss Melville hadn't spotted them yet.

Grant was becoming more insistent, made aggressive by the whisky he'd consumed. He grabbed wildly for Nell's wrist, showering her with spray from his blabbering mouth. The stench of sweat and tobacco mixed with the whisky on his breath made her wretch. As she darted under his outstretched arm, he lunged after her only to fall headlong amidst a group of women, hitherto wrapped in conversation. The music had come to an end so the entire hall turned in their direction as the women yelled their disgust at the drunken gamekeeper. Male partners came quickly to their defence, intent on dispatching the legless wastrel whilst Nell and Maggie took their chance and darted out of the back door to safety.

The girls made their way down the dark lane, out of sight of the men who were smoking and drinking behind the hall. As soon as they reached the street, they agreed to make their way straight back to Parkgate House. Nell stopped to take a stone out of her shoe then they hurried off under the chestnut trees, deciding to stick to the road as the quickest way back. They would take their chances at being spotted, absent without leave, counting themselves lucky to have escaped the clutches of disgusting, lecherous Grant.

As they looked ahead, the trees and the hedgerows were silhouetted black and fearful against the sky now that sunset had passed, though the sky was still a vivid blue and a pink glow remained above the horizon. They soon left the last of the village houses behind for fields and hedges. The road in front of them was filled with dread but the sanctuary of Parkgate lay ahead in the trees. Maggie started to say they should run for a bit when the sound of huge, lumbering feet and laboured breathing came from behind. She screamed, turning to face their assailant as he descended upon them. There was no point in running away, even further from the village. He was bound to catch them somewhere along the road.

Grant's large hand made contact with Maggie's face. He pushed her aside. She wasn't what he was after. She fell onto the hard ground then his fist connected with her temple as she tried to get back up, lying dazed in the road whilst the gamekeeper staggered off in pursuit of her friend. Maggie watched him through a fog of pain as he grasped at Nell's clothing; grabbing the hair at the back of her neck in a huge fist; lifting her off the ground then bundling her over a gate like a dead deer. Nell lay still in the soft ground on the other side, bruised and stunned, her beautiful green dress torn and streaked with dirt. Grant lifted a long leg over the gate, muttering his vile contempt for her, telling her she'd had it coming. Maggie launched herself at him as he balanced on the top spar, vulnerable for a brief moment. She screamed a heart-rending scream that came from the very centre of her being. Grant yelled his loathing for her and all the other *hoors and tails* like her. He braced himself against her onslaught with his forearm, pushed her back into the road where she landed in the gravel once again. But she was back on her feet again, quickly climbing the gate. She wasn't about to leave her best friend to her fate without a struggle. Maggie screamed and screamed as Grant dragged Nell further into the field, forcing the helpless girl to stagger with him when she regained her senses. Clutching the gate, Maggie looked up the road towards the village, vainly hoping that someone was coming to save them. Was there no one at all that could help? She ran off down the hill, jumped on Grant's back, clinging on for dear life, telling Nell to run, run like the wind. Grant held Nell's slender arm fast in his huge hand so she couldn't pull away. Once again, he let fly at Maggie with his fist then his foot. She fell backwards into the grass, screaming.

'Help! Help!' she called out, sobbing. 'Somebody, please help!'

# Chapter 17

## AN AWFUL FRIGHT

Minn and Sarah Graham sat reading at the table whilst their father dozed in his chair by the fire. The heat of the day had dissipated and the sun was now well below the roofline of the Stoneyrigg Rows making the room quite dark and the firelight bright. Much earlier, Meg had left for the dance with Will Morton who was a clerk at the pit. She had been seeing him for several months by then. Their father had remarked to her sisters that it would only be a matter of time before he lost his Meg to that young man. When Minn had asked him how he knew that to be so, he had said that he could see the signs and they left it at that.

A knock came to the door. The girls pulled back the curtain to see more clearly who it was before answering.

'Da'! Da'! are ye awake,' they said together. Tom stirred into consciousness in his chair with the mild panic of an abrupt awakening evident in his voice. 'Whit is it? Whit's wrang?'

'Da, Jenny Campbell and Sadie Healy are at the door. Can we gang oot for a while?' asked Minn. 'Da, can ye hear me?'

'Aye, I hear ye fine, Minn,' he replied sleepily with one eye open. 'Ye can gang oot as long as ye bide thegither.

An' dinnae gang near the village when there's dancin' oan.
Stay nearby, mak sure yer back afore dark. Promise?'

Those were the conditions on which freedom had been
granted and both girls nodded their acceptance of them.

'Cheerio, Da',' called Minn as she went out, chattering
non-stop to her friends before the door was even closed.

'There disnae seem tae be mony folk aboot,' said Jenny
when they were outside. 'We've looked the usual places.'

'We could go for a walk,' suggested Sarah, the youngest
at ten years. 'Whit aboot gaun back up The Law?'

'Ower faur,' said Sadie, 'An' ower steep, ma feet are
killin' me fae the procession.'

'We've tae stey awa' frae the village,' explained Minn.
'But we could gang doon by the burn for a seat. It's a
braw nicht.'

Her companions agreed so they set off towards
Craigpark. A small group of older men stood at the
steading, smoking, talking and taking the air. The girls
waved happily as they took the Station Road down to the
burn. They meandered along the path at Burnside; sat
talking for a while; throwing stones into the water and
watching small fish jump for flies. The sound of the dance
band, drifting in their direction from the hall on Main
Street, had the girls talking about what it would be like
to go to the dance when they were older. They described
the dresses they would like to wear as well as their favourite
patterns and colours. Sarah said that her sister Meg had
looked fair braw in her blue frock when she had gone out
with Will Morton that night. She explained that Meg would
soon be lost because her father could read the signs. Sadie
asked if it was tea leaves or cards that her father read but
Minn said that it was neither: her father could read the

signs in people's faces that gave away their thoughts. Jenny said that she hoped to God her father couldn't read her thoughts, otherwise she would get a slap and no supper. Her companions agreed, nodding solemnly.

They soon wandered further along the riverside, attracted by the familiar sounds of boys calling out to each other, over-exerting themselves in a game of football being played on the Meadie beyond the mill. The girls picked their way through the brambles that lined the path beside the old ruin, before settling themselves down on the grass to watch the game.

Minn was pleased to see that Andrew Brownlee was there. He had settled in well at school; seemed to be accepted by the others despite his father being the pit manager at Broadrigg. He wore immaculate clothing so he stood out in the crowd but he was throwing himself about the field, determined to be one of the lads. His beautiful tweed knickerbockers were green with grass stains, complementing the green smears on his shirt which now had a tear under the arm. Minn put her arm around Sarah, her younger sister, feeling the warm contentment of being with friends on a summer evening, whilst watching their classmates at play. When a couple of players decided it was time to call it a day, the depleted teams brought the game to an end by mutual consent. The boys collected discarded clothing then several walked off home in different directions. The remainder joined the girls.

All of a sudden, a harsh voice boomed out from the cottages at Burnside, calling out for Hector. Everybody watched in amusement as a skinny lad ran off in a panic, abandoning the company, leaping over them in his haste, long before the strains of his mother's bark had died away.

'*Hector*? That's some haunle tae have tae yer jug!' said Sandy Duncan. 'It's mair a name for a dug or a bull. Naebody doon the pit's cried *Hector*.'

'A name like thon could affect yer life,' suggested his elder brother. 'Ye ken, makin' ye staun oot in a crowd.'

'Could be a guid thing or a bad,' added Dan Potts philosophically, bringing to mind the pranks they had all played on poor Hector from Burnside in the past.

'We've a' got ordinary names, names that help ye fit in. For instance, maist men in Scotland are cried either Jim or John,' he continued looking at the twins.

John was glad to have an ordinary name that helped him to feel part of something: Scotland, this place where he lived and breathed, the place where he was alive in the world. He felt an instant connection with the many other people called John even though the connection with a particular John, who had gone before him, had been broken at his birth. He knew nothing about his birth mother and father, unlike all of his friends. His name and his brother were his only link with where he had come from.

'Ye can tell a lot frae whit somebody cries ye,' said Sadie. 'Like Robert Duncan's cried that efter his faither an' his faither's faither. But Sandy Duncan's cried efter his mither's faither, *Alexander*.'

'There's aye been a Robert Duncan in the family, an' I'm the first-born son and heir,' declared Rob, lying back on the grass, hands behind his head like a Roman emperor waiting to be fed grapes.

The girls looked on in quiet admiration.

'Ma mither maistly cries me Robert. I only get *young Rob* when ma faither's aboot tae avoid confusion.'

'Aye, she's got plans for ye... ye've tae gang faur,' said Sandy, 'She disnae cry me *Alexander* does she? What does that tell ye?' he asked, turning his head away, pretending to be jealous of his older brother.

'It tells ye, yer her wee pet lamb,' said Sarah and everyone laughed.

Sandy threw grass in her face.

'Ma mither cries me *Andrew* a' the time,' said Andrew Brownlee. 'But you lot cry me *Andra* just like we call Robert, Rob. I like that.'

'Aye, that's 'cause yer oor pal,' said Bert Broadley. He slapped Andrew on the back to confirm that he was definitely one of the gang. 'Did ye ken I was cried efter Prince Albert, Queen Victoria's man?' he said triumphantly.

'Was he yer mither's faither, then?' asked Sarah innocently, quickly working out a possible relationship based on what she'd gleaned about the tradition of naming children in Scottish families. To her surprise, everyone fell about laughing.

'Naw, Sarah,' said Bert. 'Dae ye think I chose tae bide in a miners' raw ower a palace? It was jist a brek wi' tradition, that's a'. Ma faither cried us a' efter royalty 'cause he likes the monarchy an' liked the names.'

'I like tradition,' said Minn. 'Let's ye ken whaur ye are in life. How yer connectit tae ither folk. There's reasons fer stickin' wi' the yin way o' daein things.'

'*Minn*, noo whit kinna name's that? Disnae sound ower traditional tae me!' challenged Bert, feeling slighted over the reaction to his parents' choice of names. 'Did yer Ma an' Da run oot o' names by the time they got tae ye? There's that mony lassies in yer hoose!'

'I'm named efter ma faither, Thomas,' explained Minn proudly. 'He was fed up waitin' for a son, so he cried me *Thomasina*. I could've got Ina for short but ma Ma ay cried me Minn.'

'Could've bin worse, I suppose,' said Bert. 'It should've been *Sinn* and no *Minn*.'

Everyone sniggered.

'I ken a Kennethina and an Angusina!' said the shy Jenny Campbell.

'Georgina's no sae bad, but whit about Williamina?' said Bert.

'Terrible,' they agreed, concluding that tradition maybe wasn't all it was cracked up to be. Perhaps some things should be changed for the better.

'No ower lassie-like at a',' said Sandy which just about summed up everyone's feelings. 'Hey, there's auld Aggie McLuckie,' he said pointing up the Doctor's Brae. 'Noo there's a haunle tae hiv oan yer jug!'

The long shadows of the setting sun merged into a pool of darkness that swamped the Meadie as the friends talked on about the mysteries of life in Blackrigg and beyond. The trees that lined the burn and formed the thicket further upstream rose above them, black and statuesque against the sky; the music from the dance reached them through the still air when they stopped their chatter. They listened quietly to the melodies, soft and mellow, but still audible above the flow of the river. The frantic song of a blackbird hopping across the meadow startled them, and the cawing of crows in the rookery signalled the arrival of dusk.

'The auld folk say the mill's haunted,' said Jim, bringing a few short squeals from boys and girls alike even though the story was well known. 'They say the miller went aff his heid when the estate shut the mill doon. It'd been his hail life afore that.'

'Whit happened tae him? Hoo did he dee?' asked Sadie, curiosity winning out over fear.

'They found him wrapped roon the millwheel when they cam tae evict him an' tak the machinery awa',' Jim explained. 'His heid was a' mashed frae the poundin' it got as the wheel went roon an his een were open wide in terror!'

There was a collective intake of breath.

'Have ye ever seen him?' asked Sadie. 'The ghost I mean.'

'Naw, ye dinnae see him, ye hear him – so they say – an' ye hear the mill wheel gaun roon when somethin' terrible's gaun tae happen, even though the wheel's been awa' for years,' he explained, reducing his voice to a whisper to increase the tension. 'Some o' the auld yins tell hoo they've heard him singin'. Jist about this time tae, when the daylight's fadin'.' Jim loved to tell a story and his audience had their eyes out on stalks.

'I hope we dinnae hear the miller singin',' said Jenny quietly, too scared to look round at the ruined walls of the mill wrapped in their fortress of brambles.

Sandy tried to hum without the others realising it was him. He got a shove from Rob who was listening intently for ghostly singing and didn't want the mood to be disturbed.

'When ye can hear the miller singin', that's when the heidless horsemen travel the Auld Great Road,' continued Jim relishing the power that his role as storyteller gave him over his friends. 'There's times when the spirits a' get oot o' their ghostly hell thegither, an' come back tae earth for a while.'

'Ohhh, I hope it's no' the nicht,' said Sarah who would rather be at home now but needed to wait until the others were ready to escort her, past the haunted mill.

'Heidless horsemen? Are they oan horses?' asked Rob.

'Their coach's pulled b' twa big black stallions wi' red e'en, breathin' fire frae their nostrils straight oot the fires o' hell. The auld yins speir three robbers held up the Edinburgh coach a while back. Twa were caught wi' a bag o' gold sovereigns then hung on the gallows in the toun. Their freen turned king's ransom an' got aff, an' the heidless horsemen are the twa that were hung comin' tae look for him.' Jim looked around the company, satisfied they were suitably terrified by his tales.

'Mebbe we should be gaun hame,' ventured Minn. 'It's ower late an' ma faither said hame afore dark.'

Nobody took her up on the suggestion. Fear was addictive – they hoped there was more to come.

Suddenly, a woman's scream rent the air, and again, and again. Then came a deep yell, a threatening, evil howl.

The friends looked at each other in terror; drew closer together. John pointed at the thicket that ran upstream beyond the edge of the village.

'It came frae up there!' he whispered. 'Is it the heidless horsemen, Jim?'

'I dinna ken.' Jim looked as startled as his cronies.

The heart-rending scream of a woman in need of help reached their ears once again. After a pause, it started up again. On and on and on it went.

'We should go for the polis,' said Jenny. The other girls seemed to agree.

Rob took charge. 'Richt, whau's comin tae see whit this is?' he said boldly. 'Or are ye fearties?'

Everybody looked askance. But no one wanted to chicken out and be left alone on the Meadie. Not with the ghostly miller singing away on this night when the spirits were clearly abroad in great number.

They rose from the cold, damp grass, rubbed some life back into their arms and legs, chilled by the lack of sun and the shiver of fear that had travelled up the back of their necks, brought on by Jim's spooky tales and, now, by the hellish screaming. Rob led the way followed by Sandy and the rest, bunched up together for safety against the unknown terror that awaited them.

The path to the ford was relatively easy underfoot but, further on, the group had to fight against a tangle of low, sloping branches that threatened to trip and trap them in the grip of the thicket. The familiar sparkle of the flowing river soon became a menacing lure of sprites and goblins. Minn and Sarah held each other's hand tightly. Jenny joined them, trembling with fear. Andrew hovered near the girls, reassuring them but hardly convincing himself he was safe. Sadie followed Rob and Sandy, pioneering the trail that was hard to find in places, though used by fishermen in the past. From time to time they stopped and listened as another terrifying scream filled the air, then Rob would tell everyone to stop making so much racket when they crept through the trees or they'd be caught by the evil spirits. They headed towards the light of the open space up ahead. Here in the dense woodland, the shadow overwhelmed them.

'Stoap! Everybody stoap!' commanded Rob in a loud whisper. 'SSSHHHH! Somebody's comin'!'

The companions moved at great speed away from the riverside, concealed themselves in the undergrowth, hardly able to breathe. Surely the headless horsemen weren't walking along the riverbank? They should be up on the road. That was their place.

Those who were brave enough to look kept their eyes peeled as two figures made their way hurriedly towards the Meadie. When the coast was clear, and the figures were well past, the youngsters ran quickly towards the light. One by one, they tumbled out of the thicket into the sanctuary of a field of grain, still in daylight. They lay together, their hearts racing, unsure if they had seen the headless horsemen or not but deciding that the two figures most definitely had heads. Rob and Sandy stood up bravely to survey the field for danger. There was nothing. No ghosts and no one screaming for help any more. They were safe so everyone smiled, relieved and grateful. A silly story had spooked them. That was all. Sarah hugged Minn and a ripple of laughter travelled round the group.

'Did I tell ye the yin aboot the witches' hollow up on The Law?' started Jim.

His brother gave him a push backwards for his trouble.

'Dinnae stert, you. We've had enough o' yer ghost stories,' said Dan. 'We're fine noo.'

Till a low moaning started up by the riverbank further along the trail, a barely audible drone of hate and pain that built to a crescendo of dreadful loathing and cursing.

No one needed a cue. They stood up at once, pushing up on each other for support. They fled back the way they had come, tripping and sliding through the undergrowth as fast as their legs could carry them. There might be headless horsemen up ahead or the spirit of a singing miller but whatever was making that horrible racket was surely the most terrifying thing of all.

# Chapter 18

## AFTER THE DANCE

Sunday breakfast at Parkgate House was served at nine o' clock sharp, an hour later than on weekdays, but giving plenty of time for the family to attend the church service later in the morning, at eleven. When Isabelle and Phee opened the door into the breakfast room, they were surprised to see it empty. Normally their brother was the early bird, up with the lark, half finished eating by the time they put in an appearance. They helped themselves to tea then sat back for a few minutes whilst contemplating what to have to eat. Isabelle was angry with her younger sister. She had noted her absence from the recital and no amount of interrogation later would provoke Phee into revealing her whereabouts.

'It was far too hot and Miss Shanks far too shrill, so I went outside for some air,' was all she would reveal.

But Isabelle sensed she was holding something back and would have to find out what. It was her duty as the elder sister to protect her sibling from life's temptations. Apart from anything else, she couldn't be allowed to sully the family name. Phee was altogether far too headstrong for a young woman. Isabelle fully expected her to be marching down the streets of Edinburgh one day, carrying a placard saying 'Votes for Women', like the harpies she had seen in London. How common, thought Isabelle. She hated it when people didn't know their place.

Phee drank her tea slowly, enjoying her sister's discomfort. Isabelle couldn't bear not knowing every nuance of her younger sister's life. Phee knew that Isabelle was also secretly annoyed that she'd had the initiative to avoid the tortuous tones of Miss Shanks, the soprano, whilst Isabelle had had to endure the entire performance, stuck right at the front, in full view, with the great and the good of the community. Happily, Phee decided on kedgeree and extra eggs for breakfast. She felt the need to be fortified for the day ahead. Sunday was a day she enjoyed. Helping at the Sabbath School was always fun. Children had such an amusing way of looking at things. She would meet up with Elizabeth, relive their rebellion, and the excitement of the dance. Anything to get out of this stuffy house with its manners and restrictions, she thought.

David appeared half an hour late looking the worst for wear. He poured himself a cup of tea and drank it down before remembering to say, 'Good Morning', to his sisters. His face was as white as a sheet and he was trying not to retch as the smell of kedgeree wafted in his direction. He turned away from Phee in Isabelle's direction only to be confronted with her plate of devilled kidneys.

'You look a mess, brother dear. What time did you go to bed last night? And how many bottles did you consume?' Isabelle asked, referring to his favourite tipple, Islay malt.

'Just the one,' he admitted, hardly able to bear the thought of how much alcohol had gone through his system.

Phee looked over sympathetically. They had returned to Parkgate House by themselves, at ten thirty. No guests. No

Rose. She guessed that was what ailed him. He was lovesick for the doctor's daughter and worried he would lose her to a career in medicine. Much as she adored her brother, he was a man after all. He wouldn't appreciate that a woman could possibly be a wife, yet have another calling, at the same time. That was the trouble with life, thought Phee glumly. It seemed to be a case of all or nothing: marriage or the single life. Total devotion to a husband and the procreation of children or the lonely life of a spinster, dependant on a relative or one's own money if one had any. Phee shuddered, deciding that she was much too young to worry about what the future had planned for her.

'I'll ring for fresh tea, shall I?' said Isabelle, sensing that rehydration was what her brother required.

She proceeded to talk in her usual imperious tones about this and that and everything under the sun, which was definitely not what her brother needed. Her assessment of the recital the previous evening was, *'parochial, of course, when one is newly returned from London having had luncheon at the Savoy and evenings at the theatre, and watched bi-planes overhead racing up to Manchester. Blackrigg and the Gala Day recital with Miss Shanks, and that caricature called Archibald Syme, is bound to seem... provincial'*.

Isabelle, it seemed, hardly needed to draw breath. She wasn't known for pausing long enough to allow conversation to develop.

She pronounced herself well impressed by the bravery of Captain Scott and his crew, sailing the Terra Nova across the high seas to make their crossing of Antarctica for king and empire. 'What gallant, intrepid men!'

She was lukewarm in her opinion of the Member of Parliament, Mr Ure of the Liberal Party, even if he was the Lord Advocate. 'It's a pity Mr Smith hadn't won over the constituency in January but, with so many of the working class voting now, it was hardly surprising they'd go for the radical Liberal agenda again'.

She was greatly concerned by the machinations of the Liberal Government at Westminster. 'They're lurching from crisis to crisis supported by the Irish and Labour, trying to wrestle power from the landed classes, which they'll never do of course. Talk about biting the hand that feeds! As for the House of Lords, there to keep everything on the straight and narrow, but completely gutless in passing the Budget Bill. Where will it end?! A government intent on giving a helping hand to the jobless, pensions for the aged and so on is just brewing trouble for the future when the working classes will have no incentive to get out and work at all. I'll be proved right. It will come to pass, you'll see, and as for this Labour Party, well, what do they want but revolution?'

She talked of the riot at the Bo'ness woodyards and lamented the poor availability of labour in the county. 'There's a dire shortage of good male servants nowadays because so many prefer the higher wages paid in the mines and manufactories, where they have every Saturday afternoon and Sunday off for leisure. Of course, leisure's the devil's work because the dumb ignorant choose to go off on their walks, pedestrianism so-called, and partake of other pleasures. Everyone knows that the Sabbath is the Lord's Day, one for attending church and thanking the Good Lord for all of His blessings. Without that rock in one's life there's nought but chaos ahead.'

Isabelle patted down her extravagant lace collar then checked that her brooch was in place. She waited for David and Phee to respond. Didn't they have an opinion on such important matters, she wondered?

Phee looked up from her empty plate. 'That was yummy. I must congratulate cook on a splendid dish. Could you run that passed me again, Isabelle? I got lost around the parochial gathering last night...' It was an effort to keep a straight face but she managed.

'Oh, please no,' entreated David, holding his head. 'That's lovely, Isabelle. Good show. But can we have some peace and quiet, hmmm?'

Isabelle looked at her siblings in despair. Such a deficient pair, hardly Melvilles at all, she reflected.

Jameson entered the room with a knock and his usual obsequious stoop. He was followed by a young female servant carrying a tea pot and hot water.

'Just leave them on the sideboard, please.... What's your name again?' asked David.

'Maggie Lennox, sir.' She gave a short curtsey just as she had been trained to do.

'Thank you, Maggie. Where's the other girl? The small one with the smile who normally does breakfast?' he asked.

'She's poorly, sir,' said Maggie without lying about Nell's condition. 'Cook says she's tae bide awa' fae the faimily till she's better, beggin' yer pardon, sir.'

'Ahh, good idea. We don't want to catch whatever's doing the rounds. Was there something else, Jameson? I see you hovering there,' asked David tersely, turning to the butler.

'Yes, sir. Mr Stone wants to speak to you urgently.' He noticed the master's hesitation that said it was Sunday, the day of rest. 'He has some urgent news about Grant, sir, Grant the gamekeeper.'

'I know who Grant is, Jameson,' said David perplexed. 'What can be so urgent to interrupt breakfast on a Sunday morning?'

Maggie was all ears, fussing over the placing of the teapot and the jug of hot water on the side board in order to prolong her time in the room.

'Send him in then. He can have a cup of tea while he tells us his news.'

Jameson returned with Roger Stone who wore a very grave expression. The butler clicked his fingers, the signal for Maggie to leave. As he closed the door on the conversation to come, Maggie disappeared along the long, dark corridors to the kitchen, wishing she was a fly on the wall of the breakfast room at that very moment.

When the factor was settled at the table, he told the story of Grant being found by Old Morton's men earlier that morning. The dairymaid had been sent to the bottom field to check that none of the cattle had calved in the night. She had returned distraught, claiming she could see a dead man on the opposite bank of the river. A couple of men had been dispatched to see what was up and they found Grant alive but in a very poor state. They had managed to get him to Ivy Cottage where Dr Matheson's assistant, Dr Lindsay, attended to him.

'He had been beaten severely to within an inch of his life,' explained Stone. 'A broken rib and extensive bruising on his face and his body. Several cuts to his face too.'

The Melvilles were horrified at the news.

'Will he survive?' asked Phee. She did not like Grant in the least but would not see him harmed, not even a lecherous oaf like him.

'Dr Lindsay reckons he's had a lucky escape and will recover quickly. He's a strong one after all. No obvious internal damage that he can see, apart from the rib, but one never knows how these things might develop.'

'But who would do such a thing?' asked David, pulling himself together in spite of his hangover.

'Who indeed?' said Stone. 'It looks as if he's been left for dead. He could so easily have fallen into the river and drowned. Perhaps it's just a matter of good fortune that he wasn't fatally injured.'

'Is he conscious? Surely he can identify his attackers?' Just inform the police and have them arrest the culprits.' A solution always seemed clear to Isabelle.

'It's not quite that straightforward, I'm afraid,' continued Stone. 'He claims it was dark so he couldn't see who it was, and there were several assailants. But he'd consumed a great deal of alcohol. That much was obvious, though he wouldn't admit to it. He was seen making a fool of himself at the dance in the public hall last night, annoying the women and so on. He was dispatched into the street by several young men.'

'Perhaps they followed him to teach him a lesson,' offered Phee, bringing to mind the fracas at the opposite end of the hall as she was leaving with Elizabeth and Ernest Black the previous evening.

'All the way out of the village and down to the burn from the road?' said David, 'Surely not. There must have been another motive.'

'Funny you should say that, Mr Melville,' said Stone. 'His boots are missing.' He looked at the others looking back at him. 'He was found minus his footwear.'

'Robbery then,' offered Isabelle. 'Who would have thought it? For a pair of workman's boots! We've never had a problem with crime on the estate, not until all of these new workers started to appear here from God knows where.' She couldn't let an opportunity to criticise the incomers pass her by.

'Or those responsible were trying to make the assault look like robbery by taking the boots,' surmised David. 'Do people bear a grudge against our gamekeeper, Stone? He's married with a child but he has a roving eye where the ladies are concerned.'

'Could be,' agreed the factor. 'Or was he targeted as an employee of this estate by those who bear a grudge against Rashiepark?'

'Isn't that a bit far-fetched?' asked Phee.

'Not necessarily,' replied David who seemed to be reading Stone's mind. There was the refusal to allow access to the burn on Back o' Moss land. There was also the disrespect shown to Isabelle before her London trip.

'Let's keep our eye on things, Stone. We can't be too careful when we're dealing with people we don't know,' he warned. A picture of Neil Tennant – outwardly reasonable and upstanding, from a well-respected local family – and those he had represented at their meeting came to mind.

'It seems quite obvious to me,' interjected Phee. 'Grant was as drunk as a lord at the dance, everyone could see that. If they were at the dance, that is,' she added hurriedly, almost caught out. 'He was ejected into the street and some ruffian followed him with a view to stealing his footwear and anything else they could lay their hands on. He's lying about the number of assailants to cover the extent of his own inebriation. End of story.'

'Seems simple on the face of it,' agreed David without conviction. 'But let's have a quiet word with the constable about our fears, have him keep his eyes and ears open. Got to think of our property after all, and we've a responsibility to the people we employ.'

Stone smiled his agreement, content that his influence on his employer was showing through.

'Quite right, David,' said Isabelle, impressed by her brother's resolve. 'That's what the law is there for and the police are there to uphold the law on our behalf. People just do not know their place anymore that much is true.'

David stared at Isabelle. He wondered if, perhaps, she did have her finger on the pulse after all. He had dismissed her summary of current affairs over breakfast as an overreaction to changing times but, perhaps, he should listen to her more.

Nell Graham had to wait another week before she could go home to confide in her elder sister. With Maggie's help she stayed hidden from view for several days after the night of the dance. She cried till she had no more tears. Maggie didn't know what to do at first. Nell either cried constantly or lay still and silent in her bed staring at the changing light coming through their attic room window. She slept a lot so Maggie determined that her friend needed time to come to terms with what had happened, that she would speak about it when she was good and ready. Then one day, Nell got up from her bed at five, the usual time, and said she was ready to get back to work. Maggie gave her a huge hug to let her know that nothing had changed between them, that she was very proud of her. Nell just smiled weakly as she looked in the mirror to check that none of her bruises were visible above the collar of her uniform.

The girls dreaded mealtimes in case the gamekeeper appeared but, the very next day, cook said that he wasn't going to be around for a while because he had been attacked and robbed on the night of the dance. She said that Grant had been followed along the road by six or seven robbers who had taken advantage of him in his state of intoxication, and wasn't it a sad day when a man couldn't go out and enjoy himself for fear of being set upon?

Maggie caught Nell's eye. Both were bewildered by the tale of the robbers and both disagreed with cook's sympathy for poor Mr Grant but they kept their own counsel. They had already reckoned that either Grant was so drunk that he wouldn't recollect what had happened or, if he did remember something of the events of the evening, he would have to keep his mouth shut or face the consequences of his actions towards them. Either way, Parkgate wouldn't find out that Nell and Maggie were at the dance. Their positions as servants were safe.

Nell set off from Parkgate for Stoneyrigg after Sunday luncheon. She didn't fear the walk along the road in the bright sunshine of a July afternoon but she ran as fast as she could past the gate into the field where Grant had taken her.

Meg was waiting when she arrived home. Everyone else was out and would be back soon. As Nell opened the door into the small cottage, she was overcome with emotion. Meg hugged her for a long time until she had calmed down enough to speak.

'Ye havenae telt Faither have ye, Meg?' she asked.

'No. I promised I wouldnae. Till we'd time tae talk aboot it,' said Meg.

'I dinnae want him telt,' said Nell. 'Whit guid would it dae? He'd want tae dae somethin' aboot it an' he could dae nothin' but fret.'

'He could tell the polis,' offered Meg.

'Then the Melville's would find oot an' I'd lose ma employment. I'd have tae leave withoot references,' explained Nell, worried that she wouldn't be able to find another job. Though Meg was aware of the arguments against informing the police, she wanted to let Nell be the one to make the decision. 'An' if we dae tell Faither but persuade him no tae go tae the polis,' Nell continued, 'He micht dae somethin tae Grant an' end up in the gaol himsel.'

Meg could see the wisdom in Nell's reasoning. She also knew the difficulty a girl in Nell's position could face if the gossips got a hold of the story. 'Are ye a'richt alang at the Big Hoose, Nell?' she asked. 'Ye dinnae think Grant could herm ye alang there?'

'Naw. I'm fine. He wouldnae come intae the hoose withoot gettin' found oot.' She proceeded to explain her and Maggie's thinking about Grant being too concerned about keeping his own position with the estate to do or say anything about the matter, assuming he could remember anything about the events of that evening, drunk as he was. 'Have ye heard onie gossip aboot Grant an' whit happened tae him?' asked Nell.

'No, really,' said Meg. 'Whit dae ye mean?'

'Weel, he's sayin' he was set upon by a wheen o' robbers an' they left him for deid,' explained Nell. 'He was found on Sunday mornin' half deid by the burn an' his boots had been stolen!'

'Never!' exclaimed Meg. 'He was hale an' hearty when we rescued ye, Nell. When Will and Neil gave him a bit shove, he keeled ower like a lamb. He was that drunk, the big feartie. We left him sleepin' aff the whisky in the middle o' the park!'

'He was found by the burn, near droont, wi' a broken rib an' a face like a bare knuckle boxer efter ten roonds wi' Big Wattie,' Nell explained.

Meg hugged her sister, glad to hear her humorous side coming through. That was a good sign.

'Neil an' Will didnae gang back an' gie him a hammerin', did they?' asked Nell.

'Definitely no,' replied Meg. 'They came richt back here wi' me an' had some tea. Ye ken Neil Tennant's a guid lad, Nell. He was the yin that spotted Grant gaun up the road efter the twa o' ye. An' I wouldnae have oniethin adae wi' Will Morton if he wis the fechtin kind.'

'Weel, it's a mystery as tae hoo Grant got in sic a state,' said Nell. 'Mebbe it was divine retribution for whit he did,' she suggested, starting to weep again.

'For whit he tried tae dae, Nell,' reminded Meg. 'It could've been a lot worse if Maggie Lennox hadnae focht for ye like a lion. An' yelled like a banshee, haein us runnin' up the road in time. Thon's a great freen, Nell. Mind an' let her ken,' said Meg.

'I will,' said Nell through her tears. 'She's the best. I jist cannae stop thinkin' aboot whit Grant near did. An' whit he said aboot me askin' for it, an hoo I had it comin'.'

'I ken it wasnae nice, Nell. Twa lassies should be able tae gang tae a dance thegither withoot concern, tae come an' go as they please,' she explained. 'But the world's no like that. No as long as there's ill-fowk like Grant aboot.'

Nell nodded. It wasn't her fault after all, not if Meg said so but when would the feeling of shame leave her, she wondered?

The door opened and in walked their father. He gave Nell a big smile as he asked how she was.

'Fine, Da', jist fine,' replied Nell, hoping the tears would stay away in his presence.

'I'm hearin thon gemmie, Grant is it? He was robbed o' his boots efter the dance,' their father called from the other room as he hung up his cap. 'They're lookin' for a robber wi' hellava big feet, size twelve apparently!'

Nell looked at her sister. 'Ye ken whit they say aboot men wi' big feet, Meg?' said Nell in a low voice so that their father wouldn't hear.

Meg looked puzzled, wondering what was coming next.

'Well in the instance o' Grant, it isnae true!' said Nell blushing.

When Tom Graham returned to the front room, he couldn't get an ounce of sense out of either of his daughters. He watched as they hugged each other, helpless with laughter. The tears rolled down their cheeks and they said, eventually, that they couldn't possibly let him in on the joke.

# Chapter 19

## MINING MATTERS

When working men assembled at the steading, they were often joined by those, young and old, who were permanently unemployed or temporarily idle due to industrial disease or accident. In common with every village, Blackrigg had its ancient miners and quarrymen who battled the pain of arthritis or rheumatism to make the short walk from their homes in search of banter or the latest news from the pits, wheezing and coughing up phlegm as the fresh air invaded their congested lungs. They regaled the company of younger men with tales of the bad, old days before parliamentary legislation had been enacted to improve working conditions and make mining safer. In response to the public's horror at the huge loss of life in pits across the country following explosions, roof falls and flooding, and with the appliance of science and technology, a number of measures had been implemented over the decades. A second shaft to every pit ensured safe passage to the surface if one became blocked. Trap doors and furnaces had aided ventilation and burned off explosive gases, and now there were pumps to keep the air flowing. The Mines Inspectorate had been tasked to make the country's mines safer though it often depended on workers bringing problems to the attention of inspectors and many men feared persecution if they did so.

Some of the workmen could recall family memories of pit disasters, injury and ill-health involving a father, an uncle or a grandfather but they did not feel that their own lives were any more secure when, day after day, they took the cage down into the bowels of the earth to dig for coal. The Blackrigg mines were not renowned for being gassy but the threat of explosive methane, suffocating black damp or poisonous whitedamp, never left the men. The possibility of never again seeing the light of day, entombed forever by a fall of rock or floating eternally in a black watery grave, was a nightmare they never awoke from. The black spittle hacked up from their lungs was testament to the dangers of inhaling coal dust for long hours, miners' asthma an ever-present risk that went with the job. When the younger men looked into the rheumy eyes of the old retainers, bent in half with the toil of long years spent in cramped underground spaces, they saw themselves in years to come.

'Dinnae tell me, we've got it easy,' said Alex Birse when auld Tam Pow started up about how much better things were for the miners now they had inspectors and regulations about everything from lamps to sanitation and the use of electricity. 'It's nae guid arguing that we're jist up tae oor neck in shite the day, when you were up tae yer een in it whiles past. Whit kinna argument's thon? Nothin'll get onie better if ye jist sit back an' say, 'It was faur worse in the past sae jist get oan wi' it an' stoap complainin!" His eyes bulged, his face scarlet with pent up fury. Some folk couldn't see what was right in front of their face, he raged.

'Aye, a' richt, Alex,' said Jimmy Broadley much more calmly. 'Besides, Tam, jist cause there's a law made in parliament, it disnae mean it happens ablow ground. If it suits the management, corners are cut an' there's no much we can dae aboot it.'

'The men are jist as bad,' said Robert Duncan in pursuit of fairness. 'When was the last time ye used the facilities provided when ye needed tae dae yer business, if ye tak ma meanin'? Its faur quicker tae dae it ablow a stane an' mark it wi' a bit chalk. We a' dae it an' we're no exactly followin' the letter o' the law when ye think on it.'

Alex was vexed at Robert for his remark which he didn't think suited a serious discussion. It had brought up the importance of personal responsibility underground without reference to the difficulties of the environment and the nature of the work.

'Minin' is and ay will be a dangerous business... we should be lookin' oot for oorsels. If there's a law aboot somethin', we should be keepin' tae it as best we can. It's taen lang enough tae git some things sorted in oor favour when ye think aboot it.'

'Aye, richt enough,' agreed Robert. 'Think on they poor lads in Cumberlan'. Yin hunner an' thertie six puir souls killed in a firedamp explosion at Wellington Colliery twa month back.'

'Whit are their wumen folk an' their weans daen noo wi' nae men tae bring hame the pey?' asked Davy Potts gravely. 'Some have lost men, brithers, faithers... sons an' a'. A' fae the yin faimily.'

'Aye, yon's the real price o' coal,' said auld Tam Pow shaking his head. He spoke for every man present.

A collective murmur went round the assembly as talk turned to the current concerns and conflicts about their working conditions. It was an opportunity for the men to share with each other the latest news from the various mines located in the vicinity. Reflecting the traditions of the independent collier, the organisation of the county union was devolved to each pit where officials negotiated with the Coal Company over matters brought to their attention by the workforce. Some men complained that the number of days worked was varying between just eight and ten per fortnight but other miners were even worse off, given only five or six days work over the same period with dire consequences for their living standards. In one of the pits, a conference had been held with the management about the rate of pay for drawing the roads into the coal face and to hear complaints about the single tares for filling hutches of two different sizes. In such cases, both sides drove a hard bargain. The result was a compromise with neither side achieving exactly what they wanted.

The working of the Eight Hour Act was causing particular problems for both men and management, having been controversial since its introduction. It was not always possible to complete an agreed amount of work within the eight hours of the legislation, and the use of machinery made this difficult to adhere to, since shifts were tailored more to the working of the cutting machine walls than the needs of the men as described by the Act. Bearing in mind the agreement that miners should have a Saturday afternoon off, the Miners Federation had been advocating a compromise of eleven days work per fortnight to help ease the situation but, as many men pointed out, some miners were working on *idle* days with consequences for the availability of work for others.

Mechanisation had its advantages for increased production, anyone could see that, but it cut into the bargaining power of the skilled hewers who had dominated industrial relations underground for so long. Their skill was a trump card in any negotiation over the darg since men could bargain for higher rates and lower output where the rock was hard and more time was required to hew it. Machines that could undercut at the coal face did away with the skill of the hewer making it easier for the coal masters to bring in unskilled face workers who would work for lower rates of pay.

Alex said, 'The day's comin', boys, when we'll jist huv tae git ahint the union an' let them dae a' the negotiatin', oan oor behalf. Divide an' rule is how it is in this coalfield the day, a'body talkin' tae the managers aboot the same thing an' feelin' lik they're on nettles. We need tae band thegither an' git the best conditions we can. The Federation's agin unskilled men comin' in an' drivin' doon wages.'

'Thon's why we a' should be in the union,' said Robert. 'Keep oot the non-union men an' the Federation'll negotiate fae a position o' strength. Let oniebody in an' the work'll git done for very little.'

'An' it'll no be done safely,' warned auld Tam Pow who knew the importance of a skilled hand and an experienced eye in tackling the precarious lie of the rocks in a Scottish mine.

'Thon's why the union want tae tak chairge o' the trainin' o' the young lads when they stert in the pits. Tae mak sure they're richt trained ower fower year, an' arenae used as cheap labour,' explained Alex who kept abreast of union affairs. 'The Lanarkshire boys are gonnae put in a proposal tae the Scottish Federation for every pit tae have an inspector, wi' exams for the firemen, a second checkweighman, appointit b' ballot, makin' sure yer no getting' done oot o' whit yer due.'

'Weel, yon sounds verra fine, Alex,' said Davy Potts who, like many of the men, was wary at the mention of Lanarkshire where conflict in the coalfield was endemic.

'Livin' conditions are jist as uppermaist in oor minds. The closets are stinkin' an' the rats somethin' fierce alang in Staney the noo wi' this guid weather.'

'The Union wants better hooses an' a minimum wage an a',' assured Alex. 'Eicht bob a day. Its dangerous work efter a'. The time was when we could even oot the guid an' the bad times wi' oor negotiatin' at the pitheid but they days are ower. It's an international market we're pairt o' an' the maisters want wages linked tae the price o' coal. A minimum wage's the best wey furrit for us a'.'

'Aye, the maisters have their costs tae cover, fair enough, but they have ye workin' hard when the price's low an' the wages low tae, an' they pile up the coal at the pitheid,' said Robert. 'Then they haud ontae it, tae sell when the price goes up an' we a' gae on short time. They're a wily bunch, an' nae mistake.'

'They should even oot the prices or even oot the wages an' gie us some security,' Jimmy stated. 'I'm thinkin' a kinna social wage would be fair, like mair siller spent on hooses, withoot damp an' nae rats, at a fair rent.'

'Aye, we mak the pit but we hae nae pairt o' it,' said Alex, prodding himself forcefully in the chest. 'We're workin' tae fill rich men's pockets when we should be workin' tae gie oor faimilies a decent life. Some o' they owners dae nuthin at a' for their share o' the profit. A' they done was haun ower some siller they nivver worked for in the first place.'

The men had to agree that when Alex explained his socialist thinking, he could be very convincing, though his anger and venom made many uneasy about it. It didn't seem much to ask for: a dry house that kept out the weather; wages that let them feed their children and put decent clothes on their backs; a school for learning and a doctor to tend them when they were poorly. Yet there were such loud voices raised against any proposals to change their conditions. The coal masters had railed against the eight hour day for long enough. Couldn't they see how the work wrecked a man, body and soul? Hadn't the government had a battle bringing in the five shilling pension for the elderly and creating the labour exchanges to share out the work? It was probably all down to who was going to pay for it and, as everyone knew, rich men and their money were not easily parted, otherwise how did they get rich in the first place?

# Chapter 20

## RICH MEN AND THEIR MONEY

A long, sleek motor car drove out of the avenue at Parkgate House and took the road east towards the village. It was driven by Billy Dodds, one of the stable lads who had been keen to take up the post of chauffeur to the Melvilles, ambitiously moving ahead with the times and the development of motorised transport. Billy had washed and polished the vehicle all morning with the same devotion he gave to the horse collars and brasses. He sat proudly upfront in his dark blue uniform and cap, still nervous in his new situation. In the absence of regulations beyond the payment of five shillings for a driving license, Billy had assured Mr Melville that he had practised sufficiently, quickly accelerating to a steady speed that belied his lack of skill and experience.

David sat in the back seat accompanied by Phee and her friends, Rose and Elizabeth. In truth he'd rather have been alone with Rose but, until they were betrothed, it was unseemly to be seen out together without company. He adored her and would do nothing to sully her reputation. The three friends would be pleasant company for an outing to the coast when he could be with Rose all day. He could see her, smile at her and talk with her. Longing for her every minute of the day would be the most exquisite torment. He hoped that she would feel the same about him, helping in his defeat of her resolve to attend medical school in the autumn. In truth, he'd have felt happier had he been up against another suitor in the battle for her affections but this was a harder nut to crack, a passion deeply lodged in her heart.

The countryside sped past, a flicker of sunny, green fields and hay-making beyond the hedgerows and the tall trees shading the route. The road had recently been resurfaced, making for a smooth journey. Occasional bumps brought a reprimand from David for the driver to slow down, quickly followed by encouragement from his sister to pick up some speed, to let them see what the car was capable of. Fortunately, there were few vehicles on the road, since few people owned motor cars and motorised shops were generally off the road on a Saturday afternoon. An abrupt swerve to avoid a cat then again for a group of children playing in the road made for uneasy but swift progress.

David saw the group of men assembled at Craigpark before anyone else and, as he craned his neck for a better look, his nerves jangled. What could they possibly be doing, spilling onto the road in such a large number? He pictured his gamekeeper, nursing his bruises and a burst lip from the beating he had taken at the hands of ne'er-do-weels. The newspaper report about the previous month's strike at the woodyards in Bo'ness also came to mind. A riot of men, women and children had brought about a baton charge by the police. Fortunately, they had turned up in good time and in large number, sufficient to dispel the rioters. Blackrigg had a single bobby on duty at any one time. Not much good against a crowd, he decided.

'William!' he called to his driver. 'Step on it, will you? I don't want you stopping for anyone, do you hear?'

Billy Dodds heard. He needed no more encouragement than that and pushed his foot down onto the accelerator. He honked the horn, sedately at first, glad of a chance to show off his new employment to men who probably knew him well. A prolonged honking of the horn made heads turn in the direction of the speeding car to see what all the fuss was about. At first no one moved. That was why there were so many road accidents reported in the papers, thought Billy. People weren't used to motor vehicles. Roads were still places to be walked along and used as spaces for conversation and debate.

'Keep going, William. Don't stop on any account,' came the command from the back seat.

Billy kept going but not because his master ordered it. The panic he felt as the men in the street grew near enough for him to see the alarm on their faces, petrified his senses. His eyes shut as he careered on through. He didn't see the figures throwing themselves asunder like the parting of the waves before Moses. He barely heard the screams of his lady passengers as they clung helplessly to each other in the back, expecting to see bloody limbs and bodies cast up before them.

'Well done, William,' came his master's voice when they were well beyond Stoneyrigg. David appeared outwardly calm but he was mightily relieved to have escaped the throng without leaving any physical harm in their wake. 'Now just slow down a little and let us enjoy the view.'

Elizabeth and Rose stared in David's direction with some alarm as they readjusted their bonnets. David gently squeezed Rose's hand to let her know that everything was under control. Phee laughed, a little nervously at first, then snorted her approval at the uncharacteristic recklessness of her brother's behaviour. Billy sat a little taller in his seat, content to proceed at a steady pace for the rest of the journey to Queensferry once his nerves settled and his heart beat returned to something more normal.

The passengers soon forgot the near miss, absorbed by the beautiful view as the car turned down the drove road towards the River Avon, leaving the unsightly humps and heaps of the coalfield behind. Distant ranges of hills and mountains, blue in the bright, summer sunshine lined the horizon beyond the Forth. Fields of ripening crops and grazing cattle lined the route, a patchwork of ordered calm and contentedness under a canopy of cloudless sky. The car drew onto the grassy verge at Woodcockdale to let the four passengers stretch their legs for a moment, long enough to watch a barge go under the canal bridge. A large, grey horse laboured patiently along the tow path, pulling a canal boat laden with coal for the hearths of Edinburgh. Two children sat at the back of the boat. They waved dirty hands at the onlookers on the bridge above them: a gentleman and three pretty ladies who waved back happily, delighted to be witnessing such a quaint, old-fashioned scene.

As the car started up, taking to the winding by-way once again, David pointed out the jagged shape of Linlithgow Palace and the square-towered church that stood next to it, the warm sandstone of their construction nestling in a wooded valley floor. The burgh was a straggle of houses in the older style mixed with grander edifices and people were much in evidence in the street. Children played around mothers sewing by their doors. Men stood smoking at the market cross; they watched intently as the motor vehicle swept slowly by. David gave a commentary on the layout of the burgh and its connections with Scotland's kings and queens, while his companions remarked favourably on the architecture of the buildings and the industry of the people. The ladies grimaced, holding their breath against the stench of the tannery by the loch but marvelling at the imposing facade of the Nobel Works where explosives were manufactured. To take such care over the design of a factory building was surely the sign of a successful enterprise, they agreed.

Further on and out of town, David pointed out the towers of The Binns, home of the Dalyells. He told the tale of notorious Tam, terror of the Covenanters and friend, reputedly, of the devil, as his wide-eyed and captive audience gave gasps of exaggerated horror, even though they had all heard the stories many times before. Further along the road, the well-kept policies of the Earls of Hopetoun were a delight to the eye and much admired, till Billy approached the steeply sloping road into the small burgh of South Queensferry, his trepidation obvious in a sudden application of the brakes. He didn't want to risk ending up in the Firth of Forth, a long ribbon of blue at the bottom of the hill.

'Follow the High Street to the Hawes,' said David to Billy. 'The road is winding and narrow so take it easy... do watch out for stray children. Park up at Royal Navy House, just this side of the pier, William. There should be plenty of room in the street.'

As they emerged from the warmth of the car into a cooling breeze from the sea, the marvel of Victorian engineering that was the Forth Bridge towered above them, spanning the great river estuary from north to south. Their eyes were drawn skywards to the massive iron construction, a maze of criss-crossing girders, propped up on long columns of stone. David listed impressive facts and figures about its design whilst the ladies listened. Offshore, the Home Fleet sat at anchor, stretched out along the river as far as the eye could see and it hugged the pier, just visible upstream, at Port Edgar. Battleships and cruiser squadrons made an awesome sight, decked in their brightly coloured flags. David basked in the reflected glory of the scene, as if he was personally responsible for its conception. He was delighted by the reaction of the ladies and his chest puffed up like a cockerel, before three hens. He dismissed his driver for the afternoon, eagerly sweeping his companions before him into the shelter of the grounds beside Royal Navy House where, judging by the sound of music and conversation, a garden party was in full swing.

Only a few die hards had been left conversing at Craigpark. Time was precious on a Saturday afternoon so when Alex started another of his lectures, this time about getting miners into parliament through the Independent Labour Party, some took their leave. As one group escaped to make sure their allotments were well-watered in the warm weather, Bobby Cherrie articulated a widely-held view, 'Labour Party? Why gie up yin rulin' class for anither?'

'Dae ye ken they're tae build some baths ahint the billiard hall?' asked Davy Birse, son of Alex and one of the younger miners who remained at Craigpark. 'Thon'll be an advance oan washin' in ma faither's dirty watter, in the auld tin bath afore the fire!' he joked, rubbing his hands in glee.

Laughter rippled around the small group remaining.

'I hope ye'll no be peyin guid money tae a capitalist bastard like Archie Flank for a bath!' exclaimed Alex, drawing quizzical looks from the others who saw the development as a boon to their quality of life. 'It's the Coal Company whau should be peyin for baths for their workers,' he explained.

'We'll wait lang enough for thon tae happen,' said Davy's pal, Adam.

'Whit group o' workers is in mair need o' washin' facilities but the miners?' said Alex.

No one could come up with an answer and surely that was the point, they badly needed proper places to wash.

'If Archie Flank's willin' tae invest his money for us tae hire a bath by the haulf 'oor, is thon no a guid thing?' replied Adam.

'Naw it's no. If we pey Archie Flank for baths, the Coal Company willnae see the need tae spend capital investin' at the mine oan oor behalf. See whit I mean?' asked Alex, frustrated by their lack of wisdom.

'So, we've tae gang dirty or wash in oor faithers' dirty watter till we git baths at the pitheid?' queried Adam.

'Thon's whit I'm sayin',' said Alex, laying down the law. 'Oftimes it's got tae git worse afore it gets better. If we let capitalism in tae fill the gaps, we'll nivver get justice for the workin' man.'

A loud horn took everyone's attention away from the debate to a motor car, fast approaching from the west. Heads turned as the sounding of the horn became more insistent. Half a dozen lads who had been standing in the road suddenly threw themselves out of the way as Billy Dodds mowed his way through at the wheel of the Melvilles' car.

'Bastards!' shouted Alex. 'Bastards! Watch whaur yer gaun!'

'Whit was thon aboot?' he asked the crowd, incredulous and speaking for everyone for the first time. 'Did ye see thon? Thon rich bastard Melville, never done a day's work in his life! *The class that toil not, neither do they spin!'* he spat, quoting the radical, Chamberlain.

One or two of the men dusted themselves down whilst others asked if they were alright.

'Well, thon was a close run thing,' came a new voice.

'It sure was, Constable,' said Alex, extremely pleased that the long arm of the law in the form of Big Archie McKay had been witness to the recklessness. 'Yer needin' tae get efter thon renegade in his big motor. Near killed the boys here.'

'If you lot hadnae been staunin in the road in the first place, there widnae been a problem,' replied Constable McKay, bristling at being told what to do by a workman, far less a miner. 'An' I'll decide whit's tae be done here, no you. Move on, lads.'

'We're no daen onie herm,' said Davy Birse, fast becoming a chip off the old block.

'Aye, the laddie's richt. We're jist haein a blether oan oor wey oot for the efternin. There's nae herm in thon, free speech an' that,' said his father.

'Free speech's fine, but it doesnae have tae happen here in the road,' replied the constable. 'Yer impeding the flow o' traffic. Move on.'

'We'll jist move intae the steadin' a wee bit aff the road, Constable,' offered Alex.

'Naw ye'll no,' he replied. 'The steadin's private property. Ye've a braw new public ha' for yer assemblies. If ye want tae blether get yersels a room inside. I've had complaints frae folk feelin' intimidated at the very sicht o' ye a', alang here tae a' 'oors. Move on the noo, or I'll tak names.'

The group started to dissipate but men were unhappy.

'Come oan, lads. We're no lookin' for bother,' said Alex wisely. 'But I'd like tae ken whau complained aboot us talkin' in the street. As if I didnae ken!' He spoke loudly, hoping the constable could hear.

'An' I'm still lookin' for information on the whauraboots o' a pair o' size twelve boots,' called Constable McKay to the men who were fast retreating from the steading.

'That settles it,' said Alex to the others. 'If thon rich bastard, Melville, thinks he can use the polis tae tell us whit tae dae an' whaur tae staun, he's got anither think comin'.'

# Chapter 21
## THE GARDEN PARTY

A marquee had been erected on the lawn to offer shade or shelter, in recognition of the fickle nature of Scottish summer weather, and a quintet of musicians played softly under the spreading branches of a chestnut tree in the terraced garden at Royal Navy House. Conversation and laughter coloured the animated scene as the four members of the Melville party made their way through cheerful groupings of naval personnel and local dignitaries. David was welcomed like a long lost friend by a mature gentleman in a naval uniform covered in gold braid and other decoration. Clearly the Melville name had influence at the very highest echelons of the naval hierarchy, thought Elizabeth as they were introduced to a group of young naval officers on public relations duty. She answered when she was asked a question, smiling sweetly and demurely as the young men engaged in polite conversation. Such occasions were unfamiliar to her and, therefore, quite difficult. It wasn't long before David made his excuses and, hand-in-hand with his beloved Rose, left the group. Elizabeth felt a mild panic as he went off, taking his dominance of the conversation with him. Phee, on the other hand, seemed particularly animated in the presence of handsome young men in uniform, so Elizabeth decided to let her hog the limelight. But she would try to be more than an observer herself, she determined. She would fight against her shyness and a life conditioned against hedonism of any kind though she was finding it impossible to remove the stern countenance of puritanical Richard from her mind. It would have been fine for him to make his way around the assembly in his dog collar, his passport to conversation, making the acquaintance of this one and that. Even in his absence, she could not help but suffer his disapproval at her enjoyment of a glass of fruit punch on a warm summer's afternoon in the company of the opposite sex.

'Is that you?' asked a strong, commanding voice just as David sat Rose beside him in the privacy of a rose-covered pergola. 'Swotty Melville from the senior class at the Academy?'

David bristled, annoyed that his tryst with Rose had been interrupted but he soon embraced the meddler after he took a better look at him.

'Harry Sinclair!' said David in disbelief. 'I didn't know you were destined for a career in His Majesty's Navy!' He looked the man over, taking in the smart blue serge, the white shirt, and dark tie of an officer. 'Rose, come and meet an old friend of mine from school. Rose, Harry, Harry, Rose.'

Harry took Rose's hand which he kissed lasciviously. Rose pulled away, abruptly.

'Last I heard, you were at the university, destined for a professorship or something like that,' Harry said to his old school friend. 'He was such a frightful swot you know, Rose. But a great sportsman too. Cricket, rugger, you name it, he could thrash everyone off the field! Had it all, did Swotty Melville.'

'Well, you know what they say about the best laid plans,' said David. 'After the demise of my elder brothers and my father's passing at the end of last year, my future had to be redrawn. Had no choice really but to go home and take over the estate.'

'Good luck or bad luck?' asked Harry, looking Rose up and down in a way that suggested life at Rashiepark had its compensations.

'We're making the best of things,' said David, catching Harry's reference to Rose. 'It'll take a bit of getting used to but with a good woman by my side in the future, I think I'll manage.' He looked at Rose who blushed, horrified at his candour. He squeezed her hand reassuringly, holding tight when she tried to pull away. 'But what about you, Harry? Captain is it?' he joked, studying the braid on his friend's uniform.

'Not quite yet, Melville!' laughed Harry, clearly pleased to be considered captain material by David, class-swot and sporting champion of the Academy. 'But the way this government's churning out new battleships, there'll be plenty of opportunities for promotion in the future!' He proceeded to explain the presence of the fleet in the Forth. Coast guard battleships had assembled with cruiser squadrons from around the British coast for manoeuvres and the testing of a new torpedo. After a period in the Moray Firth and the Forth, the Home Fleet was preparing to head south to the English Channel to show off the might of the British Empire to whoever might be interested.

'We're all coaled up and ready to head out of the estuary over the next couple of days,' he explained. 'A cruiser squadron has already left but the bulk of the fleet will leave together, led by the big guns, HMS Warrior, Shannon, Cochrane, and Natal, and others. They're all here. Word soon gets back to the Germans that Britannia still rules the waves.'

'How many ships does the British Navy need to prove that Britannia rules the waves, Harry?' asked Rose, bringing a surprised look to the face of her beau. Hitherto, Rose had been a shy and demure companion who rarely asked questions and never spoke of matters of national importance.

'The British Navy must always be bigger than her two next biggest rival navies and right now, Germany is building dreadnoughts at a fast rate that we can hardly keep up with. When they stop building, we'll stop building,' explained Harry, sensing a challenge from David's companion.

'It sounds like a game of one-upmanship between two schoolboys to me, Harry,' replied Rose. 'It might not be quite so difficult to finance the government's social reforms if so much wasn't being spent on building big ships with even bigger guns to blow each other to Kingdom come!'

'Do you hear that booming sound?' Harry asked, waiting for another in a series of distant bangs and crashes to illustrate his point. A blast from the other side of the river came at just the right moment. 'Well, that's the blasting in preparation for the monoliths that'll form the docks at the new naval base at Rosyth. There's no such base on the east coast. They're all on the south, positioned towards France, our old enemy. Now that the Entente Cordiale has been signed, they're no longer a threat.'

'So, you need a new enemy to justify your existence now that the Entente's been signed? Germany?' It was more of a statement than a question from Rose.

'All the social reforms in the world are worth nothing if another power can just walk in and take what they want from you, Missie,' countered Harry. 'And remember, we've got colonies to protect too.'

'Come, come, Rose. We wouldn't be spending all that money on a brand new dockyard if we didn't have evidence of a potential threat from Germany,' intervened David, looking apologetically at his old schoolfriend in his smart naval uniform.

'Wouldn't we?' she continued. This was a new Rose that David hadn't seen before and he was taken aback. 'We've made treaties with France and Russia, even Japan! Negotiate a treaty with Germany and they might not feel like we're surrounding them. They probably feel threatened!'

'Why don't you run along, dear?' said Harry with all the charm of a cornered snake. 'These are matters for us chaps. They're far too complicated and intertwined for a lovely little lady like yourself to worry your pretty little head about. Why don't you run along and powder that pretty nose of yours. You've obviously spent too much time in the sun!' He laughed as if telling a joke but his piercing stare told her to get lost.

Without a word of support from David, Rose left in high dudgeon. He watched her go, bewildered by her contribution to the conversation. He should go after her, he realised, but the presence of his old pal was like a strong magnetic force that kept him rooted to the spot, ready to apologise to Harry for any offence caused.

Lieutenant Sinclair spotted David's discomfort and tried to put him at ease. After all, it was supposed to be an afternoon of relaxation before the fleet sailed, an opportunity to make friends and influence opinion in favour of the military, an opportunity to thank local benefactors for their contributions to the new naval hospital being built on the hill.

'No harm done, David. Women tend to see these things in black and white in my experience,' he said. 'They get awfully emotional about the bigger issues. Better sticking with things they're good at like looking pretty and seeing to their man, if you get my meaning!'

David's look told the coarse lieutenant he was on sticky ground.

'A special one is she?' asked Harry.

'You could say that,' said David wistfully, wondering where Rose was now. Perhaps he had forgotten how disagreeable his old school friend could be.

'Daddy worth a fortune, then, is that it? Owns a factory or a mine or two?' offered Harry. 'You country gents need an injection of capital now and again, I suppose. Especially these days with everyone leaving the land and no sign of tariff reform on the horizon.'

God, talk about adding insult to injury, thought David. He didn't need a lesson on estate management and free trade right now. He began to wonder why the navy didn't teach their officers when to keep their mouths shut as a form of etiquette.

Harry sensed David's unease at his question about Rose's pedigree and went in for the kill.

'Don't tell me the daddy's not rich?! A shopkeeper is it? A physician?'

David bristled.

'A bloody country doctor?! You mean he's in trade?! How's that going to pay the taxes Asquith's got lined up for you landowners? Good God, Melville. You were such a swat at school! All brains and no bloody common sense!'

Harry walked off. David felt as if he had been set up and ambushed. Memories of school started to return, leaving him troubled. Whatever David had done to upset him in the dim and distant past, Harry Sinclair had taken his revenge and he had allowed the prat to treat his beautiful, intelligent Rose like an empty-headed ornament. She was anything but that. Wasn't that why he loved her? Now she was in the throng somewhere, hurt and angry. He would have to find her, to make amends.

When Rose found her friends, they were the centre of attention, surrounded by a small group of eager young officers. The quintet had been persuaded to play music suitable for dancing and several couples had taken to the floor: a rectangle of flagstones by the French doors onto the terrace. Young female dancing partners were in short supply so Elizabeth, Phee and Rose were in high demand. Newly stung by Harry Sinclair's dismissal of her as empty-headed and emotional, and, still smarting from David's failure to speak up on her behalf or even to come after her, Rose found the prospect of a dance very appealing. That was how David found her ten minutes later, dancing a waltz in the arms of a tall, dark and very handsome naval captain. She was listening attentively to his conversation during the dance and laughing at the correct times. To the onlooker, she was clearly enjoying herself. David looked on in disbelief as the music came to an end, and Rose walked off to the refreshment tent with her dancing partner, without so much as a backward glance.

# Chapter 22

## A CLOSE ENCOUNTER

Sunday morning, and the signs that the warm, dry weather was about to break were all around. A slight breeze had got up in the night and the sky had lost its blue clarity to a haze that spoke of rain coming in from the west.

Elizabeth and Richard did not speak at breakfast, such was the hangover from their argument of Saturday evening when she had arrived home from the day trip to Queensferry with the Melvilles. She decided that she had to escape the confines of the manse which had become a dungeon to her, and take time to think over all that raced through her mind. Fortunately, the Sabbath School was not in session and she only had the torment of one of Richard's sermons to suffer before she could go for a long walk to clear her head.

Sitting in her usual place, the pew at the back of the church, she observed her brother as a prisoner looks at a gaoler. His confident words of piety preached from the pulpit washed over her as she looked around the congregation. Which one had felt the need to gossip about her presence at the Gala Day dance? None of them looked young enough to have been there themselves. They were just one link in a chain of tittle-tattle that Richard tried to bind her with, caring more for the mischievous workings of small minds than the truth from his own sister's mouth about an entirely innocent encounter with the local blacksmith. She fanned herself with her hymn book and took a few long, deep breaths. The rise in humidity on such a warm day only added to the discomfort she was enduring. It hadn't helped, she had to admit, that she had arrived back at the manse the previous evening smelling strongly of alcohol. No amount of explanation on her part would convince him that she had bumped into a waiter carrying a tray of drinks for the commodore's table and that not a single drop of intoxicating liquor had passed her lips. Her dress had caught the splash of whisky as the tray went flying. His callous words of accusation had cut her to the core. But worst of all was his determination that she was his responsibility and, as such, would act in a manner that he saw fit. As the music struck up for the final hymn, she fought back tears of frustration.

Back at the manse, she made straight for the kitchen where the cook was preparing their luncheon. She made an excuse about needing to lie down but asked for some sandwiches to tide her over till evening. Mrs Tough was as impenetrable as her name. Elizabeth was sure she had heard the argument with Richard. It had been heated after all. She did not care if her story about a sore head and a fever was believed by the cook. She had to be by herself, out in the open air. Richard would be ages yet, delayed at the door of the church, debating earnestly with those parishioners who hadn't fallen asleep about the intricacies of his sermon's biblical references, and basking in the adoration of the fawning, and inevitably female, attendees of a certain age. She took a shawl from the hook at the back door, escaping along the lane to Mansefield, in the direction of the hill road. She was sure Mrs Tough had been too busy in the dining room to see her leave.

Elizabeth made her way quickly between the high hedgerows lining the footpath to Kaim Farm. Each step that took her further from her brother took her closer to a calmer frame of mind. The song of the birds and the array of wildflowers by the road brought her irrepressible joy and, in spite of her earlier melancholy, she could not help but smile. At the bend in the road past the farm, where the stream ran by the roadside, she found a rock for perching on and produced a sketchbook and pencils from her satchel. Elizabeth loved to draw flowers. She would spend hours producing a pencil sketch that could have graced any of the best botanical guides available, and her annotations evidenced a detailed understanding of the natural world.

Her pencil drifted over the page, sometimes carefully and languidly in long lines, then with short repeated bursts and curves, spotted here and shaded there. The sun was fiery. She was glad of her sun hat, there in the warm shelter of the dip by the roadside. Heat radiated onto the skin of her hands and her face from broken rocks and stones strewn all around but the grass and the stream were cool. She arched her back occasionally when she remembered to, stretching out her legs from time to time to prevent cramp. As her sketch grew to completion, hunger pangs told her the afternoon was wearing on. The sun was on her back now but still high up in the sky. She packed her bag before continuing up the road in search of a place to eat.

Elizabeth was glad there were few people around. She wanted the place to herself. The heat of the day was keeping people indoors, in the shade. Down below, on the wide expanse of peaty moorland, lay the destruction of Nature. Smoky, black, pock-marked, grey; rails of shining iron and metalled roadway cut across the moss; and channels as straight as a die drained the bog of its life blood, the living water. In places, the dark, peaty cover had been peeled back to reveal the stony, sterile foundation of pale rock that supported life but was devoid of it at one and the same time. When all of the mineral riches had been removed or when man turned his attention to other commodities, Nature would claim it all back, she was sure. The plants and the insects would move in first, then the bigger animals with the trees. She had seen it in ruins she had visited: once great houses and castles covered in shrubs and flowers, to be subsumed later to a pile of rocks, a mound of uneven ground like a small hill created by natural forces. Where was she, Elizabeth, in all of this great, never ending cycle of change, of building up and decay? What was her place in it all? She did not know. She loved the quieter places, like the hills where she walked just then; places that were made difficult by the force of the wind and the rain and the winter frosts; places that took some effort to reach, that were left to the thoughtful and the lonely.

As she focused on the road ahead, she spotted a figure on the crest of the hill. It was hard to make out because of the shimmer of heat on the gravel; a man standing motionless against the sky, looking back down the road, waiting for her approach. Then he was gone. She stopped walking and looked again. Perhaps she had imagined him, or wished for him. She started walking again, upwards towards the saddle where the road continued northwards over the muir to Woodhill or ran eastwards down to Allerbank. She wasn't sure where she would go or how far. Maybe as far as The Law or further on to the old shieling, now almost roofless and tumbled down, where she could sit in the sun with her back against a wall, out of the breeze.

'Are you going far, Miss Fraser?' asked a voice from the peat bank by the path to the top of The Law.

'Not far,' she replied, barely startled by the deep familiar tones of the man. 'Not today.'

It was Neil. He had been waiting for her.

He walked with her to the ruined shieling over the high muir on the way to Woodhill; followed a path through the heather; meandered to a flat grassy pasture, hidden from the road. Neil found some timber inside the cottage and made a makeshift seat against the sunniest wall. They settled down, laying out the provisions they had with them: her sandwiches and a piece of cake and his flask of water and an apple.

'A fine spread,' she said offering Neil one of Mrs Tough's ham and pickle sandwiches.

'A fine spread, thanks tae yourself, Miss Fraser. I've nought tae offer but some water an' a bite of an apple.' Neil was apologetic.

'But together they make the perfect meal,' explained Elizabeth. 'The sandwiches would be hard to swallow without some water to wash them down. On such a hot day, I'm glad of a drink. Thank you, Neil,' she said, lifting his flask to her parched lips.

'You're welcome, Miss Fraser,' he replied, looking at the movement of her throat as the water slipped between her lips. He ate slowly.

'Beth,' she said after a while. 'Can you call me Beth?' She turned her head, studying Neil who sat staring off to the west where the wooded slopes ran down to the moss far below, a distant dry brown in the heat of the day.

'I can call ye Beth, if ye'd like me tae,' he replied after a while, as if he'd had to think about it. He took the apple from his bag, laid it on the ground.

She spied the spine of a book within the folds of leather, asked him what it was. He handed her his bag. She extracted three books, one at a time.

'*Le Neve Foster, 'A test book of ore and stone mining'*.' She placed the book down before studying the next. '*Thomas Chalmers, 'Power of Wisdom and Goodness of God'*.' She studied his face, brown with the sun, then his strong hands, marked by daily manual labour at the forge. '*Aubert de Vartot, 'The History of the Revolutions of the Roman Republic'*.' She spied another, hidden in the bottom of the bag. '*William Wordsworth, Poetical Works*.' Each tome is more surprising than the last, she thought to herself.

'Are ye too surprised tae speak, Beth?' he asked at last. 'That a man who works with his hands should be interested in such things and want tae use his mind?' He looked straight at her, waiting for an answer.

'That's quite a selection,' she said eventually. 'A professor at the university would be unlikely to take those on a Sunday stroll.'

'That's because a professor reads this sort o' thing for his work. For me, it's a pleasure. The village library's full o' interesting knowledge and ideas,' he explained with vigour. 'Have ye been in it at all since ye cam tae the village?'

She shook her head. The idea hadn't even occurred to her.

'Mebbe ye didnae think it worth yer while, eh? A wee library in a country village full o' miners and workmen, mmm?'

214

He read her silence as embarrassment, embarrassment at her prejudice and ignorance of people like him.

'It was set up a hundred years ago to promote learning amongst the ordinary folk here. Then Murdo Maclean cam along wi' his knowledge and experience of the Classics an' he set about raising funds for the purchase o' new books to balance out the heavy bias towards the religious subjects.'

She smiled at that and thought of her dreary life in the manse under Richard's thumb. She pictured the wise and affable Mr Maclean at the dinner table at Parkgate House, a man who enjoyed his puddings, and gave his time to the promotion of self-improvement.

'It operates by subscription. Many o' the miners are members, as well as the fermin folk; an' women as well. There are books about exploration and geography, poetry and novels as well if you're interested.' Neil returned to the selection in front of her. 'I've been through all the scientific works, geology, mineralogy, chemistry, and the practical manuals on mining, surveying and engineering, that sort o' thing. The others are just for leisure.'

She smiled broadly as she picked up the book by Thomas Chalmers. Leisure, she thought. What a dark horse Neil Tennant was proving to be. 'Tell me about your work, Neil. Have you always wanted to be a smith?' she asked.

'Wanted? I suppose I wanted tae be a smith like ma faither. It was expected, Beth,' he explained. 'It's a skilful an' a useful profession. An' I'm guid at it.' He blushed, looking straight at her as he laughed at his immodesty. 'So they tell me oniewey. Whit ye have tae understand is that I'm the eldest o' four. I have a responsibility tae help ma faither put food on the table for the others. I've had less choice in ma profession than they'll have, I expect.'

He looked into the distance, said nothing for a long time. 'But I have plans, Beth,' he said after a while, looking earnestly into her eyes. He described a visiting speaker who had lectured at the continuation class and about the profound effect he'd had on his outlook. 'He was a local lad, hame visitin' his faimily, afore touring the technical colleges of Germany and Austria; a professor of engineering and electro-technics in the Transvaal who'd started his education at Blackrigg school,' said Neil.

Elizabeth understood what he was saying. But how would Neil escape his responsibilities towards his parents and his siblings?

Neil read her mind.

'Thon lad joined the army an' was trained by them. But that's not my way.' He explained that there was training available to promising young men taken on in the mines; that his younger brother was keen to start an apprenticeship with their father on leaving school the following year, which might free Neil, morally at least, to take a job with the Coal Company. He described his ongoing preparations for a future change in career. 'I'll be bringing in a wage an' they'll put me through exams in the Principles of Mining. I've done a' the continuation classes I can, an', like I said, I've gleaned whit I can fae the books in the library, everythin' on surveyin' an' minin', geology an' mineralogy, Lyle and so on.' He looked down, abashed, realising how far he had opened up to this young woman that he hardly knew at all.

'And you already have so much understanding of metals and engineering through your smithing. I think you can do it, Neil. Follow your dreams, your plans I mean,' she said. 'I really do think you could achieve whatever you set your mind to.'

'But what about you, Beth?' he asked. 'Tell me about you. I've seen ye oot walkin' many's a time, sittin' drawin' for hours on end.'

'Have you? But I haven't seen you!' exclaimed Elizabeth, wondering when he had seen her and how often.

'You've been too engrossed in your drawin' to notice me,' said Neil. 'Can I see what ye did the day? Is it in yer bag there?' he asked, pointing at her satchel.

She thought about it for a moment then retrieved her sketchbook from the bag. She watched him pouring over the detailed drawing of a common spotted orchid.

'It's quite common in the county,' she told him. 'But it's unusual to find it here on the hill where the soil is so poor and acidic.'

'Why, it's beautiful!' he exclaimed. 'A beautiful flower, a perfect work of nature so perfectly represented by your own fair hand.' He read the labels while she listened, studying his reaction to her work. '*Leaves, broad and elliptical, purple spotted; stem leaves narrow; conical flower spike, pink with purple streaks, two petals and one sepal forming a loose hood, lip with three well-separated lobes.*' He looked up at her in admiration.

'Where did I learn about flowers?' She spoke the question that was on his mind. 'From my mother when I was younger. She gave me a set of books on botany before she passed away. I've taken it a stage further and I draw them: the shape of the flower, the pattern of the leaves on the stem and the arrangement of the petals and the sepals. Each one is such a wonder of Creation with its own place in the world, the place where it thrives.'

He looked at her, thought she looked sad. 'And do you have plans, Beth?' he asked her.

'No. I have no plans, Neil,' she said sadly. 'One day I will.' She gazed off into the distance. I have hopes and dreams but no plans. Not yet, she thought.

'I think one day you will have plans,' Neil told her. 'You will know when the time comes, and you will find your place in the world.' He returned her book and they prepared to leave the sanctuary of the ruin on the hill. 'We'll leave the swallows in peace,' he said, pointing to a female with food in her beak. 'This is her place.'

Elizabeth took another sip of water and he gave her the apple. He took her by the hand, pulled her to her feet. Then they walked along the path together to the road, made their way towards The Law. The wind was rising. The clouds were gathering high up above, boiling up with the heat of the day, hiding the sun. Golden shafts of light came from the darkest clouds.

'We should get down before the rain comes,' Neil advised. 'I can hear thunder in the distance.'

'It's still far away,' she guessed, studying the sky. 'I don't particularly want to hurry back.'

He looked at her, wondering why, but she gave nothing away. Side by side, they walked down the hill. He wanted to talk to her but didn't know what to say. He wanted to ask her many questions but, at that moment, he couldn't even bring the questions to mind. He didn't know her well enough, nor she him, but it was more than that.

When they came to Kaim Farm and the footpath back to the manse, large raindrops started to fall. She put her shawl over her hair and turned to say goodbye.

'I've had a lovely afternoon, Neil,' she said, watching drops of water land on his dark hair and run down his sun-kissed face. 'I'm glad we met on the hill.'

'Perhaps we'll bump into each other again, Beth,' he replied with a wide smile that lit up his eyes. 'There's every chance we will.'

'Yes, I suppose there's a strong chance we will meet on another sunny afternoon,' she said, smiling back at him. 'I think there's a very strong chance that we'll come across each other when we're... walking.... and drawing again. I expect we will.'

'Good bye, then, Miss Fraser.'

'Good bye, Neil Tennant.' She turned to take the path, head bent against the rain, running fast between the hedgerows, back to Richard in the manse.

Neil stood in the road until she had disappeared from sight and the lane was deserted again. He turned, looked up at the hill, to where they had been. The rain was getting heavier. The parched ground seemed to hiss with wetness after the long, dry spell. The Law was disappearing into the murk. He thought he could see a figure up there on the saddle looking back at him. He squinted as water trickled down his forehead, into his eyes, obscuring his vision. He held up his hand against the rain to take a better look. Perhaps he had been mistaken. There was no sign of anyone now. He put his hands in his pockets then made his way downhill in the lashing rain. He smiled broadly, filled with the warm glow of a sunny afternoon at the shieling with Beth.

# Chapter 23

## A WOMAN'S LOT – TENDING

Peggy Duncan lay on top of her bed in the front room, feeling like a beached whale. Not that she actually knew how a beached whale felt, she had never even been to the seaside. She had read in the paper about strandings along the coast. That's how she felt: like an unfortunate animal washed up on the shore, unable to move and help itself. She was nearly seven months gone and her pregnancy had not gone well. Her ankles were swollen and she was convinced she hadn't been as big when she had carried her other babies to full term. Dr Matheson had ordered bed rest at the first signs of bleeding so there she had lain these past four weeks, barely able to do a thing but get narky at her man for getting her in the family way again. Had he never heard of getting off at Haymarket like everybody else? Maybe Highland Mary had been right. Abstinence was the best policy. Though Peggy knew that when Nature had taken her course, and the baby had arrived, she would look at her man as he got ready for bed in the firelight, tired from his work at the pit, and she would long for him again.

Peggy saw the big drops of rain land on the window and race down the dusty panes. The sky was dark, thunder rumbled in the distance. A blue flash of lightning filled the room. She counted the seconds till the thunder rolled around the skies above. Six seconds: only three miles away. It was getting closer. Her unborn baby stirred inside her and she spread her large work-worn hands across the swelling of her abdomen. 'Dinnae fret', she said quietly. 'It'll be fine.' Another flash and a peel of thunder followed almost immediately. The storm was right above her head. She lay on her side in the safety of her box bed looking up at the ceiling to make sure it wasn't going to come in on her. She was glad to see the rain though. It would take away the oppressive heat and humidity of recent days and her head would clear.

The rain brought her sons, Rob and Sandy, in from the street where they had been talking with friends. Football was frowned upon, this being the Sabbath. Peggy was frustrated that she couldn't be up and about looking after them. They were the light of her life. Sandy had been helpful when she had first taken to her bed. He went to the Co-op for the messages and he brought her a drink of water without having to be asked. Rob had learned to do his bit too, after some persuading. He was good at lighting the fire in the morning and bringing in water from the spicket in the street. Sandy would appear in the middle of the afternoon from wherever he was playing to heat up the water for his father's bath. He would fetch the tin bath from under her bed and sit it by the hearth, soap and a towel laid out on his father's chair, then set about banking up the fire with extra coal. No matter how hot the summer weather was, the fire had to be on all the time for cooking and washing. Sandy would boil up pot after pot of water, till his father walked through the door from the pit, as black as the ace of spades from his labours, ready to scrub away the grime.

If things got too bad over the next few weeks, when the boys went back to school, Peggy decided she would ask Lizzie, her daughter, to come and stay with her for a while. She didn't want to do that unless she really had to. Lizzie had a life of her own now on the other side of the county, with her husband. Peggy felt stupid for being in the family way when her eldest was married and, in all likelihood, would soon be announcing that a grandchild was expected. It was unusual for a young married woman to take so long to become pregnant. Often enough, the couple had to get married on account of the girl being in the family way but not Lizzie. She had been a good, chaste lass on her wedding day, taking her mother's advice. Now that she had been married to Archie a year past, Peggie had expected news of a grandchild by now. The thought that Lizzie and her man knew about getting off at Haymarket and other ways of delaying pregnancy occurred to Peggy for the first time. It was a possibility, she thought, but one thing was certain: she and Lizzie could never have a conversation about something so intimate and personal.

A knock came to the door. It opened before Sandy had time to reach it. In came Mary Birse with a pot of brose, hurrying out of the heavy rain. Peggy strained to see who was coming in.

'Hello, Mrs Birse,' said Sandy. Rob glowered, kept his head down.

'How ye daein, Peg?' asked Mary cheerfully, smiling at both boys. She placed the cooking pot by the hearth, drew a chair across the bare floor. Sandy and Rob disappeared into the other room without being asked. Women's talk was not for their ears.

'I'm a'richt, as weel as can be expected under the circumstances,' replied Peggy, trying to make light of her situation and failing badly. Mary helped her to sit up, rearranged the pillows, enough to let Peggy move onto her back for a spell.

'I seen ye oot at the closet earlier on, emptying the chanties.' Mary's tone was severe.

'Thon's a job I cannae ask o' the boys. An' somebody's got tae dae it,' replied Peggy defensively.

'Mind ye've jist tae ask if ye want else done.' Mary paused, brows knitted. 'Think oan, Peg. Ye'll be nae guid tae man nor beast if ye kill yersel haein this bairn.' She fixed Peggy with a steely eye. 'Whit would yer boys dae withoot ye?'

'Thanks for the broth, Mary,' said Peggy, quickly changing the subject. 'In truth, I'm climbin' the wa's in here. Lyin' on ma back when there's sae much tae dae.'

'I ken how it is, Peg,' replied Mary, although she had never known what it was like to bear a child herself. It had simply never happened for her but she had seen many women who'd taken to their beds in Peggy's condition or with a variety of ailments and conditions, frustrated by their immobility when there was so much work to be done. 'I seen Meg Graham taen yer slot at the wash hoose boiler, the ither day. Was thon your washin' she was daein?' she asked brightly.

Peggy cheered up at the thought.

'Aye, she done a' ma' bed claes as weel as the shirts, this week,' she replied. 'Fowk have been that guid tae us. I'd be in a richt guddle itherwise! You wi' yer broth an' Meg washin' for me, the ither Graham lassies sweepin' oot an' washin' up for me.'

'Their mither would be a proud wuman if she was alive the day tae see them, an' nae mistake!'

'Ellen wis in yesterday cause Minn was readin' tae Geordie tae gie her a spell. An' hey when I mind, Mags

Cherrie brocht me a pot o' soup this week. Her wi' eicht weans, a man an' twa ludgers tae feed! I've guid neebors,' said Peggy gratefully.

'Aye, yer thankfu' but ye'd raither be up seein' tae yer ain business,' continued Mary. 'Dinna fret. Ye'll no be lang up an' aboot efter the bairn comes an' ye'll be deein on a rest!'

The women laughed together. Their work was never ending and it pained them not be able to get on with it when they were laid low.

'As long as ye keep daein as the doctor telt ye, mind. It's yer ain health as weel as the bairn ye've tae think on, Peg. If ye need oniethin jist yell on they twa boys o' yours. Send them up for me if ye think I can help, eh?' It was an order.

'Thanks,' replied Peg. 'I'm feelin' better noo that the weather's broke. It's no sae mochie noo the rain's come.'

'Aye, it's brocht glaur tae the backs again, nae doobt. We'll tell the men tae get some mair bits o' wood, tae mak a better wey in tae the closets an' the middens,' explained Mary, ever vigilant of a decline in their living conditions. 'I'll speak tae Steeny Simpson aboot gettin' the ash pits an' the closets emptied mair often. They've been stinkin' somethin' fierce in this warm weather.'

Peggy agreed. Her house was close to a dry closet that served eleven households: nigh on a hundred people in all.

'Steeny'll bring it up at the next meetin' o' the Cooncil if we tell 'im,' she went on. 'We best tak oor concerns tae him, eh? We've a workin' man on the Cooncil whau kens whit it's like tae live here. If we dinnae speak up nuthin'll get onie better.'

Peggy felt relieved that Mary was going to bring up the matter. She had lain on her bed often, these last few weeks, almost wretching with the stench from the closets. What a place for her baby to be born into. It couldn't be good for you. Didn't common sense tell you that? Even the kye in the byre up at Kaim Farm were mucked out more often than the scavenger paid a visit to Stoneyrigg to empty the ash pits and the closets.

'Weel, I'll awa', Peg,' said Mary, emptying the brose she'd brought into Peggy's own cooking pot. 'I need tae git back afore Alex comes hame fae the allotment. He'll come in soakin' wet an' be in a richt strop. He's bein' awfy sair oan oor John the noo. I dinnae ken whit it is aboot the laddie. He just seems tae rub his faither up the wrang wey a' the time.' She gave a sigh. 'Look efter yersel, Peg,' she called as she disappeared into the pouring rain.

Peggy watched Mary leave and wished she was up on her feet just like her. She was a good friend and it was a comfort to have her nearby if help was needed. She wondered what life with Alex Birse was like: him and his socialist preaching about rights and making things better for the working man. Mary didn't say much but he couldn't be easy to live with, Peggy decided. And he was hard on the boys. Sure, he gave them a roof over their heads but sometimes they looked like tinks; waifs and strays going barefoot when they outgrew their boots. They looked half-starved at times too. Life must be a trial with that man, in spite of all the moralising that came out of his mouth. Actions spoke louder than words, in Peggy Duncan's opinion.

As the raindrops raced down through the dust on the window panes, she followed them with her gaze. There was nothing she wanted more than to be up on her feet with a cloth in her hand, washing away the grime, and making everything better and brighter for her boys and her man.

# Chapter 24

## A RIDE IN THE WOODS

It had been an unusual spell of good weather for Rashiepark. Since the weather had broken though, it had become very unsettled, much more like a normal Scottish summer. The rain had brought new green life to the brown, parched earth. As she made her way along a woodland path, Elizabeth marvelled at the carpets of wild flowers colouring the ground, lit by dappled sunshine filtering through the canopy of leaves above. She was glad to see the old towers of Parkgate finally coming into view through the tree tops but she still had a considerable distance to go.

Elizabeth guided her mount back along the trail that had taken them north passed Home Farm to the River Avon where she had cantered on the high ground waiting for Phee to return from her gallop on Prince. Gentle old Major, a Highland pony of considerable age, was feeling the pace. His head was down. Elizabeth patted his neck, spoke encouraging words over the last few miles back to the stables at the house. He raised his head, shaking his long black mane in reply. Although she had been learning the finer points of horse riding all summer, a couple of hours in the saddle was still quite a challenge and she eased herself up in the stirrup to relieve the cramp forming along the entire length of her body. A side saddle was the strangest invention man had ever come up with, she decided. It clearly was the invention of men who would never have to endure it. Her back ached from maintaining such an erect posture and her bottom was numb. She could barely feel the leg bent around the pommel or her left foot pressing down on the stirrup. Her body had lost any trace of elasticity and every one of Major's strides jarred, threatening to remove her onto the hard ground.

Horse and rider came to a halt in a large clearing where the track forked. They waited, breathing heavily. She could not trust herself to dismount without causing severe injury and she would never be able to get back on by herself. Here in the glade, it was calm but the wind in the leaves high above brought creaks and groans from the biggest trees. She patted Major once again then gently asked him if he wanted to go on. He lifted his head as if startled, pulled down on the reins with a whinny. His ears were up. He stepped back a stride. She heard the noise too; a crunch of a boot on dry leaves then nothing. Elizabeth peered into the shade of the trees up ahead and listened. She stroked Major again, long firm strokes down the length of his neck with her gloved hand. Everything was fine, she told him as if trying to reassure herself. The sound of a twig snapping underfoot came from the shadows. Her heartbeat set off at a pace and she swallowed hard. Nothing and nobody, she decided after a while. Nothing but her imagination.

'Come on then, old boy,' she said to Major as she took a final look around. 'Nothing to worry about and not far to go.' She pulled on the reins and the old grey horse set off slowly, reluctant to follow the trail home.

Major knew where the man was: hidden in the shade with a gun over his shoulder. He stepped out onto the track. He leapt forward, had grabbed the reins before she could react. Major was brought to a halt.

'Enjoying the ride then, Miss?' asked the man, holding tight to the leather straps whilst stroking the forehead of the frightened horse. Major whinnied again and stepped backwards, wanting to be free. Elizabeth gripped the reins, tensed every muscle and sinew to stay in the saddle, her heart pounding.

'Yes, thank you, could you let go of the reins?' she asked, trying to appear in control.

He held on, looked up at her with cold eyes, saying nothing.

'Mr Grant, is it?' she continued, her fear rising. 'We've never been introduced.' She stared back at him, debating whether or not Major had it in him to make a bolt for it.

'We've never been introduced?' Grant laughed as he mimicked her. It was a mocking laugh. He held the horse close as he stroked Major's nose with dirty, fat hands, mumbling all the while. Sullen, Grant glowered at Elizabeth. She noticed the purple mark below one eye, the scab on his bottom lip and the yellow stains of old bruises across both cheeks.

'I dinnae move in the same polite circles like you dae, Missie,' he said at last as if she were to blame. 'I'm surprised ye even ken ma name.'

Elizabeth knew his name because he had been described to her by Phee: a broad creature with arms that curved out from a heavy body; large hands like shovels with dirty fingernails; a raft of greasy fair hair and freckled skin, pock marked, rosy red from too much alcohol and long hours in the sun; a surly mouth turned down at both ends, matching the permanent frown; moleskin trousers held up with a length of rope under his large belly, and a thick cotton jacket, even in summer; his dinner spread down the front of his tartan shirt. It had to be Grant, the gamekeeper.

'I've spoken to your wife... at the church,' she offered, trying to find his good side.

'Pious bitch!' he called loudly, startling the horse.

Elizabeth flinched at the man's venom. Did he mean her or his wife?

'With your daughter,' continued Elizabeth bravely. 'When she brings her to the Sabbath School. Annie isn't it?'

'You leave ma dochter oot o' this,' warned Grant with a growl.

Out of what, wondered Elizabeth? Her concern had grown beyond fear. It was mounting to something approaching terror. 'Let the reins go, Mr Grant,' she commanded. She was determined not to say *please*. She felt ridiculous on her perch and prayed she didn't look as vulnerable as she felt.

'Your kind ay get's whit they want, dae they?' laughed Grant, mocking her once again. 'I was wondering, Miss Fraser,' he continued, 'if ye'd like tae learn somethin' o' ma work while ye're here in the woods?'

She stared at him but said nothing. Perhaps she should humour him by showing an interest. Saying no, right at that moment, might not be the best course of action, she surmised.

'As ye'll ken fae yer walks in the hills,' he coughed a polite cough, staring her straight in the eye, 'The rabbits are diseased hereaboots this season, and the hares verra scarce. The grouse are farin' weel up on the muir, though.'

Elizabeth felt sick at the mention of the moor. Neil's gentle, smiling face filled her mind then was gone in an instant. She pulled back on the reins. Major stepped back in a circle but was held fast by Grant.

'Ye ken whaur I mean, the muir up by the auld sheilin', ower the back road tae Woodhill. Dae ye ken the place, Miss Fraser?' he asked, taunting her. He laughed without mirth.

She didn't answer. Grant seemed to know she had been there. She thought of Neil again and the blissful time she had spent in his company. Fear gripped her throat. She stared down from above at the nightmare that was Grant, waiting for what he had to say next.

'Lost yer tongue, Missie? Or are ye jist bein' impolite?' he snarled. 'I've weys o' teachin' lassies manners.'

'Let me go, please, Mr Grant. I have done you no harm,' she ventured.

'Of coorse, it's no jist the hare an' the grouse that brings in the sportsmen, Miss Fraser,' explained Grant, ignoring her plea and continuing his lesson on the art of gamekeeping. 'I've tae raise pheasant as weel. It's a verra important job, ye ken. The income o' the estate depends on ma guid work though I git sma' thanks for it,' he said angrily before gaining his composure once again.

'Ye'll have tae come an' see them in their pens. It's jist through the trees there, alang the ither fork.' He pointed down the trail that led away from Parkgate. Grant pulled on the reins and Major followed reluctantly. Elizabeth pulled backwards. Major rose slightly on his hind legs, whinnied loudly. Should she try to kick the man away and make her escape? She teetered in the saddle. It was all she could do to remain upright. But she might have to take her chance when it came.

'Come, come, Miss Fraser. I've had a guid year, come an' see the pretty wee birdies.'

When he pulled the horse along the start of the fork, she let out her loudest scream. It startled Grant, and Major too. As the gentle beast rose up on his hind legs, the man lost his hold on the reins. He stumbled backwards out of the way of Major's hooves. Elizabeth gripped tightly, leaned into the saddle, took control once again. She pulled to the right and Major turned quickly. He knew where to go. He knew he had to get there as fast as he could. His terrified rider wobbled back and forth before regaining her upright position.

'Go, Major, go!' she urged and the faithful, old stallion went.

Grant ran beside them, swift despite his huge size. He made off through the trees at a bend in the track and reappeared with a growl, making a desperate final lunge for his quarry. He grabbed at the reins, stumbling at first. He caught the rider by the foot and pulled. Elizabeth was catapulted out of the saddle. She tumbled through the air with a scream, landing on her back with a heavy crunch. Major kicked then pulled to the side. He was off like the wind down the track.

A dark shadow fell over her as she lay, helpless. Grant's leering face, distorted and mocking, blocked out the sky. He held out a dirty, fat hand to help her up. She rolled to the side refusing his help. Aching all over but relieved that nothing was broken, she staggered to her feet. She held him in her gaze whilst trying to get her bearings. She wasn't within sight or sound of Parkgate. Elizabeth was alone in the wood with Grant.

As Phee rode Prince into the stable yard at Parkgate, she congratulated him on a fine hack with several firm strokes of her gloved hand down his sleek chestnut brown neck. Billy Dodds emerged from the stable block where he was mucking out and hurried over to take the reins. He watched as she dismounted; held the young, strong horse steady, calming him with his quiet, reassuring voice. It was impossible not to see the outline of Phee's buttocks and the tapering firmness of her thighs in the riding breeches she was wearing. She was a right one, that Miss Phee – everybody said so, thought Billy. She was a headstrong young filly with a mind of her own, not bound by the etiquette of the day, not like other young ladies of her class; though she was asking for trouble, wearing a man's breeches and leaving nothing to the imagination. It wouldn't have happened if her mother had still been alive, that was a certainty. He shook his head. Billy knew that her brother was having a bit of bother keeping her in hand. He had been in a terrible mood, Saturday past, when he had left the garden party at Royal Navy House with the young ladies in tow. Nobody had spoken all the way home. By all accounts there had been a dreadful din later on – Miss Phee and the young master going hammer and tongs at each other when they'd got into their private apartments, doors banging and all sorts. What a way to behave, thought Billy, them with all their money and breeding, acting no better than Mags Cherrie gaun her dinger when her man came home fu' on a Saturday night. He shook his head in dismay.

Phee felt exhilarated by the gallop up on the high moor north of the Avon. She had been riding astride in her brother's breeches all summer, leaving behind the limitations of the side saddle to the prim and the proper of another era. It was one of many restrictions that women were rebelling against these days and she could understand why. Lamely jolting up and down, balanced precariously atop a placid old nag could not compare with the thrill of racing across the open countryside at full pelt with a lithe youngster like Prince between your legs.

Phee looked back along the track, across the fields of Redburn Farm to the woods beyond. There was no sign of Elizabeth but she was not surprised. The poor girl didn't have much experience in the saddle and they had ridden out further than they had expected. If only she would take Phee's advice to try riding astride. It was so much easier. The feeling of stability gave the rider much more confidence, something her friend needed badly. Never mind, for a young woman conditioned by a lifetime of strict Presbyterianism, Elizabeth was doing well. That brother of hers, the holier than thou Reverend Richard Fraser, kept her on a short rein. Considering she shared a house with the man, Elizabeth was developing into her own person, faster than anyone might have believed possible, and Phee was very proud of her.

'Thank you, Billy,' said Phee, pulling the hem of her jacket down as far as she could when she noticed his eyes taking in the curve of her hips. 'Could you rub him down for me while I pop inside for a minute? Miss Fraser should be here very soon... she'll need a lot of help. Stick around till she comes, will you? She'll be wobbling along at a snail's pace, no doubt.'

'Certainly, Miss,' replied Billy.

'We'll have to persuade her to try proper riding. Won't we? And ditch the silly old side saddle!' she called back to him as she disappeared into the house to change.

Billy couldn't imagine the gentle Miss Fraser in riding breeches, astride a horse like a man. She was too much of a lady. Men knew where they were with ladies like Miss Fraser who acted like they should. 'As for that Miss Phee,' he said quietly to Prince as he led him over to his stable,

'She's somethin else.' He shook his head. 'I dinnae ken whit this world's comin' tae, Prince, neither I dae.'

Phee made her way through the dark hallway of the old house, climbed the stairs two at a time to the first floor, looking around to check that the coast was clear as she did so. She hurried towards her room, hoping she wouldn't bump into David on the way. They hadn't spoken to each other since their argument on Saturday night, after their return from the garden party at Queensferry. She loved him dearly but he had been such a spoil sport about the party, and he was being a complete idiot about Rose. She'd had to put him right and she didn't regret it. Bumping into him would be awkward and she might let down her resolve at the sight of him. She made it to the door of her room then let out a sigh of relief. But much too soon.

'What the hell do you think you're wearing?' called David as he strode along the corridor towards her. Her heart sank. She made no attempt to argue as he followed her into her room, closing the door behind him. It wouldn't do for the servants to detect discord within the family, after all.

'I'm wearing riding breeches because I've been out riding, brother dear,' replied Phee defiantly. 'I will have them returned to your dressing room if you wish.'

'That's not the point,' continued David. 'We've had this conversation before.'

'Which conversation, brother?' asked Phee. 'The one about me being a lady and letting the family down with my behaviour, is that the one?'

'What do you look like, Phee? Dressing like a man and riding astride like some barbarian out of the east!' He looked her up and down in disgust.

'For God's sake, David, times are changing. Don't you read the newspapers?' she asked, weary of his strictures. 'And I've already apologised for enjoying the garden party! Leave it out!'

'This is not just about the garden party, Phee. It's about your reputation and the opportunities you'll have to make a good match,' he explained feebly.

Phee was horrified to know that her brother was even remotely concerned about her prospects in the marriage stakes. 'I have been riding with my friend. What more innocent a pleasure can there be?' she asked. 'I danced with some very nice young officers at the garden party. An elderly couple bumped into my partner and we fell over on the terrace. It was amusing. We laughed. Everyone laughed and the old dears apologised.'

David blanched at the memory of Phee landing on top of the young naval officer as they tumbled to the ground, her dress about her hips revealing her silk undergarments. He tried to interrupt his sister but she was livid and having none of it.

'It was not my fault and Lieutenant Gibb apologised profusely. Several people came to our aid and we all made light of it,' she continued. 'Family honour was restored. My reputation remained intact.'

'Not from where I was standing, it wasn't. Anyway, you shouldn't have put yourself in that position in the first place,' stated David haughtily.

'How could I have escaped it?' she probed. 'By sitting at the side like a wall flower all afternoon? It was a party!' She looked daggers at him as she pointed at his face. 'This isn't about me at all. This is about you and Rose, isn't it? You're upset because the love of your life was dancing with someone else! Well, why was she, brother dear?

Perhaps because you let the school bully, Lieutenant Harry Sinclair, treat her like she hadn't a brain? Like she can't think for herself? Like it was improper to express an opinion just because she wasn't born a man like you and your old school mate? Like she was some bit of fluff that you happened to have on your arm for the afternoon, like a mark of your manhood, huh?' Phee could tell from her brother's gaping mouth that she was saying much more than she should, that she was cutting deep with every thrust and parry.

'And the first thing she does is go off with another man,' he said, riled to his own defence. 'Within five minutes, she's dancing with someone else then off for a drink with him at the drop of a hat!' He pictured his beloved Rose strolling off, laughing on the arm of another man. David's jealousy peaked. 'She's just a trollop like the rest of her sex!'

The look on Phee's face told him he had gone too far. She was horrified to think that her brother held the same prejudices she had seen in so many other men.

'He is her cousin,' she replied at last.

David looked back at his sister as if he hadn't quite heard her correctly.

'You heard. Captain Andrew Matheson R.N., her first cousin. She hadn't seen him for some time and hadn't expected him to be there.' Phee stared back at her dumbstruck brother, savouring his discomfort, egg all over his face.

'How do you know this?' he asked eventually, much diminished.

'Because I asked her,' replied Phee, almost feeling sorry for him. 'Didn't you ask her? No, you didn't,' she continued. 'You judged her without knowing the facts. You put her in the category of all women, didn't you? The one marked *"not to be trusted"*, *"not to be let out on their own"*, the one labelled *"keep under control at all times"*.' Phee could feel tears welling up in her eyes.

That was how he had treated her friend, the beautiful intelligent Rose. That was what women were railing against in their different ways. It wasn't just about *Votes for Women*. Not being able to vote was only one symptom of a society that held women under the thumb. Rules and regulations, ties that bind and control, dressed up as etiquette and manners. There was no point in explaining it any further to him, Phee thought. He might understand one day if he opened his eyes. You had to be a woman to understand: a woman like her, who had a strong spirit and a mind of her own. You had to live with it every day as she did. You had to know what it was like to live with the expectations: expectations that had gone unquestioned for long enough because of tradition and class. You had to live with the frustration that life as a women brought, waiting for other people to make decisions that would affect your future, for good or bad.

David looked defeated. He didn't know what to say.

A knock at the door brought a welcome interruption to the awkward silence that had descended between brother and sister.

'Come in,' called Phee.

Nell Graham stood in the doorway.

'What is it, girl?'

Clearly, Nell had heard the battle that had taken place a few moments earlier and was afraid to speak.

'What is it? Spit it out!'

'Beggin' yer pardon, Miss. It's Miss Fraser, Miss. Her horse came back withoot her jist a meenit past. Billy Dodds's lookin' for her. He telt me tae let ye ken, Miss.'

'Thank you, Nell,' replied Phee. 'Thank you very much. That'll be all.'

Phee looked at her brother and gave a loud groan. He sat dejected in the corner, his head bowed. She grabbed her riding hat then ran swiftly out of the room.

Phee stood in the stable yard looking across the fields to Paddy's Wood, hoping to see Billy emerge with Elizabeth at any moment. Billy must have gone off on Prince when Major appeared without his rider, she decided. Phee felt a dreadful guilt at leaving her friend behind but she had been so slow. She had felt sure Elizabeth would eventually amble into the yard. She had just needed time to jiggle along on old Major, that was all. She was proving to be a competent rider with great empathy for her aged mount. They were just slow. If only Elizabeth would agree to ride astride – it was so much more stable – so much more fun when you could ride like the wind with the horse between your knees. Phee crossed to where the grey Highland pony had been tethered. She stroked his neck, then his forehead. He gave a nod and a snort as she looked him in the eye.

'Where is she, Major?' she asked. 'What did you do with Beth? Dump her on the ground, hmm?' She patted his head, stroked his neck again. 'Is she alright, Major?'

The horse seemed agitated as he lifted his hooves in turn. Phee walked around him, checking for signs of a fall. She slapped his rump, watched him move his legs. There was no obvious sign of injury. She looked back at the woods, at the place where she hoped to see Elizabeth at any moment. But, when she did not appear, a wave of dread turned Phee's stomach. Her friend could be lying hurt somewhere, unable to move or even call out for help. If she had stuck to the right path, Billy would find her easily. So, they should be here by now. But they weren't. She started to take off Major's saddle, unbuckling the straps and hauling it off his back.

'Let's get rid of this ridiculous contraption, old chap,' she said to him. She disappeared into the stable where she heaved the side saddle onto a rack. She returned with a normal one, still searching the edge of the trees for her friend as she set about preparing the old horse for another foray into the woods.

'We'll find her, old boy,' she promised, producing a lump of sugar from her pocket. 'Yes, we will.' Major shook his head and snorted. She untied him, led him over to the mounting block. Then a final glance in the direction of the woods before she got ready to jump onto his back.

Suddenly there they were, Elizabeth walking out of the forest followed by Billy leading her beautiful Prince. What a wonderful sight! Phee dropped Major's reins and ran to meet them. She waved and called out as she hurried along the track. She was relieved to see Elizabeth, safe and sound, perhaps limping a little but at least she was walking by herself. That was a good sign, wasn't it? Phee resolved never to be impatient again. She would think about other people more carefully and she would never ever again leave her friend in a situation where she was vulnerable.

Eventually, Phee stopped running and waited at the gate into the low meadow. She watched them approach, solemnly walking towards her, one behind the other with Prince in tow. Things didn't seem quite right, Phee realised. Neither rescued or rescuer was responding to her calls. Not even a wave. They just plodded on in her direction.

'I've been so worried about you. Thank God you're safe, Beth?' she called when they were close enough to hear. Phee ran the last few steps and hugged her friend.

Elizabeth just stared ahead glumly, expressionless, hardly responding to Phee's presence. Phee put a reassuring arm around her shoulder as she walked with her.

Dust and dried leaves covered the back of Elizabeth's riding habit. Her jacket was dirty down one arm and her blonde hair, normally so precise with every hair in place, was dishevelled.

'Did you have a fall, Beth?' Phee asked when no information was forthcoming.

There was no reply.

'Are you alright? Nothing broken then?' she tried again.

'Seems Major bolted for it an' Miss Fraser was thrown aff,' explained Billy.

'Oh, dear,' replied Phee. 'I hope this isn't going to put you off riding for good, Beth. Not when you've been doing so well!'

When Elizabeth didn't reply, Phee started to worry that she had taken a blow to the head. 'Were you knocked out, Beth?' She turned to Billy for an answer. 'Did you find her on the ground, Billy?'

'No, Miss. Luckily, Mister Grant found her afore I got there. He saw to her,' he started to explain. 'Seems she was in a richt state when he tried tae git her up aff the ground, screamin' an' shoutin' an' a' thing, so he says.'

'Do you think she took a bump to the head, Billy?' asked Phee, becoming even more concerned at her friend's lack of response. She took a pace back, holding Elizabeth with both hands, and looked carefully into her eyes. Phee could see that she had been crying from the dirty tide marks of old tears down each cheek but she continued looking straight ahead. She would not or could not speak.

'Let's get you back to the house, Beth. Perhaps you'll feel better when you've had a lie down.'

She put a comforting arm around her friend's shoulder as the pair made ungainly progress towards the house, along the path through fields of ripening barley.

'Where did you find her, Billy?' Phee called back as the groom led Prince homewards with encouraging words and promises of fresh grazing.

'Seems Major made aff at the fork in the track, middle o' Paddy's Wood,' Billy explained. 'Thon's whaur Mister Grant says he cam upon her, oniewey.'

'Okay, Beth, here we are. Looks like you had a lucky escape,' she said to her friend who remained too dazed to speak, as they entered the stable yard. 'Thanks, Billy. I'll leave both horses to you, shall I? Who would've thought old Major had it in him to rush off like that, eh?' she called over her shoulder.

'Come on, dear one,' she continued gently, turning to Elizabeth. 'Let's get you upstairs and see what's what.'

# Chapter 25

## A NARROW ESCAPE

As the two women entered the bedroom set aside for guests, Elizabeth suddenly let down her guard, much to the other's astonishment and great relief. Tears slipped from her tired eyes and her shoulders shuddered with emotion.

'Never mind,' comforted Phee. 'You've had a nasty fall and maybe a bump to the head but you're safe now. Billy brought you back safe and sound.'

Elizabeth let out a wail of despair that had Phee patting her friend's shoulder, encouraging her to lie down on the bed.

'And it's just as well Grant was there to pick you up, isn't it? You could have wandered off in a daze and we might never have found you,' she said gently into Elizabeth's bowed head.

Elizabeth shook her head from side to side.

'Please, Beth. Whatever is the matter? You're safe now. No harm done, eh?'

'It wasn't like that,' said Elizabeth, wiping her wet face with the back of a hand.

'It wasn't like what, Beth? Whatever do you mean? Tell me.'

Elizabeth sniffed and kept her head bowed. 'I feel so ashamed.'

She started to cry again, her shoulders moving up and down.

Phee gave her a handkerchief.

'Ashamed? Don't be silly. You fell off a bloody horse. There's nothing to be ashamed about.' She looked closely at her friend. Elizabeth nodded her head up and down. 'What do you mean, Beth? What on earth's happened?'

Elizabeth held out her hands and showed the bright red marks circling her wrists. She started to take off her jacket, the one she had borrowed from Phee, and the long rent around the neck of her silk blouse became obvious.

Phee gasped.

'Major didn't bolt. He's the kindest, most placid creature.' She started to cry again as she thought of the old, faithful horse but Phee encouraged her to go on. 'It was Grant. He stopped us in the woods, wanted me to go with him. I tried to get away. I tried but Grant cut us off. He pulled me off Major.' She looked at her friend who sat beside her horrified. 'I screamed and scratched and hit out but he's so strong, Phee. He's so strong.' She started to cry again as the memories came flooding back. She held out her wrists again, examining the places where the skin had been broken. 'He was leading me off to his place in the woods – where he rears the birds – when we heard Billy calling my name. Grant tried to put his hand over my mouth but I called out just in time.'

Phee put her arm around Elizabeth's shoulder again.

'I feel so ashamed,' she continued, the tears subsiding.

'You have nothing to feel ashamed about. Nothing whatsoever,' Phee stated emphatically. 'I'll get David onto this and the man will be brought to book.'

'No, please, no,' implored Elizabeth, reaching out to her friend. 'Please don't say anything. I feel that I'm to blame, somehow.' The tears started again. 'Just by being there, I mean, I'm to blame. Please don't tell anyone. I want to forget the whole thing ever happened.'

'But we can't have a crazed lunatic like Grant stalking the women of Rashiepark, Elizabeth! He's got to be punished for his actions. You've nothing to be ashamed about, for Goodness sake! Nothing at all.'

'But that's how I feel,' Elizabeth explained. 'I shouldn't have been there on my own. If I hadn't been there, this would never have happened, don't you see?'

'You mean, if you'd been at home with Richard, doing your embroidery, this would never have happened?'

'Maybe something like that, I don't know.'

'Or maybe you're to blame simply because you're a woman!'

Elizabeth hadn't thought about her feelings in that way. She hadn't analysed how she felt and why she felt as she did, shame and guilt wrapped up together and Richard's stern face judging her from on high in her mind's eye, his finger wagging, telling her it was all her own fault. She only knew that she felt ashamed and she didn't want anyone else to know what had happened to her in the woods. She thought about what might have happened if Billy Dodds hadn't come along when he did, if she hadn't managed to call back to him in time, and she started to cry again. Hot tears burst from her eyes and ran down her face again.

'I won't tell anyone. Not right away,' agreed Phee. 'I want you to lie down and I'll have some tea brought up. We can talk about it again later if it will help.' She helped Elizabeth take off her boots, comforted her until she stopped crying.

As Phee left the room, she gave her an encouraging smile before closing the door and heading for the kitchen.

Something would have to be done about that gamekeeper, she decided as she made her way along the dark corridors of the house. She had never liked him that was for certain. There had always been a look about him. He made her feel uneasy whenever she was anywhere near him and she had been right. How many other women had Grant upset or left in an even worse condition? If Billy Dodds hadn't been quick off the mark when old Major arrived back, things could have been quite different for Elizabeth. Very different indeed. She was so wrapped up in her thoughts, that she didn't notice the young servant coming up the stairs from the kitchen with a large basket of fruit. Each was as taken aback as the other when they collided, sending the contents of the basket flying into the air.

'Terribly sorry, Nell.' Phee apologised to Nell Graham who was horrified to have bumped into one of the Miss Melvilles.

'Beggin' yer pardon, Miss,' said Nell, embarrassed. 'Didnae expect ye tae be there. Sorry, Miss.' She started to chase pieces of fruit up and down the stairway and return them to the basket. 'I'm tae put fruit in the dining room, Miss,' she continued, feeling the need to explain herself.

'No harm done, Nell, my fault entirely.' She watched the girl fetch apples and pears from all around. 'When you've done that, could you take a tray up to Miss Fraser in the guest room? You know the one she always uses when she visits? She's had a bit of a fall. Some tea and a few biscuits to cheer her up would be good.'

'Certainly, Miss. I'll see tae it,' replied Nell. 'Sorry tae hear she's hurt hersel, Miss. It's no awfy bad is it? She'll recover quick-like, will she?'

Phee hurried away. 'I hope so, Nell,' she called over her shoulder. 'I hope so.'

Later, when Phee returned to see how Elizabeth was faring, she found a much brighter person, more like her old self. She looked tired, even after a short nap, but the tea had helped and she was feeling stronger.

'After Nell brought the tea,' explained Elizabeth, 'I got to thinking about what I'd said. You know, about not wanting anyone to know, about feeling ashamed and so on.'

'Yes, yes,' agreed Phee, encouraging her to continue.

'Well, it's wrong, isn't it, to feel ashamed, I mean? It's Grant that's in the wrong, isn't it? It's not right that he should get to plague women's lives like this,' She brought to mind Grant's cursing of his poor, cowering wife and wondered what his daughter's life was like with him in the same house. 'I looked at young Nell Graham who brought me the tea and then asked so kindly if I was feeling better and I thought about her sisters and all of the others in the village just like them. And I thought for the sake of all the young women like me who might be prayed upon by Grant, I should be strong and speak up so that nothing awful can happen to anyone else in the future.'

'Well done, Beth. You're so brave,' Phee said. 'I'll speak to David and see what he has to say about it. He'll know what to do.'

'But can we not involve Richard?' said Elizabeth. 'Please!' Then, at the sight of her friend's disappointed face, 'If at all possible... You see... I'm not that brave. Can this be dealt with.... quietly, please? I'd rather not let the whole village know if it can be helped.' She stared at Phee with red-rimmed eyes. 'But especially not Richard,' she implored. 'Please don't let Richard know.'

Phee understood. 'Don't worry, Richard doesn't need to know,' she said reassuringly. 'You have another nap. I'll be back as soon as I've spoken to David. Just ring for anything you need meantime.' She pointed to the bell-pull by the bed-side.

Elizabeth felt more relaxed, feeling she was doing the right thing, as she watched her friend go out of the room. She sank into the soft mattress, let the bed covers envelop her like a cocoon. She buried her face in their coolness, the smell of rose and lavender filling her head with calm. A light breeze lifted the lace curtain back from the window and birdsong lifted her spirits. Then as she went to close her eyes, the nightmare of her encounter with Grant returned. The tears welled up, ready to spill over once again.

# Chapter 26

## IN SEARCH OF JUSTICE

Phee was stopped short by the butler as she made to enter the study where she hoped her brother was working as usual.

'Excuse me, Miss,' said Jameson with a bow. 'Mr Melville is in a very important meeting.'

'Important? What I have to discuss with him is very important. In fact, its urgent, Jameson,' she insisted. 'Who is he meeting with?'

'Mr Imrie of the Coal Company, Miss. Mr Stone and the lawyers are there too.' Jameson lifted one eyebrow to emphasise the importance of those in attendance.

'Oh, alright. I get the message,' she replied. 'Be a good man, ask the kitchen to fetch me up something, will you? I'm famished. Missed luncheon because Miss Fraser fell off her horse.'

Jameson departed in his usual silent fashion.

'I'll be in the drawing room,' she called out, watching him disappear down the passageway into the old house. She stared after him, wondering if he was capable of walking like normal human beings. He seemed to glide off silently across the floor into the gloom. She shuddered. This business with Grant had put her on edge. She was starting to see threat and malice where there was none, even in old Jameson who had given faithful service for many years.

Phee sat in the drawing room, staring out at the beautiful view across the gardens to the west wall that held back the wilderness of the Black Moss, on the other side. The lawns were perfectly manicured to a smooth green, despite the drought of the earlier part of the summer. She was heartened that just a hint of rain could bring the parched earth back to life so quickly. The flower borders were looking splendid, a profusion of colour and scent, and the trees trained on the lattice across the south-facing wall looked certain to deliver an abundance of fruits, groundwater soaking into every fibre, dilating small green blisters into a sweet, luscious harvest.

Phee began to wonder, as she often did, what she might do with her life. Her earlier encounter with David had riled her beyond belief. Next time, she would be more prepared. She knew that she didn't want to sit around waiting for a husband. She had to have a goal in life. It wasn't enough to want something, or to not want something for that matter. She would have to make it happen. She loved horses. Perhaps she could breed horses? She loved walking on the moss. Perhaps she could study and become a naturalist, an expert on moths and butterflies? Then she could travel the world, discovering new species and new countries. She loved visiting new places. Perhaps an explorer then, like Captain Scott or Dr Livingstone? The extreme cold and frostbite facing Scott and his men didn't attract her much. But to battle against the elements and hoist the Union flag at the Pole where no man had been before, for King and country, now that was noble and heroic. Livingstone's accounts of his travels into the African

Interior had caught the imagination of a nation, for over fifty years. Taking Christianity to remote tribes who had never seen a European face, and opening up opportunities for commerce and learning, seemed worthwhile reasons for an expedition. Then there was that mill girl from Dundee, Mary Slessor, who had convinced the Mission Board to let her travel to Calabar where she preached God's Word to the tribes in their own language, and had saved twins from the savagery of sacrifice to evil spirits. What a brave and devout soul that girl must be: courageous and driven! However, that wasn't who she was. Euphemia Melville hadn't been chosen by God for missionary work in Africa. She wasn't too keen on the privations of life outside of Parkgate House or Parisian Hotels for that matter, she had to admit, a bit of a drawback for a would-be explorer. She looked around at the sumptuousness of the drawing room, so carefully redesigned and decorated on Isabelle's instruction. Phee knew she was privileged. Yet how could someone so privileged feel as restrained and restricted as she did?

When Jameson appeared with her tray, she asked him to place it out on the terrace, in the shade.

'How long do you think they'll be?' she asked him. 'In the meeting, I mean. David with the lawyers and Mr Imrie.'

Jameson looked confused. God, the man was getting past it, she decided, feeling irritable and impatient.

'They've been in there two hours already, Miss,' replied Jameson, unable to say more.

Phee guessed they were discussing leases and mineral rights and percentages for Rashiepark which were pretty important for the future income of the estate, so it might take all afternoon.

'Well, Jameson, tell my brother I need to see him about a very urgent matter as soon as the meeting's over, will you? It's very important indeed. Don't forget. I'll be here with my book waiting for him.'

Phee returned to the view, tucking into the food provided. As she quenched her thirst with some lemonade, her thoughts returned to her future. She wondered what life had been like for the devoted Mrs Livingstone. Travelling all over Africa with her husband, into the Interior, along great rivers and through forests; finding great treasures of Nature like the Victoria Falls and naming them after the queen; making love under Southern skies. Mmm, now there's a possibility! Plodding, pregnant with child after your beau into deserts or mosquito-infested swamps; giving birth under acacia trees in the heat of the mid-day sun. Hmmm, not so good. She came to her senses. She would have to find a husband to accompany to Africa and that went against what she was trying to achieve. Still, one never knew who might come along at the right time. Best not dismiss it out of hand completely, she decided.

When David found his sister, she was asleep with her head in a book out on the terrace. It was late afternoon. The sun was well over the roof of the house, lighting up the rose garden and the terrace where Phee was slumped, one side of her face fast becoming a very unbecoming shade of bright pink.

'Well, sister,' came David's voice from the depths of her dream. 'What can be so urgent? I've just spent four hours in a meeting and, frankly, I need a break.'

Phee stirred. She gave a start as the events of the day came flooding back to her. David drew up a chair beside her then flopped into it. Phee explained about old Major returning without Elizabeth and about Billy Dodds going off on Prince to find her in the woods, apparently being helped to safety by Grant.

'However, Elizabeth is very distraught about what happened,' continued Phee. 'It seems Grant actually pulled her off the horse.'

'He what?!' exclaimed David, sitting back.

'Yes. He was leading her off into the woods against her will. If Billy hadn't appeared in time and if Elizabeth hadn't called out before Grant put his hand over her mouth, God knows what would have happened to her! Something's got to be done about the man, David. I have to say, he makes my flesh creep whenever he's around.'

David stared at his sister for a moment without saying a word. The way he had seen the man look the young servants up and down came to mind. He rose from his chair then leaned forward towards Phee, his face sombre.

'Elizabeth is making a very serious accusation against this man,' he started. 'It might be best if the police were involved.'

'No!' replied Phee quickly. 'Please no, she wants it dealt with quietly if at all possible, David. You can understand that can't you? Above all, she doesn't want Richard to know.'

'She can't just go around making accusations about the man and expect to have him dealt with, without recourse to the law.'

'But thanks to Good Fortune, Elizabeth was found in time. The best the police will do is tell him off and Elizabeth's reputation will be torn to shreds by the gossips,' explained Phee. And her pious brother will keep her under lock and key forever more, she thought to herself.

'So, what do you want me to do?'

'At least investigate the matter. Do you want such a man working here on the estate? Who knows what he might do next?'

'I'll speak to Billy Dodds. I'll find Grant and confront him with Elizabeth's accusations,' David agreed, his manner one of resignation. 'What a day! Lawyers and leases and now this. Now I've to solve the case of the gamekeeper and the minister's sister.'

'Goes with the territory, I'm afraid,' replied Phee, trying to sound understanding, to make amends for their recent disagreements. 'Lord and Master of all you survey!' She laughed tentatively.

He gritted his teeth and stormed out of the room.

'Glad to see you've changed out of my riding breeches into something a bit more ladylike, sister,' said David Melville as he entered the drawing room much later, just before dinner.

Phee tried to decide if he was being belligerent or conciliatory. 'Don't start that again, brother dear,' she replied, unimpressed by his humour.

'How is Elizabeth? Have you been up to see her?'

'She's calmed down a lot,' replied Phee. 'She slept for the rest of the afternoon and is a bit brighter. I sent word to the manse that she's going to stay here for a couple of days.'

'Is she joining us for dinner, then?' asked David from his stance by the windows, his hands in his pockets as he looked out across the lawns.

'She'd rather not. I'll have something sent up.'

'I've had a word with Billy, you might be interested to hear,' David began. 'Grant was there, at the stables, when I went down. Asking after Miss Fraser, as it happens.'

'What, Grant? At the stables? The cheek of the man!'
Phee was incensed.

'I took Grant aside, interviewed him separately. Both
men confirm exactly what you told me, all bar one detail.'
He looked across at his sister who was waiting expectantly
for the punch-line. 'Both men describe a tired, hysterical
woman who was unwilling to accept help. A woman who
lashed out, screaming and shouting at Grant when he tried
to help her up off the ground.' He glanced back into the
room where his sister sat appalled by the way in which
Elizabeth was being represented. 'You should see the
scratches down Grant's face. And on his hand,' he added.

'Well, of course he'll be scratched! A woman might
scratch her assailant if she was being attacked!' Phee sat
confused for a moment. Elizabeth's account of what
happened had been perfectly clear to her.

'What detail?' she asked. 'You said both men confirmed
the story except for one detail,' Phee demanded, speaking
to her brother's back as he gazed out at the sunlit gardens.

'The one about Grant pulling her off the horse as it
galloped off. He claims he ran to catch her, to break her
fall. He was convinced she was going to do herself an
injury.' David waited for his sister's response.

'You don't believe him, do you?' she asked, confronting
him by the window. 'He tried to lead the horse off into
the woods, against her will.'

'He says he was going to show her the pens where he
breeds the game birds,' countered David. 'Apparently, they
were discussing his work. He made the offer, started to
lead the horse down the track, she suddenly became
hysterical, started screaming and the horse bolted.'

'And Billy came upon a tear-stained Elizabeth, distraught
and embarrassed after falling off the horse.' Phee took over

the story from the stable hand's point of view. 'She didn't say anything to Billy about how Grant had acted towards her. She walked with Billy out of the wood looking dazed. Billy says that when he caught up with them, he saw Grant helping Elizabeth who was upset.'

'Exactly, right,' agreed David. 'We see what we want, or what we expect to see, mostly. Don't we?'

Phee looked puzzled. 'Meaning Billy got it wrong.'

'Could apply to Elizabeth just as easily as it could to Billy,' suggested David.

'What are you trying to say, brother?' asked Phee, aghast. 'Are you suggesting that Elizabeth misinterpreted Grant's motives? That he was, in fact, being friendly? That she'd nothing to fear from that pleasant, helpful gentleman?'

'I don't know,' replied her brother. 'I wasn't there to interpret what happened. But Grant has a witness who says he saw him helping a young woman who was clearly shaken. She had come off her horse. Everyone's story coincides, more or less. It all hinges on Elizabeth's interpretation of Grant's motives, as far as I can see.'

'No, it doesn't! It hinges on who is telling the truth. It hinges on what Grant's motives were in the first place, surely?' retorted Phee. 'You're saying there is some doubt about Elizabeth's story. Why? Because she's a woman and women, according to people like you, are unreliable. They're too emotional about things. They become hysterical and don't always know what's going on round about them! And they start accusing men of trying to waylay them when, in fact, their motives have been entirely honourable!'

'Look, Phee. Elizabeth is a young woman without much experience of the world and with even less confidence,' David said firmly. 'You saw how upset she was at the garden party when the waiter bumped into her and the drinks went flying! And you said yourself, Grant gives you the creeps. But that doesn't mean he's out to do harm.'

'I cannot believe what I'm hearing,' Phee replied. 'Maybe I should persuade her to go to the police after all!'

'Listen. Do you think the police would say anything different? What would it achieve? It's her word against Grant's, and Billy's for that matter. Grant may be a slob but he has no record of doing this kind of thing, has he?' David paused, thinking. 'The best that can be done at the moment is if I instruct him not to go anywhere near Elizabeth, otherwise his job is on the line. How does that sound?'

Phee studied her brother. She asked herself if that was that the best that could be done. 'I'll have a word with Beth and see what she says,' she said eventually. 'I'll emphasise that we believe her but it's a case of her word against another and all that. I'm saying nothing to her about the possibility of her misinterpreting Grant's motives because I don't believe she did. And Richard mustn't hear any of this, agreed?'

David agreed.

The dinner gong sounded as Isabelle entered the room.

'Evening all,' she gushed, newly arrived home from a trip to Glasgow. 'What news? Have I missed anything? Nothing ever seems to happen around here.'

'Nothing to report, Isabelle, nothing at all,' David assured her.

She examined her siblings, sensing they were keeping something from her. 'Shall we go into dinner?' she asked brightly.

'Yes, let's,' said David and Phee together.

David offered his younger sister his arm. They gave each other a knowing look and the merest fragment of a smile, then walked together arm-in-arm towards the dining room.

# Chapter 27

## THE SABBATH SCHOOLS' OUTING

The summer outing of the Blackrigg Sabbath Schools was always held on the last Saturday of the school holidays, a bittersweet occasion for many of the children who attended. They looked forward to the event but not too much, as it marked the end of freedom and a quick return to the colder days of autumn, to getting out of bed on cold mornings, and to sitting once again in rows, without being allowed to speak for hours on end. Also, the summer outing of the Sabbath Schools divided the children of the community in a highly visible way: the children who took part and the children who stood by the roadside, watching their friends go off for the day.

The outing was an unusual example of the churches joining together for an event. For the rest of the year, they tended to compete for people's souls and the clergy rarely spoke to each other on a day-to-day basis. Handed down through history, divisions within the protestant faith ran deep and were maintained by each new generation that came along. Congregations tended to form on the basis of class or family tradition and incomers to the area often chose to stay away, rather than confront the dour, unspoken rejection meted out by the regular attendees. Those of other faiths, notably the Roman Catholics, made the weekly trek to the neighbouring village where a chapel had been established. The small trail of quiet devotees, making their own particular pilgrimage every Sunday, marked them as outsiders who chose to leave the village for the purpose of worship. Meanwhile, the disaffected and the disinterested chose a long lie in bed or a quiet Sunday morning of contemplation by the fire, till morning worship was over, when the churches had disgorged their congregations, and it was acceptable to be seen out and about again.

Minn and Sarah walked to Craigpark hand-in-hand, accompanied by their elder sister. Meg gave them each a hug then handed over their picnic in a paper poke before retreating to the Co-op for the messages. She waved from the opposite side of the street, telling them to enjoy themselves. The girls stood excitedly as more and more children joined the group. Girl friends from school congregated together, watching the growing group of boys who naturally assembled further along the road. Everyone looked along Main Street, eagerly awaiting the arrival of their transport.

The adult supervisors appeared one by one, checking the sky for signs of rain, even though there wasn't a cloud in the sky. It had been a most peculiar Scottish summer, they agreed. First of all, the Gala Day had been blessed with sunshine and warm weather, and now the Sabbath Schools outing to Wallace's Cave looked as if it might be similarly favoured. Miss Foulkes, ever the Presbyterian, spoke for many when she declared that they would all pay for such glorious weather at the end of the day.

'We're a' gaun tae pay for it at the end of the day,' whispered Daisy Gowans who hung on her teacher's every word.

'Pay for whit?' whispered back Pansy, Minn and Sarah all at once.

'The guid weather, of coorse,' replied Daisy.

'Why?' asked Sarah, perplexed.

'Cause we're enjoyin' it,' said Pansy wisely.

'It's just how the auld fowk say things ay turn oot,' explained Minn brightly. 'Ye ken how it is in Scotland, guid weather ay turns tae bad?'

'An' yin day yer happy, the next day yer sad. It's hoo life ay turns oot,' continued Daisy who was twelve going on seventy.

Sarah looked up at the clear, blue sky. 'It's a braw day. Best enjoy it while we can, then,' she said with a broad smile, casting off the shadow that the doom-laden words threatened to cast over a day that held so much promise.

Minn hugged her sister, laughing to let her know that it was alright to enjoy herself. In the excitement of the occasion, the dour words of wisdom, handed down the generations to keep everyone in line, were soon tucked away for another time. When a succession of small stones rained on them from the direction of the boys, the girls threw them back at the perpetrators: Rob and Sandy, Bert and Dan. They were immediately chastised by the teachers for behaviour unbecoming of young ladies. Sarah stood open-mouthed as the boys got off scot-free.

Richard Fraser, the incumbent chairman of the Sabbath Schools Outing Committee, paced up and down, looking at his pocket watch then surveying the empty street for transport by turns. Local farmers had been encouraged to donate the use of a horse and cart and the services of a horseman for the day. It was a lot to ask at this time of year when there was so much work to be done in the fields. But they were five minutes late! Why, oh why, did the committee vote for a local trip this year, he asked himself, anxious that everything go to plan. Last year's visit by train to Aberdour had been very enjoyable, although he had to admit, numbers had been much reduced because of the cost.

He looked along the lines of children, pleased to note the large number present from his own church, comparing very favourably with attendance from the other denominations. A couple of teachers had called off at the last minute but his sister and her friend, Phee Melville, were there reliable as ever.

Elizabeth had been very quiet and subdued over the past weeks, he reflected. She seemed to take his criticism of her attendance at the dance earlier in the summer very badly but it was for her own good, he was sure. Then there was their argument after her visit to Queensferry with the Melvilles. He thought that she had been looking brighter afterwards, that their spat had somehow cleared the air, then came a dip in her mood again. The few days spent along at Parkgate House hadn't cheered her up at all. In fact, she seemed to return to the manse more downcast than ever. Perhaps today would bring back the old Elizabeth. She had such a way with children, always brightening in their company. And Phee Melville was an attentive friend whom his sister had grown very fond of, he admitted with reluctance. Unfortunately, there was an indifference about the young woman he couldn't warm to at all.

A cheer from the massed ranks of the children soon indicated that transport was in view, bringing broad smiles to everyone's faces. Six hay carts festooned with colourful flags and pulled by workhorses made a wonderful sight as they arrived from different directions to line up by the roadside. Children, picnic hampers and sports equipment were loaded swiftly. Once the adult helpers were distributed around to maintain order, the procession was soon ready to depart. Impatient to be off, everyone strained to see what was causing the fuss up ahead, delaying the start. They witnessed an indignant Rev Fraser having to pull rank and eject a lady teacher from the seat up front on the leading cart, much to her embarrassment. As soon as he had established himself in pride of place beside the driver, he gave the command to proceed with a flourish of his outstretched hand, accepting the cheers from behind as thanks for all of his hard work in organising the day.

Minn loved the smell of the hay that lingered in the cart, and the sight and sound and the smell of the horse as he tramped along through Stoneyrigg. The wind in her hair, the creaking of the leather, the clinking chains of the harness and the gentle up and down motion of the cart rolling along the dusty road, combined to generate a joy at being alive in the world on such a fine day. She waved to everyone who came out onto the street, to her friends who didn't attend the Sabbath School, to Sadie Healy who was RC, and to the dejected looking Jim and John whose father didn't let them go to church. Geordie Broadley and his mother got a special wave. In fact, Minn had to be told to sit down by Miss Fraser, in case she fell off and hurt herself. Geordie gazed up adoringly into Minn's eyes. She had spent a lot of time with him over the summer, reading to him, playing marbles in the street on days when he was feeling stronger. It gave Ellen time to walk to the Co-op to buy her groceries, to enjoy adult company, and visit Peggy Duncan for a blether whilst she helped her out with some housework. Ellen gave Minn a special smile.

The procession of carts soon left the village, heading east past fields of grazing cattle behind dry stone dykes or hedgerows covered in ripening berries; over the Red Burn bridge and the railway bridge that crossed the line to Allerbank. People came out onto the main street in Rowanhill and waved back as the carts ambled along at a steady pace. It was such a happy and unexpected spectacle, that it roused a smile in those not normally disposed to displays of emotion. Old women wearing the black weeds of widowhood and bent from a long life of toil, bid the merrymakers *God speed*. Customers and shopkeepers alike, emerged from under the shade of red and white awnings, to return the cheers of the children in mutual celebration of their special day. The bartender of the Gothenburg, already dressed in his white apron in expectation of a busy Saturday afternoon, waved his dish towel and laughing heartily. The Rev Fraser recoiled at what he viewed as a den of iniquity, regardless of its role in the temperance movement, and social improvement more widely. He ordered the lead driver to make haste whilst teachers warned their charges to hold on tight as the horses were manoeuvred carefully around the corner at The Cross then down the steep hill of the drove road towards Linlithgow.

Occasional patches of coppiced woodlands and wide pastures gave way in places to quarries and cottages. Workers taking a break from their tasks leaned against a dyke to smoke their pipes and share the news of the day. They raised a hand in salutation. People labouring in the fields, with horses or sickles or pitch forks, took time to mop their brows and acknowledge the passing parade of cheerful day trippers. A steam train heading north tooted as it puffed by. On one side of the road, the high towers of Bridgecastle projected upwards above tall trees planted to please the eye whilst, on the other side, the Bathgate Hills stood stark against the sky, stripped of their woodland to fuel industry that had brought prosperity to some and hard work to others. Only the ancient settlement of Torphichen retained a collar of protective cover that held back the worst of the winds on stormy days. At the sharp turn onto the Westfield road, progress slowed down and came to a standstill. The first horse slowly led the way up the farm road to Crawhill followed by the others, rocking from side to side on the stony, rutted track. Those in the know pointed to where the river snaked through the trees below – somewhere down there was Wallace's Cave! Eager faces gazed around at their destination, hardly able to contain their excitement.

The workhorses waited patiently in line to enter the farm yard where they would have their precious cargo of children unloaded by the men ready to assist. Elizabeth told the children on her cart to wait and stay seated until it was their turn.

'Here we are,' she said as the cart finally moved into place, pulled gently by a large black and white Clydesdale, clip-clopping onto the cobbled yard.

'Woah lass, Woah up!' said a deep voice, commanding the horse to a standstill. 'Steady lass, steady.'

A man made his way around the high side of the cart where he unhooked the tailgate at the back.

'Be careful. Take your time,' called Elizabeth as the older children started to spill out of the cart, ready to catch their younger brothers and sisters. 'Watch you don't fall.'

'One at a time, please,' said the man, his voice kind and very familiar.

Elizabeth looked up, surprised to see Neil Tennant standing with a small child in his arms, smiling broadly back at her. No one smiles like him, she thought. He held out his hand towards her. 'Miss Fraser, allow me to assist.'

Speechless, Elizabeth held out her hand and Neil took it in his. Memories of the evening at the dance came flooding back, when he had birled her round the dance floor, catching her when she came back to him from another dancer, smiling broadly with that same happy smile that lit up his dark eyes. For all of their dashing good looks and impeccable manners, not one of the naval officers at the garden party had been able to dance like Neil Tennant.

'Mr Tennant,' she said eventually, as if wakening from a dream.

He took her other hand, looked straight into her eyes. 'The very same,' he replied.

As Elizabeth poised on the end of the cart, ready to make the jump, he reached up and clasped her firmly round the waist. She held her bonnet in place, one hand on her head, allowing him to steady her as she jumped onto the ground.

'Run along, run along,' she said quickly to the small group of girls observing the scene. 'Follow Miss Melville into the bottom field,' she ordered, pointing towards a gate where a line of children was filing through. 'I'll bring the hamper with Mr Tennant.'

Daisy, Minn and Pansy loitered a little, convinced they were seeing something illicit – and appealing – take place before their eyes.

'Come oan, git aff wi' ye,' said Neil, clapping his hands to get a reaction. The girls ran off giggling, sharing the well-known joke.

'Dae ye get it, Sarah?' asked Minn as they ran away giggling. 'Come OAN, git AFF! Aye? Och, niver mind!'

'You turn up in the strangest of places, Mr Tennant,' Elizabeth said once they were alone. Neil slid the hamper off the back of the cart, held it in front of him with strong arms.

'Just a coincidence, Miss Fraser,' replied Neil. 'I've been here at Crawhill daein some work for them these past twa days. Just a coincidence,' he laughed.

'Of course it is. A coincidence, of course,' replied Elizabeth, a little embarrassed that he should take her remark as alluding to anything other than that, a coincidence. But God works in mysterious ways, she said to herself.

They walked together towards the middle of the bottom field where everyone else was congregating. Her bonnet provided welcome shade from the bright sunshine and her skirt swished against the summer flowers in the meadow grass. She tried not to smile too broadly and give herself away. Phee saw them first and greeted Neil cordially. She would have a word with her friend later; quiz her about where on earth she had been hiding Mr Tennant on the trip over from Blackrigg.

'Just put the hamper down, my man,' said Richard Fraser in a booming voice, never one to miss a chance to appear in command. He looked at his sister's beaming smile, then quickly back at the workman with her, recognising him in an instant.

'That'll be all, thank you,' he said, dismissing him. 'The farm hands are not expected to stay with the party,' he added witheringly.

Neil turned his back on the fatuous Mr Fraser and faced Elizabeth. He bowed his head of thick dark hair, giving her another of his delicious smiles.

She nodded back, embarrassed for him and for herself. She followed him with her eyes as he walked back up the field to the steading in long strides.

Her brother observed her closely.

The adults surveyed the park they had been allocated for sports. The bottom field, as it was called, would catch the sun for much of the day but it sloped steeply down to the river, bordered by a long fringe of trees. It was decided that the field was far too precipitous for games and the Rev Fraser let everyone know how disappointed he was that the landowner hadn't provided a flat site. His communication had expressly requested a site suitable for sporting activities. The Duncan boys suggested trying the meadow on the far side of the river. After a comparatively dry summer, it might be suitable for games, they reckoned. They had been to Wallace's Cave before with their father and knew the area well.

As chairman of the Outing Committee, Rev Fraser said he should scout on behalf of the party but as soon as he made a move, a tide of children swept down the hill like a hundred lemmings, charging towards certain doom. No amount of shouting on his part could stop them. The adults had no choice but to follow on, treated to the delightful sight of the minister hoarsely calling for attention whilst running gamely after his charges as they disappeared into the trees. No one could criticise him for not taking his responsibilities very seriously indeed.

After the brightness of the bottom field, the wooded glade that held the River Avon in its grasp was cool and shaded. A rickety bridge of wood spanned the stream, leading to an open meadow on the opposite side. A steep river terrace bordered the wide expanse of flat land, for the most part closely cropped like a lawn by grazing livestock but presently unoccupied. Only a small group of cattle browsed further downstream, close to the water, unperturbed by the tumult that had descended on their quiet space. And judging by the number of girls already sitting on the ground, the meadow was dry enough for picnicking.

Mr Smith and Mr Brown from the other churches present were tasked with organising some games and several of the female teachers dutifully joined them to help out. Rev Fraser fanned himself with his straw hat as he assembled the small stool he had brought with him. He sat with his arms folded, content that the day was at last going well.

Phee and Elizabeth checked the hampers to ensure there was adequate food for the adults. The children had been instructed to bring their own.

'Ooops,' said Phee. 'I think we've forgotten something.' She lifted napkins and cups. She found the cakes to surprise the children with later in the day but not the refreshments. Elizabeth looked up puzzled. 'The cups are here but there's no lemonade,' said Phee. 'Weren't we supposed to provide refreshments to prevent spillages and breakages in the carts?' she reminded her.

'There were two crates by the roadside when we waited at Craigpark,' said Elizabeth. 'Have we left them behind?'

'I hope not,' replied Phee. 'Perhaps they're up at the farm. If they're not we'll need some water or the children will be thirsty.'

Phee looked at Elizabeth and Elizabeth looked at Phee. 'Richard!' called Phee.

The minister looked in her direction from his seat in the shade of an old ash tree.

'I'm just going up to Crawhill! Up to the farm,' she indicated with her hand. 'Seems we may have left the drinks behind! Back soon!'

Elizabeth stared after her friend who was beckoning her to follow as she crossed the bridge. She glanced back at her brother to find him engrossed in a game of cricket, now in full swing. He sat dressed in a white cotton jacket with his arms folded, a straw hat shielding his eyes from the sun, with all the look of a colonial surveying the natives. She picked up her skirts then raced after Phee. They giggled conspiratorially, hurrying along the path through the trees to the gate that led into the bottom field.

'You go,' Elizabeth said half way up the slope, suddenly stopping to catch her breath. Phee was faster, a little ahead.

'Come on, Beth,' she replied looking back, studying her friend's face. 'Neil Tennant's up there and you'll be down there!' But Elizabeth had that determined look, the one that said she was dealing with some deep inner turmoil; the one that almost stopped them from going to the dance; the same one she had on her face when she returned from her encounter with Grant in the woods.

'No,' Elizabeth said, emphatically. 'I'm here to help with the children. I'll go back and supervise.' She turned away.

'I'll go then,' called Phee, knowing there was no point arguing. 'I'll be as quick as I can.' She started swiftly up the steep slope. That poor girl, she thought of her friend, a slave to her conscience and to duty.

Phee found the farmyard, now crowded with abandoned hay carts and swallows that swooped back and forward, in and out of their nests of mud tucked under the eaves. The horses, unhitched from the carts, stood grazing in a small paddock for the afternoon. Their ears twitched and their tails swished off the flies as they munched on sweet grass. She looked around, located the crates of lemonade stacked in the shade but the place seemed deserted. The farmhouse was an obvious place to seek assistance but it was the help of one man she really wanted. The sound of laughter and conversation led her behind the byre. She ventured through a narrow alleyway between the buildings and peeked round the corner.

Neil sat outside the bothy, talking with several young men and women of a similar age. A young girl held out a shallow basket full of jam sandwiches and the company helped themselves. Another poured tea from a tinny into chipped cups laid out on a rustic table. Neil removed the scarlet cloth from around his neck, wiped his brow with it. The stains and sweat of hard work, in the fields and around the steading, showed on everyone. One of the men took up a fiddle from its place beside the bench then drew the bow across the strings ready to play a tune. Neil drew his fingers through his dark hair, leaned an elbow on the table, turning to converse with his companions.

'Can we help ye, Miss?' asked the girl with the tinny when she noticed the smartly dressed lady standing by. Everyone looked up.

'I'm so sorry,' replied Phee. 'I didn't want to disturb you. You're having your meal.'

They stared in her direction.

'Dae ye need a hand wi' somethin', Miss Melville?' asked Neil. 'Can I be of assistance?' He put up his hand to shield his eyes from the sun.

One of the lads looked up; a worn cloth cap sitting back on his head signalled he was off duty. 'Is it thon crates o' ginger? I meant tae bring them doon when I saw them an' I forgot.'

'Ginger? Oh, yes, it is… the ginger… as a matter of fact,' said Phee shyly. She wasn't someone who was normally lost for words. 'Could someone help me carry them down to the riverside? No, don't get up,' she begged, 'When you're ready of course.'

'Certainly, Miss Melville,' replied Neil. 'Come and have a seat while I have ma tea. Then I'll see to your crates.'

Phee hesitated. It wasn't what she was used to: sitting with ploughmen and serving girls in the sun, talking about horses, telling tall tales of what they got up to on Saturday nights, and discussing the best tunes for dancing. She didn't want to intrude on the happy gathering but the offer to join it was inviting. Phee overcame her reticence, made her way to the place on the bench made vacant by a red-haired lad who duly perched on the table. For the first time in her life, she felt awkward in her own skin. In her expensive hat, she stuck out like a sore thumb amidst the ordinary working attire of everyone else. She fiddled with the locket of gold that hung round her neck, wishing it would disappear.

'I'm sorry to disturb your luncheon,' she offered awkwardly.

'Nae problem, Miss. This isnae oor denner,' said the fiddler, correcting her terminology. 'We had oor denner ages past. We've been up since the crack o' dawn, ye ken,' he explained. 'This is oor tea. Maist days we'd hae it in the fields but we were nearby so here we are.'

The young girl with the basket stared in awe at Phee's dress, hypnotised by the sight of such beautiful silks, and lace too rich to grace the window of any shop she had ever seen. She held out the truckle with the remaining sandwiches.

'Would ye like a piece?' she asked.

'A piece of what?' enquired Phee.

Everybody sniggered.

'A piece oan jam,' came the reply. 'It's rasp, jist new made.'

Phee looked perplexed.

'A sandwich spread with raspberry jam, Miss Melville,' Neil explained. 'A piece is a sandwich.'

Phee declined politely. The girl with the tinny ran off for fresh tea and another cup.

'Dae ye have a favourite tune, Miss?' asked the lad with the fiddle. He held it up ready to play at her bidding.

'Gosh! I like them all! But I couldn't tell you the names, I'm afraid.' She felt out of her depth when it came to the finer points of strathspeys and reels. 'You choose, please.'

A medley of well-known tunes followed as the small audience clapped, tapping their feet in time to the music. The girl with the tinny returned to replenish everyone's cup. Phee was handed a cracked blue and white cup decorated in the willow pattern. She took it with a white gloved hand, noting the absence of milk or lemon. She drank and it tasted divine. As the conversation ebbed and flowed, Phee was content to sit in the sun and listen in.

'Are ye gonnae read the tea leaves the day, Nellie?' asked the lad with red hair who sat perched on the table.

Nellie blushed, folded her arms. Everyone joined in, encouraging Nellie to tell them their fortunes but she was not to be persuaded.

'I'll tell ye yer fortune, Davy, withoot even lookin' at yer cup,' replied Nellie, her face coming close to his own. 'Whiles, yer gonnae get a great big skelp fae a gorgeous wuman.' His guard down at the mention of a beautiful woman, Davy wasn't quick enough to evade the full force of Nellie's hand as it came flying through the air and met with the side of his head. 'Tak that, ye gormless gowk ye!'

'Whit was thon for?' he groaned, nursing his head with one hand whilst defending himself against another onslaught with the other. 'Ach, I can tell ye've a richt passion for me,

NellieTamson! Dinnae haud back!' said the brave Davy provocatively.

Amidst the laughter and another slap at the poor lad, Nellie announced that she had already read their tea leaves many times before. Their fortunes couldn't have changed that much since the last time.

'Whit aboot Neil?' asked the girl who had brought the tea. 'An' Miss Euphemia here,' she added giving Phee her Sunday name. 'They havnae had their fortune telt.'

Neil caught Phee's eye with a smile.

Nellie relented, taking Neil's cup in both hands. She looked up at him several times before speaking. 'There's a lot o' talk,' she said after a while. She stared at him, her face serious. 'A lot o' talk, Neil, tak heed,' but she gave no further information. That was as much as she could tell him on the subject, she said. She turned the cup carefully in her hands, screwing up her eyes as if making sense of the patterns and shapes in the leaves. 'An' there's a journey,' she said at last. 'Yer gaun somewhaur faur awa', Neil. Faur awa' an' soon tae.' She put the cup down.

'Aye, thon'll be the road back tae Blackrigg,' laughed Davy. He got another slap for his cheek from the fortune teller.

Davy placed Phee's cup in front of Nellie who took it reluctantly. Everyone waited patiently for her pronouncement.

'It's no awfy clear, Miss,' said Nellie eventually. She pushed the cup away and looked from Phee to Neil and then back again. She took the cup back after much persuasion from the female members of the group. 'Ye've a secret.' She looked Phee in the eye then back into the cup. 'Ye're close tae somebody, Miss. Look efter them,' she warned.

Phee shivered slightly. 'Male or female?' she asked but the girl would not be pressed further.

Phee nodded. Her brother and Elizabeth, her friend, came to mind immediately. She could see the girl was disinclined to continue but Phee had been drawn into the game. She was intrigued, wanted to know more.

The girl who brought the tea stood up abruptly with a loud shudder. 'Richt thon's plenty! Gie me yer cups,' she demanded. 'This fortune tellin' stuff gies me the creeps. It's a load o' auld rubbish!'

Phee was disappointed but Nellie stood up to leave, letting everyone know that was the end of it, she would say nothing more.

'I hate tae brek up the pairty,' said a voice from the stack yard. 'But this isnae gettin' the work done, you lot.'

'Jist comin',' said the musician, putting down his fiddle. 'We're near feenished oor tea.' He turned to Phee. 'Thon's the gaffer, Miss,' he whispered. 'There's nae rest for the wicked, as they say.'

'No when the sun's shinin' an' there's hay tae be brocht in, oniewey,' said one of the women, retying the red and white checked scarf that covered her blonde hair.

The serving girls gathered the cups into the basket for washing. They didn't need to be told twice by the man in charge and hurried off in the direction of the house.

'Thank you, girls,' Phee called after them. 'The tea was most welcome!' I've had such a lovely time, she said to herself.

'Thanks for yer help wi' the horse, Neil,' said one of the lads as he adjusted the pieces of string round his trouser legs. 'We'll gang turn the hay in the west field noo. Are ye jist gaun hame efter ye assist Miss Melville?'

'I'll hing aboot tae help see the horses back in harness for the day trippers,' replied Neil. 'An' mebbe get a lift hame wi' them.' He looked enquiringly at Phee, hoping she had understood what he was asking.

'I'll see ye afore I go, lads.' He gave the haymakers a cheery wave as they left for the west field, hay forks and scythes at the ready.

'Well, Miss Melville,' he said, turning his attention to her. 'Yer charges'll have built up an almighty thirst by now, don't ye think?'

He led her along the small alleyway to the farmyard where the haycarts had been left, leaving her momentarily before returning with two large enamels jugs of water.

'From the dairy,' he explained. 'Cold water, freshly drawn. Some o' the bairns might prefer a drink of water.' He held out the jugs for her to take, noting her hesitation. 'Can ye manage tae haud thur a' the way doon the brae?' he enquired, assuming she was willing to do her bit. It was more of a statement than a question.

'Of course,' she said, a little taken aback. She took the water, which proved heavier than it looked. 'Yes. I'll manage,' she stated, eager to be seen as capable.

Neil manoeuvred a crate onto a shoulder, carrying the other in his free hand. He marched off down the hill taking big strides with his long legs. Phee struggled manfully behind, doing her best to keep up, working harder than she had ever done before. Apart from riding out on Prince, she couldn't remember breaking sweat, not since she had captained the school hockey team at any rate.

'Could you slow down a little?' she called after him but he gave no response. 'Excuse me young man, but are you laughing at me, Neil Tennant?'

He continued down through the grassy field.

'Yes you are. I can see you're laughing at me!' she said with pretended petulance, hardly able to stop giggling at her predicament. Good God, Phee Melville, she thought, you are such a useless entity. How ever did you get to this stage in life, hardly able to carry two jugs of water?

Rev Fraser was pleased to see the arrival of refreshments, at last. The children had finished their games for the moment and he had already fitted in a small session of hymn singing. The picnic could begin. He was less than pleased to see the young man who was helping to carry the supply of lemonade and was forced to say thank you. The minister ordered him back to his work up at the farm but the chorus of children's voices imploring Neil to stay was overwhelming. It infuriated the minister that Neil was popular with the children of the village. They were delighted when Miss Melville explained that his work on the farm was done and she had invited him to stay for the picnic. A cheer went up. And, she added, perhaps Neil could patrol the bank of the river later, if anyone wanted to go for a paddle. Neil blushed but agreed to stay. The minister stomped back to his chair.

'What took you so long?' Elizabeth asked her friend as they helped Neil to pour out lemonade and water for the thirsty multitude.

'Was it a long time?' asked Phee. 'I didn't realise.' She would keep Elizabeth guessing, tell her later about the jolly time she had spent, drinking tea outside the bothy and having her fortune told.

'I was starting to get worried about you,' continued Elizabeth.

'Nothing to worry about, Miss. Nothing at all,' Neil assured her with one of his smiles.

'Miss Fraser's been telling us about the secret messages in flowers,' said Daisy Gowans, interrupting the adults.

'Secret messages?' asked Neil with exaggerated interest. 'Now what's that about?' He lay down on his side, propped up on an elbow waiting to be told. 'With a name like yours, yer just the person to tell me, Daisy Gowans.'

Daisy blushed that such a handsome man should know her name. She pointed to the daisy chain around her neck. Daisies stood for *innocence* in the secret language that the Victorians had created, the girl explained. She pointed to the line of tall beech trees growing along the riverside then asked Neil to guess what type they were. After he had guessed correctly that they were beech trees, Daisy told him they were all the same age. That was because the Victorians had planted them because beech trees stood for *prosperity* in the secret language. Everyone would know how prosperous a family was, if they had lots of these trees on their land, she explained. The avenue of beeches leading up to Parkgate came to Neil's mind; he nodded at Daisy's remarks to show he was in agreement. She told him about ash trees standing for *greatness*, another tree often seen in the parks and gardens of the wealthy; but the yew tree meant *sadness* or *immortality* so it was often seen in graveyards. Neil nodded again. He had seen several graveyards with yew trees in them, he told her.

'Well done, Daisy. You've remembered so much of what I said,' congratulated Elizabeth, proud of her pupil.

Then Daisy explained that the secret language of flowers had come over from Europe, especially France, so that lovers could pass messages back and forward to each other without anyone knowing. She was whispering now to emphasise the covert nature of the information she was providing.

Miss Fraser interrupted, horrified. 'Daisy, dear! That's not quite what I told you!' But when all of the girls backed Daisy's version up, their teacher sank back into silence.

'Quite right girls,' said Phee, hoping for more. 'Go on, Daisy, go on.'

Neil tried hard not to laugh. He kept a straight face, encouraging the girl to continue the lesson.

Elizabeth sat blushing.

'You see this big daisy?' asked the young girl of Neil. She selected a large bloom with many white petals around a bright yellow centre, on a long stem.

'Aye, that's a marguerite or a gowan dependin' on where yer frae,' answered Neil, sounding quite fascinated.

'It says *Dost thou love me?*.' She used a very affected accent to emphasise her point.

'Look!' said Minn holding up the flower. 'He loves me, he loves me not, he loves me,' she said as she removed one petal at a time.

'I believe I've heard that rhyme afore noo,' said Neil, catching their teacher's eye.

Daisy held up a small blue flower that Neil knew to be speedwell. 'It means *fidelity*,' she told him, nodding wisely. Neil nodded back to show he was taking it all in. 'And this?' She gave him a long strand of honeysuckle but he could not guess its meaning. '*The bonds of love!*' She swooned backwards, quite overcome with excitement and intrigue.

Neil made to get up. 'I'm thinkin' I'd better leave you lassies tae yer blethers,' he said, laughing. 'This is clearly no place for a man.' He excused himself to the ladies. The girls giggled as they watched him join a large group of boys. One of the other ministers shook his hand and Neil settled down beside him.

'Beth! Whatever have you been teaching these young girls?' Phee asked after Neil had left the group. 'I'd no idea botany could be this interesting! Now what about this one?' she asked the girls, quickly picking up a jagged stem of bramble between her fingers. 'Bramble isn't it? Too late for the flowers, they've turned to fruits.'

'*Envy*, Miss Melville,' said Sarah. 'It's a pretty floo'er in the spring but its meanin' isnae verra nice.'

Phee had to agree. The girls continued to regale her with their new knowledge. Bindweed for *humility* and hazel for *reconciliation*, they explained; the thistle for *harshness* and the nettle for *cruelty*.

'Well, I can quite understand how those meanings came about,' she ventured, carefully picking up the thistle and the nettle from the array of botanical specimens spread out on the grass. 'Ouch!' she feigned making the girls laugh.

'This is whit ye need, Miss,' said Daisy, offering her a dock leaf. 'It means *patience* an' ye rub it oan the nettle sting tae tak awa' the pain.'

'Ah, and you need patience while it works its medicinal magic, yes?' Phee held up a sprig of hawthorn with its cluster of green berries that already showed signs of turning red. 'Its flower comes out in late spring, doesn't it?'

'Aye,' said Pansy. 'It's the mayfloo'er and it means *hope*. Mebbe fowk hope for a guid summer when they see it!'

'Ne'er cast a cloot till may is oot!' recited Sarah.

'Don't throw out a cloth till the month of May is passed?' suggested Phee, puzzled. The girls were astounded that she didn't know what the old proverb meant.

'Miss Melville!' said Sarah, 'It's aboot when tae tak aff yer woolly simmit an' it's naethin at a' tae dae wi' the month o' May. It means hing oan till the floo'er comes oan the hawthorn, Miss.'

Phee looked at Elizabeth for confirmation. She nodded

'Jolly good advice then!' agreed Phee. She couldn't help giggling at this wonderful, innocent and earnest girl.

'Mebbe Miss Melville disnae need tae pit oan a woolly simmit up at the Big Hoose, richt enough,' ventured Sarah. Minn dunted her sister for her cheek but it had been a remark made in all sincerity. 'Weel, it'll be warm a' the time up there,' said Sarah, feeling the need to explain herself.

Phee smiled to show that no offence had been taken. Perhaps living up at the Big House, we Melvilles have lost a lot of very useful knowledge, she decided. A privileged life had its sacrifices. She pictured the group of farm workers enjoying a simple meal together up at Crawhill, outside the bothy where the lads slept during their term on the farm; a mattress of chaff on a wooden platform and a kist to keep their meal in; four stone walls and a roof to keep out the worst of the summer weather. No maids or bone china cups for them; no silver tongs for the sugar bowl or oil paintings of disapproving ancestors watching your every move, expecting a good marriage into another respectable family. No formal dinners and assemblies with the latest fashions and impeccable manners on show. Instead, the sound of the fiddle playing tunes handed down through the generations, tunes that spoke of sadness and loss and the sheer joy of living, celebrating the big occasions like weddings or the brief happiness of a jig with a nice lad on a Saturday night, a brief respite from the long days of toil in the fields or in the house.

The girls had moved away and were searching out wild flowers. They made flower chains with gowans and red poppies, scabious and burdock. They decorated each other's hair with wreaths of innocent daisies and purple vetch. When Miss Foulkes tutted her disapproval at such frivolous ornamentation, Phee praised the girls loudly for both their beauty and their artistry. She encouraged the girls to decorate Miss Foulkes' straw bonnet but the schoolteacher strode off petulantly, unimpressed by the notion.

'Let's have a look at Wallace's Cave everyone,' she suggested instead, in clipped tones, already practising for another term in the classroom. 'A little history lesson is overdue.' She called on Mr Smith, as a renowned expert on Scottish History, to lead on. A stream of children followed him back over the bridge, into the shade of the tall trees, eager to hear the tale of how the great Scottish patriot, William Wallace, had come to this place a very long time ago.

# Chapter 28

## THE LESSONS OF HISTORY

Jim and John sat at the table in the middle of the day, waiting for Mary Birse to dish up the simple dinner she had prepared. At the weekend, meals reverted to the traditional order of rural life, subverted on work days to suit the shift patterns and demands of the mining industry. On weekdays, the mid-day meal was a *piece*, usually a thin smear of jam on white bread, or cheese if working hours and wages were regular and families could afford it. Dinner was eaten later in the day, on return from the pit or from school.

John watched his mother stir the pot of brose on the fire, his mouth watering as he waited. His stomach grumbled, sounding out the hunger he always felt. He was growing fast; there wasn't an ounce of fat anywhere to be seen on his skinny form. A skelp across his head, delivered from behind, indicated Alex's annoyance.

'Stoap yer belly rumblin',' he snarled. 'I can haurdly read ma paper! An' stoap watchin' yer mither, ye look like yer aboot tae bite aff her haun, ye gutsie midden ye.' Alex added another swipe for good measure. 'Ye can haurdly wait tae git it ower yer thrapple.' He added a loud *tut* for good measure.

When John's stomach rumbled yet again, Alex hit him on the head with his paper. It tore across the middle to his great annoyance. He held it up for John to see. 'Look whit ye've made me dae,' he growled.

John knew it was pointless to say anything in either protest or defence. It just riled the man further and John would come off worst. He kept his mouth shut, his head bowed. He was glad when Jim started to talk about the Sabbath School outing to Wallace's Cave. The boys had been speaking to Rob and Sandy who had been excited at the prospect of a trip in a haycart pulled by a fine horse and a day by the river at a place of adventure and legend. Together, they had discussed the tale of William Wallace many times; how he had escaped from the rout by the English army at the Battle of Falkirk and taken shelter in the cave beside the River Avon until it was safe to make the journey to Perth. The Duncan boys had visited the cave in the past with their father. He often took them on rambles through the countryside, telling them the names of the birds and the trees, reciting the stories and legends of places they visited. They'd said it had been a long walk to Wallace's Cave but it had been worth it to see the place and hear the tale.

'The cave's concealed in the trees, Jim. Ye cannae see it doon by the Avon an' it's got twa ways in,' John reminded his brother. 'Wallace an' his best captains kept watch for the enemy comin' alang the riverside. If they saw them comin', they could jist nip oot the ither way an' escape up the burn.'

Jim had already heard his brother retell the tale several times but, as usual, he indulged John's imagination and interest in the past since Jim's own delight in the telling of ghost stories was tolerated in return. John loved to tell tales from Scottish History, about the exploits of Bruce and Wallace, about the battles won and lost by the Stuart kings to keep Scotland free from English tyranny. He liked to imagine what it was like to put down the tools of everyday life to follow the king on his proud stallion; walking to the site of battle with hundreds of others, with Rob and Sandy and Jim beside him just like in the Gala Day parade, waving goodbye to his proud mother who would stand wiping away her tears beside Mrs Duncan, Mrs Broadley, and the other mothers. All the girls would line the route, admiring the brave sons of Scotland, marching off to send the invading army back to where it came from. To wield a pike or a bow, to kill the enemy for glory and freedom, that surely was a fine thing, he decided.

'I hope ye dinnae think for yin minute, that thon William Wallace had oniebody bar his ain interests at heart,' said Alex, interrupting John's imaginings.

John said nothing. He had been told often enough to *shut his geggie*, so he had learned to keep his mouth shut. Whatever he said was wrong, and it usually brought another blow.

'They're a' the same, ye ken,' Alex continued, determined to destroy the boys' enjoyment. They were old enough to hear the truth about life, Alex decided, and that included putting them right about myths and nonsense told as historical fact.

The twins listened but said nothing. They were about to get a lecture and they knew it.

'His kind were efter power for thursels an' fowk like you twa were jist cannon fodder, or whitever the weapon o' the day was,' he said with feeling. 'Ye would jist be there tae mak up the numbers; left for deed on a bloody field wi' women an' wee bairns greetin' at hame, waitin' for ye; left tae git oan wi' it or starve.' Alex glared at the twins to ensure he was having an impact. 'Thon's the real story o' yer Scotch History,' he continued. 'An' the sooner the workin' man sterts tae tak power intae his ain hauns the better.' He held up his work-weary hands with their calluses and scrapes till he was sure the twins had had a good look at them. 'Else history'll jist keep repeatin' itsel ower and ower and ower again.' He paused before pointing at the boys with his spoon. 'Yous mark ma words.'

John was learning to close his mind when he heard Alex rant. When he sensed the release of more venom, he shut off the sound as best he could. He recognised the cynical worm of disillusionment that could find its way into his heart and crush his spirit. He had felt it in the past, as it burrowed into his gut and gripped hard. He had felt the life blood of youth being squeezed out of him by the man's anger. He tried his best to block the words out; though it was hard not to hear what had been said about his hero, William Wallace, a man who had made a stand for good against evil, justice against tyranny. That's what the teacher had told him so it had to be the truth. Once his father's words were out though, they were alive in his head, battling for his understanding of what was true, chipping away at the innate optimism that got him out of bed every morning, alive to the promise of each new day.

Mary put plates of brose on the table. 'Leave the lads alane, Alex,' she told him. 'If they like tellin' the stories, there's naethin wrang wi' it. Ye're ower hard on them.'

Alex glowered at her but made no reply. The twins kept their heads down. John felt his face grow hot and his pulse quicken, the sound of his heartbeat loud in his ears. He waited for Alex to lose his temper but he didn't.

'So, the Holy Wullies are awa' for a day oot,' said Alex after a while, referring to the Sabbath Schools outing. 'Disnae seem fair that some weans are left ahint,' he went on, finding something else to complain about.

'Weel, it's for the weans that gang tae the Sabbath Schools,' explained Mary, sounding exasperated. 'The twins dinnae gang tae the church so they cannae gang oan the trip. It's you's against them gaun tae the church in the first place.'

'Haud yer wheesht, Wuman,' he ordered. 'We've been intae this afore. Ye ken whit I think aboot the kirk an its fancy weys. The rich stole God but he belongs tae us a''.'

'It's no jist for the rich,' rejoined Mary. 'Robert Duncan's lads attend, an' the Broadleys, Davy Potts' lad an' mair besides.'

'There's a Bible there on the shelf if fowk want tae read it.' Alex indicated the mantelpiece with his spoon. 'We dinnae need a buffoon like yon minister, Fraser, tellin' us whit tae think or hoo tae lead oor lives.'

John could see his father's colour rise, though his head was bowed. He watched him stuff more brose into his mouth. A spray of spit and oatmeal rained down on the table.

'We dinnae need tae be judged by yon buffoon when we've the Day o' Judgement comin' at us!' Alex pronounced after a while.

'Weel, stoap complainin' aboot them leavin' weans oot,' argued Mary. 'It was yer choice tae keep the boys awa' fae the kirk in the first place.'

It was unusual for the boys to hear their mother argue like this. They sat still, their senses peaked by her sudden rebellion.

'Organise yer ain trip for the weans that arenae awa' the day,' she challenged. 'If ye can be bothered.' A long silence followed. 'Aye, that'll be the day. Yer a' talk, Alex Birse. A' bloody talk.'

Alex ate the rest of his brose in silence, nursing his wrath. Nobody dared say a word. He wiped his plate with a piece of bread then held out his cup for tea without speaking. His wife poured the hot dark liquid from a height. He ladled in three spoonfuls of sugar, stirring vigorously; sucked up the too hot tea with a loud sook. Then he rose from the table, and taking his cap from the nail by the door, slapped it onto his head.

'I'll organise a trip for them,' he said forcefully as he opened the door. 'Thon's jist whit I'll dae!'

The window shook as the door slammed shut. They listened to the loud scrape of the nails on the soles of his tacketie boots outside on the stony road as he marched off into the distance.

'Mair brose, boys?' asked Mary, smiling. She scraped the pot clean into their plates. 'Haud up yer cups an' I'll pour the tea.'

The twins saw the twinkle in her eye when she raised her cup. They held up their cups to hers, wondering what was coming next.

'Here's tae William Wallace, boys,' she said. 'Slainte! Cheers!'


The children of the Sabbath Schools assembled on the flat ground by the river bank, crowding around Mr Smith as he assumed an advantageous point for the delivery of the story about William Wallace and the glorious defeat that had led him to hide in such hostile surroundings.

Miss Melville supervised the seating of the girls on one side of the large audience. She sent Minn and Sarah to a space on the bank where children sat comfortably with their feet on a sandy beach, only to see them usurped by Daisy and Pansy who shoved their way in to take up position beside Rob Duncan. Phee watched in amusement as Daisy rearranged the frill on her smock and ensured her ringlets dangled evenly down each side of her face. Her ribbons in place on the top of her head, Daisy gave Rob a soppy smile as she handed him a sprig of honeysuckle. Rob almost jumped out of his skin. He edged closer to the other lads, brushing off the offending flower as if it might burn or bite.

'I don't think Robert Duncan is ready for the secret language of flowers, Daisy dear,' said Phee from behind, in her most imperious voice. Then whispering in her ear, 'Best not to wear your heart on your sleeve, dear. It generally comes to nought.'

Everyone turned to witness the colour rise from the depths as Daisy blushed a bright pink.

Mr Smith waited for the children to settle down before starting his lecture about that brave and true son of Scotland, William Wallace, Guardian and defender of freedom whose struggles stood, he said, as an example to them all. His audience latched onto every word, shutting out the noise of the fast-flowing water nearby.

'Edward 1 of England had already invaded Scotland, believing he had a right to rule here,' explained Mr Smith, painting the wider picture. 'He refused to recognise Scotland as a separate nation, seeing her as simply another feudal barony to be ruled by him. The Scottish people had already had a taste of life under Edward during his first invasion. His troops had burned towns and villages and even the crops growing in the fields, leaving people to starve in the cold. The weak John Balliol, had surrendered the country to the English king,' explained Mr Smith in a sad and disappointed voice. 'No wonder they called him the Toom Tabard – *empty waistcoat*!'

A murmur of disappointment wafted around the audience, showing their distaste for the traitor with the empty coat.

'But William Wallace raised and led an army against the English at Stirling Bridge in 1297. Even though the Scots were greatly outnumbered, they were victorious and the defeated Edward was sent packing!' Mr Smith punched his enthusiasm into the air with his clenched fist. 'The Scots were canny, ye see, boys and girls. They led the mighty English army into a trap by meeting them on the other side of a bridge, picking off the great English knights as they filed across. Ahh, the canny Scot,' he continued almost thinking out loud, 'A formidable enemy when he's got *Right* on his side!'

No one cheered or even looked happy. They knew it wasn't the end of the story. It never was with Scottish history.

'But Edward was determined to have Scotland for himself and he came back for more,' continued the storyteller. 'He held a Council of War at York and the Scots nobles didn't turn up! A good excuse for a war! He invaded Scotland for a second time with a great army, raiding towns and burning people out of their homes. William Wallace, the canny Scot, knew the English were too strong to be met in all-out battle. He waited for them to weaken, and so they did. They ran out of supplies, started to fight amongst themselves.' Mr Smith surveyed his captivated audience, pausing to let hope and expectation emerge in the listeners.

'Now you might think,' he went on, 'that all should have ended happily for the Scots. But no, I'm afraid not.

The Scots suffered a great defeat at the Battle of Falkirk. That led Wallace into hiding which brought him here to this place.' He indicated the arch of rock behind him.

Andrew Brownlee put up his hand to ask a question. 'Whit happened tae the canny Scot at the Battle of Falkirk? Why did he not win then, Mr Smith?'

'A good question, boy,' said Mr Smith sounding impressed. 'They were defeated by betrayal, I'm afraid. Wallace didn't intend meeting the English at Falkirk. He was encamped there. But a traitor told Edward where Wallace was.'

Mr Smith responded to the whisperings amongst the children. 'He betrayed his own people.' He looked around the audience, communicating his disgust through piercing eyes. 'The English knights and the superior strength of the Welsh archers with their long bows, saw the Scots defeated. Many were left dead or dying on the field.'

The children sat quietly. A great sadness hung over them like a shroud.

'They fell like blossom in an orchard before the fruit has ripened, it was said,' continued Mr Smith, adding to the misery. 'Wallace fled but was captured some years later, thanks to yet another traitor, Sir John Menteith.' The story of Wallace's ultimate betrayal was well known, written forever in the placename, Lake of Menteith.

The children's heads were bowed, their faces glum. The betrayal of Wallace weighed heavily on young shoulders.

Miss Foulkes intervened to bring the tale to a conclusion. 'Do tell us what happened to William Wallace, Mr Smith. Just to finish the story for us.'

'Oh, joy!' called Phee. 'Nothing like a happy ending!'

Neither Mr Smith nor Miss Foulkes could hear Phee's comment above the rush of the river but returned her smile, glad she was enjoying the storytelling.

Mr Smith related with great relish and in great detail Wallace's bitter end, sparing the youngsters no detail of his torture and subsequent impalement at sites across the two kingdoms. Even those who knew about the great martyr's demise had never had it explained so graphically. Finally, it came to an end.

'Now, off you go everyone,' Phee said brightly to the children, hoping to change the mood in an instant. 'You can go and enjoy yourselves now!' She hugged a weeping child, telling them not to worry, it was all in the past after all. 'Have a look around then get back into the sun for some games.'

As the children wandered up and down the river and in and out of the cave, the site that had once represented hope and adventure for themselves as much as it had for the fugitive Wallace, took on the gloomy inevitability of grief and pain. No one felt like asking if they could paddle in the river. It was suddenly cold in the shade. Small groups made their way through the arch of rock, disappointed that it hadn't lived up to the cavernous sanctuary of their imaginations. They paused to examine the smooth, water worn walls, covered in moss and ferns, seeping with water even on a summer's day.

'Whit a place tae spend yer days, hunted doon like a sly fox waitin' tae flee tae anither lair quick as a flash,' commented Dan Potts, avoiding the drip of water from above.

'No much o' a cave,' said Bert, assessing its protective qualities. 'The wind would whistle through like naebody's business. I'd ask for ma money back.'

'Mebbe it was the only yin left in the shop. Or the rent was a' he could afford,' suggested Sandy in his usual droll fashion. A drip ran down the back of his neck. 'God, it's worse than Staneyrigg.'

'Aye, but no much worse,' murmured Andrew Brownlee who lived elsewhere.

Sandy heard him, gave him a thump.

'It's better than Staney in some respects,' said Andrew, expanding his point. 'Ootside cludgie,' he pointed to the river. 'But wi' built-in flush an advantage. Damp wa's but nae rats, no that we can see oniewey.' He had everyone casting a critical eye over the cave, imagining what life would have been like there. 'God, Wallace must've been desperate tae bide here!' added Andrew.

'Weel, it's still a guid place tae hide fae the enemy,' said Sandy, feeling the need to defend Wallace's choice of residence. 'Look, ye can see the enemy comin' frae a mile back.' He pointed his stick in the direction of the group of girls approaching along the path. Daisy and Pansy, Minn and Sarah, and Annie Grant at the coo's tail as usual. He looked at Rob, 'Ye can either run oot the back like a scaredy cat or staun an' fecht for freedom and honour!'

The boys assessed the situation. The sight of Daisy Gowans approaching with her ringlets and a posy of flowers brought a collective intake of breath. She had her beady eye on Rob, they could tell.

'To the death!' shouted Rob, raising his stick like a sword.

'For honour and glory!' called Bert.

'For Scotland!' shouted Rob, 'Charge, men! Charge!'

'For freedom!' called all of his companions together as they belted from the cave, yelling at the tops of their voices. They made a desperate break for the bridge to the sunny side of the river.

The girls helped each other up from the ground where several had landed. They dusted each other down, tutting all the while.

'Grow up, boys,' shouted Daisy. 'Grow up!'

# Chapter 29

## FOUNDATIONS OF THINGS TO COME

In the cool of the early evening of the Sabbath Schools outing, a large group of children of all ages had assembled at Craigpark, awaiting the return of their pals on the haycarts. One of the best things about growing up in Stoneyrigg was that there was always someone on hand to play with. The birth rate was high so children were a feature of the landscape. Women usually went through several pregnancies in their lifetime and some had as many as fourteen or fifteen children. By necessity, mothers dispatched their offspring out into the street to play from an early age knowing that the older ones would look after their younger siblings, entertain them, and keep them safe. Teenage girls would often be seen wrapped in a shawl that held a baby brother or sister, like apprentice mothers in training. Knowledge passed on, combined with a liberal dose of imagination, led to play that kept youngsters occupied for hours. It continued till either darkness fell or a mother's voice was heard calling curfew. Then the shout of resignation would go up, *'the gemm's a bogey!'* and a long trail of children could be seen wending their weary way home.

The team game of choice was football, the preserve of boys, but the absence of a ball on that particular day had been something of a drawback, thwarting attempts to get a game going. Instead, a game of hide and seek was in full flow. John Birse searched high and low for the others who hid quietly behind walls and bushes. As those who were caught joined him, the excitement of catching the diminishing number of children still hidden grew, and as each one was found, shrieks and yells rang out when they raced to get back to the den first. If the seekers were unsuccessful in this regard, those at large were rewarded with another life and the search went on. Games of hide and seek were all-inclusive and could, as on this cool evening in late summer, involve huge numbers of individuals of all ages roaming the area late into the evening, hunting down that elusive person who hadn't yet been caught. Wee Geordie was legendary for having, at the age of seven, gone home to his bed without informing the multitude looking for him, leaving them to search till after dark, by which time his brother had been in tears for fear of having lost him forever. On the evening of the Sabbath Schools outing, because of his weakened state following his illness earlier in the year, Geordie sat on a make shift seat at the side, a gleeful look on his face as he watched his friends playing. His mother had assured him it wouldn't be long before he would be back to full strength and he would be running about like the rest of them.

Eventually, there was only Jim left to find, a situation that heightened his brother's competitive streak. Jim was John's greatest rival and his best friend at one and the same time. Strategies were shared amongst the seekers who swept the area, checking the most likely nooks and crannies for the fugitive, silently creeping around corners and signalling, with exaggerated arm movements and desperate looks on their faces, for each other to go this way or that.

John crept round the back of the steading to inspect the field behind the dry-stone dyke. He made his way through the brambles towards an overgrown ruin, ravaged by nature and plundered by man, and barely recognisable as the old farmhouse it had been long ago. Sadie Healy appeared round a corner and pointed vigorously. John went left and she went right. They crept along, careful to minimise the noises made by their feet on broken slates and dried stalks in the undergrowth.

When Jim jumped out with a rumble of rock and stone underfoot, the shout went up that he was found. Dozens of children headed back to the den, like a swarm of bees intent on a honey pot. John was ahead and ran till his heart thumped in his chest and his legs ached. Jim was behind, faster and stronger. The younger brother threw himself across the dust, landing on the den first, his knees skinned and his elbow bleeding. A cheer went up, bringing a huge smile to John's face.

'John won! John won!' shouted Geordie from the sidelines. Such a victory would live long in the memory, bringing joy long after the day was over.

A large crowd gathered on the ground, breathing hard and describing to each other who they had caught or how they had found the best hiding place, if only somebody hadn't found them, of course. Rarely had John felt as good about himself as he did then but victory was its own reward. He thought it was a great feeling, lying on his back in the dirt, getting his breath back, looking up at the blue sky that went on and on, out into space forever.

Small pairs and knots of children soon rose to engage in other games: bools and chuckies for the boys; peevers or skipping for the girls. The group of boys playing bools swelled in number. Most carried one or two marbles in their pocket as a matter of course and the Birse twins were no exception. The competition to take an opponent's bool was fierce, especially for the best colours or for the big 'steelies' that looked for all the world like ball bearings from the store in the railway maintenance shed. When a prized bool was at stake, great skill and concentration were employed. To the victor the spoils and losses were keenly felt in an age when even a small sphere of glass or metal was hard to come by.

Sadie Healy had procured an old rope from the washing lines at Stoneyrigg. A long line of girls of widely varying ages and sizes assembled and stood patiently, waiting their turn to skip in and out as two of the older ones were selected to turn the rope.

'Ready?' shouted Sadie. When they shouted back that they were, she said,' Richt, caw the rope, caw!' and the singing started. They sang songs that had been passed down to them by their mothers and grannies: songs about love and longing and pieces on jam. If you jumped into the rope when the chorus of the song started up, you had to skip till the end of the refrain. Everyone got their chance to skip to the chorus. It was a chance for your friends to let the boys know who you were sweet on and no one, except the boy, ever complained. When they sang loudly that John Birse was Sadie Healy's *'boy with the tartan tie'*, he had just lost his best steelie to his brother. He put his hands over his ears as he rolled over on the ground, dying in exaggerated fashion after his friends gave him a shove. Why girls had to embarrass you like that was a mystery to him but there was something quite nice about it all the same, not that he would ever admit it to his pals.

'Here they come! Here they come!' shouted Geordie at last as the first of the carts came into view.

The children abandoned their games then lined up at the roadside to watch the line of horses approach with tired but happy day trippers in tow. They watched as the adults worked hard to maintain order and ensure safety, glad to be back and soon to be relieved of their responsibilities. Presently, friends reunited with friends made off in the direction of their respective homes in a huddle of excited voices.

'It was great! It was great!' said Sandy Duncan from on high, when he spotted the twins. 'Ye should've been there!'

Jim and John gathered around and as each of the pals joined the group, new information was added to the description of the day's events.

'Wait till we tell ye oor news,' said John, with the emphasis on *'oor'*. He was too excited to wait for the whole story of Wallace's Cave to be acted out with sticks on the battlefield of the Craigpark steading.

'Aye,' said Jim. 'Wait tae ye hear whit's happenin' the morn.' He had everyone's attention.

'We're haen a big picnic,' explained John. ''Cause the morn's the last day afore we gang back tae the school.'

'Whau's haen a big picnic?' asked Rob.

'A'body an' oniebody,' explained John. 'Oniebody that wants tae come! Ma faither's organised it for the hail village,' he said proudly.

'So whaur's this takin' place?' asked Neil Tenant as he helped his younger brother down off the nearest cart, ushering him off to the Smiddy.

'At the Meadie, Neil,' said Jim. 'In the efternin, as lang as the weather stays fair.' He examined the sky to the west. 'I hope it disnae rain.'

'Ye hae tae bring yer ain picnic,' continued John. 'There's tae be a fitba' competition, an' cricket. Will ye come, Neil?'

As he helped the last child down off the cart, something white caught Neil's eye. He reached into the empty hay cart where his brother had sat next to Miss Fraser on the way home. He retrieved a small piece of folded cotton, edged in lace. A delicate letter 'E' embroidered in white, indicated the owner. He opened it up to reveal a green stem with broad, spotted leaves and a long spike of tiny, perfect flowers: a common spotted orchid. He recognised it from the drawing she had shown him by the shieling. He turned in the direction of the church. She was watching him from a distance, her hand on top of the wide-brimmed hat that shaded her eyes. He lifted the handkerchief for her to see. She waved back. She seemed happy. Then she turned away, and walked off.

He studied the flower in its bed of lace and cotton.

'Will ye, Neil?' came an insistent voice.

'Whit did ye say?' asked Neil, as if coming back from far away.

'Will ye come tae the picnic, Neil?' pressed John. 'Last day o' the holidays,' he said persuasively.

'Aye,' said Sandy. 'Ye can be in oor team.'

'Aye, the swimming team!' offered Bert.

'Thon's an offer that's hard tae refuse,' said Neil laughing. 'I'll think aboot it.' He put the flower wrapped in the handkerchief into his waistcoat pocket for safekeeping. 'I'll mebbe come alang. We'll see.'

'Great, we'll see ye the morn,' they replied and the Staney lads took their leave, their chatter not stopping all the way along the road to the Rows.

# Chapter 30

## FOR THE SAKE OF RASHIEPARK

A large brown work horse pulling a hay cart clip-clopped his weary way along the avenue leading to the front door of Parkgate House. Sandy Scott, ploughman at Craigpark Farm, pulled on the reins, bringing his transport to a halt outside the main door of the big house. David and Isabelle Melville looked on in horror. Their younger sister gave them a cheerful wave from her place next to Sandy, perched up on the cart with its bunting, now torn, flapping in the breeze.

'Woah, boy! Good boy! Woah, Charlie,' called the ploughman. He jumped down from his seat, settled the horse with a reassuring stroke down his strong neck before holding out a helping hand to his passenger. Phee jumped lightly to the ground and readjusted her skirts.

'Thank you, Sandy,' she said, beaming. 'The children had a wonderful time. Thanks to old Charlie here and yourself, of course. Do thank the gaffer when you get back.' Phee was pleased to be able to use one of the words she had learned earlier at Crawhill. 'I know what a busy time of the year it is with the harvest starting early and everything but the outing couldn't go ahead without the farmers' goodwill.' She stroked Charlie's forehead with affection.

'I'll pass on yer thanks, Miss,' said Sandy, tipping his cap at all three Melviles before leaping back into his seat and driving Charlie and the cart back down the avenue at a fair lick.

Phee turned her attention back to her brother and sister who looked like thunder. A middle-aged couple hovered in the background.

'Mr and Mrs Imrie, our sister Euphemia,' said David by way of introduction. 'Euphemia, Mr and Mrs Imrie of the Coal Company.' He stepped aside with his hand outstretched to reveal their dinner guests, newly arrived for an evening at Parkgate House.

The couple stepped forward into the light to shake Phee's hand. 'It's a pleasure to meet you, Euphemia,' said Mr Imrie, an uncertain smile on his face. Mrs Imrie said nothing but held out a limp hand with all the enthusiasm of a cold fish. Disdainfully, she looked the younger Miss Melville up and down, noting the hay stalk in her unkempt hair.

'Do call me Phee,' she implored, trying hard not to giggle. 'All my friends do!'

There was no response. A silence followed.

'Phee helps out at the Sabbath School. It was their outing today,' explained Isabelle on her behalf. 'In hay carts,' she added, raising an eyebrow. 'Such a good cause, don't you think, Mrs Imrie?'

Mrs Imrie did not reply.

'This is our daughter, Catherine,' said her husband proudly, beckoning a shy, young woman who lurked in the shadows close to the door. 'Come, dear. Come and meet Miss Euphemia, she's about your age. How fortunate!'

Catherine Imrie held out her hand with the same lack of energy shown by her mother.

'Pleased to meet you, Catherine,' said Phee in her usual friendly manner, vigorously shaking the girl's hand. 'Please call me Phee.'

Catherine said nothing but looked away, her face a blank canvas.

'I'm sure you two will get along famously,' said Isabelle as she watched Phee greet the indifferent Miss Imrie. Isabelle quickly swept mother and daughter inside. David followed with Mr Imrie, leaving Phee to follow on.

'You don't have your hat on!' Isabelle fumed at her sister when they were alone in the hall.

Phee looked at the bonnet in her hand. 'Neither I have. Ever tried sitting on a hay cart trying to keep your hat in place, Isabelle? Impossible!'

'Don't be flippant. Your brother has spent a lot of time negotiating with Imrie over the leases on farms that look promising to him. David needs to keep on good terms to ensure the maximum amount of investment is made.'

'Jolly good,' replied Phee, a little more subdued but unimpressed.

'Until any mines start producing, there's little return for the estate beyond what the farmers pay at the moment in rent,' Isabelle went on. 'Imrie and his shareholders take all the risk. It can take years before a mine pays and, at every turn, there's the chance the shareholders will get cold feet and pull out. In which case, we lose out. Understand?'

'Not really,' replied Phee. Her elder sister removed the straw from her hair.

'The estate receives a percentage of the value of any minerals produced,' explained Isabelle. 'We need the Company to invest sufficiently, and quickly. Enough capital as is required to ensure any mining is highly productive.' She studied Phee's face to see if further explanation was necessary. 'All sorts of factors influence business decisions about the investment of capital.'

'AAAH! Like coming for dinner with the local gentry,' said Phee whispering, pretending that the penny had finally dropped. 'And being able to call on the laird for shooting and fishing parties, to entertain potential shareholders.' She rolled her eyes in her head feigning boredom.

'Exactly, little sister,' continued Isabelle. 'And the laird's sister cultivating her friendship with Miss Frosty Face in there would help.' She pointed at the drawing room door, behind which the Imries and their daughter sat being charmed by David.'

'No! Oh, no! Spend time with her?' replied Phee. 'Yuch! She has all the personality of a dead rat!'

'Just play the game, Phee,' said Isabelle in her most superior voice. 'Just play the game. Now go and tidy yourself up. Dinner's in twenty minutes.'

Dinner was less of an ordeal than Phee had imagined. The factor, Roger Stone, was present to assist David in the charm offensive against the wealthy Mr Imrie, and mother and daughter seemed to thaw at the sight of Parkgate's impressive dining room, splendidly arrayed in the family silver and glass. By the time the jugged hare was being served, Mrs Imrie had quaffed enough claret to warm even the coldest heart, and the faintest of smiles was discernible on Catherine Imrie's face by the end of the lemon syllabub.

After dinner, the men moved onto the terrace with port and cigars whilst the ladies remained inside the drawing room with coffee and sweetmeats, for a game of cards. In spite of the considerable quantity of alcohol she had consumed, no one could match Mrs Imrie's talent for card playing and the foursome soon made their way through the entire spectrum of games, without finding her weak spot. Phee decided that alcohol was the best means of attack and made Mrs Imrie an offer she could not refuse. Isabelle followed her sister to the dresser where she began pouring a large glass of port.

'Good, Lord,' said Isabelle. 'She's been soaking it up like a sponge all evening. If alcohol's the key to Imrie's money, we've got it made.'

When Phee added a splash more port with a snigger, Mrs Imrie's face lit up at her hosts' generosity. They returned to a game of whist that was not turning out at all well for the Melvilles.

Outside on the terrace, the men were enjoying an animated discussion of the economic realities of the age, voicing their concerns about the government's handling of fiscal matters, especially relating to the taxing of land. Fists were brought down on the table and voices were raised in protest, though all three were in agreement. The ramifications of higher taxes were of major concern to the Laird of Rashiepark and his factor, already dealing with the repercussions of skilled people leaving the land in favour of employment in industry. A land tax could only make things worse for the rural economy, they believed. The free trade issue had Mr Imrie up in arms, castigating the Germans and their burgeoning industrial sector for undermining the British state with their ungentlemanly practices. British industry was being threatened to extinction, he explained, by undercutting the price of British goods with cheap imports from German manufactories that were not subject to tariffs. At the same time, Germany slapped massive import taxes on British exports, effectively removing the main market for British goods abroad.

'Of course, any practice that impacts adversely on manufacturing is going to reduce the demand for fuel,' continued Mr Imrie looking extremely grave. 'As the owner of twelve coal mines that makes me extremely unhappy.' He raised an eyebrow at his host. 'As it should concern you, David. The prospects for the extension of mining onto your estate are tied to the fortunes of the wider national and, indeed, international economy.'

'It's not just Germany, though, is it? France and Belgium are as bad,' David pointed out. 'Cheap imported coal from the United States is a concern is it not? Even the Russians are at it, with their attitude towards Scotch herring. The herring ports could be completely sunk with the loss of such a big market as Russia, no?'

Imrie nodded sagely, agreeing but saving much of his anger for Germany.

'Hopefully, the government will see sense sooner rather than later,' interrupted Stone, sensing the discussion, now focusing on fish, had veered too far away from anything connected directly to Rashiepark. 'Eventually, the Liberals will be forced to recognise who puts bread on the tables of every family in Britain one way or another: the landowners and the entrepreneurs, of course.' He caught Imrie's eye. 'And policies will be enacted for all our best interests.'

'Here, here,' agreed Melville and Imrie together.

'Or a government of more favourable hue will be elected,' added Imrie. 'Now tell me about this estate of yours. I've a notion for a spot of shooting now that the season's underway.'

Laird and factor happily regaled him with a list of Rashiepark's attractions, telling tall tales of the biggest trout caught in the Black Loch, and the greatest number of game birds shot in a single shoot.

'We've a fine gillie looking after the lochs and burns, Mr Imrie, and our head gamekeeper,' explained Stone, 'keeps the estate well stocked with game. A day's shooting on Rashiepark never disappoints.'

'Speaking of our gamekeeper, Mr Imrie,' interrupted David, 'he's had a spot of bother over the summer from some of the locals, we assume men employed in the mines or thereabouts.'

'What sort of bother? What do you mean?'

'Actually, he was rather badly beaten up one evening earlier in the summer. And he reports problems with poaching quite frequently. There have been a couple of arrests and, yes, they were miners from Stoneyrigg.' Imrie looked thoughtful as he listened intently to his host. 'There's also been a bit of trouble around the estate. You could call it a crime wave compared with what it was like here in my father's day.'

'Crime wave?' laughed Imrie.

'Break-ins at farms, wash houses, isolated cottages and so on. And just last week one of the tenants came upon a fire in his hay barn just in time to put it out and save half his winter store from going up in smoke.'

'Sounds very serious. I hope you're not suggesting I bear any responsibility here, sir. Remember, I'm their employer, not their keeper. Sounds like a matter for the police.'

'The police have been involved, for some time in fact. Constable MacKay has been in touch frequently, keeping an eye on the situation and reporting back to me. We had a bit of a problem with large numbers of the men congregating in the street. Quite intimidating for the rest of the community, I have to say.'

'Sounds like you're doing what you can then.'

'Wouldn't like to get on the wrong side of the community as a whole though,' explained David, opening up to a concern he'd had for some time. 'Especially if we're to develop our mineral interests here on the estate. Wouldn't like to affect the labour supply, if you get my meaning?'

'You mean you're worried about people refusing to work in Rashiepark mines?'

David nodded. 'Yes, that and wouldn't like to start off on a bad note. Might lead to discontent at every turn. I'm well-versed in the problems caused by dissent, especially when labour is organised, as in the other coalfields.'

Imrie gave the biggest and loudest guffaw imaginable, for such a short man. Laird and factor looked on in awe.

'Did I say something funny?' asked David suddenly feeling embarrassed and more than a little naive. He glanced into the drawing room to see the ladies craning their necks in his direction. 'When Labour combines and they support each other, mines can be idle for long enough. I've read the newspaper reports about instances in Lanarkshire and Fife,' ventured the younger man.

'Not so much here in Linlithgowshire, young sir. The federation is organised pit by pit, not regionally as elsewhere. Foreign labour's plentiful and contractors can be brought in if things start to hot up. And there are ways of dealing with troublemakers. They can soon be identified and sent packing or left for the community to deal with. The great majority simply want to work and live quietly.'

David did not look convinced and Imrie gave another enormous laugh.

'Nothing to worry about, young man,' explained Imrie when he had calmed down. He leaned over, looked David square in the eye. 'Ultimately, starvation is the limiting factor to any choice or action made by the working man.

The demands of capital will always win out against the needs of labour.'

He paused while David took in what was being said.

'There will always be people willing to work in Rashiepark mines, mark my words, Mr Melville. As for your crime wave, the police have a job to uphold the law on your behalf. Take your concerns to Constable MacKay. It can only reflect well on the estate under your leadership, if you are seen to be strong.'

David nodded thoughtfully.

Conversation ceased as the ladies appeared on the terrace, intrigued. The Melville sisters certainly felt that the discussion outside might be more interesting than Mrs Imrie's increasingly unintelligible slurring inside. Nervously, Catherine told her father that it might be time to head home. He took a swift look at his wife and agreed.

Phee and Isabelle followed the others out under the portico whilst the Imries took their leave and their car was summoned. In admiration, the sisters watched their brother and Roger Stone continue to cultivate good relations with the coalmaster and his family.

'The wife's weakness is alcohol. That's for sure,' said Phee, keeping her voice low. 'And the daughter couldn't keep her eyes off the terrace all evening.'

'Yes, I saw. You mean she has a soft spot for our dear brother?' replied Isabelle. 'That could work to our advantage.'

'Meaning what?' Phee understood but looked for clarification.

'Golly, gosh. You are so slow at times, dear sister. Meaning a liason between Imrie's daughter and our brother could be what this estate needs.'

'You must be joking. I wouldn't wish her on my worst enemy! Miss Frosty Face?

'I've never been more serious in my life, sister!'

'But! But he doesn't.... I mean he hardly knows her!' Phee was horrified.

'You are so naive, dear Phee. Someone in David's position can't marry for love! He's got to marry money.'

Lost for words, Phee looked on as Isabelle joined the others.

'So lovely to have met you at last!' said Isabelle, gushing. 'Do come again, soon. Perhaps Catherine would like to join my sister and myself for luncheon one day?'

Catherine nodded, looked over in Phee's direction for approval. 'What a lovely idea!' she agreed, animated for the first time that evening.

Oh joy, thought Phee. 'Yes, do,' she called, feigning enthusiasm, her heart sinking. 'Do come!'

# Chapter 31

## CHANGING TIMES

Mrs Gow and the Widow MacAuley helped each other down the steps of the church after a particularly uplifting morning service. They marvelled at the minister's skill in turning news of every day events and seasonal changes, in this case the harvest, into lessons about life, responsibility, retribution, and judgement. For two women who went to sleep every night wondering whether they would wake up in the morning, it was a comfort to know they had lived blameless lives and that, one day, the rogues and ragamuffins of the world would get their come-uppance in the fires of hell. They made their way slowly along the street, curtailed by the limitations imposed by old age and the long, black coats and fox furs they wore to church all year round regardless of the weather, and took up their usual posts in Main Street to survey the midday scene.

As a small number of people passed their way, mainly in twos and threes, the ladies remarked that it was a lovely summer's day for a stroll. Personally, they had never spent the Sabbath walking for pleasure, even before arthritis limited their range as it did now. It seemed an innocent enough activity, they agreed. However, the trickle of strollers became more of a tidal surge when joined by whole families, especially when these numbered up to twenty individuals laden with bags and blankets. The sight of children carrying cooking pots and kettles along the street was most unusual. It was clear that the steady stream heading down the Doctor's Brae was no coincidence. Something was afoot. Both ladies were as much perturbed by their complete ignorance of any planned local event as they were by its timing on the afternoon of the Lord's Day.

'Would ye look at yon,' exclaimed Mrs Gow, pointing along the road. 'They're no gaun tae the same place as the ither fowk.'

Widow MacAuley stared as three ladies on bicycles wobbled past on the opposite side of the street.

'I dinnae ken whit the world's comin' tae,' she replied, tut-tutting. 'Young women oan bicycles. It cannae be guid for them.'

The cyclists gave a friendly wave.

'It's yon schoolteacher, Miss Foulkes,' said Mrs Gow, nodding back in disbelief. 'Would ye credit it? I widnae have thocht she was the kin' for sic brazen nonsense as yon. Tut, tut. Whit's she teachin' the weans? It maks ye wonder.'

The old women watched the lady cyclists as they wobbled along the road to Stoneyrigg and out of sight.

'Richt oot the kirk an' awa' tae God kens whaur, tae meet God kens whau,' lamented the Widow MacAuley. 'Widnae hae happened in oor day. Tut, tut.'

'I cannae comprehend whit it's like tae perch up high on a wee totie seat like yon. Its gallus, yon. No richt at a'.'

But the old widow looked almost wistful. 'Here, dae ye think it's straightfurrit gaun yin o' thon contraptions, Mrs Gow?'

Her companion tutted her disapproval once again before changing the subject back to the steady flow of people heading down the brae in the direction of the burn. 'Here's twa o' Tam Tennant's lads comin' this wey. They'll maybe ken whit's gaun oan.'

'Afternoon, ladies,' said Neil as he approached with his brother. 'Guid day for a cycle in the countryside. I see Mr Brogan's got customers for his new range o' ladies' bicycles.'

'I've ne'er seen sic a thing. Women let loose like yon,' complained the Widow MacAuley.

'Whit's gaun oan, Neil? Whaur's a'body gaun the day?' asked Mrs Gow, indicating the general direction of the Doctor's Brae with a gnarled hand.

'I was jist aboot tae ask the verra same question.' The women looked up to see a stern-faced Constable MacKay hovering beside them.

All eyes focused on Neil and his brother.

'Its jist a wee gaitherin', I believe,' said Neil, unsure himself but feeling the need to emphasise the informality of whatever was happening down by the burn. 'I'm takin' Billy here tae play in a fitba' tournament wi' some o' the lads. That's as much as I can tell ye, I'm afraid.' He turned to leave.

'Whau's ahint it?' asked Constable MacKay before Neil and his brother had gone more than a few steps. 'Whau's organised it?'

Before Neil could say that he was unsure of the details, Billy piped up excitedly. 'It's Mister Birse ower at Staney's organised it. A' body's comin' tae the Meadie for a picnic. Are ye comin'?'

Neil pulled his brother away, retreating quickly before another query could come their way.

As a dozen more people passed, all heading for the Doctor's Brae, the constable turned to the two elderly citizens beside him. 'We'll need tae see aboot this, ladies. Oan the Sabbath!? This'll no dae, ladies, no it will not!'

Mrs Gow and the Widow MacAuley smiled contentedly at each other with the same moth-eaten grimaces borne by the dead animals hanging round their necks. They were never happier than when there was a to-do about something or other. And today, there was definitely something in the air.

# Chapter 32

## THE BIG PICNIC

Alex Birse had mentioned his idea for a village picnic to be held on the Meadie to whosoever he had met immediately after leaving the house in a temper. Some folk pointed out that, as the day in question was the Sabbath, it might upset some of the older villagers if a large number of people congregated in the open air for the purpose of enjoyment. Alex said that attendance was voluntary so those who objected could sit at home with their doors and windows shut if they didn't want to join in. The weather was set fair, he had said, and he didn't think God would mind if people gave humble thanks by spending the afternoon outside in the glory of God's creation. When he had looked in on the Saturday evening meeting of the Orange Order, several of the brothers said that they would tell their wives and consider dropping by with their families. Brother Timothy of the Rechabites agreed to let his associates know as long as there were to be no alcoholic beverages present. Alex assured him that it was to be a picnic with some games for the children, nothing more. Other folk reminded him that the shops were closed, and wouldn't reopen till Monday morning, which might restrict what families could bring to the picnic so Alex said that people could bring what they had and share it with those who had little. Wasn't that what a community was all about?

It did Alex proud to watch a steady stream of neighbours and workmates arrive at the Meadie with their families on Sunday afternoon. The Cherries appeared pushing an ancient, rickety pram piled high with sandwiches and blankets for sitting on. Other families, where there was a dearth of bread at home, brought pots and pans full of peeled potatoes and large kettles for the brewing of tea. A group of the younger men disappeared into the woods beside the burn in search of fuel for the fire. They soon returned with armfuls of sticks and twigs, dragging behind them enormous dead branches, at the sight of which a work party of younger lads set about breaking them down into a suitable size for burning. Children of all ages raided the shallows of the burn for large stones to ring the hearth, thereby keeping the fire contained. Soon, out of the chaos of everyone's arrival, came order. Families staked claim to a suitable spot on the ground then settled down on a blanket. Food was prepared on a roaring fire and children played a variety of games wherever space between the adults allowed.

Constable Mackay arrived at the fire. He soon spotted Alex Birse and his wife, sitting on a tartan shawl in conversation with a large group of friends and neighbours. His presence cast a long shadow, even though it was still early in the afternoon.

'So whau's in chairge?' he asked, arms folded over his ample belly. He looked straight at Alex Birse.

'Naebody's in chairge,' came the reply. 'We're a' in chairge o' oorsels.'

'I'll hae nane o' yer cheek, for a stert,' replied the constable. 'Whit's gaun oan here? I've telt ye afore aboot assembling in public, there's a public ha' for activities like this.'

'Ye've telt us men aboot assemblin' in the street, Constable. But we're no in the street.'

'An' we're no a' men!' shouted one of the women present.

'There's a public ha' for activities like this, I telt ye,' stated the constable.

'I think ye'd be the first tae complain aboot us burnin' doon the public ha' wi' a fire for brewin' the tea an' cookin' the tatties, officer,' said Mary before Alex could say more and get himself into bother with the law.

'Have ye got permission tae be here?' he asked, trying a different tack.

'It's oan the public path oot the village,' explained Alex. 'Dae we need permission? The weans play here withoot permission of'en enough. Its Coal Company land, in't it? An' maist o' us work for them. It's no yer pal Melville's land, is it?' It was a rhetorical question.

The policeman bit his tongue. 'This is no richt, no oan the Sabbath. Some fowk'll be affrontit, so they will.' He felt the need to find fault. 'Ye should've telt the cooncil or somebody, an' asked permission.' He surveyed the busy scene. Families sat with a picnic in the sun. Grown men tended pots of potatoes nestling into the glowing logs around the edge of the fire and kept curious children at bay. Women made tea as girls lined up to have empty cups filled at the behest of older relatives. A football tournament was underway on the stretch of grass below the sloping gardens of the cottages up on the ridge. There was nothing untoward that MacKay could see, nothing to justify clearing the park anyway. Also, he was on his own, without back up, and he was greatly outnumbered. There were more than two hundred people present, he surmised, probably many more.

'If oniebody complains, Constable,' suggested Alex, 'jist tell them we're re-enacting the parable o' the loaves an' the fishes.'

'Except it's no loaves an' fishes, its breid an tatties!' added one of the women with a cackle. A peel of laughter resounded round the company.

'A' richt, verra funny,' conceded the constable. Feeling the need to depart before his aura of power diminished further, he made to leave. 'Mak sure there's nae bother, or I'll haud you responsible, Alex Birse.' He stabbed a finger at him. 'Nae drinkin' in public, nae fechtin, an' pit oot thon blaze afore ye leave in case ye stert a gress fire. Is that clear?'

'Verra clear, Constable,' several voices said together.

'Shame ye cannae stey for a cooked tattie,' added Alex, fishing a big charred potato out of the embers with a stick.

Cheeky shite, thought Constable MacKay. He'll come a cropper yin o' thur days. He made his way slowly through the multitude, making sure as many as possible had spotted him. That was the best way to keep order, by maintaining a high profile, reminding people they were subject to the law of the land and that he, Constable Archibald Fergus MacKay, would be down on them like a ton of bricks if they got too big for their boots.

He made his way over to the football match. It was keenly fought. Lines of ardent spectators shouted advice to the players and kept the referee right. Taking off his peaked cap, MacKay lingered for a few minutes. Some of these lads were good, nippy on their feet, and skilful with the ball. Then he remembered his purpose and quickly replaced his hat on his big bald head, before striding off up the hill as if pressing matters needed attention. He didn't like large gatherings like this, however innocent the motives appeared. There was something about this one but he couldn't quite put his finger on it. Maybe it was simply that Alex Birse was involved. He was a troublemaker that one, and no mistake. He had come to Blackrigg from across the county, with a reputation. So far, he hadn't done anything untoward but the minute he did, the long arm of the law would be there.

Alex watched MacKay leave the field through narrowed eyes. The remark about the parable of the loaves and fishes had been a joke but he couldn't get the image out of his head: Jesus taking some bread and a few fish from a small boy and the disciples sharing it around the assembled multitude. When everyone had eaten their fill, there had been enough left over to fill many baskets. Alex looked around the villagers on the Meadie. They had brought what little they had and had shared it around. Everyone had enough, though it wasn't what could be called a banquet. Was that what Jesus had been trying to say through his parable about loaves and fishes? That everybody could have their fill if they shared it out? And didn't expect anything fancy – that was important too. Not like the Melvilles with their fancy big dinners up at the Big House. Or the Imries who owned the collieries and lived in splendour whilst the miners' families rarely saw a piece of meat from one year's end to the other. Maybe just a bone for a pot of soup or some potted hough as a special treat on Hogmanay.

'Weel, ye saw him aff, Alex,' said Mags Cherrie, guessing where he had been looking. 'Whau needs thon big creeshie bastard, eh? Look at a' the fowk here, policin' theirsels.'

'Them that's got ower muckle abin whit they can use, thon's whau needs the likes o' him,' explained Alex.

'Aye, like the laird wi' his Big Hoose an' his fantoosh weys,' added Mags, mother of eight, reading his thoughts.

'An' sae muckle land, he lords it ower the birds an' the beasts thereof, an' the rivers an' the streams that rin ower them.'

'Maks ye wonder, richt enough. Hoo can oniebody hae sae muckle land? An' hail rivers forby?! Yin family when ithers have got sae little?! It disnae mak onie sense tae me an' niver will.' Mags gazed across to the river flowing past the Meadie, to the deep pool where Wee Geordie Broadley had almost come to grief. 'Ma lads would like tae learn hoo tae swim,' she ventured, studying Alex with cat-like eyes.

'An' there's nae reason why they shouldnae learn, Mags, nae guid reason at a'.' He eased himself up from the ground then turned to his neighbours. 'Come oan. Oniebody whau wants tae learn their weans hoo tae swim, follae me.'

'Alex!' called Mary when she realised where he was heading. 'Come back! We dinnae want onie bother!'

He was undeterred. He marched over to the football match where he grabbed each twin by the wrist. She watched helplessly as he strode back towards her, both boys struggling to free themselves, wondering what they had done wrong this time. He propelled them along the path to the ford, beyond which was Melville land.

'Weel, Mags. Whit are ye waitin' for?' he called back. 'There's only yin bit o' the burn that's guid for swimmin' an' it's alang here!'

# Chapter 33

## THE BEST LAID SCHEMES

A single cloud drifted over a blue sky, blocking out the late afternoon sun, and bringing welcome shade to many. Those who spent their working day down a pit, inside a works or a family home were not used to the sunshine. A steady trickle of revellers began to leave the field. First a mother with a fractious bairn, then a granny with a wet hankie on her head worried about sunstroke, and a whole procession gradually followed with their eye on the start of the new school session the following day, and all of the bathing and preparations still to be made. Those women whose men and children had followed Alex and the twins up the burn for a swim, were duty bound to wait for their return. They collected around Mary and chatted, patiently at first, then with mounting ire. Most would have left the men to it and returned home to their chores but the involvement of their children in an illicit activity kept them glued to the spot. It had seemed quite a good idea at the time, with the sun shining, conversation and laughter filling the air. However, with more and more time to reflect, the reality and the consequences of trespassing on Rashiepark land started to dawn. It wasn't as if ignorance could be used as a defence if they were caught. The Melvilles had turned down the request to have access to the burn when approached earlier in the summer, making their opposition to any such activity on their land quite clear.

Mary sensed the other women's angst. She felt it herself. Living with Alex Birse had inured her to it: though not entirely. He had been hot-headed as a young man. That was what had attracted her to him: his passion. She first found out he couldn't read on their wedding day when he had made his mark, a simple cross, on the marriage register. He had looked deep into her eyes and she into his. She had loved him all the more for it: his vulnerability. At first, he had let her teach him to read. It had been a slow process but he was keen to learn. They had sat close together in the light of a small candle, laughed at his mistakes, and made love when the light grew dim and the words disappeared into the darkness. But life changed Alex and the anger and bitterness grew. He talked more of his parents, of their struggle to feed ten children, moving from one pit to another, wherever the work took them, his mother making a new home each time in houses not fit for purpose. That was why he had never learned to read: all the moving, never settling in a school for any length of time, and a mother and father who couldn't read or write themselves. His own life hadn't turned out much better, he raged at her: the same hard graft in the dirt and glaur of the bowels of the earth to pay high rents for a damp hovel with rats for lodgers. He had wanted a family of his own, children who would give his life purpose, who could advance in life, taking his name forward into the next generation. But they never came. For all their love and passion for each other, Mary had never borne him the children he craved.

As a rule, he had never been a drinker but that night, when he had gone out in a temper, he had been out of his mind. He said he couldn't remember what had happened but the facts were played out in court clearly enough and it was six months before she had seen him again. He was a changed man when he came back from the gaol.

She remembered the night he appeared at her sisters' house. He had walked all the way in the driving rain to claim her, without so much as a coat on his back; more than ten miles on a bitter night in February, the kind of raw winter's night that Scotland does so well. She vividly remembered the vision of him standing in the doorway, a drip on the end of his frozen nose; his hands stinging and purple with cold, stuck under his oxters for warmth; his brow knitted and bowed against the icy blast. He had insisted she come with him at that very moment. He had a place for them at a pit, newly opened with the promise of years of work ahead. She told her sister not to fret and out into the teeth of the storm she had gone in the dead of night, following her man to God knows where.

A small fire greeted them when they finally got there and he made her tea. The place was decent, dry at least. She rolled out the blankets she had brought on her back and he helped her take off her wet clothes. But it wasn't the old Alex she lay with that night; not the gentle, loving man who could laugh at what life threw at you; the one she had longed for during those months apart. This Alex would never again ask her to read with him. He was angry and brutish and, afterwards, he lay silent, staring into the cold, black night.

The presence of Highland Mary on the Meadie had a calming influence on the other women waiting for the return of the swimmers. She had helped bring many of their children into the world and it was to her they turned when their children fell ill with one of the many diseases

320

of childhood that regularly visited the community. She spoke up about matters that affected them all, like having the dry closets emptied more often and bringing a Co-operative store to the village. She wasn't frightened to approach the men on the council to tell them what needed to be done. The other women watched her bring a pot of water from the burn and dowse the fire, kicking at the unburned logs to ensure no embers remained to cause havoc later when they had all gone home. She retrieved a child's jumper and a shoe from the fringes of the field. She held up the shoe for them all to see and shrugged her shoulders. They all laughed. Who would've gone off with only one shoe? She would reunite it with its owner and that just about summed her up: always looking out for other folk. However, her husband was responsible for the swimming expedition and many of the women were starting to turn their growing anxiety and diminishing patience on him, though they held their tongue for long enough in deference to Mary.

Mags Cherrie was the first to speak up. 'I kent I should've went up the burn masel' an' no let ma man go,' she griped. 'I wouldnae've stayed as long. Your Alex'll hae them a' up there till yon time, Mary.'

'Ye were keen enough on the idea tae stert wi', Mags,' countered Mary in her husband's defence. 'I seem tae mind it was yer idea in the first place!'

Mags felt stung. 'Naw, it wasnae, Alex instigated it!' she said, ignoring her part as catalyst to the notion of swimming lessons in the burn. 'Oniewey, I'm jist sayin', men tak things tae extremes, Mary. I'm stertin tae worry. Why are they takin' sae lang? The gemmie'll hae heard fae Auld Morton that they're there, an' he'll have the militia oot tae hunt them b' noo.'

A small number of men appeared in the distance, through the trees, bringing a collective sigh of relief. The women craned their heads to get a better view and several mothers stood up ready to leave straight away, relief etched on their faces. Their happy smiles soon turned to angry grimaces as they prepared to give their men what-for. How dare they keep them waiting as long?!

'Are the rest comin', Joe?' asked Mags of the first man on the scene. 'There's no been onie bother has there?'

'Naw, Mags, nae bother at a',' said Joe as he approached, dragging a small waterlogged boy by the hand. 'The ithers are jist comin' or thereaboots.'

Joe's wife slapped a blanket and a blackened cooking pot into his arms before hurrying their child towards the Doctor's Brae.

The women who remained watched as more men gradually appeared with their sons. Alex and the twins were greeted by Mary. She hugged the boys as they told her they'd had a great time, then they started to argue about who'd been the better swimmer. Alex gave each an affectionate slap and they ducked out of the way, eagerly taking their share of the things to be carried home.

Mags Cherrie and three women were left waiting as Mary and Alex took their leave.

'They're jist comin, Mags,' Alex reassured her. 'Dinna fash yersel, yer man was the last tae get oot the burn. They were gettin' ready when I left them.'

'Fine, Alex, fine,' Mags replied, glancing along the empty path. 'As long as they're no droont nor nothin'. Ma man cannae even swim hissel, nivermind learn his bairns!'

She watched the Birses weave their way home across the deserted Meadie and disappear up the Doctor's Brae. A feeling of quiet desolation remained after the hubbub of the afternoon's activity. The noise and the chatter of many people had gone, replaced by birdsong and the rush of the stream flowing by.

The squealing voices of frightened children brought her attention back to the missing swimmers. Mags gave a start. Several boys, red faced, with alarm in their eyes, were advancing along the riverside path. Arms went round bewildered mothers and some burst into tears. It was left to Billy Tennant, who was on his own, to tell the tale.

'They've taen some of the men awa',' he explained, close to tears himself. He pointed back upstream.

'Whau's taen them, Billy?' asked Mags, a lump in her throat.

He pointed at the river again. 'The gemmie, Mr Grant, an' some ither men. They'd guns an' taen the men awa'. They said we were trespassin' on private land. They made them gang wi' them.' He pointed again, 'They went up the hill, headin' for the Big Hoose.'

# Chapter 34

## CRIME AND PUNISHMENT

Constable MacKay was sitting in the police station on Main Street, drinking tea and eating fruit cake with colleagues who had dropped in from the main office in Bathgate. Sergeant Orr observed that, as Sundays were such quiet days, it had been a fine opportunity to take the new officer, Constable Anderson, on a tour of a less familiar part of the county.

MacKay had been delighted to see them, puffing out his chest like a proud peacock as they rolled up in the latest motorised vehicle for the conveyance of policemen and criminals alike. He had stepped out into the street, admired the shiny, black vehicle with great aplomb, taking a quick glance up and down the village to ascertain how many of the local population bore witness to its arrival at his door; further proof if it was needed, of his importance within the community. Then he had beckoned the officers inside for a tour of the premises.

He was proud of his newly constructed police office, in commission for less than a year. Along with the churches, the school, the public hall, and the Big House, it was one of the most solid and striking buildings in the village. He pointed out the attention given to security in its design, showing his visitors every conceivable room, cupboard and recess in order to impress. Two cells for holding those taken into custody nestled in the basement, half sunk into the ground with only small barred windows visible at ground level on the side furthest from the road. Through the wall from his office was the home he shared with his wife. It was a commodious dwelling commensurate with his position as keeper of order and upholder of the law.

'Mair tea, Sarge? Constable?' MacKay refilled their cups, offering each man another piece of Dundee cake. Half way through his first bite, he was interrupted.

'Are ye there, Constable MacKay?' came a voice from the counter in the front office. 'Mr MacKay, are ye there?'

MacKay couldn't help being irritated at the interruption but here was an opportunity to impress the sergeant. He put down his cup with a flourish and donned his cap. The senior officer returned his smile sympathetically.

'I'm here,' replied MacKay, making his way through to the front of the building. 'Oh, it's yersel, Billy Dodds. Whit can I dae for ye, lad?'

'Mr Melville sent me, Constable. He says can ye come up tae Parkgate the noo?' Billy took a sharp intake of breath at the sight of Sergeant Orr and Constable Anderson emerging from the back room. He addressed all three men in uniform with a tremble in his voice, his eyes wide. 'There's been a bit o' bother wi' folk trespassin' oan estate land.'

'Dinnae tell me the gemmie's caught a poacher,' laughed MacKay.

Billy laughed nervously. 'No a poacher, Mr MacKay. Naw, no a poacher. Ye better come an' see for yersel. There's fower o' them but ithers got awa'.'

All three policemen looked at each other. This sounded like a serious breach of the peace, perhaps a riot thwarted by an alert gamekeeper, in the right place at the right time by Good Fortune.

'I can see why the Board invested so heavily here, MacKay,' said Sergeant Orr, indicating his surroundings with a roll of his head. 'Lucky we're on hand to assist on this occasion. We'll gang wi' ye in the vehicle.'

'Aff ye gang, Billy Dodds,' said a very serious MacKay to the nervous young man. 'Dinna fash yersel, son, we'll sort this oot an' nae mistake.'


On arrival at Parkgate, Billy signalled for the police vehicle to proceed round the back of the house to the stable yard. David Melville moved forward from a small group of estate workers and spoke to the officers as they lowered the window.

'Thank you for coming so promptly, Constable.' He acknowledged the accompanying officers as MacKay introduced them. 'We've four men from Stoneyrigg in the empty stable at the end.' He handed over a piece of paper with four names on it then pointed to the last doorway where a rough-looking character stood guard with a shotgun. Several more of his kind hung back when the policemen stared in their direction, barely out of sight round the corner of the steading. 'That's Grant, my gamekeeper. Thank God he was around. Don't know what might have happened if he hadn't been there.'

'Yer man, Billy Dodds, says plenty mair got awa',' said MacKay. 'Whaur were they and whit were they daein, exactly?'

'Seems the rest scarpered at the sight of Grant and his fellows,' explained the young landowner.

The police officers surveyed the other men in Grant's vicinity, rustic characters, each looking more dissolute than the next.

'The grieve at Back o' Moss alerted Grant on the tenant's instruction. A hoard of men appeared out of nowhere and started roaming over his land, by all accounts.' David turned to the unfamiliar officers, Anderson and Orr. 'MacKay knows about some of the problems we've been having recently. We've been in close communication and he's been keeping an eye on things for us, for which we are eternally grateful.'

MacKay puffed up at the laird's warm praise.

Melville continued. 'I'm sure he'll explain the background in more detail, gentlemen. A deputation from the village asked for access to the estate for recreation a while back and we refused. However, it seems that some people cannot take '*no*' for an answer.'

'Ye said that some folk got awa', Mr Melville,' interrupted Sergeant Orr. 'Oniebody in particular ye could name?'

'Good question, Sergeant. There are a couple of people I could name but perhaps you should hear it from the horse's mouth, so to speak.' He called Grant over.

The officers watched carefully as a curmudgeonly figure made his way towards them. It was hard not to stare. The remains of several dinners were plastered down the front of his tartan shirt, the buttons of which strained to contain his belly which overflowed moleskin trousers, tied up with rope. Constable MacKay brought to mind the image of Grant on the day after the Gala Day dance when he had been found beaten to a pulp, covered in cuts and bruises, and minus his boots. MacKay tried to set aside his other dealings with the man. He was renowned for his quick temper after a night in the Village Inn and it wasn't uncommon for him to be seen sleeping off the drink in a convenient hedgerow.

'Congratulations, Mr Grant. Seems you averted a serious breach of the peace or worse.' The policeman looked across to the place where Grant's compatriots stood guarding the stable. They seemed like the type he locked up in a cell of a Friday night but he didn't recognise them. MacKay checked the names of the prisoners listed on the paper he had been given, disappointed to see that a certain name wasn't there. 'Dae ye ken the name Alex Birse, Mr Grant? He's a miner ower at Staney.'

'The name's familiar but I cannae say if I'd ken his face,' replied Grant. 'He micht've been there richt enough but ye'll need tae ask the ithers. There was a wheen o' them, that's for sure. But they got oan their marks at the sicht o' us comin' doon the burn. Disappeared like rats aff a sinkin' ship, so they did. Ower monie tae put names tae.'

'There's the pity,' said MacKay turning to his colleagues. 'I spoke to Birse earlier this efternin aboot a potential breach o' the peace doon at the mill. I could tell he was up tae nae guid an' I'm sure he's had somethin' adae wi' this business.'

'Grant has another name that might interest you, Constable,' said David rather too eagerly. He gave his gamekeeper a nod of encouragement.

'Aye that's richt, Mr Melville, sir. A richt troublemaker but no the type tae hing aboot an get caught. Mair the type that leads ithers oan an' leaves them tae it.'

Melville took over earnestly. 'He was one of the deputation who came to ask for permission to trespass on the estate. The cheek of the man. Couldn't take no for an answer, obviously; a self-taught expert on all things, including the law. You know the type I'm sure, officers, full of socialist nonsense about rights but no notion of responsibilities.' He turned again to the gamekeeper.

'Seen him wi' ma ain e'en, officers. Goes b' the name o' Neil Tennant. Bides alang at the Smiddy.' Grant could see that MacKay was taken aback at his accusation against the clean-cut village blacksmith. He went in for the kill. 'Acts like butter widnae melt in his mooth, yon yin. But ran aff an' left the ithers tae tak the rap, so he did.'

Sergeant Orr stepped forward and took over the proceedings. He felt sure he had a good enough grasp of the day's events and the background leading up to them. He thanked the laird and the gamekeeper, explained that statements would need to be taken, sooner rather than later. Either he or Constable MacKay would be in touch. He would take the four prisoners to the police station for questioning and bring in this agitator, Tennant, straight away.

The constables got to work, retrieving the four trespassers from the stable then settling them in the back of the motor transport, conveniently available for that purpose.

As the sleek, black vehicle left the scene, David Melville turned to his gamekeeper. 'Well done, my man!' He slapped Grant's greasy back then immediately thought better of it, removing his hand and examining it with distaste. 'That was a good day's work, was it not, Grant? Do thank your companions for me. It's jolly good luck you were out and about together. There'll be a bonus in this for you.' Grant's dirty attire caught his eye. 'Perhaps the estate could purchase a new set of work clothes for your use? Jolly well done indeed.'

'Nae problem, Mr Melville,' replied Grant, hiding his conceit. 'It's ma job tae rid Rashiepark o' vermin, is it no?'

The laird shivered at Grant's choice of words. He wasn't a likable fellow, just a glance at his dishevelled form was enough to turn the stomach. As for his companions, Melville decided he wouldn't like to meet them on a dark night. They looked an unsavoury bunch, though one shouldn't judge a book by its cover, as his old school master used to say. He wondered if, perhaps, his gamekeeper had suffered from the beating he had received earlier in the summer. That sort of incident could leave its mark on a man's self-respect. Then there was the warning he'd had to give Grant following the complaint from Elizabeth Fraser. He was glad he hadn't dismissed the man as Phee had asked him to do, and instead given him the benefit of the doubt. It was fortunate that Grant had been on the spot to take control of the situation and prevent any widespread damage to Rashiepark property.

Grant watched his employer through narrowed eyes. He waited until the laird had disappeared into the house before going over to join his friends. Grant found it hard to contain his delight. He bent double with laughter, had to prop himself up against the nearest fellow, a man with a scowl and all the charm of a hungry ferret.

'Weel done, lads. Whit a great day! Someb'dy's aboot tae get their come-uppance!' He held his sides and leaned over again to stifle his laughter. 'I've a bottle or twa back at the howf an' I feel the need tae celebrate. Come oan, lads, come oan!'

# Chapter 35

## THE ONE THAT GOT AWAY

Since arriving to take charge of the new police station, Constable MacKay had not had occasion to visit the Smiddy in the line of duty though he had introduced himself one day at the forge, located behind the cottage. A farm cart sat without a wheel, he remembered, and father and son were busy at the tyring platform, banging at the metal tyre and heating it at the forge. They had shouted back and forward at each other over the noise as they hammered it into place then quickly dowsed the hot metal in a water butt to prevent the wooden wheel from burning. The policeman had waved politely, moved on when he realised he was in the way, leaving the smiths in a loud hiss of steam as the iron rim shrank for a tight fit. The family had always seemed pleasant and upstanding: hard working parents with an elder son following in his father's footsteps and younger siblings who had never been brought to his attention for the wrong reasons.

He stood at the door of Smiddy Cottage ready to knock, bemused by the picture painted by both the dour gamekeeper and the earnest new laird of Rashiepark. Neil Tennant, a political agitator? He would never have guessed. But when Constable Anderson had described the same type of self-educated young man he had come across when policing demonstrations and strikes in Glasgow, spouting revolutionary talk and high ideals, MacKay had opened his mind to the possibility that the well-mannered Neil Tennant could indeed be a wolf in sheep's clothing. After all, hadn't he spoken to him earlier in the day in the presence of Mrs Gow and the Widow MacAuley, when he was blithely taking his brother by the hand to play football on the Meadie? Tennant was down by the mill with Alex Birse and the other workmen who had decided to go together onto Rashiepark land. They had decided to take part in a collective trespass on private land. If that wasn't a political statement, then Constable Archibald Fergus MacKay didn't know what was.

When young Billy Tennant opened the door, he nearly fainted at the sight of the local bobby towering over him. Billy was as guilty as the men who had been taken away from the Red Burn at gun point and here was the proof. The local constabulary in size ten boots had come to take him away.

'Who is it, Billy?' came a woman's voice from a room at the back of the cottage. 'Queer tae get visitors on a Sabbath nicht.' Mrs Tennant appeared behind her son. She looked bemused at the sight of MacKay.

'Sorry tae disturb ye, Mrs Tennant.'

'Has there been some bother, Constable? How can we help ye?' She had the kind and generous face of a loving mother who had led a blameless life.

MacKay felt uneasy.

'Can I come in, Mrs Tennant? It's best if I can say what I've got to say in private.' He felt the eyes of the neighbours burrowing into the back of his head.

He dipped his head under the door lintel then followed her into a small, neat parlour. She ushered her daughters into the kitchen at the back of the house and closed the door. Their brother tried to join them but MacKay called him back. Billy returned to the front room, sat bolt upright on a hard chair with his legs and his fingers crossed, aware that his mother was glaring at him. He dared not look in her direction.

'There's been a bit of bother on the Melville estate, Mrs Tennant.' MacKay could see she was perturbed so he got to the point. 'Is yer elder boy, Neil, at hame at a'?'

'Neil?!' she looked at Billy, her brows knitted in confusion. She shook her head. 'Naw, Constable, he's no in yet. He's been oot maist o' the day but I expect him onie minute. Whit dae ye want tae speak tae Neil for? Whit's happened?' She looked as if the bottom was falling out of her world.

'It seems that earlier the day, a large number of men deliberately trespassed on Rashiepark land, Mrs Tennant, even though they were denied permission by the landowner. It seems your son, Neil, headed up a delegation that went to the laird earlier in the summer, asking for access to the burn where it crosses Back o' Moss Farm. The laird refused permission.'

'Aye, he went to speak up for the local folk. He's aye been guid at speakin', has Neil. But that isnae a crime, Mr MacKay, surely.' She waited for what was to come. There had to be more.

'Billy, you were on the Meadie this efternin wi' yer brother, were ye no?' MacKay asked softly.

Billy nodded, almost paralysed with fear.

'I saw ye masel, playin' fitba', eh? Ye've a rare left kick, I have tae say.' Billy wasn't taken in by the policeman's friendly approach. He heard him say, 'An' Neil was wi' ye, wasn't he?'

333

Billy nodded.

'Was he on the Meadie wi' ye a' efternin, Billy? I saw him refereein' yin o' the matches early oan in the proceedings.'

Billy moved his head slowly from side to side. 'Naw, he went awa'.'

'Whaur did he gang, Billy? Tak yer time, son. Whaur did he gang?'

'I dinnae ken, Constable. I came aff the pitch an' he wasnae there. I dinnae ken whaur he went.' Billy turned to his mother with tears in his eyes. 'Honest, Ma, I dinnae ken whaur he went.'

'I believe ye, Billy. Jist tell the Constable the truth an' naebody can fault ye fur it.' She patted his shoulder, meeting MacKay's gaze.

Billy continued. 'He telt me when he taen me doon tae the park that he had tae gang somewhaur. He niver said whaur an' I niver asked him. He telt me he had tae gang somewhaur an' I was tae gang straight hame efter the fitba'.' He looked at the adults for their reaction. 'Neil's no in bother, is he?'

'Weel, I've heard naethin this faur tae suggest he's done oniethin wrang,' answered his mother. 'Dinnae worry, yer brither's a guid man.' She studied the policeman's face as she said it. 'That's fine, Billy,' she said kindly. 'I think the constable's heard a' he needs tae hear fae ye. Awa' ye gang, ben the hoose.'

Billy didn't need to be told twice and he fled out of the parlour. He thanked God that they hadn't asked if he had been with the men who had gone up the burn. Was it a criminal offence to keep information like that to himself? When he went into the kitchen, his sisters looked at him as if he was already on the road to the fires of hell, or the gallows at least. He could hardly speak for the lump in his throat. When he saw Neil's kind, smiling face coming through the back door, Billy had to blink back the tears. His little sisters were quick to inform Neil about Constable MacKay's presence in the front room and Billy sat tongue-tied, unable to warn his brother about the nature of the visit.

'Just the man I'm lookin' for,' said MacKay as Neil entered the room.

Neil looked intrigued. 'Can I help ye, Officer?'

The policeman said that he hoped he would be able to help and proceeded to revisit the same ground already covered in his absence, explaining about the mass trespass, the four men in custody and Neil's role in seeking access to the burn for recreation on behalf of these very same people.

'Where have ye been this efternin, Neil? asked MacKay.

'I was doon on the Meadie wi' ma brither, then I went walkin'.'

'Whaur did ye walk?'

'He's ay walkin' on the Sabbath, Constable,' interrupted his mother. 'Lookin' at rocks an' fossils. Him wi' his books.'

'Whaur did ye walk the day, Neil?' he asked, repeating the question. 'Did ye see oniebody oan yer travels?'

'I went up the road past The Law an' ower by the shieling on the muir, alang the road tae the Avon for a bit but no jist as faur. Jist roon aboot, ye ken.'

'Naw, I dinnae ken, son,' replied the policeman in a much less friendly tone. 'Can oniebody speak up on yer behalf, I asked ye?'

'Somebody mebbe saw me, I suppose,' Neil replied. 'But I cannae gie ye onie names,' he added.

'Yer wee brither says ye telt him ye HAD tae gang some place. Ye HAD tae gang somewhaur. He was verra clear.'

'Aye, I HAD tae gang fur a walk. I like tae walk wi' ma books an a'. It's an innocent enough past time, lookin' at the birds an' the hills an' a'thing, is it no?' Neil showed no emotion.

'Weel, Neil Tennant, I've a witness, possibly mair than yin, swears he saw ye doon b' the Red Burn, trespassin' on Melville land when ye kent fine ye didnae have permission. Thon same witness swears that ye scarpered when ye saw the men come tae apprehend ye, an' ye left ither poor buggers tae tak the blame. It seems tae me that ye were yin o' the instigators o' this collective trespass. I'll have tae ask ye tae accompany me tae the station for further questionin'.'

MacKay couldn't make out who was more taken aback, the man or the mother.

Neil composed himself then spoke slowly and clearly. 'I did not trespass on Melville land. Nor did I incite ithers tae gang on Melville land.' He turned and spoke directly to his mother who sat with tears in her eyes. 'That is the truth, Mither, so help me God.' As he stood up to go with the constable, she could see there was no fear in his eyes.

'He's tellin' the truth, Constable MacKay,' said Mrs Tennant firmly. 'I think ye'll find this has been a terrible mistake.'

It crossed MacKay's mind that he would be a rich man if he had a pound for every mother who had said that very same thing to him but he held his tongue. He liked Mrs Tennant very much and felt sorry for her.

Neil hugged her tightly, telling her everything would be fine. She stood at the parlour window and watched through a veil of tears as he left the house with MacKay. She followed the two figures walking side by side along Main Street in the direction of the police station until they finally disappeared from view.

'Oh, Neil,' she said quietly as if he could hear. 'How has this come tae pass?'

# Chapter 36

## TRUTH AND LIES

The mood in the Birse house that evening was lighter than the twins could remember for a long time. Their father had seemed happy during the swimming session at the burn. Some of the men had rolled up their trouser legs and waded into the water with their boys, holding them round the middle, telling them to kick their legs up and down and make their arms go like Davy Broon's dug when she swam for a stick. Alex had stripped down to his underwear and swam back and forward across the burn to show everybody how it was done. He had looked like a boy without a care in the world or a sleek otter, dipping and diving with ease. He had held his boys one at a time by the chin, standing upstream of them, telling them to copy his swimming action. When it was their turn, they had pushed their arms and legs through the water until they ached. John, who thought there was nothing better than getting out of the house to play with his pals, had hardly been able to wait for his father to finish with Jim and call him over for another go. John had tried to swim on his own, undeterred by the mouthfuls of water he was taking on board. And when Alex had told him how well he was doing, he thought it might be the best feeling in the whole world. He had swelled up with pride till he felt he might burst, smiling broadly at the other lads all the while.

On the way back to Stoneyrigg, his parents had talked and laughed as Alex described the antics of some of the inexperienced swimmers, mimicking desperate calls for assistance with exaggerated arm movements. John couldn't remember the last time he had seen his mother and father walking out together. They seemed to do everything separately as a rule, and he was sure he had seen them holding hands for the last bit of the road home.

Mary put a simple supper of bread and jam on the table then she filled the teapot, leaving it to brew on the hearth. She put on extra water for the twins to wash in afterwards.

'Ye'll jist need a dicht the nicht,' she told them, 'Yer face an hauns first, ahint yer lugs an' roon the back o' yer neck, nae tide marks mind. Ye'll have had a guid wash in the burn when ye were swimmin'.'

The boys thought that was a great idea. The benefits of swimming were many if it meant you didn't have the palaver of a full Sunday night bath by the fire in front of the whole household, when Davy and the boarders could walk by at any moment and make fun of your manhood. They talked about what a good day they'd had and about how it made you feel better about going back to school when you'd had such a great time. There would be loads to tell their pals about, pals like Rob and Sandy and Bert and Dan who had missed an unforgettable day at the village picnic.

Alex went to answer a knock at the door. He was ashen faced when he came back to the table. The twins studied him and knew to say nothing. There was silence until his fist suddenly came down on the table with a bang. Mary told the boys to stop blethering and eat up their supper. They saw her studying their father's face and they watched him avoid her eyes while he finished his meal.

'I need tae gang oot,' he said eventually. He took his cap from the nail by the door. 'Dinnae wait up.'

The boys looked at their mother but she gave nothing away. The three ate in silence for a while. She looked out of the window in the direction her husband had disappeared but soon returned to her seat where she nursed her cup of tea, deep in thought.

'Drink up yer tea an' feenish yer piece, boys. An early nicht afore the school the morn's jist whit ye need. Doctor's orders.'

She took down a towel from the line above the fireplace. 'Richt, whau's first for shavin?' she said. She wasn't inviting them to shave. They weren't of an age for it. It was what she always said at washing and bathing time. The boys knew it meant that they had to decide who was getting washed first and there was to be no arguing about it. She poured hot water into a tin basin with a sigh.

'Whaur's Faither gaun?' ventured Jim at last, unable to contain his curiosity.

'He's awa' tae see a man aboot a dug,' she replied. Jim and John knew that he wasn't really away to buy a dog. It was what she always said when they weren't supposed to ask.

A small group of women had gathered at the front of the police station. They wailed like banshees at the sight of him. Alex marched on past but they followed, talking all at the same time. It was like running the gauntlet, he imagined. He shut his ears to their pleas, telling them he was here to sort the whole thing out.

He was glad of the peace and quiet that met him inside the front office. There seemed to be no one about so he banged the bell on the counter several times to let them know he meant business. Two policemen appeared from the back room. Neither was Constable MacKay and that threw him for a moment. He introduced himself as Alexander Birse, the organiser of the picnic on the Meadie. He explained that the decision to go onto Melville land for the purpose of swimming was his and his alone, and that it had been a spur of the moment decision on account of the good weather. He hadn't meant any harm and no harm to Rashiepark property had been done. So, if the police could simply release the men in custody, they could all be on their way and nothing of the kind would ever happen again, thank you very much.

Constable Anderson and Sergeant Orr stood with their arms folded as they listened intently to Alex's story. Unfortunately, they explained when Alex stopped to draw breath, it wasn't quite as simple as saying sorry, and that it wouldn't happen again. The landowner had made a formal complaint to the police about a large number of people trespassing at the one time on his land, and the four men in custody had already been charged with what was, after all, a very serious offence. In fact, they continued, it would be up to the Procurator Fiscal to decide if a breach of the peace or incitement to riot had been committed, and perhaps consider bringing even more serious charges that they hadn't even thought of yet.

Alex could not believe his ears. It was a swimming party, he insisted: a bunch of fathers teaching their sons to swim. What could be less of a disturbance than that, he asked? The officers stood looking unimpressed, still with their arms folded, as he continued to insist that if anyone should be in custody it should be him.

Then the door to the street opened and Constable MacKay entered with Neil Tennant in tow. Alex made to speak but he was told to keep his mouth shut as Neil was roughly pushed through another door into the back of the building. Sergeant Orr left the front office for a moment but Constable Anderson stood guard.

Alex was perplexed. He asked the constable why Neil Tennant had been brought in for questioning and was told it was none of his business but that Neil was helping them with their enquiries. Alex explained that they were wasting their time because Neil Tennant had nothing to do with the incursion onto Melville land as he hadn't even been there. If they wanted to charge anyone, he insisted, they should be charging him as it had been his idea in the first place. Alex leaned both hands against the counter. He looked down at his feet, sighing and shaking his head. God, how many times did he have to tell these eejits, he thought to himself, no wonder the polis had a reputation for being thick.

To Alex's consternation, Constable Anderson also left the office, though he was back with his sergeant in a moment. At last, thought Alex, they've seen sense. Not a bit of it. Sergeant Orr told him to go home and keep his head down. They appreciated that he was only trying to take the blame for his friends but that they, the constabulary, were satisfied that they had the right men in custody. Alex could hardly believe what he was hearing. The trespassers had been caught in the act, red-handed so to speak, by a number of witnesses who could corroborate each other's account of events. Those same witnesses had placed Neil Tennant at the scene. It was clear to the police that Mr

Tennant was behind an orchestrated attempt to incite a breach of the peace on a large scale, which was tantamount to mobbing and rioting, in their opinion. The common purpose of those involved made it mobbing and rioting, the constable confirmed. Although it was fortunate that such activity had been thwarted, explained the sergeant, it was certain that a judge would take a poor view of such political activity and come down on the perpetrators like a ton of bricks.

'Political activity?' spluttered Alex. 'Whit nonsense! Neil Tennant wisnae even there, I'm tellin' ye!'

'An' I'm tellin' you, Mr Birse,' said Sergeant Orr, leaning menacingly across the counter, 'Tae gang awa' hame afore I put ye in the cells for the nicht an' charge ye wi' causin' a breach o' the peace in this very police station.'

Alex's mouth opened and shut like a fish on a hot day.

'Git!' ordered the sergeant, his finger pointing at the exit.

Alex made to leave. He knew when he was defeated.

'Ye've made a terrible mistake!' he shouted back when he opened the door. He was confronted with the women camped outside. 'They jist widnae see sense, ladies,' he said to his audience, now frantic with worry. 'They wouldnae listen at a'.'

Back inside the police station, Anderson and Orr tried not to laugh as they were joined by their colleague, MacKay.

'Are ye sure we're daein the richt thing?' asked MacKay. 'Birse is a troublemaker. He was involved, by his own admission.'

'Troublemaker? He's a bit o' a blaw mair like,' replied the sergeant. 'We've fower men chairged wi' trespass, caught at the scene and chairged. Richt? They'll serve as an example tae their freens. Birse wants a bit o' the action, wants tae be the Big Man. A'richt, so even if he was there, dae ye want tae mak a martyr o' him?'

'Dae ye want him tae get aff scot-free?' asked MacKay.

'He'll no get aff scot-free, Archie. His neebours'll tear him tae shreds for getting' the ither lads intae bother, an' at the same time bein' let aff himsel.'

The penny was dropping inside MacKay's head.

'If oniethin, yer man Tennant's the real troublemaker,' continued the sergeant. 'Mair than yin witness identified him at the scene yet he swears he wasnae there. That maks him a liar an' a coward.'

'Yet, yer man Birse comes tae tak the blame on his behalf, he's that much looked up tae b' the rest,' interjected Anderson. 'I've seen it as often in Glesgae wi' ma ain een. Boys like John MacLean, he's yin tae watch let me tell ye, wi' their slick-tongued speeches an' their philosophisin' aboot better times comin' an staunin up for yer rights.' He paused briefly, looking grave. 'Thur educatit lads are dangerous when it comes tae public order, let me tell ye.'

'He cannae accoont for his whauraboots, richt enough,' added MacKay, bringing to mind his meeting at the Tennant house. 'Him an' his story aboot bein' oot for a dauner an' readin' his books.'

'Knowledge an' learnin's a dangerous thing in the workin' man, Archie,' warned the sergeant. 'Time tae tak Tennant doon a peg or twa an' put him in his place afore he gets ither boys intae even bigger bother, dae ye no agree?'

MacKay agreed with a sigh. It saddened him to think that he had been fooled by Neil Tennant's clean-cut image and good manners. It was always such a pity, he thought, when people who had been born into good families turned out to be trouble.

# Part Three
# Autumn

# Chapter 37

## CHOICES

Elizabeth was polishing some of her late mother's brassware when Mrs Tough came into the room to tell her that she had a visitor. There was no indication of who it was. That was the way of the old cook, a permanently disapproving look carved into her ancient face that gave nothing away, and that was the nature of their relationship, distant with few words spoken between them. Elizabeth's face lit up as she whipped off her sleeve protectors and wiped her hands as best she could on her apron. She didn't have many visitors, stuck here in the manse keeping house for her brother, and looking out at the world through the parlour window. She was overjoyed when she saw that it was Rose Matheson. As they hugged, Elizabeth ushered her into the parlour.

Rose explained that she had come to Blackrigg with her father who was covering whilst Dr Lindsay was on holiday but she had changed her mind about actually visiting his patients with him. Although she was due to start her medical training soon, Rose felt it an imposition to accompany her father on his rounds. To be invited into people's homes and to see them at their most vulnerable and most intimate, she told her friend, was a privilege that only qualified doctors deserved.

'I think he'll be a while. In fact, I've said I'll make my own way home,' said Rose. 'I thought I'd pay you a visit, catch up with your news. Are you busy?'

'I'm never busy,' said Elizabeth a little too honestly. 'Well, not too busy for a friend at least!'

'Have you heard from Phee?' asked Rose.

'I got a letter from Perthshire. She's been visiting a cousin for a late summer ball. They seem to live an incredible social whirl up in the glens. Didn't she write, Rose?'

'Oh, yes. She wrote all about it. I wondered if you'd seen her since she'd returned, that's all.' Rose seemed hesitant.

'No, I haven't seen her. She should have been back these last few days. I expect she'll appear at the door one day and brighten up the day! She's such good company, don't you think?'

'It would be nice to see her,' ventured Rose. Elizabeth sensed that her friend was, in fact, thinking of another member of the Melville family.

'Have you seen him much over the summer?' Elizabeth inquired after a while.

Rose sighed. 'Was it so obvious?'

'You mean, was it obvious that you were really talking about David? Yes it was, I suppose. How do you feel about going off to do your medical training? Is it what you really want out of life?'

Rose paused. 'In answer to your first question, no, I haven't seen David much over the summer. The naval garden party was a bit of a disaster but he still drops by at the house, ostensibly to see Daddy. I think he sees him as a bit of a father figure, to be honest. And there's the fact that he's a doctor, so there's a connection back to

David's student days, when he was so happy studying in Edinburgh himself. But I'm always left feeling he's actually coming to see me when he visits. Perhaps that's just wishful thinking, I can't be sure.'

'And what about my second question? Are you still intent on becoming a doctor?'

'Oh, I'm so mixed up, Beth,' she blurted out. 'It's all I've ever wanted to do with my life. I admired what my father did and one of my teachers encouraged me to think of it as a career. Then, when it's all organised and I can't wait to get started, David Melville appears on the scene, gives me long lingering looks across the dinner table, his eyes searching me out across crowded rooms and church halls, holding me with his eyes when I take him tea on his visits to my father.'

'You seemed so determined in your decision to study,' continued Elizabeth, wanting to help her friend work out her feelings. 'There is such need out there, Rose, the children who die or are maimed by the most frightful conditions, and discoveries being made all the time that might help in the future. You've wanted to play your part for so long. And their mothers too, Rose, dying way before their time from overwork and too many births.' Elizabeth was quietly shattered by her friend's predicament. Rose had been such an inspiration to her, an example she had hoped to follow when she found her own vocation, perhaps. She had set an example as a strong woman going out into the world, making her own decisions.

Rose agreed and seemed to pull herself together. She had seen the conditions in Rowanhill and Stoneyrigg and they appalled her. You would need to have your eyes closed not to see the effects of poverty and poor living conditions on people's health. It was all around, everywhere you looked.

She told Elizabeth about the pioneering work done by the Edinburgh Association in promoting university education for women, a twenty-five year campaign to have women admitted to higher education. Women like Sophia Jex-Blake who aspired to treat other women had eventually been admitted to read medicine, standing up to vociferous male opposition manifest in the Surgeon's Hall Riot, for example, when men protested against women studying and practising. At that time, the voices raised against them had been too strong and the law was used to keep them from qualifying. It took more than twenty years before Edinburgh's female medics prevailed and eventually gained equality with the men. Only single-mindedness and self-belief on the part of those women had made the changes come about, opening the door of opportunity for people like her, Rose Matheson, to follow on.

'What on earth would those women think of me, Beth? I should be grasping this opportunity with both hands? Shouldn't I?'

'I'm afraid I can't answer that for you,' replied Elizabeth kindly. 'You must be true to your heart, true to yourself, Rose. You have only one life and you are the one who must live it.'

'So many women don't have the choices I have because they don't have the opportunity; women like my own mother, who would have made a brilliant doctor but spent her life making tea and supporting my father.'

'But she was she and you are you and things are different now,' replied Elizabeth, encouraging Rose to be positive. 'Remember, you have the choice of whether or not to study medicine. Just because you can do something doesn't mean you have to do it. The thing is, this has to be an informed decision. You need more information, surely?'

Rose understood. That was the difficult part. 'How?' she asked.

'By visiting Parkgate House and speaking to David Melville, of course! Let's pay Phee an unexpected visit and see who else is at home!'

Elizabeth raided the kitchen and packed a small knapsack with bread and cheese, cake and plums. Mrs Tough looked on disapprovingly. She didn't like the way Miss Fraser was tramping around her kitchen, ignoring her in her very own kingdom. She had witnessed quite a change in the girl over the summer, she thought, preferring the demure shrinking violet she had been in the past to the bold and assertive young woman she was fast becoming. Mrs Tough determined to have a word with the minister about it. It would end in tears if she wasn't brought to heel, she decided.

As she left the manse with Rose, Elizabeth suggested they take the long route to Parkgate House, up the hill on the road to Woodhill, across the muir and down towards Paddy's Wood, picking up the track across Redburn Farm and into the stable yard at the back of the house. Rose agreed that a long walk would give them a chance to talk. Also, it would be better if they dropped into Parkgate 'by chance', rather than boldly walking up to the front door as if they had deliberately set out to pay a visit. Sometimes, it paid to be discreet.

The autumn had brought a distinct change in the weather. It was noticeably colder in the mornings and had been breezier of late. White clouds scudded across the sky; the wind blew in waves through the long grasses at the side of the road. The horse chestnut trees down by the public hall were already turning a brilliant shade of orange, and the rowans and hawthorns were laden with bright red berries, a sure sign of a hard winter to come.

Elizabeth knew the countryside better than Rose the Academic, so she pointed out landmarks as they came into view the higher they climbed. They left behind the chimneys and spoil heaps that peppered the southernmost part of the county for the empty swath of moorland that clothed the higher land. The more fertile land much further north formed a distant patchwork of fields: the greens and yellows of interwoven pasture and harvested crops were embroidered with fringes of woodland tinged with the first signs of autumn, like threads of gold and copper in a coat of many colours.

Rose was impressed by her friend's knowledge of the countryside and, in particular, her skill in identifying plants. To begin with, Elizabeth seemed to have an endless list of names tucked away in her memory but it soon became obvious that she was much more analytical in her approach, classifying them by the shape of their leaves, the arrangement of their flowers and, even by their habit, occupying different nooks and soils. As they left the road and headed across the moorland towards the shieling, Elizabeth warned her friend to keep to the path if she hoped to keep her feet dry. Although it had been a dry summer, the recent rains were filling up the peat. Extensive areas of bog were forming. She bent down to pick up a handful of green which she held out to Rose.

'Looks like a funny sort of moss to me,' said Rose.

'Correct, it's a bryophyte,' replied Elizabeth. 'Sphagnum moss or peat moss to be precise. There's thousands of different mosses, you know.' She squeezed her hand, producing a copious amount of water. She presented the same moss, now light and feathery like down from a pillow.

'Do you know what the tribal women of North America use this for?'

Rose was intrigued. This appealed to her enquiring mind though she was stumped for a practical usage for a plant with such sponge-like qualities.

'Napkins!' said Elizabeth. 'For babies, before they're trained to.... you know... keep it in!'

'How clever!' said Rose impressed. 'I wonder if we've used it here for anything like that.' She paid more attention as she followed the path across the muir, noting the large number of different plants all around, from the tiny insectivorous sundew to the various grasses that were so beautiful when she took time to look at them properly. The heather was about to burst into bloom, already painting the hills with a purple hue. It had always seemed such an unattractive, empty space to her before, not much good to anyone, just tough grass and heather clinging to the soil and to life, enduring the harsh weather in a place where more useful plants couldn't grow.

By the time they reached the ruined cottage, both were famished and thirsty. They sat on a long piece of wood on the sunny side with their backs against a tumbled-down wall, sheltered from the breeze. They shared the food in Elizabeth's bag, sipped the water from her flask. Nothing was said as they drank in the view.

Elizabeth noticed that the swallows had gone.

'Are you sure it's alright to come up here?' asked Rose after a minute. 'You seem to know the place well, Beth.'

'It's quite safe, I think,' she replied, not sure what Rose was getting at. As a picture of Grant the gamekeeper invaded her thoughts, she shuddered. She brought Neil to mind instead and smiled. 'I love it up here. It's a special place. I never feel lonely here, even when I'm on my own.'

She bit her tongue, waited for Rose to ask who she visited with. But the remark had gone unnoticed.

'What I meant was, is it allowed?' asked Rose, 'For us to walk here.'

It had never occurred to Elizabeth that walking here wouldn't be allowed. She shrugged.

'Haven't you heard about what happened to the men from the village?' Rose continued. Elizabeth hadn't, so Rose told the story of the trespassers who had been caught on Back o' Moss land whilst swimming with their children in the burn; and about how four had been charged and were waiting to be tried in the Sheriff Court. Apparently, David Melville and the police had taken a very dim view of the men going onto estate land without permission, she explained, so they were to be made an example of to discourage widespread trespassing in the future and to prevent interference in the work of the estate.

'Gosh,' said Elizabeth when her friend had finished her account of the incident. 'I hadn't heard the least thing about it. Nobody tells me anything, it seems.'

She realised more clearly how cut off from the world she felt in the manse. Mrs Tough had no conversation, just eyed her suspiciously whenever she went near the kitchen. Even in the early days of Elizabeth's arrival in the village, when she had tried her best to make conversation, the cook had simply grunted and kept her communications to matters related to food. Mealtimes with Richard were often taken in silence, after grace had been said. He seemed to have the scriptures and church matters constantly revolving round in his head. He didn't have much to say to her at all. After their arguments in the early part of the summer, she felt quite estranged from her brother and it saddened her.

'So that's why I was asking,' Rose interrupted her friend's thoughts, 'Is it alright to be here?' We can't be arrested for trespassing, can we?'

'I hadn't thought of it like that,' said Elizabeth. 'There's no wall or fence to speak of around the area so maybe it's alright. It's not as if the land's much used for anything anymore except when they come up to shoot. Maybe that's the problem with people going onto the farmland lower down, you know, they could be interfering with someone's livelihood. And in the past, before this was a shepherd's cottage, people probably came up here in the summer with their cattle so maybe we still have an ancient right to walk here, even though nowadays it belongs, strictly speaking, to the Melvilles.'

The two friends relaxed a little, brushing aside any thoughts that they might be trespassing, then talked once again about Rose's future. They discussed what they had heard about women in the cities campaigning for female suffrage. It was a gradual process, taking many decades. Men, it seemed, were not willing to see tradition overturned easily. Rose told the story of the Scottish Women Graduates Appeal to the House of Lords, when Jessie Chrystal MacMillan debated the contradiction of women graduates being excluded from voting in the election of the universities' MPs. Rose said that the women's movement was benefiting from the many changes and triumphs already achieved: women had spoken out for changes in the law relating to control of their own earnings and about the ownership of property, and had been successful; they had achieved the right to sit on governing bodies and even some local franchises had been granted. These many 'quiet' achievements were like trickling streams, Rose explained. They flowed gently into the raging torrent that was the clamour for women's suffrage.

The friends laughed with excitement borne of possibility. They talked about the opportunities for study that had been opening up to women but also about how much progress they still had to make when it came to careers, business, and family inheritance. They confided in each other, sharing their thoughts on marriage and children and love.

'Love – romantic love – is such an all-consuming force,' ventured Rose. 'It can leave you blind to all sensible action.' She studied Elizabeth's face for reassurance. 'It can come along at just the moment when you need to be able to see most clearly.'

'I know,' Elizabeth said at last, swallowing hard. 'Don't ask me how I know but I do. That's why it's so important that we, I mean you, find out if the other person feels the same way.' She looked into the distance, thinking of Neil.

'But men can have it all, Beth. They can have marriage, children, and a career. How long will it take for that to change in our favour? How long will it take for us to be able to choose both?'

'Perhaps *you* can have both, Rose.'

'But only if a certain man decides that I can!' Rose groaned. 'I feel like a pathetic fool, completely dependent on a man to decide my future.'

'Mmm, yes, women have a long way to go when it comes to choices in life!'

Elizabeth started to pack her bag, making ready to continue their walk.

'Come along, then, Miss Matheson,' she ordered, 'Can't hang about here, waiting to be arrested for trespassing. Let's go and see where your future lies! Watch out, Mr Melville, here she comes!'

They made their way downhill, off the moorland towards the edge of Paddy's Wood. On their last visit to the shieling, Neil had pointed out the way, in case Elizabeth hadn't wanted to walk back down the road. She hadn't seen him for what seemed a very long time. Even when she had boldly taken the long road back to the manse, past the forge, he hadn't been at work with his father as she had expected. It occurred to her that she wasn't meant to see him again, that it wasn't part of God's plan for them to meet and spend time together. If Fate could intervene for them to meet up, then it could surely intervene to keep them apart. She had decided that Fate or God's plan, call it what you will, sometimes needed a helping hand. That was why she had left him the flower in the hay cart after the Sabbath School outing. It was a message as clear and as loud as the restrictions and conventions of the day allowed her. But wasn't it now up to him? Wasn't it his turn to give Fate a helping hand? If he wanted to, of course, and that was by no means certain.

Elizabeth led Rose along the edge of the wood, glad to be giving Fate a push when it came to her friend's future, leading her to a possible assignation with David Melville and a better idea of his feelings for her. They walked quietly, each with their own thoughts.

Rose wondered if David would be at the house and what he would say when he saw her. The late summer flowers in the hedgerows and the sweet song of the woodland birds gave her hope for a happy reunion.

Elizabeth couldn't help looking around for Grant. As the tallest trees swayed gently with the wind, the sounds of creaking timber made her pulse quicken. This place did not have happy memories for her and every shadow brought a threat.

For different reasons, both women were glad when the towers of Parkgate came into sight and the sounds of servants busy at their work reached their ears. Billy Dodds gave them a wave as they entered the stable yard from the direction of Redburn Farm. When he asked Elizabeth how she was keeping, she assured him that she was very well but hadn't been back on a horse since the last time. He smiled broadly at the mention of the last time, when he had found her in the woods. He led out and tethered two horses, already saddled up and ready for riding. Elizabeth recognised them as Phee's mount, Prince, and old Major, the horse she had been riding when she had had her encounter with Grant in the woods. She stroked his forehead to let him know that she had no hard feelings against him.

'Is the family at home, Billy?' asked Elizabeth.

'Aye, Miss,' replied Billy. 'They are that. Seen Miss Isabelle a meenit past. Mr Melville should be in. He's no asked for the caur onieways so he'll be aboot the hoose some place. An' yer jist in time tae catch Miss Phee afore she gangs oot for a gallop.'

He smiled broadly at Rose. He thought she was a beautiful young lady, fresh-faced and rosy cheeked from her walk in the breeze and with the loveliest smile, one that could melt any man's heart.

The ladies thanked him as they went into the house through the rear entrance. Elizabeth was more familiar with the layout and led the way. She spotted Phee at the other end of the dark corridor that led through the old part of the house.

'Going out for a ride, Phee?' she called, pointing at her riding breeches and laughing when Phee looked back, obviously startled to see her.

'Oh! Oh, my! It's you Beth, how lovely to see you! I've been meaning to come and visit.' A smile lit up her face until she spotted that Elizabeth was not alone. 'And you've brought Rose. How... lovely!'

The visitors assumed they had caught her unexpectedly, that she had been slightly thrown by their sudden appearance when she was intent on a ride out with Prince. Though it wasn't like Phee to be caught unawares by anyone or anything. She ushered them through the darkness, into the drawing room where light flooded in from the garden. Elizabeth saw how quickly she closed the door behind her.

'We're sorry to interrupt when you're about to go out on Prince,' apologised Rose. 'But we were out for a walk and hadn't seen you for ages. So here we are!'

'Well, that's super!' exclaimed Phee, kissing each girl on the cheek. 'It's lovely to see you both. We must catch up properly sometime soon.'

Though not right now, thought Elizabeth, reading Phee's mind and sensing she was ill at ease. Rose looked out of the French windows, into the garden.

'Do you mind if I, sorry we, have a quick look at the garden before we go?' ventured Rose.

'Oh, alright, I suppose... if you really must.' Phee opened the windows for her friends to exit onto the terrace.

Elizabeth's suspicions grew when she noticed Phee take a furtive glance back into the drawing room. Perhaps they should just leave straight away; but Rose was intent on studying the lawns and the borders.

'Just a very swift visit, Rose. We've been walking for hours and we don't want to keep Phee back,' called Elizabeth. 'We'll come back another day when we've more time.' She watched as Rose stood, a lone figure, absorbing the vista of lawns and flower beds. What romantic thoughts were going through her mind? Was Rose remembering the dinner in early spring when David couldn't take his eyes off her. She had been dressed in a green silk dress and he had been drinking her in, causing her to blush with delight.

Elizabeth turned quickly to Phee. 'Is David in at all?' She hoped Phee would understand the true purpose of their visit.

She understood perfectly. 'Yes, he's here. But he's awfully busy, Beth. It's really not very convenient today. Couldn't you come back another time?'

Not convenient, thought Elizabeth. Your brother's been stringing our best friend along and it's time he made his intentions clear. 'Couldn't he see her? Just for a few minutes?' She kept her voice low so that Rose couldn't hear.

'Absolutely not, Beth. I can't explain right now but you must leave immediately. Both of you!' Phee nearly choked on her whisper.

'Rose! We have to go, Rose, I'm afraid,' called Elizabeth. She watched as Rose hurried back from the arbour where fruit hung ripe for the picking. Elizabeth could see how hopeful she looked, uplifted by the search for times past. They climbed the steps back onto the terrace.

'Thank you, Phee,' said Rose. 'I'm sorry if we've held you back. Can we come back and visit later in the week, when you haven't any plans?' She hugged her friend warmly.

'Of course, you can! I'd love to see you both, to catch up.'

She held the French door open for Rose to go ahead of her, into the drawing room. Phee drew back onto the terrace for a moment. She was about to say something to Elizabeth when she heard Rose gasp. They both rushed in behind her, almost knocking her over. Rose was rooted to the spot, staring at the chaise longue in the corner where David Melville and Catherine Imrie held each other in a close embrace.

# Chapter 38

## A WOMAN'S LOT – PROMISED JOY

When Dr Matheson called on Peggy Duncan, he found
Mary Birse cleaning the floor and keeping her company.
Peggy was sitting up in a chair, trying to find a comfortable
position but her back ached, she told him, regardless of
whether she stood up, walked around, sat up straight or
lay in her bed. Mary offered to leave but Peggy insisted
that she stay and listen to what the doctor had to say. In
all likelihood, it would be Highland Mary who would see
her through the long hours of childbirth when it came to
it.

The doctor watched his patient laboriously get onto her
bed and swivel onto her back with the help of Mary
supporting her legs. Whenever he saw a woman in the
advanced stages of pregnancy, as Peggy was, he thanked
God that he had been born a man. He listened to her heart
beat, took her pulse then counted her breathing. Then he
felt around her huge bump, praising her for reaching the
advanced stages of pregnancy without mishap. It had been
touch and go, he said to her, but she seemed to have come
through very well. Peggy said it was down to the help she
had received from her sons and her man but most of all,
from her friends and neighbours who had taken it in turns

to visit every day, bringing soup and brose, a helping hand, and good cheer.

'Well, you're as strong as an ox, Mrs Duncan. And the baby has turned into the right position, head down, ready to make his way into the world at any time. Maybe another week or so yet, right enough. There shouldn't be any difficulties with the birth since ye've had three bairns before.'

'Five, doctor,' Peggy interrupted putting him right. 'Mind I had twa stillbirths years back atween Lizzie and Rob. An' I lost a couple o' bairns that didnae come tae term afore I had Lizzie.'

'Well, ye've had two fine lads since all thon, so I'd say whatever was causing it has sorted itself oot, Mrs Duncan. Dinna fret about the birth, it should be fine.' He looked at her, a very serious look in his eye. 'But ye are getting on a bit, I think ye'll agree.'

'Aye, doctor. It wasnae ma choice tae have anither bairn. Bit ye've jist tae tak whit God gies ye an' he or she'll be loved like the rest.'

'I know, Mrs Duncan, I know. Your bairn will be much loved and cared for. But it's you I'm thinking of. I'm just saying, in light of the time you've had these last few months, having tae tak tae your bed and so on, another pregnancy wouldnae be sic a guid idea.' Doctor Matheson spoke with the clear burr of the educated Scotsman, peppering his message with Scotticisms in a way that endeared him to his patients, letting them know that, at the end of the day, he was one of them.

'I'll tak heed, doctor, I ken whit yer sayin,' she looked across at Mary, still busying herself with dishes in the corner.

'An' I'll mak sure she disnae gae mad afore the wean comes, an' she steys in her bed or close by,' offered Mary.

The doctor took his leave. The two women looked at each other for a while after he had gone.

'Can they vaccinate against bairns, Peg?' said Mary, breaking the silence. 'Then ye micht hae a choice aboot haein anither yin.'

'Och, dinnae stert oan aboot yon again. I've learnt ma lesson. There'll be nae mair bairns in this hoose, no efter this yin, mark ma words.' Peggy had made up her mind. 'Robert'll jist have tae be telt.'

'If they niver mak ye laugh, they niver mak ye greet, Peg.' It was an old saying more suited to her own situation than Peggy's but it was out before she realised it. Mary knew its meaning better than most. It had been little comfort in the first few years of her marriage, till she had realised that childbearing wasn't what Fate had in store for her. Alex had found it harder to accept. His years of disappointment rested sadly in her heart. It's an ill-divided world right enough, she thought. That was another saying, so true to life. She cleaned up the grate then added a lump of coal to the fire. Keeping busy was her cure for life's shortcomings.

Nothing more was said between the two women until Mary took her leave. She promised to look in the following day but Peggy was to send for her straight away if the bairn decided it was time to make its way into the world.

'I better gang hame an' get ma ain guddle sorted oot, Peg.' She put on her coat, turning the collar up against the cold autumn wind that whipped in through the open door. 'Och, here's young Meg Graham comin' tae see whit else needs daein. Cheerie, Peg.'

Mary stepped into the street, happy to have been of service to a woman, and a friend, in need. It was a south-westerly wind so the smell from the privies was blowing away from Stoneyrigg. In its place came the waft of soot and sulphur from the coke ovens on the other side of the road. If it wasn't one thing, it was another. That was yet another of the old sayings, she thought with a wry smile.

She spied Davy Potter's wife coming towards her and was about to ask how her youngest was keeping, since coming down with the croup. At the sight of her however, Davy's wife put her head down, her collar up, and hurried on past. Mary stood stock still. She looked after the woman, until she was completely out of view. Mary wasn't invisible the last time she had looked though she felt like it at that moment. She wasn't surprised though, not really. It had been like that since the incident at the burn. Bobby Cherrie's wife, Mags, was another one. She had pretended not to see her at the Co-operative store the previous week but Mary could tell that she had. Both their men were awaiting trial for trespassing, along with two others. She reflected on all of the help that she had given those families over the years, especially the women and children, and it saddened her to be punished for something she hadn't done. Guilt by association, was that it? Besides, Alex could never have foreseen the outcome of the swimming session, a piece of naughtiness rather than malice. Surely folk knew his heart was in the right place?

That was folk for you, she decided, and you just had to live with it. But she was a grown woman. She could take what life threw at her, even if it seemed so unjust. It was harder to watch the punishment being meted out to the twins. On several occasions, they had come home from school with new cuts and bruises. John had a rare keeker courtesy of one of the Cherrie lads. He was a big strapping lump like all the Cherries but at least the twins could stick up for each other in a scrap. When other boys, with no connection to the trespassers, had started on them, she had briefly considered going up to the school but that wasn't her way. It wasn't the school's business and what could the teachers do anyway? The boys had to learn to stick up for themselves – that was all there was to it. Her heart was heavy and her stomach churned at the thought of her boys being punched and kicked by the bullies but that was life. They would come out of it stronger in the end, and as long as they didn't turn into bullies themselves, she could thole it.

# Chapter 39

## CONSEQUENCES

Alex made sure as many people as possible knew about his visit to the police station and that he had tried his best to persuade the officers that the swimming expedition had been an innocent activity, not intended to cause damage or to make a political statement about the ownership of land. He had even offered to take the blame himself, he stressed, offering himself up as a sacrificial lamb at the altar of the law. He brought up the subject at the steading though fewer men stopped for a blether these days. When he stood in the queue for the cage with his fellow miners at the start of a shift, he had a captive audience. Similarly, when he was packed in with the other men for the drop to the underground roads, he told his story.

In the early days after the incident, much of the talk between the men was about whether the trespassers would lose their jobs and, by definition, their homes. There was gossip that Mr Imrie of the Coal Company and Melville of Rashiepark were cosying up to each other. It didn't take a brain like Isaac Newton's to work out that Melville could exact even more damage on the men by having them sacked. Also, it would send out a stronger signal, if it was needed, that Rashiepark land was private and that they had better keep off in future. However, within a few days, the men had been told that they would keep their jobs. Their representative had spoken up on their behalf. Mr Brownlee, the senior mine manager had asked for clarification of the names of the men involved and said he would consider their position. By the end of the day, he was able to confirm that the men were hard working and of good character, according to the testimonies of the supervisors. The company, therefore, saw no reason to let them go. Mr Brownlee's reputation grew as both a decent man and a hard but fair task master. His compassion in allowing the men to stay did the company's industrial relations no harm whatsoever.

As the time grew nearer for the court to hear the case of The Crown versus Cherrie, Brown, McColm and Potter, Alex had become more acquainted with the law and how it had worked. He could summarise the basic tenets of The Trespass (Scotland) Act 1865, explaining that the Stoneyrigg Four were being prosecuted on the evidence of the witnesses, Grant the gamekeeper and his attendees, who just happened to be in the vicinity at the time. The presence of the men in *'an inclosed space'* when Grant and his men had arrived, meant they were almost certain to be found guilty of trespass. Alex said that it was such a pity that the men had tarried by the burn long enough to be caught, whereas, if they had left in good time like the rest of them, there would be no case to answer since there would have been no witnesses to the fact.

He told everybody who would listen that the men were likely to receive a fine of no more than twenty shillings or a period of imprisonment not exceeding fourteen days. Since this was a first offence for each of them, it was most likely that they would be fined a smaller amount and that would be an end to it. Alex announced that he was willing to take charge of any donations to help the men pay their fines. Even though some might argue, he went on, that the men had only themselves to blame by staying too long at the burn. It would be a shame, he continued, for the men to feel that the fine was way beyond their means and opt for a short prison stretch instead. No matter how short, prison was to be avoided. The punishment should fit the crime and prison, so it was said, robbed a man of his soul.

The day after the trial, the mood in the cage was sombre. The news from the court had come through late at night the previous day and had spread like wildfire. Alex stood in the huddle of men as the metal cage dropped like a stone to the underground roads. The clanking of bars and metal grills being pushed back and forward seemed wholly appropriate under the circumstances. No one had much to say and Alex had enough sense to keep his mouth shut on this occasion. He had been more shocked than anyone else when he had heard that the judge had sentenced each of the Stoneyrigg Four to the maximum period of imprisonment.

In his judgement, the judge had explained, it was clear that there was common purpose in what the men had done. Although no damage to property had occurred, it was the timely arrival of the gamekeeper that had prevented an escalation from the mere presence of many individuals on farmland (interfering with the business of the farmer notwithstanding) to a full-scale riot, the consequences of which could only be imagined. Given that the men had earlier in the year, through intermediaries, made a request for permission to access the enclosed space in question, and given that said request had been turned down by the landowner, the men could not claim to be ignorant of either their rights and responsibilities under the law or the rights of the landowner to go about his lawful business on his own land. Although some might feel that a mandatory prison sentence was harsh in this case, the judge had continued, it should be remembered that Mr Melville had specifically sought leniency, asking that the charges be limited to trespass, rather than pursuing more serious charges, leading to heavier sentences.

Down the pit, the work carried out on that day was done with a great deal more vigour than was usual. Hutches seemed to be flung along rails with extra effort, borne of frustration. Boys shouted for more care and more patience, jumping out of the way as the loaded wagons clashed and bounced off each other. Men hewing at the coal face swung their picks as if justice could be wrought with every ding. Every noise sounded louder, every inhalation of dust-laden air penetrated deeper into the lungs and every movement in the cramped conditions of the semi-darkness was more awkward when anger was present and fairness was absent. They felt the injustice of the Stoneyrigg Four keenly. It multiplied with the injustice of their own working and living conditions. Yet there was nothing that could be done about it. They had no influence over what went on above ground. Here, deep in the earth, they were far away from the green spaces and the living air, closer to the fires of hell than anyone. Deep underground was the place where they spent their time and their talents, hidden from the world, and born to live like moles.

'But we're no moles,' said Alex under his breath as he trudged from the cage along the main underground road in the direction of the coal face. A mole was designed for life below ground where few other animals except worms lived. In fact, moles thrived in the darkness; near blind it was said. They didn't mind the darkness, nor the dirt and the tunnels running with water. He recalled how he had caught one as a child, digging down into a molehill and grabbing the animal with his small inquisitive fists. Its closed eyes and pink face with twitching whiskers had fascinated him as he stroked its sleek, black fur. It was as clean as a whistle even though it had been plucked from the earth. He had asked it, how come? He had put his finger up against the back of its large hand and felt its strength. It didn't like being held, he could tell, and there was nothing to tell its whiskers where it was. So, he had placed it back on the mound of earth, watched as it buried its snout in the warm soil, excavating with its shovel-like hands and disappearing back into its own world.

Here he was, he thought, a grown man hundreds of feet down in the land of the moles, peering through the pitch black and breathing in dust till he wheezed and coughed and spat. His clothes were caked in dirt, and padded at the knees. He was an animal in the wrong place but with no one to rescue him, no one to lift him up into the fresh air where he belonged; not till he had hacked at the coal face for eight hours, sufficient to fill half a dozen hutches. Then he could go back to his own world, the one he was made for; back to Mary and the twins, his neighbours and his allotment; an hour at the football on a Saturday afternoon, perhaps, and a good plate of soup made with a bone from the butcher. That was what he looked forward to.

Alex joined the other men at the fireman's station till they were told that the coast was clear. They stepped onto the bogeys, lined up ready to take them down the steep slope to the dook. The rope pulley controlling their descent creaked and stretched as the bogeys rolled downhill full of men. At the bottom they walked down the main tunnel together, the air cold and fresh at first. Small teams of men peeled off to the left, made their way to the coalface along several different tunnels. The machine man and the hand strippers kept on ahead towards the part of the coal face where one of the new coal-cutting machines had been installed. The machine would undercut the seam then shot would be placed to bring down the coal. The untrained strippers would move in and take out the coal with relative ease. Then a skilled man would appear to prop up the roof under the watchful eye of the foreman. Bringing in the new machines hadn't been popular with the skilled miners but the work had been contracted out by the Coal Company so there was nothing that could be done to stop it.

Alex, Robert Duncan and Davy Potts peeled off to the left with their team of young labourers. They followed rails they had laid themselves to the rail head where a rake of hutches stood ready for filling. Their eight-hour shift started as they made ready for work at the face. The older men were skilled facemen. They could turn their hands to any job underground and could read the lie of the rock. The youngsters were employed as fillers and drawers. They shovelled out coal into the hutches, pushing them back along the track to the drawing roads where they would be collected, taken up the steep incline to the tumblers at the bottom of the shaft, and uplifted to the surface for sorting and picking.

The small team stripped off to their vests and laid down their piece tins and tinnies of tea. It would be fully four hours before they could come back for a rest and a bite to eat. The road to the coal face was short but the roof was lower here, and everyone had to bend double. They were working on a section of the mine where the coal seam was thin, too thin to justify the installation of a machine, but still winnable by men. As long as the coal could be sold for more than the cost of its production, the management deemed the area workable. The older men set about examining the pit props that secured the roof and got to work on their allocated section of the face whilst the boys shovelled out the coal piled up from the previous day. It was hard work and hot, lying in the wet on one side then the other, undercutting an eighteen-inch seam with a small hand pick. The rock underneath was clay, a mudstone resembling shale, so relatively easy to excavate. The clay reddings from the main roads were drawn out then taken up to the brickworks for the manufacture of bricks, though not here, where the roof was so low and there was some doubt about the future of the face.

The three skilled workers made good progress, helped by the structure of the clay thereabouts, and aided by the comradeship between them. They relied on each other for their safety, reading the conditions, and reacting to the possibility of danger. They were piece workers, paid by the yard and by tonnage, depending on the bargain struck. Working hard was to their mutual benefit. As was normal, some of the coal collapsed as the undercut progressed and boys were called in to help with clearing the debris out to the rail head.

Sometime into the shift, a low, resounding rumble stopped everyone in their tracks. Small vibrations could be felt as rocks settled somewhere in the bedrock around them.

'Back tae the rail heid, boys,' called Robert calmly but firmly. The younger lads scurried away on all fours. Davy joined them, staring back along the faint beam of light from his lamp. Alex and Robert remained prone as a small shower of rock dust came down from the roof and rattled off their caps.

'Whit dae ye think boys?' called Davy softly, keeping his voice low in deference to forces in the strata that could bring the whole jing-bang down on them in an instant.

Alex called for another tree. A lad scampered in with a pit prop, retreating as quickly as he had come.

'It'll be fine, I'm thinkin',' Robert said as he helped Alex wedge the strut into place. 'We'll leave it for a bit, mak sure it's no gaunae come doon oan us.'

'Aye, cornin time, boys,' announced Alex. 'Time for a brek. It'll settle doon in a bit,' he added confidently. Or it'll come down with a crash and a cloud of dust, he thought to himself, worming his way slowly along the ground.

The others went ahead of him into the bigger road where there was more headroom and fresher air. They turned the corner, settled down with their backs to the tunnel wall, reaching for piece tins and opening tinnies for a long draught of warm tea.

Alex joined them, stretching the ache out of his legs and his neck. He settled back with his eyes shut for a moment. It had been a hard morning's work but satisfying for all that. Knowing you had done a good job kept you going, gave you self-respect. Everybody needed to know their life was worthwhile, even miners, or especially miners, working in the land of the moles. The team had made good progress, cutting under the coal face along a decent stretch and the young lads had drawn out the debris as well as the coal from yesterday. They could all take it a bit easier for the rest of the day. They would bring down the seam with a blast after the break. Boring holes for the explosives and firing the shot was straightforward enough and took less effort. Then the coal would be shovelled out from the face, ready for drawing out by the young lads.

The warm, sugary tea slipped easily over his dry tongue and down his parched throat. It didn't need to be hot to satisfy his thirst. It tasted like nectar. He wanted to have a moan about the government – tariffs on the sugar and the tea he drank, and tobacco and coffee too for that matter; goods that were bought in large quantity by poor working men like himself. Was it fair to tax the poor so heavily? He kept his mouth shut. For the first time since the start of the shift, the plight of the Stoneyrigg Four came to mind.

Prison was a harsh punishment for walking up the burn through a field of grazing cattle, only a few hundred yards further on beyond the ford and the old south road that folk had walked for centuries. The kye hadn't so much as flinched at the sight of the happy group. Fathers had warned sons to stay clear and not spook the animals, he remembered with a smile, and the boundary wall was just a heap of stones where it led into the water, easy to climb over without doing a bit of damage. They had only wanted to swim with their boys. But the law was the law, made by the rich to protect what they had, and it had to be administered or upstarts like him would get the idea that Scotland was actually his land because he lived and breathed there, working his fingers to the bone. It didn't exist for his use or his pleasure, that much was clear. His forefathers had been illiterate workers, labouring in the fields or in the mines, whilst other folk had had the time and the inclination to grab a bit of it for themselves and their families, by hook or by crook. He shook his head at the thought of it.

Alex picked up his piece tin and made to open it. The top was ready to spring off but that wasn't how he had left it. He always made sure the lid was secure before he tucked it under his arm for the walk to the pit. His stomach rumbled, telling him to hurry up with the pieces but something made him hold back. He looked at the rest of them, his fellow workers, like docile cattle chewing the cud, quietly staring into the murk and the shadows cast by a single lamp. He watched their mouths attack the bread and jam they had brought for their lunch, a bit of cheese if they were lucky. His fingers gingerly prised his tin open. The stench hit him first but he peeked in to make sure he had been right and wasn't imagining things. There were no sandwiches; just a large coil of excrement, newly laid. He snapped the tin shut again.

'No hungry the day, Alex?' asked Robert, making conversation. 'It's no like ye tae leave yer piece.'

Alex paused, hiding his anger in a slow intake of breath. 'Naw, no hungry the day, Robert. I'm leavin' it till efter.' His stomach churned and he tried not to boak. The message left for him was loud and clear. It hurt more than one of Big Wattie's fists at the dancing on a Saturday night. He sipped his tea to stave off the pangs of hunger and take away the smell of keech from his nostrils. He wondered who had done it. All of them or only one of them. It didn't matter, not really. He had tried to take the blame at the police station. Everybody knew that. How could they think he was responsible for the plight of the four men languishing in prison at that very moment? Anyway, could people not see the bigger picture? It was the law that was to blame, and the people who made it; the people who held land and made profit from it but who had done nothing to earn it in the first place; people like Melville who had inherited the wealth of his father, and who felt his position threatened by a bunch of workies and their weans going for a stroll along a burn.

Alex announced the end of corning time and went to collect the shot. He felt weary. Might as well get on with the job in hand, he decided. It was all they could do. It was all they had it in their power to do.

The shift passed quickly. Blasting, shovelling, scraping, filling and drawing, then inspecting the next part of the seam, newly revealed and glistening in the light of the lamps. There was plenty of work for them to be getting on with the next morning, and that left everyone with a feeling of satisfaction. The skilled men retrieved their tools which they stashed near the face. The younger boys collected a rake of hutches, stood them ready for filling. Then they joined the steady stream of men on the main road back to the bogeys for hauling up to the bottom of the shaft. Another day of toil over, they stood patiently in the queue for the cage.

Alex was subdued, all of his talk knocked out of him. He listened to the others waiting in line and pricked up his ears at the mention of the trespassers. It seemed no one was very sure about the fate of Neil Tennant. Someone shouted an enquiry back at Alex but he shook his head saying nothing. Neil seemed to be up for more serious charges, someone said, although the Stoneyrigg Four were adamant that they hadn't seen him by the burn and had stressed that he hadn't encouraged them to go on Melville land. As far as the four detainees were aware, Neil had headed up the deputation to the Big House and that was all. Over and over again, the men had been questioned by the police about Neil's political activities, and what they knew about them – which was nothing, of course.

Someone remarked that Neil had always seemed such a quiet, respectable lad, pleasant and well-mannered, quite bookish and not given to joining clubs or societies. No one could remember seeing him in the later part of the afternoon after he had left the Meadie, they agreed. So where had he been? Maybe he had been trespassing with the others, someone suggested, but they had forgotten or not noticed him being there. After all, said another, wee Billy Tennant had been at the swimming so Neil had probably taken him there. There was no smoke without fire, people were saying. Still waters ran deep as the saying goes, said others. Someone else made a connection between Neil and the outbreak of trouble around the Melville estate during the summer. Fire raising and breaking windows could have a political motive if the perpetrator felt a grudge against the estate for not allowing access to land when asked. Someone complained that the miners had been under suspicion for weeks because of these acts of vandalism, yet the bastard could have been right in their midst all along, keeping quiet whilst watching the unease grow.

As Alex crowded into the cage with a dozen others, and the doors slammed shut, he could hardly believe his ears when he heard several men agree that Neil Tennant must be as guilty as sin and all the more so for leaving other innocent lads to take the rap.

Crushed into the middle of the throng, Alex craned his neck upwards fighting for air. He sought out the daylight far above with tearful eyes. The cage reached the surface not a moment too soon. As the banksman drew back the grill and men spilled out into the winding house, Alex pushed through the surge of bodies in front of him. Noise converged from every direction; conveyors, cages, tumblers, workers, steam, hissing, shrieking, clanking, grinding, clashing and shouting. His head hurt. He felt sick and ran for the open air. Robert shouted after him, was he alright, but he kept running. He had to get away.

He ran through the heavy rain. It washed black dust into his eyes and chilled him to the bone. Not till he reached the long track up to the Rowanhill road did he stop. He bent over, retching, holding himself steady against the fence and sucking in air with deep, controlled breaths. Then he glanced back to make sure no one was nearby. The others were some way behind, a surge of blackened faces just visible through the murk, like an army straight out of hell. Alex opened his piece tin with clumsy, trembling fingers then emptied out the contents. He had had enough shite for one day and hurried home alone.

# Chapter 40

## THE REVELATION

Reverend Richard Fraser sat at one end of the dinner table while his sister sat at the other. Mrs Tough would be through with the main course in a minute and neither antagonist wanted to risk another argument in front of her. She was a woman who never had much to say in their presence but she was all ears.

Richard surveyed the heavy furniture and the decorative brassware that crowded out the room. He counted himself much blessed. A large aspidistra erupted from a porcelain planter by the window. He had carefully positioned it himself, to connect the room with the wondrous gifts of God outside in the natural world. A white linen cloth, embroidered but not ostentatiously so, covered the table. A dark, patterned rug on the wooden floor added colour to the otherwise austere surroundings. He felt pleased by the overall effect: a balance of solidity, status and severity that reflected both his nature and his calling.

Elizabeth would not look at him but he decided that he could play her at her own game, so he sat in silence. He aimed to look serene, clasping his hands together on his lap and holding his head erect, as if great thoughts were coursing through his brain. When the soup plates were being collected earlier, they had been arguing about the fate of the trespassers. He felt Elizabeth had become rather shrill at his refusal to agree that the men's punishment was harsh. He decided that his sister took delight in taking the opposite view from him in everything. It was the only possible explanation for her refusal to understand the importance of strong discipline and the need to enact the letter of the law when it came to the labouring classes, both in this case and in every case. Otherwise, chaos and anarchy would reign, he was convinced. When she had invoked the concept of a loving and forgiving God in support of her point of view, he had to admit he had been incensed. However, impertinence and irrelevance were typical of the female mind, he believed. It was a mind that was subject to all sorts of hysterias and imbalances, depending on the phases of the moon. He had read about it in a book.

The cook entered the room with a ham on a platter. It was placed in front of him for carving. She returned with a dish of mashed potato, the lumps clearly visible from ten feet away. Steam rose from a bowl of cabbage that had all the charm of hot, green slime. It looked as if it had been boiled to within an inch of its life, the product of a scientific experiment rather than a recipe for delighting the palate.

Richard gave Mrs Tough a hearty vote of thanks for her hard work and culinary skills and she retreated with what might have been a smile on her face. It was hard to tell. He picked up the carving knife and fork but they made slow impression on the meat. He tried to retain a modicum of control as he sawed away at the unforgiving ham.

Elizabeth was laughing at him, he was sure. He wondered if she needed more to do than simply keeping house for them both. A bit of cleaning, polishing, dusting, laundering and ironing might not be enough for her. She needed more to keep her occupied. The congregation paid for the services of a cook but perhaps, he mused, if he were to dismiss Mrs Tough, his sister could take on that role also and be much happier and contented with life as a result. When the first slice of ham finally gave way to his knife, he deposited it on a dinner plate. He swept back his hair with the back of his hand, patting beads of sweat from his brow. The minister fixed his sister with his eye as he passed over her plate. He was sure she could become a very good cook, with a little practice.

Elizabeth accepted the plate of ham cordially then added several lumps of mashed potato and a slop of boiled cabbage. She stared out of the window, though it was hard to see the daylight because of Richard's confounded aspidistra. She reflected on the recent disastrous visit to Parkgate House, feeling sad for Rose whose dreams and desires for life with David Melville had been dashed in the most cruel of ways.

She remembered feeling proud of her when David had offered them the use of the Melville car to get home, and Rose had refused saying that she had come under her own steam and would return the same way. When she had fled along the road to the village, it was clear that her heart was broken. Elizabeth could hardly bear to hear her sobbing. By the time they had reached the far side of Stoneyrigg, Rose had pulled herself together though. What was unbearable, she had raged, was feeling so deluded, and so stupid. She told Elizabeth that she was meant to be a doctor all along, of course she was, and how glad she was that things had turned out the way they had. Fate had intervened at exactly the right time. Now she understood what her path in life was to be. She would feel awful for a few days, that much was true, but she would be boarding the train for Edinburgh at the weekend, ready to embark on her studies at the university. She wouldn't have to worry about bumping into David or seeing him when he visited her father. She wouldn't be reminded of what might have been every time she saw the towers of Parkgate through the trees because she would be many miles away.

Elizabeth felt glad for Rose. Men, it seemed, were not to be trusted and could be so fickle. Her mind drifted back to her visit to the shieling where Neil had been waiting for her on that beautiful afternoon. They had shared cake and fruit from her satchel. He had been ravenous, she remembered, and they had laughed at his mouth crammed with plums. He had offered her wild strawberries, collected from the bank by the burn. He hadn't let her take them when she had tried. He had placed one in her mouth and she let him. Then he had kissed her as she lay in the warm, dry grass. He had stroked her fair hair whilst they watched the swallows whirring and circling, gathering in the blue sky above, getting ready to leave for the winter. He had told her that the same birds returned to the same place every year. The place where they had hatched and spent the summers of their lives was special, engrained in the memory. He had pointed to the nests in the broken eaves of the shieling.

People were like that too, he'd said, about places where they were born and were nursed by their mothers. The small kindnesses of long ago were never truly forgotten and the happy, innocent pleasures of youth remained in the heart even when the eyes grew dim, no matter how far away the person had travelled. She had thought he sounded sad but then he had taken both of her hands in his, told her that the shieling would always be a special place for him: special on account of the long views across to the mountains, because of the orchids and the butterflies, the swallows and, most of all, because of her, Beth Fraser, whom he loved with all his heart.

Elizabeth turned her attention back to Mrs Tough's cooking. She pushed food around her plate with little enthusiasm then looked out of the window again. The rain had started. The evening was drawing in, grey and cold. A shiver ran through her body and a tear threatened to spill onto her cheek. She had returned to the shieling several times but Neil hadn't come again. She left him flowers: messages of hope and joy. They were always there when she returned, withered and scattered by the wind. She had waited every time, huddled by the wall against the cold, where she had listened to the report of guns in the east, across the moss and in the woods, slaughtering the beauties of Nature for man's pleasure. On her final visit, she had seen Grant in the distance, his dark shape silhouetted against the top of The Law, watching her as she made her way home, weary and lost.

That was when she had realised that the blissful day with Neil, when they had watched the swallows gather in the sky, had been the last day of summer.

A loud knock at the front door brought Elizabeth's attention rudely back to the present. She heard Mrs Tough patter along the hall from the kitchen, moaning mildly about having so much to do but greatly interested in who could be visiting the manse and why. Then came the sound of women's voices and the parlour door opening. It'll be for Richard, Elizabeth decided – a parishioner in need of comfort and blessing at a difficult time. She returned to her plate, head bowed. Mrs Tough opened the door and looked straight at her. Perhaps it's Phee, thought Elizabeth when she looked up, her heart leaping. But it wasn't.

'It's for you, Miss Fraser,' announced Mrs Tough, turning briefly to meet the minister's enquiring eye. 'It's Mrs Tennant to see you, Miss. Mrs Tennant from the Smiddy.'

Richard Fraser sat with a pout, his features etched in bewilderment and disapproval. Mrs Tough stood stony-faced as ever, saying little but thinking plenty. Elizabeth ignored them both as she hurried from the room, a hundred questions running through her mind, her heart racing. She closed the parlour door behind her and tried to appear composed for the visitor.

'Do take a seat, Mrs Tennant,' she said.

The woman left her stance by the window. She sat in an armchair by the fire.

Elizabeth sat opposite and remarked on the weather.

'I hav'nae come tae talk aboot the weather, Miss Fraser.'

'No. No, you haven't. How can I help?' Elizabeth studied her visitor who looked anxious and drawn, the dark shadows of many nights without sleep circling her eyes.

The woman stared back at Elizabeth, taking in every detail of her, from the colour of her eyes to the cut of her clothes.

'Ye're acquainted wi' ma faimily, Miss,' she said eventually. 'We're modest folk whau work hard.' She was hesitant. 'I've aye worked hard for ma bairns an' I've taught them richt fae wrang.'

Elizabeth searched out the older woman's eyes and saw Neil in them. She wondered what was coming next and why this mother was finding it so difficult to speak about her children. She seemed to be taking great care over her choice of words, finding it hard to get to the point.

'I know that, Mrs Tennant. Billy's such a happy boy… he's doing well with his catechisms. And your daughters have only just arrived at the Sabbath School but I'm getting to know them very well. They must be a delight and a comfort to you and your husband.'

Mrs Tennant nodded. 'They're a blessing. We are much blessed, Miss Fraser. But it's no Billy or his sisters I've come to speak tae ye aboot.' She caught the younger woman's gaze and would not let it go.

At last, thought Elizabeth. She felt relief and closed her eyes. 'No. I didn't think it was. Is Neil well?' Suddenly there was an explanation for his absence. 'He's not unwell, is he? Ill, I mean.' Concern showed in her face, unease that was magnified in the shadows cast by the firelight in the darkening room.

'He's no ill, Miss. An' he's as weel as can be expected under the circumstances.'

'The circumstances?' Elizabeth looked perplexed. She frowned, desperate for an explanation.

'The circumstance of bein' in the gaol, Miss, these several weeks past.'

Elizabeth gasped in horror and put her hands to her face. 'Gaol?!'

'Ye didnae ken, then?' Mrs Tennant could see that Elizabeth hadn't known. It was only too clear that this was news to her. When she had come to the manse, she hadn't expected to feel pity for the girl. Now that she saw her in this cavernous house, cut off from the world, she seemed as much of a prisoner as her own dear son, locked up at that very moment and awaiting trial.

Elizabeth shook her head in disbelief as Neil's mother told the story of his arrest on the evening of the picnic on the Meadie when some of the workmen had taken their boys swimming on Melville land.

'But I thought only four men had been tried for trespassing,' explained Elizabeth, confused by Neil's place in it all.

'Yer richt enough. Jist fower have been tae trial thus faur. But Neil's still in the gaol waitin' his turn, even though he swears he wasnae there at the burn. An' a'body else who was there, even the men who've been tried an' convicted, swear that he wasnae there.' Mrs Tennant blinked back tears of frustration born of injustice. 'Ma younger boy was though, he was at the burn. He's telt me he went wi' the ither lads an' their faithers tae swim. Billy swears Neil didnae gang wi' him cause he had a'ready gang aff tae some ither place.' She stopped gesticulating, leaned her head forward on her hand with a sigh. She looked weary. 'An' Neil jist says he was walkin'. He likes to walk in the hills.'

'I know that,' said Elizabeth softly.

'He says mebbe somebody seen him walkin' while the men were swimming, Miss Fraser. But he cannae gie ony names. He gies the impression he was by himsel yon efternin. Neil's awfu' guid wi' words, an' it's whit he's no sayin', thon's whit I need tae ken.' She leaned forward and looked straight into Elizabeth's eyes, searching out the truth. Her hand uncurled from where it held her shawl closed around her. She held it out for the younger woman to see. A white handkerchief edged in lace, embroidered with the letter 'E', lay in the palm of her hand. There was a flower too, withered but still recognisable.

'It was in amangst his things.'

'Yes, it's mine.' Elizabeth took it carefully and lovingly with trembling hands.

'Can ye help him, Miss Fraser?' She was pleading. 'Whit are we if we dinnae hae Truth?'

'Yes, I can help him, Mrs Tennant. He was with me on the afternoon of the trespass.' Her love for Neil swelled in her breast. Now she understood why he had not been to meet her at the shieling in recent weeks. And she understood that he would not say where he had been or who he had been with to protect her, even when it left him in a cold, dank cell awaiting trial for something he could not have done; but she was left puzzled by it all. There were questions that remained unanswered such as why Neil hadn't been tried and convicted with the rest of the men for trespass; and why he had been arrested in connection with the incident at all, when other men who had been there hadn't been arrested later like he had. The authorities seemed content with convicting only the four men caught at the scene yet they had seen fit to come for Neil.

'On what grounds have they arrested Neil? They must have testimonies saying he was at the scene. Who spoke against him? And why was he not tried with the other men?'

Elizabeth listened intently as she was told about how the gamekeeper, Grant, was the main witness for the prosecution and about how Neil's participation in seeking access to the burn had been used to suggest that, somehow, he had a grudge against the estate and a wider, possibly political, motive.

'A story's been concocted tae discredit ma son who is a guid man, Miss Fraser. It seems that people jist see whit they want tae see an' I dinnae ken hoo or whit wey this has come tae pass.'

The light was beginning to dawn on Elizabeth, however. She could not be sure of all the detail but the picture was becoming clearer. 'I know what has to be done, Mrs

Tennant, never fear. I promise that I will do everything in my power to see that justice is done for Neil.'

Night had descended without either woman realising it. Firelight danced around the room as they hugged, two women united in their love for one man. Smiles lit up their faces and tears flowed: tears of relief and joy.

'Thank ye kindly, Miss. I'm richt gled I come by. Ye'll sort it, will ye no?'

Elizabeth gave a nod and they hugged once more.

Mrs Tennant put her shawl over her head before hurrying out of the manse, bowed against the rain and the howling wind. Elizabeth gently closed the door. She put the handkerchief to her face and inhaled the smell of him, Neil. Then she turned to face her brother. He stood motionless in the dark hallway staring back at her. She knew what had to be done.

# Chapter 41

## A WOMAN'S LOT – HARVEST

The children of the village, in common with their peers all across the country, were looking forward to the mid-term holiday in October, a welcome break from the routine and hard discipline of school, and an opportunity to get out into the fresh air before winter set in and the nights became interminably long. It was only when the Friday afternoon bell rang and released them into the playground that the reality of what was ahead dawned on them. It was tattie week, a week of hard, back-breaking work when they helped to bring in the potato harvest. When the teacher had been detailing the list of farms where labour was required, Jim Forrest had put up his hand to tell the class that in Fife, the tattie holiday was two weeks long, such was the magnitude of the potato harvest in those parts. At the gasp of envy that rippled round the class, Miss Foulkes had warned everyone to count their blessings. After just one day of lifting potatoes, they would all remember what hard work it was and would be longing to be back in her class sitting in a fine wooden chair, specially provided for their use. People have such short memories, she had declared, and told them she would pray for good weather for their sakes, suggesting that they do the same.

The farms immediately adjacent to the village had only small areas of land given over to the cultivation of potatoes, such was the poverty of the peaty, acidic soils thereabouts. However, further out towards Rowanhill and north, towards Bridgecastle, two centuries of improvement by ploughing and liming had rendered the ground more suitable for arable production so larger areas were given over to the crop.

On the first morning, a crowd of women and children waited by the road for transport out of Stoneyrigg. In many cases, mothers accompanied their own and Meg Graham was there with her younger sisters, Minn and Sarah. The household chores would need to wait for a week. An opportunity to augment the family income in the potato fields could not be passed up. Peggy Duncan and Mary Birse being notable by their absence, the women present asked the Duncan boys how their mother was doing. They looked embarrassed, said they didn't know but the bairn must be close because Highland Mary had been there in the house all night. The Birse twins beamed with pride at the mention of their mother, her having such an important role in the community, but it had its downside. She hadn't been at home when they had left that morning. Their breakfast had amounted to a piece of dry bread and there was no hot, milky tea on the go, not like they were used to. Their mid-day piece amounted to a couple of slices of bread, thinly spread with syrup. Not much to keep you going all day in the fields but they loved the prospect of being with their pals whilst earning a bit of money for their mother in the process.

Everyone was well wrapped up against the cold wind but at least it was dry, someone remarked. You had to look on the bright side, after all.

'Miss Foulkes must've been prayin' for us, richt enough,' said Dan.

'Aye, but no ower hard,' remarked Sandy. He pulled his jacket close about him, tightening his woollen scarf against the biting wind.

They piled into the carts when they arrived, smaller children sheltering against their mothers; older boys hanging onto the tailboards at the back because there wasn't enough room for everyone. Just as the horses started to pull away, Minn spotted her friend running beside them, waving for a lift. Jenny hadn't been tattie-howkin before so she had been nervous about coming.

'Haud on, haud on!' called Minn. 'We forgot aboot Jenny. Stoap!'

The second horse slowed down and Jenny was pulled aboard by Mags Cherrie who gawped at the girl's snow-white apron.

'God, hen!' she gasped, 'Are ye comin' tae pick the tatties or tae bile them?'

Jenny fell in amongst the girls as a mother started singing to calm her fretful child. The girls soon joined in such was the happy mood. Before long, the singing was loud and cheerful. It got even louder after Mags prophesied, 'Aye, yer singin' noo but ye'll be greetin wi' the pain in yer back afore the day's past.'

But nothing was going to dampen their spirits. They sang the songs of the tinkers who always appeared for the tattie-howkin.

*"Dae ye see yon bonnie high hills,*
*A' covered ower wi' snaw?*
*They pairted mony's a true love,*
*And they'll soon pairt us twa*

*Busk, busk bonnie lassie an come awa wi' me*
*An I'll tak ye tae Glen Isla and bonnie Glen Shee."*

A highly polished motor car swung into the roadside just in time, before the corner at the brae. Dr Matheson wound down his window and gave a cheery wave. The tattie-howkers waved back vigorously. The women in the carts gave each other knowing looks as they peered after the car. Why was the doctor out so early? They looked at the Duncan boys but said nothing.

The driver of the next vehicle on the road wasn't as patient. A loud horn sounded incessantly from behind, causing both carts to pull onto the verge to give it room. As it passed, the glum expression of David Melville stared at them from the back seat. The singing subsided briefly then started up again, much louder than before. Perhaps the Laird o' Rashiepark could hear them? The boys gave it laldie this time.

*"Dae ye see yon bonnie sodgers*
*As they marched alang,*
*Wi' their muskets on their shooders*
*And their broadswords hingin doon?*
*Busk, busk bonnie lassie an come alang wi' me*
*An I'll tak ye tae Glen Isla an bonnie Glen Shee."*

When they arrived at the field, work was already in progress. The tinkers had been up early, following the horse that pulled the digger. The pickers put potatoes in baskets then ran up to their foreman when they were full. The grieve stood on the back of a cart, recording the amounts delivered by the foreman.

Straight away, the Stoneyrigg crew divided into teams and was following the same procedure. It didn't take long for it to be going like clockwork. The cold wind was forgotten as everyone warmed up, full of intent and purpose. Along with the crows and the gulls, they followed the digger, spying the small, pale mounds in the soil then tossing them into the baskets, quick as you like. The women, even more than the children, found the work arduous and were often to be seen standing up and arching their backs to ease the pain. They were carrying on the tradition of many generations. It had always been women's work, picking potatoes or cabbages, and gathering in the stooks of corn for storage in rucks or in barns whilst men gaffered, worked the horses and machines, and saw to the livestock beyond the confines of the farmyard.

When stoppage time came for a bite to eat and a drink of water, the small army of potato pickers gravitated to the edge of the field seeking refuge from the biting wind, raw and unforgiving. They nestled in the shelter of a hedgerow: a mix of tall trees and smaller bushes. Grey clouds blocked out the sun but it felt warm, huddled together, breathing hard from the morning's work.

Minn Graham loved tattie-howkin. Her father often said she was destined to work on the land, she took such delight in being out in the fresh air. She loved the smell of the newly turned soil, thick and black and moist, to see the tubers peeping out ripe for the picking, and to watch the jackdaws strutting around in search of worms, checking her out with a pale blue eye. She loved to be with her sisters, helping them to pile the potatoes high in the baskets – kind Meg with a brightly coloured scarf round her hair and Sarah, laughing with delight when she fell over clods of earth and her apron got dirty.

The tinkers always sat a little apart from the rest of them, Minn noticed, as she ate her bread and cheese. They had a tent of sorts, stretched over birch branches, and a small fire going with a pot hung above. They were more like the birds and the beasts of the fields than the Stoneyrigg people, she decided, living in the open air like they did, eating berries and the small animals of the hedgerows, and making and mending things for a few pennies. They seemed contented enough. An old man sat stripping wood from a willow wand for mending the pile of potato baskets beside him and Mags Cherrie – she had gypsy blood it was said – sat in conversation with an ancient wife whose skin was the colour of the tobacco they were smoking in the pipe they shared.

Minn watched the boys, already back on their feet with a piece of bread in one hand, exploring a stream that ran downhill beyond the hedge. The Birse twins, Bert and Dan, and the Duncan boys: they never sat down for long and always seemed to be on the go. Andrew Brownlee wasn't there. It wasn't the place for the son of the pit manager. She wondered if Mrs Duncan had had her baby yet. Rob was a quiet one these days, embarrassed when you went to the house with a message and nothing to say if you spoke to him on the way to school. She was glad that Daisy Gowans wasn't there at the tattie-howkin. Her father was tenant at Redburn Farm so she would be helping there, if the work wasn't beneath her, of course. That day, Minn had Rob all to herself.

She lay back in the grass, enjoying a few minutes peace before the work started again. The wind rustled the withered beech leaves, high up in the trees. The hawthorns carried a bounty of berries but were otherwise bare, a tangle of branches, black against the grey sky. Field fares and wax wings, newly arrived from far-off shores, sang in the bushes and on the ground. As she studied the clouds, it occurred to her that this might be the last time she would be here like this: at the potato harvest with her friends and neighbours. This would be her last year at school. The following year, she would be working for a living and life would never be the same.

She watched Mags Cherrie with her gypsy blood cackling like a witch with the tinkers. The younger mothers were enjoying a blether and a joke together, their youngest children wandering in safety nearby. The boys by the burn had found a branch to swing on and John Birse had already fallen into the water up to his knees. Most of all, Minn studied her sisters: Sarah, the comedian in the family who struggled with her schoolwork but was so good with her hands, and Meg, her eldest sister and second mother.

Tears pricked Minn's eyes when she looked at Meg. She was to be married to Will and they had plans to go to Canada. They were saving for the passage then would leave in the spring. Minn couldn't bear to think of Meg on the other side of the ocean, far away where she couldn't see her or speak to her. Why did everything have to change? Sometimes things changed for the better but not always. This was where she would live her life, Minn was sure: here in the parks and the hills and the wooded valleys of Scotland. Meg would leave one day, searching for pastures new like the geese flying high in the sky above, a new life in a new place, following her heart. But this was where Minn's heart was, for better or worse, for richer or poorer, here was where she wanted to be and here she would stay.

Lowsing time came at last and the tattie howkers bid the men farewell till the following morning. There was no lift home but the carts would come for them again, early the next day. That was the arrangement. The walk home was less of a trial than expected. The walking let them stretch out their backs and they could take the shorter route home, over the hill. Friendly banter and good company made time fly. The wind was stronger higher up though, out of the shelter of the parks. It left the cheeks scaddit and ears sore with the chill of it but it spurred everyone on to walk faster, and they soon warmed up.

By the time the village was in sight, the women remembered that Peggy Duncan had been in labour. They geed up the Duncan boys with cheerful chat about the prospect of a new baby in the house though, in the backs of their minds, was concern about whether Peggy would be alright or not. She'd had a difficult time of it these past few months and childbirth was a risky business, even for the youngest and fittest of them. However, the prospect of a new life coming into the world filled everyone with optimism. A new life was a new start, full of possibilities and purpose. So, the talk all the way down the hill road was about babies and families and hope for the future. Even Mags Cherrie, proud mother of eight, didn't feel inclined to give one of her dire warnings and they were all grateful for that.

They left the countryside behind as they crested the hill then descended the road below The Law. Tall Scots pine trees were replaced by chimneys belching smoke; the patchwork of fields and the open moorland became a maze of works and sheds; and instead of green hills, heaps of spoil and mounds of coal rose out of the ground.

At the bottom of the road, wee Geordie Broadley was waiting for them by the steading. He leapt out to tell them there was news. The tattie-howkers gathered round, eager and expectant but with bated breath. They pushed the Duncan boys to the fore.

'Rob and Sandy have a baby brither! An' it's a girl!' he announced proudly.

Bert corrected him, 'They've a sister.'

Everybody cheered and gave a round of applause.

'He's called Margaret!' said Geordie.

Everybody laughed, and Rob and Sandy smiled broadly.

'An' whit aboot Margaret's mither? Whit aboot Mrs Duncan? Is she fine?' quizzed Mags, thinking it was better to know sooner rather than later.

'I dinnae ken,' replied Geordie with a shrug. 'But she was hingin oot the washin' earlier oan this efternin.'

# Chapter 42

## THE PROMISE

Elizabeth faced her brother across the vast expanse of the dark hallway. Mrs Tough had been sent home. The two were alone. The wind howled around the eaves and rattled the windows in every room. A door upstairs slammed shut in the draught.

Richard broke the silence between them. 'What did the smith's wife want?'

'You knew that he was imprisoned,' she glared at him, her eyes full of anger and contempt. 'When we were talking earlier, you knew and you chose to say nothing. Yet we spoke of the trespass affair at length. Why?'

'I told you to stay away from him.' Richard's face was hidden in the shadow, his voice as dark as the night. 'What did the smith's wife want?' he repeated.

'Why did you say nothing about his imprisonment when we spoke earlier?' Elizabeth waited for an answer but none was forthcoming. 'The minister's sister is asking a question!' she yelled. 'I am asking a question and I expect an answer! Why did you not tell me that Neil Tennant was in prison awaiting trial?!'

'And I told you to stay away from him. His affairs are of no consequence to you but his mother seems to think that they are. Otherwise, she would not be paying you a visit.'

'He is a good man, better than you by far.'

'You are in my care and you will do as I command.'

'He is a far better man than you, in spite of all of your preaching and holier-than-thou affectations,' she said failing to appear calm. 'He is a good man,' she repeated.

'Who does not attend the church he was brought up in!'

'He thinks for himself. He makes up his own mind. Why is that such a crime, such a threat?'

'He is self-seeking and devious, proved by his present situation. He is charming, doubtless, and you have been fooled by him. You are a young woman remember, one dance at a village fair and you are besotted. You have no experience of life and are easily swayed in your opinion.'

'I know my mind very well, Richard, but you are far too quick to judge. It is you who is self-seeking and devious, not him. You hypocrite!'

'You live in this house at my discretion and will temper your language, sister. Else I will have you dealt with. There are ways of dealing with wayward and highly strung women who become difficult to handle.'

She could see that she had gone too far but his threats landed on stony ground. She could not think of the consequences for herself, Neil was uppermost in her mind. 'I know that Neil Tenant is a good man and would never do what they are accusing him of. He would never incite others to do anything untoward and, certainly, would never leave others to take the blame had he been involved in any way whatsoever. I will testify on his behalf.'

Richard walked away from her laughing. He went into the kitchen forcing her to follow.

She made her way along the long, dark hallway in close pursuit.

'He'll need more than a testimony of good character from the likes of you, dear sister, to get himself out of a mess such as this – a mess of his own making.' Richard's tone was mocking.

'That's right, he will need more than a good word spoken on his behalf,' she agreed. She watched as he prepared the oil lamps for lighting. 'I am his alibi. I was with him on the afternoon of the trespass. And this mess is someone else's making, not his.' She could see her brother's face better now. He was having trouble taking in the magnitude of what she was saying. 'Those who bear witness against him are lying, Richard. I know this to be true. I do not know why they are lying but I know that they are. I know because I spent that afternoon in his company, at the sheiling up on the road to Woodhill.'

He spun around and faced her, the look of shock on his face clear to see. 'You Jezebel! Yer nae mair than a slutterie tail!' Then he thought better of it; continued in a more thoughtful vein. 'If that were true, he could have saved himself before now. Why has he not told the police of this, then the matter would never have been taken to this advanced stage? Instead, at the last minute, he sends his own mother to plead for your assistance.'

'Are you so turned against him in your opinion that you cannot see the simple truth when it is staring you in the face?' She studied her brother whom, it seemed, she hardly knew. 'Neil has said nothing of my tryst with him because he is a good man. He does it to protect me. Don't you see? He has kept his mouth shut to protect my reputation, even when the cost to him is so dear.' She let the truth sink in. 'Richard, I am asking for your help.'

'I will not help in this.'

'Alternatively, I can go to the police with my story and your reputation will be sullied as much as mine.'

'What do you mean?'

'Scandal, Richard. It taints all who are near. I am asking that you accompany me to Parkgate House for a meeting with David Melville. He has the power to bring all of this to an end. If I go directly to the police with my evidence, they might not believe me, in which case I will have risked your reputation as much as my own for nothing.' She knew she had to appeal to her brother's own self-interest. Nothing else would hold sway in his deliberations.

Richard stood, considering his position. The wind whistled eerily in the chimney. The windows rattled.

'As you say, I am a young woman,' she continued. 'Men, and some women for that matter, might question my judgement, my recollection, and my motives. I know this because I have experienced it already in my short life. Listen to what I have to say, Richard. Do not judge me, just listen until I have finished.'

She told him about her experience with Grant in the woods, and about how David Melville had decided that her version of events and her assessment of Grant's intentions might not be believed; not against the account given by both the gamekeeper and the stable hand who had rescued her. Perhaps David Melville himself had not believed her. That was entirely possible. It showed her how difficult it could be for a woman like her to be taken seriously and that a man's assessment of a situation would often hold sway. It proved to her that people only see what they want to. Somehow, she was certain, David Melville's assessment of Neil Tennant's character had played a part in his wrongful imprisonment, accused of something that he couldn't possibly have done. Since her testimony contradicted that of the gamekeeper so completely, the other charges were likely to be trumped up too, she explained. The case against Neil would fall like a house of cards.

'But what is Grant's motive in all of this? He has stated that he saw Tennant with the others. Why would he lie like this and ensure an innocent man was wrongfully imprisoned?'

She was too concerned with Neil's welfare to be stung by Richard's questions, which challenged her evidence so directly.

'I do not know the answer to your question. Only Grant knows what his motive is... revenge perhaps, a long-held grudge, jealousy, or simply to impress his employer, knowing the laird is impressionable and suspicious of Neil because he led the deputation that was denied access to Melville land?'

For all his own suspicions about Neil Tennant's intentions towards his sister, Richard Fraser could not contemplate the possibility of an innocent man going to prison. At the same time, he wasn't entirely taken in by Elizabeth's protestations. What to do? He faced a moral dilemma and would need God's help to resolve it. If he did not offer to accompany her to Parkgate however, Elizabeth would surely go to the police and the entire community would hear of it. He would be left with his reputation sullied by his silly, lovesick sister, hell-bent on lying to save her sweetheart from justice. The stench of immorality would follow him, preventing him from doing God's work. What would the elders make of it? He felt backed into a corner though an opportunity was presenting itself, and he seized it.

'I will accompany you to Parkgate as you request, Elizabeth. We will meet with David Melville to discuss what you have told me.' He hesitated then drew himself up to his full height. 'But only on one condition.'

'Condition?' She was suspicious.

'You must promise me that you will not have further acquaintance with this common workman, this Tennant character.' Richard saw her despair and enjoyed it. 'That is my condition, Elizabeth. Judging by your previous experience at Parkgate, David Melville is unlikely to believe what you say without my assistance.'

Her hands came together by her lips as if in prayer.

He ignored the tears that welled up in her eyes. 'Take it or leave it. That is my condition. Promise me that you will have nothing more to do with Neil Tennant in the future.' He lifted his lamp then made to leave. 'Or risk letting him rot in gaol for a very long time.'

# Chapter 43
## IN SEARCH OF JUSTICE CONTINUED

David Melville entered his study in a flap. So many estate matters required his attention and plans for the development of Rashiepark's mineral resources were being agreed. Securing the investment of other people's money was a very time-consuming business, it appeared. Not content with having the run of the estate, with the gamekeeper and the gillies at their beck and call, the financiers seemed to want – and to expect – the laird's company at the same time. It was a very fluid situation, giving cause for great concern. The future prosperity of the Melville family depended on it. There was so much to be done and yet here sat the minister and his sister, insisting they had a very important matter to discuss with him, something that could not wait.

'I've asked for tea. It's been a hectic morning. You'll have some, won't you?' He sat in his large leather chair, gave a sigh then rubbed his eyes with the heel of his hands. 'Do forgive me. Such a busy time of year and Isabelle's plans for a Harvest Home are just adding to the guddle.' He gave a mild chuckle, happy that he had impressed upon his visitors just how valuable his time was.

'It's very kind of you to see us at short notice.' Richard Fraser was at his most obsequious. 'We would not impose ourselves upon you at this busy time if the matter were anything other than urgent, requiring your prompt attention and,' he stressed, 'extreme discretion.'

David looked at the brother and sister. He couldn't take to the minister at all but he had his uses in keeping the flock in order and so on. However, he seemed to be fighting a losing battle with the great unwashed who were moving into the village in search of work. Recent events proved that. As for the girl, she was a pretty little thing but, otherwise, she was hard to fathom. He brought to mind her accusations against Grant, made earlier in the summer. That matter seemed to have died a death, proof that the actions he had taken as laird had been sufficient and well judged. Now here she was once again, with her brother, asking for help with another matter that required *'extreme discretion'*. What could she possibly want of him this time?

Richard Fraser gave a mild cough.

'What can I do for you then? What is so urgent?'

'It's in connection with the trespassing incident, David,' explained the minster, hoping to appear friendly rather than impertinent in using his given name.

'Rather late to be discussing that, I'm afraid. It's just about done and dusted.' He frowned. 'Unpleasant matter, I must say, but soon to be concluded to our great benefit.'

'And satisfaction,' added Elizabeth. She returned his gaze, her eyes cold, accusing.

David was surprised at her directness. 'Not at all, Miss Fraser, not in a personal sense at any rate. But satisfied that justice will have been done, as I'm sure, you will be. Or should be.' What was this, he thought, some deputation asking for leniency based on misguided Christian principles?

'An innocent man is awaiting trial,' Elizabeth stated. 'Neil Tennant has been wrongfully accused and imprisoned.'

David signalled for the tea tray to be deposited on his desk as Nell Graham entered the room. She gave a short curtsey, smiled softly at Elizabeth.

'Thank you, close the door please,' he ordered as Nell walked away. He bore in mind the Frasers' request for discretion, waited until they were alone before proceeding. 'I'll be mother, shall I?' He began to pour tea, listening for further explanation, a little thrown by this sudden turn in events.

'It would appear that Neil Tenant has an alibi for his movements on the day of the trespass,' explained Richard. 'My sister is correct. Neil Tennant could not have been trespassing as your gamekeeper has testified.'

David called to mind Neil Tennant's look of anger when he had burst into the room on the evening of the dinner party in early spring. He had visited the house in search of a doctor for an ailing child – Isabelle had kept him from his mission. He was an angry young man, envious at the sight of wealth and plenty. David had long ago decided that his refusal to grant the community access to Rashiepark land for recreation, had combined with the experience at the dinner and crystallised into some sort of political fervency on Tennant's part. This was not uncommon in these days of social change, he had heard from friends in the law and elsewhere, and knew it had to be resisted.

'Grant is lying,' interjected Elizabeth in response to David's silence. 'Or he is mistaken. I can swear to Mr Tennant's presence elsewhere on the afternoon in question.'

'Several of Grant's party have also spoken against Tennant,' David reminded her.

'Then they are lying or are mistaken also,' she replied.

David gave an exaggerated sigh.

Richard took up Neil's defence on Elizabeth's behalf. He could see the doubt in the laird's mind. When he had finished, he appealed to the younger man's good sense for support in preventing a travesty of justice.

'We hoped that you could go to the authorities, that is, outwith the police. That you might use your influence to have Mr Tennant released. You can understand our wish for discretion, I'm sure.'

'And what might Grant's motive be? Does he bear a grudge against this Tennant individual?' he enquired, looking quizzically at Elizabeth. 'It seems rather far-fetched that Grant is spiting you, Miss Fraser, for your earlier accusations about him, by having Mr Tennant wrongfully accused.'

'We cannot know or understand the workings of an evil mind, David,' offered Richard. 'Who knows what legacy Elizabeth's rejection of him has engendered? Who knows how such a man might act in not getting his... way?' Richard winced at the thought of it. 'Perhaps he is aware that Elizabeth is... acquainted with Mr Tennant.'

'If I am to intervene in this matter, I need to know something of Grant's motive? It's not that I don't believe you, Miss Fraser, but if... I am to be discrete, I need more information to convince the Fiscal of the truth of the matter.' David studied Elizabeth Fraser, here proclaiming against his gamekeeper for a second time. Perhaps this demure young lady had an ulterior motive in speaking up for Tennant. He had to be sure the scoundrel, if that was what Tennant was, wasn't going to be let off scot-free and go on to cause further havoc in the name of so-called social justice.

A knock at the door and the appearance of Phee Melville interrupted the silence that had developed between her brother and his visitors.

'Not a good time, Phee,' David said with a hint of despair, assuming she had come to socialise with her friend.

'Actually, a very good time, brother dear,' countered Phee. She caught Elizabeth's eye.

'Just for once, Phee, will you take the word of your brother and not challenge it so spontaneously?' He turned to Richard Fraser for empathy.

She ignored him. 'I don't know what you've been speaking about, not exactly. But I have someone outside who has information you should hear. It is relevant to your discussion.' Phee did not wait for an answer but walked over to the door and beckoned. Nell Graham came into the room.

'Little Nell? One of the servants?'

'Listen, David. Just listen. Now Nell,' Phee said gently, 'tell them what you've just told me. Don't be embarrassed. You've nothing to be ashamed of and no harm will come to you, I promise.'

Nell related her tale of what had happened on the night of the Gala Day dance when Grant had followed her and Maggie out of the village. She told of Neil Tennant's role in rescuing her from the clutches of Grant and about how he had been left to sleep in the field. He had been hale and hearty but very drunk when they'd left him, she assured her audience.

'Mr Grant was that fu', sir, fleein he was. We thocht he widnae mind a' whau was there. Mebbe he minded Neil had helped me. Then when he came tae the next mornin', beaten tae a pulp, he thocht Neil had done it.'

'There's a clear motive,' said Elizabeth to David.

'Clear? Clear as mud!'

'It's adding up to something not very nice in the man, this Grant character; a pattern in his behaviour that can no longer be overlooked,' said Richard.

'I hope I wasnae speakin' oot o' turn, sir,' said Nell. 'I heard ye were talkin' aboot Neil Tennant when I brocht in the tea. There's somethin' no richt aboot they chairges against him. Neil is a guid man an' Mr Grant isnae. I can vouch for that.'

'Yes, thank you, Nell. Your testimony has been very useful. You may go now.'

Nell thanked her employer, leaving the four to their deliberations.

'If I hear once more that Neil Tennant is a good man, I think I'll scream.' David sounded defeated.

'I'll second that, David,' agreed the minister. 'Believe me, I'll second that.'

# Chapter 44

## THE GATHERING

Isabelle had spent much of the summer planning her Harvest Home, a traditional celebration that had not taken place in these parts for nearly fifty years. She wanted it to be as authentic as possible so had spent hours poring over the family archive in the attic of Parkgate House, delighting in the detail of old guest lists and invoices for comestibles. The festival would be a link back to the good old days when the role of the gentry was more clearly defined. The social changes she witnessed in Rashiepark and in the village were occurring with such rapidity that it was hard to bear at times. On the face of it, the party was an opportunity to give thanks to the tenants and estate workers for all of their hard work during the farming year, to let them know how valued they were by the Melville family who were not just employers but also guardians of the estate lands, its traditions, and its history, offering continuity into a prosperous future, God willing. Her brother was the new head of the family, with Phee and herself in support. It had been almost twelve months since the passing of her mother and father. Isabelle hoped that the celebration would help bring attention to the new generation of Melvilles, highlighting the successes of this, their first year in charge.

She had intended to commandeer the barn at Home farm of Dunmore for the occasion but circumstances had dictated that the barn at Back o' Moss was a more pragmatic choice, not least because the contents had gone up in one of several arson attacks made on estate property during the summer. It was a fine space, she had decided, and several men had been dispatched to prepare it for the evening's entertainment. The walls and the floor had been scrubbed and rafters and window sills dusted down. Huge garlands of greenery decked the walls: holly with its bright red berries, Scots Pine covered in cones, juniper dripping with purple berries scented the air, and dried honesty from the garden at Parkgate added a shimmer of silvery white. A few sheaves of corn, mixed stalks of barley and oats tied with bright red ribbons, gave a finishing touch that left Isabelle proud. A small, wooden stage had been constructed, positioned in one corner for the speechmakers and, afterwards, it would be used by the musicians. After several enthusiastic recommendations on their behalf, Walter Heggie and his Band from Airdrie had been hired. She hadn't been convinced at first, preferring a classical quintet herself, but such was the band's reputation in the village that even Phee had heard of them.

When she arrived at the barn in her favourite ivory silk and lace gown, Isabelle was well pleased with the transformation. A variety of long tables had been lined up under white cloths and seating for nearly two hundred guests had been procured. Oil lamps and candles had been arrayed along the tables and placed in the small window recesses, painting the entire space with soft light and shade. She hugged her brother and sister, her own dear flesh and blood. What could possibly go wrong, she thought?

Guests arrived promptly, stepping out of the cold of a dark October night into the warm glow that enveloped the barn. Lady Moffat appeared with her son and heir, twenty-year old Arthur. Isabelle was delighted. She led them straight over to where her younger and very eligible sister stood in lilac tulle, rapt in conversation. This is going to be a night to remember, she decided excitedly as she dragged herself away from the great Lady and her baronet son to greet other guests.

All of the principal tenants were there with their wives and children, and a selection of their labourers and servants, chosen by the tenants according to the priorities of their particular farms. Selected members of the business community and local organisations arrived with their wives, joining the unmarried Richard Fraser of the manse and Mr Black representing the educational establishment, and still a bachelor after so many months at the village school.

'Your sister couldn't make it then, Reverend?' David Melville asked when they were alone. He observed the merry gathering, returning the salutations of guests by raising his glass. 'Cheers! Good to see you! Thank you for coming!' he called.

'No, she's been quite quiet and restrained since the business with Neil Tennant. Doesn't go out much at all at the moment, I'm afraid. It's upset her greatly, I feel.' The minister's face was grave.

'Quite a business. But Tennant's been released so no harm done, I suppose. The four trespassers have done their time. That will serve as a warning to others who think they can flout the law.' David stuck out his chest, looking every bit the new laird. 'We must have order, Richard. Civilisation requires it.'

'What about your gamekeeper, Grant? I see his wife and child are here.' Richard waved across to Mrs Grant and her daughter, Annie, already seated at a table. 'Don't think I've ever seen the woman smile before now.'

'Police are still looking for him, I hear. By the time they got to his cottage, he'd scarpered without a trace. Even left his family behind as you can see.'

'It's so good of you to give the poor woman employment up at Parkgate, David.'

'We couldn't leave her destitute, could we? No, Rashiepark looks after its own, I'm proud to say.' He puffed his chest out a little further.

'So, the fact of Grant's disappearance rather tells its own story, doesn't it? Guilty as we suspected?'

'The Fiscal took a very dim view of him conniving to put Tennant in gaol for so long, not to mention all the time he'd wasted. But it's worse even than we feared. When Stone and I searched his hut, out by the aviaries in the woods, we found all sorts of evidence that he was responsible for this summer's crime wave.'

'Shocking!' replied the minister, his eyes out on stalks, and proud to have played an important part in the scoundrel's undoing.

'Indeed. A stack of stolen items from homes and farmsteads, paraffin and rags for use as accelerants in arson attacks. All sorts. The charge list against him's as long as your arm! But until the police can interview him, we can only guess at his motives.'

'You'll be hoping the police pick him up soon.'

'Yes, let's hope they get him sooner or later. But he'll be long gone. I think we've seen the last of Grant the gamekeeper by a long shot.' David looked very pleased with himself. He waved to Murdo Maclean who sat nearby with his wife.

'Keep the speech short so we can get to the puddings, young David,' called Murdo jovially from behind his hand.

Isabelle flitted around giving orders to servants and guests alike as people began to settle down, waiting for the evening's programme to begin. The Imries had arrived, suitably late, just in time to be introduced to the top table before Richard Fraser stepped up on stage to start the proceedings with a prayer. The laird's greeting of Miss Imrie was lost on no one, and looks of *'I told you so'* between female guests reverberated around the room.

Mr MacCullough, tenant at Mosside, had been elected to speak on behalf of the tenants and, by definition, all who were employed by the estate. After only one glass of alcohol, his complexion was florid, his manner genial. He tapped his glass with a spoon hoping for quiet.

'Mr Melville, Miss Isabelle and Miss Euphemia, Lady Moffat, Sir Arthur, ladies and gentlemen,' he began to a few calls of encouragement and whistles of delight, 'Ye've asked me tae mak a speech oan behalf o' the tenants an' estate workers o' Rashiepark.' He wiped his brow, taking a deep breath to calm the tremble in his voice. 'We would like tae thank the Melville family for their fortitude and their steadfast loyalty tae the tenants ower the years.'

A loud guffaw erupted at the far end of the barn but it was quickly hushed.

'The present generation is nae different fae their forebears,' he said to suppressed laughter from the audience. 'An' we would like to express oor admiration for the strength o' leadership ye've shown in takin' ower the estate at a very hard time for the fermer and the landowner. The leadership ye're showin' tae bring the estate into the twintieth century is maist heartenin'. Yer advice in the new fermin weys is gratefully received an' the programme o' improvement, long overdue in the opinion o' some, is a sign o' yer belief in the future.' He paused for a quick refreshment of his parched lips but quickly added, 'B' the wey, can I hae ma road sorted afore the winter blast sets in?' Laughter resounded round the company. 'We would like ye to ken o' oor great affection for the Melville family, past and present, an' tae thank ye maist sincerely for yer generosity and kindness, which are evident here the nicht but seen in yer dealings wi' us at a' times. Ladies an' gentlemen, staun up! I gie ye the Melvilles o' Rashiepark.' He lifted his glass and everyone stood to do the same.

'The Melvilles o' Rashiepark.' Applause and a cheer went up.

It was a very proud David Melville who stood up, asking for calm. 'Thank you very much indeed, Mr MacCullough, for your very kind words. But I'm afraid you'll have to wait in line for your repairs to be done like everyone else!' The audience appreciated the joke and laughed loudly. 'Everyone! Thank you very much for coming along tonight and supporting our restoration of the ancient tradition 'Harvest Home'. A special thanks goes to her Ladyship, Lady Moffat, and her son for gracing us with their presence tonight and I would also like to thank my dear sister, Isabelle, for arranging the festivities this evening.' Applause started up and a few spoons were rattled. 'But you've heard enough talking for now, let's make a start with our meal and then, perhaps, you will indulge me with a few minutes of your attention later on, before the dancing and merriment gets properly underway. I have words of some importance to say.' The assembly was intrigued. 'No later,' he joked holding up his hand, 'I'll not be pressed. Let the feasting begin!'

Richard surveyed the happy gathering from his place beside David Melville at the top table. He poured wine for Mrs Imrie who seemed to like a glass or two, and he enjoyed congenial conversation with Lady Moffat and Catherine Imrie till the food came. The lamb had been roasted to perfection – it almost melted in his mouth. Mrs Tough could learn a thing or two from the cook at the Big House, he thought, remembering her Beef Wellington, which was more wellington than beef. He tried not to laugh out loud but he really did have such a clever sense of humour. He congratulated himself on his recent dismissal of Mrs Tough. It had taken considerable courage to stand up to the woman but needs must. He had been losing weight! Who else but her could render cooked ham from the Co-operative inedible? Elizabeth was already a much better cook and would soon develop her skills. She seemed to have the instinct for good food that women were naturally born with. All it needed was practice and he would ensure she got plenty.

By the time the apple pie was served, Richard was itching for the dancing to begin. He cared not for the notion that ministers should be dusty and conservative in their habits. Sober, steady, humble and gracious, yes, but he saw no argument against dancing on occasion, in proper company, to connect with the faithful. To show a little *joie de vivre* let people know that his was a broad church open to all, a church that celebrated all of God's gifts. He would be much in demand, he knew, but had the stamina for it. Mrs Smith of the Tea Committee would expect a dance as would Miss Silver from the Public School Board. He would make a point of asking Mr MacCullough's daughter, now fully grown into a rather comely young woman. He spotted where she was sitting beside her mother then gave a friendly smile. He might try a jig with Ruby Gowans from Redburn Farm too – not really his cup of tea but buxom and bonny, and quite stunning in her blue dress. He was glad that the gentle Miss Gibson wasn't in attendance. She was rather over-attentive and submissive, which he disliked when it came to romantic assignations, unlike the haughty Phee Melville here at the top table, busy flaunting herself at the young baronet in front of everyone.

It was a pity, he admitted, that Elizabeth wasn't present at the celebration. Such a shame to think of her in the dark house all by herself but she needed to be taught a lesson. However, she was missing out on a wonderful opportunity to find a life partner, someone suitable for a girl of her upbringing. Someone like Mr Black perhaps. 'Eureka!' he exclaimed to himself. A schoolmaster was a very respectable profession indeed, he decided, for the brother-in-law of a minister.

During dinner, David had been in deep discussion with Mr Imrie. They congratulated each other on the signing of the leases by the Coal Company. It had been fortuitous that the old leases on two farms had run their course so there could be no legal impediment to their transfer from the present tenants to the Company. Mr Imrie confirmed that his surveyors had their eye on the other farms, where the leases were due to expire the following year, but he counted himself very happy with those procured thus far. Adjacent to his existing pits, Back o' Moss Farm was guaranteed to be productive, he explained to David's great satisfaction. The trials by his surveyors and mining engineers had proved most satisfactory and Baird & Sons, a firm of pit sinkers, had been contracted to start work within a matter of weeks. There was less certainty about the potential for mining on Redburn land, though the orange colour of the rocks in the burn, where it flowed across the farm, suggested the presence of a chalybeate spring that originated in iron bearing strata below the surface. The historical record did show interest in Rashiepark Ironstone in the past but, seemingly, nothing had come of it.

David stood up to give his speech, well pleased with what he had just heard from Mr Imrie. Heckling at the far end was shrugged off, quickly put down to over-consumption of his good beer. 'Better Scotch beer than imported French claret,' he joked, raising his glass of red Bordeaux to the audience. 'The tradition of the Harvest Home developed in this part of Scotland as a celebration of the harvest, safely gathered in,' he explained. 'It was held, as it is today, to thank everyone who, through their hard work in ploughing, sowing, harvesting, and in animal husbandry throughout the year, helped to create such riches as we have enjoyed in our meal tonight.' He lifted his glass to his audience. 'That's you by the way!' and he laughed as a parent laughs with a child. 'Rashiepark is blessed with many riches, ultimately God-given of course, not just above ground on the land but also below ground.'

A murmur of disquiet was heard around the barn. They feared what was coming next.

'Whilst I promise to continue to reward your trust in me by supporting your endeavours in the sphere of agriculture, it should be remembered that the riches of this estate extend below ground also. It is this sphere which will have to be developed, if our future prosperity is to be ensured.'

'Whau's prosperity's he talkin' aboot? Aye, no mine,' said a tired voice loud enough for everyone to hear. The sounds of hushing and a scuffle at the far end were brief but caused a stir along the top table.

David continued as if nothing had been said. 'As two of our tenants have recently discovered, the legal arrangements between us may change. But what will not change is your personal relationship with me and the rest of the Melville family. You will always be valued members of the Rashiepark family. I can assure you of that.'

'B'Jesus! Whit a' load o' guff,' shouted the same elderly voice.

The laird continued, undeterred. 'We have new people at our table tonight, ladies and gentlemen, new members of our Rashiepark family who will help to realise the great underground riches of the estate for all our benefit. Please welcome Mr Imrie of the Coal Company, his wife, Mrs Imrie, and daughter, Catherine.' He lifted his glass to a perfectly silent and unresponsive audience.

'The legal ties between Rashiepark and the Imries are two fold: both business and personal. It is with the greatest pleasure that I announce to you tonight my engagement of marriage with Miss Catherine Imrie.' David took his fiancée by the hand then invited her to stand. Her diamond ring sparkled in the soft lights illuminating the top table. He kissed her lightly on the cheek as his audience looked on. A sharp intake of breath travelled all around before applause rang out and voices called, 'Congratulations, David and Catherine!'

A group of ladies soon collected around the future Mrs Melville, conveying their good wishes, each hopeful of a closer look at the engagement ring. The cluster of yellow diamonds, it was announced, was a family heirloom, first presented by David's grandfather, an illustrious soldier of the Indian campaigns. Catherine professed her great humility at being the recipient of such a beautiful piece of Melville history as Isabelle kissed her future sister-in law with every ounce of affection she could muster. She was fulsome in her praise of her brother's choice, telling his fiancée she couldn't wait for the day when they would be living under the same roof together. Phee cemented Catherine's acceptance into the fold with an exaggerated embrace and kisses on both cheeks but she secretly prayed that any future offspring might take after her brother in both looks and charm.

Meanwhile a group of men, including a delighted Mr Imrie, gathered around David, congratulating him on his fine choice of partner with much back-slapping and firm shaking of hands. Glasses of claret were raised to toast his future happiness.

Murdo Maclean thought the time ripe for philosophising as he brought to mind the conversation they'd had earlier in the year at the dinner party. 'Little did you know at that time just how quickly you would find out what your future held, David... even though the young lady in question wasn't even known to you back then! Do you remember what you said?'

David smiled fondly at the memory of the dinner party, when he was only just beginning to come to terms with the huge change taking place in his life, from medical student to Laird of Rashiepark with all of its burdens and responsibilities. Suddenly, he had seen only the possibilities in life, the disappointments swept aside by a girl in a green dress. Rose Matheson's grey eyes had filled him with hope and optimism that his new life might be filled with love and happiness after all.

Murdo said the words for him. '*Whatever may happen to you was prepared for you from all eternity; and the implication of causes was from eternity spinning the thread of your being.*'

'Or as they say in the vernacular, '*Whit's fur ye'll no go by ye!*'' Ernest Black gave a chuckle that was met with silence. 'Oh, I hadn't meant to be superior or patronising,' he said blushing from head to toe. 'It's just that... it translates so effortlessly into the local language.' He saw blank faces and thought that further explanation might bring about understanding so he started up nineteen to the dozen.

'Ernest, old chap! Steady on. Why so serious? You are obviously spending far too much time listening to your pupils and not enough reading Ovid and Aristotle!' said Richard, coming to his rescue.

Murdo gave a great guffaw and the others joined in the fun.

'Remember this is a time for celebration. Let's toast the future,' suggested Mr Imrie, happy father of the future Mrs Melville. 'The future's looking rosy for this community, I can assure you. They're gaining more than they're losing, I'll wager!'

'Cheers!'

David Melville looked thoughtfully into his empty glass. He stared over at the ladies clucking around his wife-to-be. Phee was staring back at him. He smiled meekly as he raised his glass in her direction. She smiled back but her eyes said it all. Dearest Phee, he thought sadly, you have always been able to read my mind.

Another group had formed at the opposite end of the barn, amid a flurry of activity intent on rearranging the floor space for the dancing to come. The principal members of two families huddled deep in conversation, all except Old Morton who had been responsible for much of the heckling during the speeches. He had eventually been persuaded to leave, to the great relief of his family. The Gowans of Redburn and the Mortons of Back o' Moss had much in common, stemming from the loss of their tenancies to the Coal Company. The Gowans, at least, held onto the vague hope that the mineral trials on their land would come to nothing. After all, prospectors had looked for riches for decades and found nothing of note. But the loss of the tenancy meant the family would answer directly to another master, one they were less acquainted with and no less suspicious of.

The Mortons, however, had a clearer notion of their future. The company would develop a new coal pit on land they had farmed for three generations – the house and the outbuildings would be requisitioned at the turn of the year. No wonder Old Morton had got himself in a right state with the drink. Seventy years devoted to a farm, like his father and grandfather before him. To have it taken away without so much as a by your leave, was a sore thing to bear. To sit listening to the laird's platitudes about relationships and family and trust, well it amounted to nothing short of a pack of lies and a punch in the teeth. Melville could salve his conscience with a promise of good testimonials that might help the family secure a tenancy on another estate; but how could Morton start again in another place at his advanced stage in life with his vital spark at a peep? He would follow his son to a different farm. He would walk the parks and smell the air, give his tuppence worth about what to grow and which beasts to buy. But to all intents and purposes he was finished. It would be sore to watch the lorries move in and strangers come to dig up the ground. Seeing the men walking around the yard at the farm roup, looking over his carts and his implements with an eye for a bargain out of all that was left of a lifetime's work, could be too much for a man to take.

A long chord on the accordion announced that it was time for a dance. Walter Heggie and his band sat up on stage atop a pile of hay, grinning from ear to ear, ready to entertain another Blackrigg gathering. Couples reappeared from outside where they had retreated earlier for either air or privacy and people gravitated to the benches along the sides of the barn, waiting for the first dance to be called.

The huddle of Mortons and Gowans melted into the crowd as if nothing was amiss. It stuck in the craw to be treated so ill by the laird, they all agreed, but what could you do? You had to accept it and make the best of it. The other tenants didn't want to know. They just looked embarrassed when you caught their eye. It was hard for them to know what to say. They were busy thinking of their own positions, hoping the same wouldn't happen to them. Every last one of them went to bed at night thinking, *'There but for the grace of God go I'*, even though, as everybody knew, it had nothing at all to do with the Lord.

# Chapter 45

## THE FUGITIVE

Grant stood in the lane that led from the hill road towards Mansefield. He lurked in the shadows of the tall hedge where it turned the corner and continued down the side of the manse to the kirkyard. That way he could be sure of hearing someone approach before they spotted him – he could hide till they had passed. He looked back and forward, breathing heavily. When the last of the daylight disappeared over the Black Moss, he peered through the moonless night. He watched the back of the house as he had done so many times before, waiting in all weathers for a glimpse of her.

Grant knew every window and what was behind them. The kitchen with its big range overlooked the garden where she had dug up a square of turf in the summer to plant vegetables for the minister's table. The scullery window was smaller and to one side. On the far side, the pantry window was smaller still, too small for his bulk to get through so he ruled it out as a possible way in. The tall stair window with the coloured glass led up to the bedrooms, two at the back, three at the front. Her room was the one on the left at the back. He had seen her shadow in the lamplight often enough when she had been getting ready for bed, devoid of shame, the curtains open for anyone to see. She wanted him to see her. He could tell. She wanted him to know she was there, just out of reach, waiting for him. Well, he had waited long enough. He had been lying low with the help of his cronies but he couldn't disappear just yet, though he knew that he should. He had to claim what was his, what had eluded him for so long.

It was cold. The wind blew through the trees with a long sough. Autumn leaves skittered across the garden and about his feet. He drew his jacket around him, turning up the collar a little more. He didn't want to wait much longer. It could cool a man's fever to wait too long for a bit of skirt but there was no sign of her. The house was in darkness though the sun had gone down ages before. When would she light the lamps? And where was that arse of a brother of hers? They would be in there sitting in the darkness, the two of them, he decided. Holy Wullie would be saving on the price of oil for the lamps. It didn't matter that the minister would be in the way of what he had to do. A man of the cloth couldn't put up much of a fight. All that book learning had made him soft. The most work he ever did was to lift the big Bible in the church. No, Creeping Jesus would be no match for him. Besides he had something that no one could argue with. He lifted his gun from where he had stashed it in the hedgerow. Maybe I'll make him watch, he said to himself.

Grant moved along the lane towards the gate into the back garden of the manse. It squeaked as he turned the handle and pushed it open on rusty hinges. The shrubbery was low on that side of the lane. He would have to be careful that no one saw him there, where he had no right to be. He glanced back up towards the corner at Mansefield then tried the back door. It was locked as he thought it would be. What sort of Christian doesn't trust his fellow man enough to leave his back door open? Nobody locked their door in these parts. That showed Holy Wullie up for the hypocrite he really was. Grant heard a noise, footsteps coming along the lane before the corner. He dived into the laurel by the gate. It was evergreen, giving suitable cover. He lay stock-still, waiting for the person to pass but they didn't. Whoever it was had stopped half way up the lane, a little beyond the shrubbery. If they looked down they might see him. He squinted through the leaves. Someone else had their eyes on the manse – a man, young and fairly tall. Was he going to stay there all night, and who the hell was he?

Grant got his answer when the stranger walked on down the lane. It was yon fool, Neil Tennant, he realised, still sniffing about her, like a dog after a bitch in heat. He wondered how the sap had enjoyed his stint in the gaol. Pity it hadn't been longer. It was hard not to laugh but the situation demanded it, lying there under a bush in the leaves and the wet grass. Grant had guessed who had helped get the idiot released, all charges dropped. It was that clatch that lived in the manse like a nun. He knew her for what she really was. He had seen her up on the hill with Tennant and he, Grant, wanted a bit for himself. Besides, if she hadn't interfered, he wouldn't be hiding under a bush like a worm, a wanted man hunted down by the police, hounded out of the place he had lived all his life. She was to blame and she was going to pay for it. He would make sure of that.

He approached the scullery window and found it was locked. The kitchen was the same. Which one would he break open? More footsteps came down the lane and voices this time, folk making their way into the village from Kaim

427

Farm perhaps. He dived for cover again and waited. Two lads and two lassies, off to a Friday night dance no doubt. He strained to hear what they were saying; something about a big celebration; the names Melville and Morton and lots of giggling by the girls. He remembered about the plans for the Harvest Home. They had been discussing it along at Parkgate all summer. It must be tonight, he decided. The minister would be there. No show without Punch. The sister would be there too. Holy Wullie dragged that whore with him wherever he went. She must be at Old Morton's place and not at the manse after all. That was why he hadn't seen anyone at home all evening, he realised. The house was empty.

Bastards! He swore under his breath. He had been standing in the cold for nothing.

Grant got up from his hiding place then went over to the back of the house. He felt bolder now. There was no need to hide anymore. He peered in through the windows and saw no one. A table and chairs, the glow of the range and a clock ticking on the wall. Round to the front where the two front rooms were in darkness too. He squinted past the pot plant in the window; a whole room just for eating your dinner; and another, this time with fancy chairs just for gabbing in. His hatred for these hangers-on burned like a fire. Them with their airs and graces. Who did they think they were? He checked his gun and his pockets. Only two shots. He should've gone up to Parkgate earlier but two would be enough to get him what was his and no mistake. And woe betide anyone who stood in his way.

# Chapter 46

## HARVEST HOME

Isabelle was delighted that her arrangements for the Harvest Home had been carried out to the letter and that everything was going so well. The barn looked jolly and festive, everyone agreed, and the principal guests seemed to be having a very happy time, dancing and conversing with each other. Even Lady Moffat had stayed for the first few dances. She had joined David and Arthur in a reel but the gout was the ruin of her, she claimed, bidding farewell long before midnight with thanks for a wonderful evening's entertainment. Arthur Moffat was enjoying Phee's company, it seemed, and David and Catherine made a lovely couple out on the floor. Now that Isabelle knew that her future sister-in-law couldn't dance, she would endeavour to teach her in time for the celebration of marriage, the following year. One or two of the servants would be press-ganged into helping, she decided. Little Nell Graham and her friend, Maggie Lennox, could teach them all something by the looks of things. They could fairly birl the young men round and throw them off their feet, she noticed.

Isabelle felt a great swelling of satisfaction in her bosom as she surveyed the merry scene. History, legacy, and duty had all come together in a traditional celebration that should never have been left to die, in her opinion. She could not understand why it had been allowed to fade away when it did long ago. However pride, it is written, goes before destruction, and a haughty spirit before a fall; and Isabelle was guilty of both.

It took Walter and his band a few moments to realise that something was up. The accordion player played on longer than everyone else but the music soon stopped. The dancers gasped when they caught sight of Grant, evil incarnate, and the crowd parted down the middle like the Red Sea before Moses. The uninvited guest lumbered into the middle of the barn. He stood with his arms apart, holding a gun in one hand, a big oil lamp in the other. He spun round with a demonic look on his face, enjoying the fear in their eyes. Parents pushed their children behind them, the brave endeavoured to shield others with outstretched hands.

'Dinnae come near,' he warned. 'I micht jist hae the yin gun but whau would want tae be the yin I tak oot wi' it? An' mind, a fire could dae damage tae a wheen o' ye.' He swung the oil lamp on its wire handle and laughed. 'I've jist come for whit's mine an' tae gie somebody whit's comin' tae them.'

Heads turned. They looked in the direction of Mrs Grant and Annie, her daughter. Both were ashen-faced, a mixture of fear and shame.

'Naw, no her!' exclaimed Grant. 'I'm well shot o' yon dried-up witch!' He spat on the ground.

Women gasped in revulsion, and in pity for a wife who had endured such hatred and contempt in her many years with him.

'Do the right thing, man. Give yourself up.' The words were out of Richard Fraser's mouth before he knew it. He astounded himself.

'Why, it's the bold meenister, Mr Fraser. Giein me advice for the sake o' ma soul, nae doobt!' He laughed a great belly laugh that ended as quickly as it had begun. 'Whau dae ye think ye are, giein me advice? Or oniebody for that matter. When ye cannae keep yer ain sister in order.'

All eyes were on the minister.

'You keep her out of this when she isn't here to defend herself. You are not fit to mention her by name.'

Everyone then turned to Grant to see how he would take the rebuke.

'Elizabeth!' Grant called in a ridiculous voice, searching the crowd for her.' Or Beth tae them yer sweet oan.' He turned directly back to Richard. 'Dae ye think she'll let me cry her Beth, meenister? Whaur is she? I've come for her. She's comin' wi' me.'

The crowd stood open-mouthed, perplexed at Grant's intentions towards the minister's diffident sister.

'She's not here. Now put the gun down and give yourself up, man.' Richard Fraser tried to appear calm but inside he was a quivering wreck.

David Melville stepped forward. 'He's right, Grant. For your own sake, put down the gun.'

Grant turned to the laird. 'Aww, meenister, it's yer best pal, wee Davy Melville. Found his tongue at last. Cam back tae Rashiepark tae tell us a' whit tae dae when he didnae ken the first thing aboot it!' He glared at David. 'Jist cause yer a Melville. Jist cause ye were born on the richt side o' the bed. No like some o' us, eh?'

All eyes were now fixed on the laird, waiting for a reaction.

'Put down the gun, Grant. You've done a great deal of harm to a lot of good people around this estate. Enough is enough.' David waited, watching the man's face for signs of rational thought.

Grant turned to the audience. They stood wide-eyed and open-mouthed, completely entranced by the drama being played out before them.

'Enjoyin' yer celebration are ye?' he asked as if they were children, contempt in his voice. 'Jiggin' in Auld Morton's barn, ye micht as weel be dancin' oan the man's grave! Coorse, it's no his barn at a', is it? He'll be oot in the cauld afore the end o' the year. Does thon gie cause for celebration? Niver mind, it could be yer ain turn next. Whau will it be?' He turned to MacCullough of Mosside. 'Yersel, Tam?'

Grant aimed his gun. MacCullough put up his hands, his eyes out on stalks.

'Aye, thon's whit ye'll dae when they come for yer place. Ye'll pit up yer hauns. Roll ower at their bidin' lik a wee dug. Jist lik Auld Morton's daein, cause he's nae option.'

'I'll speak for masel,' said a tired, old voice from the doorway. 'I dinnae require the likes o' yersel tae fecht oan ma behalf.'

Grant turned carefully and looked down the barrel of Old Morton's shotgun. He gave a grunt and a snigger.

There was a click then a blast. Grant fell, a spreading blot of blood across his chest. The crowd gave a gasp of horror and relief. They crowded around his body before turning their stare towards the old farmer. He looked ill, defeated by life and unmoved by what he had just done.

'I think we owe you a debt of gratitude, Mr Morton,' began David.

'Save yer thanks, yer Lairdship,' replied Old Morton. He let his gun fall out of his hand. 'I was comin' tae shoot you, no the gemmie.' With that he dropped to the ground, frothing at the mouth, unable to move. His family moved in around him.

As farmers and servants stood in awe and turned to each other to make sense of what had happened, the principal players took control of the situation. The minister closed Grant's lifeless eyes and prayed for his soul. David Melville dispatched a messenger to fetch Dr Lindsay and the constable from the police station. He told the Morton family how brave their father had been. Arthur Moffat, Mr Imrie and Murdo Maclean ensured that the ladies were alright while Ernest Black sought to comfort Mrs Grant and her daughter.

Isabelle stood distraught, unable to hold back the tears. Her wonderful Harvest Home, which had been such a success, was in tatters and unlikely to be repeated because of the actions of two insufferable men, one lying dead on the ground before her.

'Thank God, Lady Moffat wasn't here to witness this debacle,' she whimpered.

# Part Four
# Winter

# Chapter 47

## A FRIEND IN NEED

Mrs Gow and the Widow MacAuley stood blethering outside their homes in Main Street, undeterred by the bitter chill in the air. The business of the trespassers had given them food for thought throughout the autumn but what had happened at the Harvest Home had them in a feeding frenzy that was sure to sustain life through the cold, dark days of winter ahead. There was plenty to talk about, and no amount of picking over the dead bones of other people's lives could satisfy their appetite for more gossip and intrigue. They stood by the roadside, happed up against the winter weather in shawls and woollen jackets, like two black crows after carrion. They pecked together at the morsels of information each could provide but with a weather-eye open for who was about to offer further sustenance.

Theirs was the perfect view. Vehicles coming and going from Parkgate House passed in front of them. The church and the path up to the manse were across the road. The Smiddy was further away towards Stoneyrigg but easy to see from where they regularly stood, smoking their pipes and sweeping the dirt from their doorsteps. The women coming and going from the shops often provided stimulus for a change in conversation and could sometimes be relied upon to drop a crumb or two of news in their direction. The postman or the delivery boys passing on their bikes could be called over and grilled if an update to a situation was required.

Just when the women decided that the day was offering very slim pickings, a large, shiny motor vehicle drew up outside the church. It had come from Parkgate House, they were sure. They stretched their necks, watching with beady eyes as Billy Dodds made his way round to the far side to open the door for his passenger. Euphemia Melville emerged from the back seat and exchanged a few words with her driver who returned to his seat in the front. He pulled the peak of his cap down a shade before sinking into a comfortable position as if he might have to wait for some time. The old crones toddled a few steps along the street, sufficient to follow the visitor's journey to the front door of the manse, just visible beyond the kirkyard. The minister opened the door where a conversation took place before the young woman was eventually admitted. Mrs Gow and the Widow MacAuley cast each other knowing looks. They would have to return to the warmth of their respective homes because of the snell wind but they would be back out directly, they agreed, when the visitor decided to leave.

'Elizabeth is not taking any visitors,' said Richard Fraser, the door only half open. 'She doesn't want to see anyone, not even you Miss Melville.'

'Ridiculous!' proclaimed Phee. She wasn't used to taking no for an answer. 'You've turned me away once before and I will not be deterred this time, Richard. I want to hear it from her own lips.' She peered round his bulk hoping for a sign that her friend was about.

'You can understand how she feels, can't you?' he persisted. 'The whole thing has proved quite too much for her.'

'What she needs is a friend to talk it over with, someone who can help her put it all into some sort of perspective. Now open the door and let me in!'

'My sister is not able to receive visitors. Now leave.' He stepped back to close the door but Phee was too quick for him. She took a step inside making it impossible to shut her out.

'Why, thank you, Richard,' she said sarcastically. 'Beth! Beth! Are you there?'

At the end of the dark hallway another door opened. Elizabeth emerged in a halo of light. 'I'm here, Phee. Come into the kitchen – I'll make some tea.'

Phee almost ran towards her friend and they embraced warmly.

Richard looked on askance as the door was closed on him. He was left in the dark.

'It's so lovely to see you. It seems ages....' Both women spoke at the same time and laughed when they realised they were in agreement.

'I've tried to visit before, Beth. But Richard wouldn't let me see you. Are you alright?'

'Yes, I'm fine.'

Phee studied her friend who didn't look fine in the least. 'You didn't come to the Harvest Home. I missed you!'

'I wanted to come, Phee. I truly did.'

'You've shut yourself away here forever. You haven't even been to the Sabbath School. It's not good for you!'

'It's not entirely my doing,' Elizabeth offered. 'But I'll tell you about that later.'

'So much has happened, first the business with Neil Tennant, arrested and left to rot on Grant's evidence, which exposed Grant for what he really was, and now the awful business up at Back o' Moss. It's all such a mess.' Phee paused with a glint in her eye. 'I don't think Isabelle will ever mention the words *Harvest Home* again, far less try to organise another.' She caught Elizabeth's eye making them both giggle.

'Poor Isabelle,' replied Elizabeth. 'All that work and planning then look what happened!' They tried to stop sniggering. Elizabeth poured hot water into a tea pot and set out cups for them both. 'I know it's not funny,' she admitted wearily, 'Two men have died, after all. Will you tell me all about it? I only have Richard's sanitised version to go on.'

'Did he tell you about David's engagement to Catherine Imrie?'

'Yes, he did. I wonder what Rose will think of that. She sent me a letter from Edinburgh. I'll give you the address of her rooms if you like.' Phee nodded whilst Elizabeth continued. 'She seems to be settling in very well. Writes that her classes are interesting... a challenge, but she's loving it all.'

'I am glad for her. I felt so awful that day, when she came upon the lovebirds in the drawing room. You will tell her I'm sorry, won't you? I'd hate anything to spoil our friendship.'

Elizabeth nodded. 'Of course, I'll tell her and she wouldn't blame you in any way, I'm sure of that. You were caught in the middle of it, after all. I expect she's glad she found out in time. She'll get over it... she's got a brilliant future ahead of her.' She smiled at the thought of Rose taking control of her life. 'I feel quite inspired by her example.' She paused, staring out of the window at the lane. 'Sometimes,' she added with a sigh.

Phee studied her friend who looked so sad. She waited for Elizabeth to say what was going through her mind but she didn't.

Elizabeth came back to life as she poured the tea, encouraging Phee to tell her everything that had happened at Back o' Moss on the night of the Harvest Home. Phee related the tale as best she could, hoping she wasn't leaving out any important details.

'He was looking for you, Beth,' Phee said. 'Grant was looking for you. Thank God you were safely tucked up here.'

Elizabeth paused for a moment before she spoke. 'He came here first.'

Phee gasped in horror. She put both hands over her face, dreading what was to come next.

'It's alright he didn't get into the house. But he tried every door and window… then something made him change his mind and he went off.'

'You were here alone, while Grant was trying to get into the house? How awful!'

'You're right,' Elizabeth shuddered. 'It was terrifying. His big face pressed up to the kitchen window while I hid in the pantry with a poker in my hand. I had to crawl along the floor out of sight.'

'How terrifying! Lucky you had the door locked!'

'No, I mean yes but no, that was Richard's doing,' she studied Phee's puzzled face. 'He's so angry with me about seeing Neil Tennant up at the shieling. Now he's trying to keep me under control.'

Phee couldn't believe what she was hearing. She looked around the kitchen: vegetable peelings in the sink, a pot of soup cooking on the range and no Mrs Tough. The reality of her friend's life began to dawn on her.

'That's right.' Elizabeth answered her friend's unspoken question. 'I am Mrs Tough now. I cook and clean for my brother. It's his way of curing a wayward sister.'

'That's ridiculous, Beth! And he locks you in the house! I've never heard of anything so cruel.'

'He makes sure I have plenty of work to do, to keep me busy and my mind occupied. He's been inviting eligible bachelors for dinner hoping to marry me off, eventually.'

Phee looked aghast. She hardly knew what to say.

'Mr Stewart from the Presbytery's been twice: small, squat and forty.'

Phee made a face, still speechless.

'And Ernest Black's been a couple of times too.'

Phee studied Elizabeth for her reaction to the possibility of a romance with Mr Black but she gave nothing away. Everything she'd said had been told in a very matter of fact way, almost as if she had no opinion about it all. She seemed resigned to her fate, as decided by her brother. Phee couldn't make her out.

'Oh dear!' said Phee at last. 'Can't you simply tell him what's what? That you're having none of it!'

'Think about it, Phee. I am entirely dependent on my brother, for everything. It's only right that I earn my keep. Richard will calm down when he's learned to trust me again.'

Phee wasn't so sure that Richard would let go. She embraced her friend. 'And what about Neil Tennant, Beth?'

'What about him?'

'You like him, don't you? You met him up at the shieling, didn't you? Hasn't he been to see you since coming home from... oh, dear.... from prison? To thank you and.... you know, thank you.'

'He has tried. But Richard won't let him over the door.' She looked very sad. 'I know he wants to see me. Sometimes he walks down the lane and looks up at the windows. He stops and waits. He waits for a glimpse of me, I know he does.'

'Really? How utterly, utterly romantic, Beth! And what do you do?'

'I hide. I step back into the shadow so that he can't see me. Or I turn away. I can hardly bear to see him.'

'Don't you want to see him anymore?' Phee couldn't believe that she wouldn't.

'Don't want to?' Elizabeth's stony exterior crumbled. She cried like her heart was broken. Tears flowed down her face. 'I want to. Of course, I want to. I want him to kiss me and tell me that he loves me, just like he did that day at the shieling. I want him to hold me in his arms and read to me and dance with me. And I want to tell him how much I love him.' She cried some more, her head resting on the table, her shoulders heaving.

Phee gave Elizabeth a handkerchief. The solution seemed quite obvious to her but she hesitated from saying the wrong thing.

'But I can't Phee, I can't. Because I promised Richard that I would never see him again.' She looked into Phee's astonished eyes. 'That was the price I paid for Richard's help in having Neil released.'

Phee hugged her friend and thought for a while. 'Well, a promise is a promise, I suppose.' Elizabeth's shoulders started to heave once more but Phee wasn't finished. 'However, given that this promise was exacted under very difficult circumstances, under extreme duress and for totally the wrong reasons, namely to suit your brother's ridiculous prejudices and affectations, I declare such a promise to be null and void.'

Elizabeth smiled wanly. 'Thanks for trying, Phee.'

'No, I mean it! Why are you sitting here when there is a lovely, lovely man along there in the Smiddy, who loves you and cares for you and wants you as much as you want him? You could go away together, build a life away from Richard, do anything you wanted, together.'

Phee studied Elizabeth's face for a reaction. 'Can't you see what's right in front of you, there for the taking?' Phee implored. 'Not everyone will be blessed with such a love. And you will never find it again, Beth! Go and take it with both hands!'

Elizabeth started to remove her apron. 'Do you think so? Do you really think so?'

They hugged until it hurt.

'Yes, I most certainly do think so. And if you don't hurry up, I might have him for myself! Don't think I'm joking about that,' Phee said earnestly. 'I'll deal with Richard, now go, hurry, vite! She watched Elizabeth run out of the kitchen, along the dark hallway and exit through the front door.

Richard was on the scene in an instant.

'Don't worry, Richard. She's had to run an errand that simply couldn't wait a moment longer.'

'What's she gone for?' he asked rudely.

'Something that she needed very badly, something very important indeed that can't wait a moment longer.' Phee drained her cup before standing up. She looked around the kitchen that was her friend's prison cell. 'Please tell Beth I'll be back to see her very soon. I hope not to be kept waiting at the door next time. Clearly, visitors agree with her. I've never seen her look better, don't you agree?'

She didn't care to wait for his reply. Richard was left with his mouth open, as she turned abruptly, closing the door behind her with a flourish.

Mrs Gow and the Widow MacAuley were back out of their homes and onto the street the instant they spied the manse door opening again. They watched intently as the minister's sister came running down the path at great speed, a huge smile lighting up her face. They followed her with their beady eyes like two birds of prey watching a rabbit. They saw her turn left onto Main Street and continue running until she reached the junction with the hill road at Smiddy Cottage. She darted round the corner where she disappeared from sight.

The old women barely had time to give each other a knowing glance when Miss Fraser was back in view. They watched enthralled as she took up position at the front of Smiddy Cottage, casting her eye over the white-washed building, at the small skylight in the slate-covered roof and, deep-set into the thick walls, the windows on either side of the heavy wooden door. She stood for a moment, apparently composing herself, arranging the loose ends of her hair, and getting her breath back. She stepped forward then gave a confident knock at the door. When it was answered, she spoke only for a moment before being invited in. The door closed again.

'Weel, Mrs Gow, the lassie's come tae her senses at last, it would seem.' The Widow MacAuley gave a cackle that showed her delight. Her face broke into a toothless grin.

'Aye, an' aboot time tae. When the richt lad comes alang ye've tae grab him, else he'll be awa' an' there'll niver be anither like him.' She joined her friend in a broad smile.

'Let's hope she's no ower late, Mrs Gow. We'll pray she's got there in time.'

# Chapter 48

## A WOMAN'S LOT – GUESS AND FEAR

Mary Birse had dropped in to see how Peggy Duncan was coping with her baby daughter. Wee Maggie had been fretful and the women decided it might be the colic or teething, even in one so young. There was no fever, no cough or rash so it couldn't be anything to worry about, they agreed. Mary made tea while Peggy fed her baby. The boys were at school and the men were at the pit so they had time for a blether.

They talked about the new boarders they had taken into their homes. Mary now had four and Peggy had two, all biddable and grateful to have a roof over their heads. The Coal Company had urged the tenants to take in more lodgers in order to help with the housing shortage. Some men were walking many miles in the morning – they were tired and soaked to the skin before they got started their work below ground. Boarders made extra work, reasoned Peggy, but helped to pay the rent and people needed a place to lay their heads at night. It must be a terrible thing to have nowhere to live. Mary told the story of the homeless lad who had slept on a bench in the furnace room of a pit where Alex had worked many years before. He lived by the light from the flames, cooking his dinner on a shovel pushed into the fire. The miners had quipped about how fortunate he was. He had the driest and warmest accommodation in the place.

The women talked about how cold the weather had been lately and how difficult it made life when it came to your turn at the wash house. Hanging out washing for it to freeze straight away, or having to take it in almost as soon as you had put it out because of the rain or the sleet, was not one of life's pleasures. Peggy had her work cut out for her with so many nappies to wash but, having spent many weeks confined to her bed or sitting in a chair during her pregnancy, she was happy to be up on her feet again, able to get on with her work.

Mary talked about the business surrounding the trespass; about how it had affected Alex who had taken it all to heart. He had been like a bear with a sore head for weeks because of it. He felt that he was responsible for the men's fate, she explained, even though he could see that Melville had been unreasonable and extreme in his reaction to a group of fathers and sons going for a swim together, just because they'd had to walk a few hundred yards across his land to do so. All that time, the laird had known that a coal pit was to be developed on the land, so his arguments about people interfering with the tenant's legitimate business were shown for what they were, nothing but a sham. Melville was damn lucky he hadn't been killed by Old Morton before the farmer had taken some sort of fit at the Harvest Home. The poor old soul had lain insensible in his bed for days, unable to speak, but had passed away in the night which was surely a blessing under the circumstances.

The women agreed that the gamekeeper had got his just desserts when the old man had shot him. He seemed to have been a wicked character, intent on doing damage to a lot of people's lives and no one would miss him, especially his wife and daughter who were well rid of him. Mary said that she had spoken to Mrs Grant only the other day in the store. She seemed to be coping very well indeed, with a cottage on the estate for her and Annie, in return for some work in the laundry and the kitchens at Parkgate House. It just showed how contrary these landowners could be, Peggy remarked, coming down hard on the men on the one hand and being so kind to Mrs Grant on the other. You never knew where you were with them, Mary said, that was the trouble.

They began a discussion of Neil Tennant's terrible experience at the hands of the evil Grant. The role of the minister's sister in it all was still an enigma that had a lot of tongues wagging, including their own. But a knock at the door brought their conversation to a halt, just when it had come to the most interesting bit, as Peggy remarked with a chuckle.

She opened the door to the cheerful face of Dr Matheson who had dropped by, he explained, on his way to meet with Dr Lindsay and he was wondering how things were going with the baby and so on. Having been present during the final stages of Peggy's confinement, Dr Matheson thought he would pay her a visit. He only stayed for a minute or two, just long enough to ask how Peggy was feeling, whether she had any problems following the birth, and long enough to take Maggie in his arms and give her a look over with a big smile, telling her to say *cheese* which, of course, she was still too young to understand. The women looked on in admiration. It meant a lot that he wanted to know how Peggy and the baby were and that he had taken time out of his busy schedule to visit.

It left them feeling more secure that if anything was amiss, he would be there for them.

'Now mind, Mrs Duncan, Dr Lindsay's just along the road if you're ever worried about anything,' he said as he made to go. He knew that it would have to be something serious before she would contact the doctor, however. Consultations had to be paid for, though subsidised by the Coal Company, her husband's employer. 'But I'm sure Mrs Birse here is a great support to you as well.'

'Aye she is, Doctor,' replied Peggy. 'We dinnae ken whit we'd dae withoot her.'

Mary followed the doctor out of the door. 'Can I have a quick word wi' ye, Doctor Matheson?' she asked when they were outside.

'Is this a suitable place, Mrs Birse? Do you want me to come up to the house?'

'Naw, this is fine, jist here, Doctor,' she replied closing Peggy's door behind her. 'It's no aboot me, exactly. It's aboot everybody here,' she explained. 'I dae whit I can dae, ye ken – confinements, lookin' in on the auld yins fae time tae time and advisin' mothers worried aboot their weans. I've seen maist o' the common complaints in ma time, ken?'

'You do a grand job, Mrs Birse,' said the doctor. 'And you ay advise sending for the doctor when it's a serious matter. You've an experienced eye for matters relating to folk's health.'

'Aye, but I think the time has come for a trained eye, Doctor. A community o' this size, an' Lord it's growin' every day, it's in need o' a nurse, trained in the new weys an' a'thing. Dae ye no agree, Doctor Matheson?'

'Great minds think alike, Mrs Birse,' he replied. 'Dr Lindsay and myself were discussing that very matter only the other day. Is that a position you would be interested in yourself?'

'Naw, no me, Doctor.' She shook her head. 'I have ma ain responsibilities at hame. I couldnae tak the trainin'. Besides, I could haurdly stert chairgin folk for daein whit I've been daein for years, could I?'

'I understand, Mrs Birse,' he replied, studying her with even greater admiration than he had before. He understood her position and the family ties that had prevented her from becoming a trained nurse but he'd had to ask. A trained nurse working in the community would interfere with her role as Highland Mary, who they all went to for advice. It was a role established over many years dedicated to helping others. However, her priorities lay with the best interests of the community, not in maintaining her own position.

The doctor explained what needed to be done as if he was thinking aloud. 'I'll speak to the Council, the School Board, Mr Imrie and so on, Dr Lindsay too, of course. The usual way of it is for a committee to be formed by some interested men in the community. Funds to pay a salary and provide accommodation would have to be raised. The ratepayers and the employers, in this case mainly the Coal Company, would pay towards the fund but a fee would still be charged to the patients for a consultation or a visit at home.'

'Weel, I'll have a word wi' Steeny Simpson on the Cooncil an' mention it tae folk here in Staneyrigg. We'll soon get the ba' rollin', Doctor.'

'As well as the main committee, there would need to be a women's committee to oversee the work of the nurse, to clean her accommodation and so on, Mrs Birse. I hope that someone of your experience would be interested in taking charge there.'

Mary didn't have time to give her response. A loud hooter sounded, making her start. It blasted the air, not once but over and over again. They both looked in the direction of the pits, even though their view was blocked by a row of houses. Mary's face went white.

'We'll speak again soon, Mrs Birse. I'll have to go.' The doctor didn't waste any time getting into his car.

Peggy appeared at the door of the house, her baby in her arms. She didn't speak but looked over her shoulder in the direction of the terrible noise, fear in her eyes. She looked back at Mary unable to say what was hurtling through her mind.

'Aye, hen, it's the siren ower at the pit. Get yer coat, Peg, an' we'll gang see whit's up.'

# Chapter 49

## WAITING FOR NEWS

Mary Birse and Peggy Duncan joined a trickle of women all making their way between the rows of the Stoneyrigg miners' cottages. They left their homes, abandoning their chores, unable to speak to each other as they hurried along still donning coats and scarves against the harsh winter chill. Something was amiss but if they didn't speak it, then it might not come to pass. The trickle soon became a flood, joined by grandparents and very young children not yet of school age, all heading down the long track to Broadrigg Numbers 1 and 2 where the siren continued to rend the bitter air. The noise stopped as a crowd formed at the main gate into the complex of sheds and other structures where the men worked, close by the winding house to the first pithead. The calm induced by deliverance from the awful racket was soon filled by voices asking if anyone knew what the matter was. Someone pointed out that the wheels of the pithead gear for both mines were running as normal, giving no clue as to the location of the problem. When someone else shouted out that Doctor Matheson's car was parked by the manager's office, a gasp of anguish went up. Dr Lindsay drove in behind the crowd, now clamouring for news.

'I know as much as you do, folks,' he said as he emerged from the vehicle to be surrounded by concerned faces. 'Let me through... I'll ask someone to come out and let you know what's going on.'

They watched as he disappeared into the office then followed his progress when he came out with one of the clerks before running off between the sheds where work on the picking tables and the tumblers rumbled on. They had passed the winding house for pit Number 2, some remarked. Rumours spread that the problem, whatever it was, was probably in Pit Number 1. This brought a little relief to some and greater fear and trepidation to others but no one was willing to count their chickens until they were hatched. To do so was sure to bring misfortune. Arrogance brought downfall and ruin, whereas humility might bring a favourable outcome.

At last, one of the under-managers arrived back at the office and approached the crowd. He was inundated with questions; had to ask for quiet. He put up his hands, waited, swallowing hard. His face was kind.

'If ye've men in Pit Number Twa, ye can gang hame. Please, can ye mak yer wey hame an' be assured they're fine.' He waited for people to start leaving the scene.

It was hard to go and abandon your friends and neighbours to hear bad news on their own. No one felt like celebrating. Some of the women with younger children did leave, grateful for their own good fortune, but with heads bowed, unable to look those who were left in the eye.

'Is it an explosion?' asked an aged voice. It was old Tam Pow, fearful for his grandson.

'Naw, it's no an explosion,' the man replied.

'Thanks be tae God,' said a woman. An explosion was every mining family's worst nightmare.

'A section o' the roof's caved in doon the ither pit, Number Wan,' he explained in his Glasgow twang. 'There's been an ingress o' watter in wan o' the sections. The rescue lads are doon there the noo an' we're waitin' for word aboot whaur it is precisely. I'm sorry, ye'll jist hae tae wait till word comes up fae ablow.' He made to go. He couldn't bear to see the anguish on their faces and he'd no more news for them in any case.

'Dae ye ken hoo many men are doon there? Is onybody hurt?' Mary Birse spoke for many.

'There are casualties for sure,' he replied. 'I'm sorry, I can tell ye nae mair. We're bringin' up a' the men fae the side o' the pit affected so there'll be news by an' by. I'm awfy sorry, so I am,' and with that the Glasgow man turned, leaving them in the cold. A crowd of small forlorn faces watched him until he had disappeared out of sight, into the office building.

'At least it wasnae an explosion,' remarked old Tam Pow.

'Aye, could be worse,' said a woman.

It didn't feel like it could be worse, waiting there in the winter cold without news. It was hard to be optimistic about the outcome. All they had was hope and silent prayers for the men down below. An ingress of water was not uncommon. The men at the face lay in the wet as they dug out the coal. Water dripped through the roofs of the underground roads then ran down to its lowest point to be pumped out if it looked like it was going to lie. Experienced miners could tell tales of whole peat bogs disappearing down shafts or through tunnel roofs when the rocks gave way, entombing lads in a black, watery grave for evermore. The watchers turned their backs on the Moss, surrounding them on the lower lying land where the pits had been sunk: the vast expanse of blanket bog with its web of streams and rivulets, trickling water across the land and down into the underground where the coal seams lay. Instead, they watched the wheels above the mine shaft, constantly rotating back and forth, a sign that something was being done to bring the men out.

Mary and Peggy hugged each other for reassurance and to keep out the cold. Ellen Broadley joined them, unable to put her thoughts into words. They admired wee Maggie, snug in her shawl, sleeping her way through the crisis like only a bairn could do; her eyes closed and her mouth pursed like a small rosebud that brought joy to her doting father, so Peggy said. They stamped their feet, moved up and down a few paces, always with an eye on the road past the sheds to the pithead. That was the road their men took at the end of every shift and that was the road they hoped they would take today when they walked back to them, to come home later in the day.

The Glasgow man appeared again, at last, with a grave look on his face and a list in his hands. He read out the names, telling everyone else they could go home. One had died and five were injured but the doctors were attending to them, he explained. Four remained unaccounted for and the rescue team was still trying to get to them. More men had been caught up in the incident but had suffered nothing more than a soaking and a few bumps and bruises. He said it could have been worse but for the quick action of the rescue team and the pump men.

He held up the list in front of him then cleared his throat. The crowd were silent, waiting for the names. '*James Anderson, Alexander Birse, Robert Duncan, William Kennedy, John McNab, Seamus Murphy, David Potts, John*

*Purdie, James Pow, John Thomson, John Wilson.*' The man said, 'Could the relatives come wi' me, please?'

It was strange to hear the name of your man or your son read out, there in that grey place where the works rumbled on and the wind whipped round your ankles. Your life was changed forever in the second it took for the name to be spoken and then to be heard, hopes dashed in an instant. Ellen hugged Mary and Peggy. She told them not to worry about the boys when they came home from school. She would make sure they were warm and had something to eat. The women nodded, numbed by the news, hardly hearing what she had said. Wee Maggie stirred in her sleep. She would soon need fed.

'Dinnae fret,' Peggy murmured softly to her baby. 'It'll be fine.' Hadn't she said those same words to her before she was born? And she had been right. She followed the small group making their way into the manager's office where more news awaited.

# Chapter 50

## THE DELUGE

That day underground had started like every other day. After a hurl down to the dook in the bogeys, the men had peeled off in groups going their separate roads to the coalface. The team led by Alex, Robert and Davy had taken the last tunnel off to the left on the downward slope, leaving the machine man and his group of coal strippers to walk further into the mine to their own place of work.

Electric lighting had been installed along the main road but not on the side tunnels. As always, it took a time for the eyes to adjust to the gloom and the much dimmer glow from the lamps on their caps. As he always did, Davy reminded everyone to watch their heads now that the roof was lower, and Alex chastised him for saying the same thing each and every day. He asked him if he thought they were all dafties. Alex wasn't in the best of moods. When he clattered his head off a piece of rock projecting from the roof, the younger lads laughed loudly till Alex conceded with a snort that he had probably deserved it. They discarded their clothes and tinnies on arrival at the railhead then collected their tools: shovels for the drawers; picks and shovels for the skilled men. By the time they had made it to the face, they were bent double and Alex had told Davy to mind his head at least half a dozen times.

The team made good progress that morning. The coal was coming away from the country rock with ease and the young lads seemed to be full of energy, requiring little encouragement to keep shovelling from the older, more experienced members of the team. Jamie Pow claimed it was down to it being a Friday – the thought of the Friday night dance in the public hall was keeping them all going. He took a great deal of ribbing from his peers who let it be known that he was sweet on one of the Johnson sisters and rumour had it they would be getting married soon. If his thoughts were on the dance, declared Jimmy Anderson, then they all knew what activity Jamie was really thinking about, and it wasn't dancing, that was for sure. Jamie's face blushed a brilliant shade of red, visible even in the gloom. He said no more but the smile on his face was there for all to see and to comment on from time to time.

The men were clearing out ready for corning time when a sudden crack in the rocks above stopped them in their tracks. They listened to the creaking of the pit props and the low rumble that reverberated around them. No matter how long a man spent underground, the response was always the same. The heart rate increased and breathing decreased. It was common to smell urine at such times, on account of the fear. On this occasion, they remained silent and motionless, ready to shift quickly if necessary but trying not to provoke the situation with unnecessary movement or sound. Beads of sweat pierced the brow as they listened, swallowing hard. A trickle of water appeared from the roof. It splashed onto the ground some way in from the railhead where the hutches stood full of the morning's coal. Then it stopped. Nothing to worry about.

It was common for rocks to settle and the ground to be wet. The skilled men set about examining the trees whilst the youngsters finished off the shovelling.

'They'll hae tae get the brushers tae put a proper linin' oan these wa's,' observed Robert. 'The tunnel's lang enough tae warrant it.' Brushers were workers who lined the roofs and walls of the passageways used for drawing out coal. They made them secure and suitable for the small wagons filled by the lads.

'They'll be waitin' tae see if the face is gaunae peter oot, Robert. The roof's awfy low, it micht no be worthwhile, eh?' commented Alex.

They watched and listened, tapping here and there with their hands.

'Nae worries, Jamie ma lad,' called Alex, after having had a good look back and forward. 'Lizzie Johnson an' yersel will have a fine time the nicht, oot the back o' the village ha'.'

The younger lads gave a whoop that was more relief than delight.

When the deluge came, they were caught by surprise. A long crack rent the roof for several yards along the length of the tunnel before two huge blocks of shale broke apart, collapsing into the space below. Several pit props splintered then cracked with a bang. Alex and Robert, who were checking a tree, hung on for dear life, praying it would hold. They watched as a waterfall poured down from the roof filling up the underground passage, sweeping men and boys off their feet on either side of them, and launching shovels through the tumult in all directions.

'Git oot! Git oot!' shouted Robert. 'Thon wey!' he yelled to lads disorientated by the suddenness of the flood. He pointed in the direction of the railhead, glad to see Davy helping Jimmy Anderson. Blood poured from the younger man's temple.

Alex looked round in the opposite direction, towards the coalface. He saw two heads sticking out of the water, Jamie Pow and John Purdie, alive and well but with terror etched on their faces. Jamie had lost his cap.

'Ower this wey! Come oan!' Alex called above the noise of the cascade and the yells of frantic men. Jamie and John crawled through the stream, spluttering and coughing as the flow surged against them. Alex held out his hand. John was able to grasp it. He pulled himself onto the prop holding the older miners in place against the surge. When they looked round for Jamie, he was nowhere in sight. An avalanche of rock plunged into the rising water where they had last seen his panicked face in the flood. Alex made to go after him but Robert pulled him back.

'He's awa', Alex son,' declared Robert. 'I seen him just as the rock cam doon. He's awa'.' He turned to John Purdie who was staring back at where Jamie had been, now a wall of rubble. 'We cannae help him, John,' he said kindly but quickly. 'We've got tae git oorsels oot.'

The older men took John by the arms, ready to make their way to safety. The flood level rose around them. The roof was low forcing them to kneel in the water but it was too deep to walk on all fours and neither Robert nor John could swim. They extended their necks upward, faces pushed above the surface, into the diminishing airspace. It was impossible to stop water going into their mouths so they inhaled plenty at times. It was hard to cough it up in a gap of only a few inches. The three finally let go of the pit prop when they realised that the stream was now going in the opposite direction, towards the railhead and beyond to the main underground road. Water continued to pour in from the roof but now that the tunnel behind them was blocked by fallen rock, the flow streamed out of the passage the other way.

'It'll run doon tae the level they're machinin' at!' shouted Alex, a positive note in his voice. 'It's ablow where we are here... the pumps'll be oan b' noo. We'll soon see a difference in the level o' the watter.'

They peered through the gloom, glad to see that the roof was higher just ahead. They struggled on, shouting to anyone who could hear that they were coming. Nothing came back to them, only the sound of the deluge, gushing out of the roof. They pushed through the waterfall, then out the other side. Alex shouted again, hoping someone would hear them now that they were on the right side of the commotion.

'I can hear somebody,' said Robert, making the others stop. They listened. A man's voice called back to them.

Their relief was short-lived. Another avalanche of rock came down, this time ahead of them. John made to out-run it but Robert held him back.

'There's tons o' rock comin' doon, John. Ye'll no beat it,' he yelled at him.

The landslide made waves that washed over their heads. The water was cold and getting colder. Robert started to shiver. They stayed back from the rockfall till it settled down then went for a closer look.

'There's nae wey through yon,' pronounced Alex. They looked over the pile of rock impeding their passage to safety. The faint loom from their lamps played over the stony surface as they investigated every crevice. An impenetrable barrier of rubble blocked the way.

'Best ca' canny for a bit an' let the rescue lads come for us,' suggested Robert. 'There's naethin we can dae oan oor ain, except tire oorsels oot an' dee o' the cauld.'

'The watter micht stoap in a meenit,' said Alex. 'They reservoirs build up unner the ground but they dinnae gang oan forever.'

John Purdie's face lit up. It was the face of a young lad, barely out of school and blackened by coal dust.

In the pale orb of light from his lamp, Robert looked closely at the boy's youthful features: long eye lashes that were sure to be dear to his mother's heart and a smooth chin with barely a sign of hair. 'Whit age are ye, John?' he asked kindly like he might speak to his own child.

'Fifteen, Mr Duncan,' John replied. Then he thought better of it. 'Weel, nearly fifteen oniewey.'

The men turned away, hiding their tears.

When the coldness grew they jumped up and down, slapping their arms with their hands across their chests. The water was only up to their oxters and the roof was higher now, where they stood waiting. Robert and Alex took it in turns to rub warmth into John's back, his angular shoulders and long, skinny arms, with their big powerful hands. It got the blood going they told him, and it helped them as well.

It seemed they had been there for hours but they had no clue as to how long exactly. They asked each other questions about their favourite pastimes, foods, places they had been, memories, birds, beasts, fruit, flowers, and fish. Then they chose a letter of the alphabet and had to name all of these, beginning with the chosen letter. It was a game they played with their families, at home by the light of the fire, and the memory brought a warm glow whilst the cold water lapped around them.

They spoke about the lantern lectures they had seen in winters past and about whether they would like to go to any of the places featured. John said he would like to go to Africa, to see all the animals and the natives with their spears but he didn't fancy that Manchuria place as much, where the missionary had been. He was quiet for a bit, said he had talked about emigrating with his brother but would probably stay in Scotland when he was grown, though maybe not in Stoneyrigg. That made him think about his mother and he started to bubble. So, they told each other all the funny stories they could remember. Which was a hard thing to do, joked Robert, because they went straight out of your mind when you were put on the spot.

'Why does the sun niver set on the British Empire?' shouted Alex above the sound of running water.

'I dinnae ken, Mr Birse. Why does the sun never set on the British Empire?' asked John and Robert together, their teeth chittering with the cold.

'Cause God couldnae trust the imperialists in the dark!' replied Alex. It was his favourite joke and he laughed his head off. If there had been more light, he would have seen that John was baffled.

'I dinnae get that joke, Mr Birse,' ventured John, thinking he might as well own up.

'See yous youngsters,' replied Alex, sounding vexed. 'Dae ye no tak an interest in political matters? I dinnae ken whit the world's comin tae, neither I dae.'

Robert explained the joke to John but the boy wasn't that impressed, something had been lost in translation.

'I've got a better joke,' John announced.

Alex and Robert waited for it, rubbing their arms vigorously to get warm.

'Dae ye want tae hear a dirty joke?' asked John.

'Aye, oan ye gang, then,' said Robert, knowing full well what was coming next.

'Jock the Coalman! Get it? Dae ye? Joke the Coalman?' John laughed and laughed till he lost his footing and disappeared under the water. He came up spluttering.

'Have ye noticed the watter isnae getting onie higher?' he asked the men when he had regained his composure. 'I near got pu'd under oan thon side.

Alex shone his light into the stream. It was flowing strongly through the wall of rubble at floor level. He thought for a bit. 'Since I'm the swimmer oan this team, I'll gang hae a gander,' he announced, disappearing under the water without further ado.

Robert and John waited, wondering if they would see him again. He seemed to be gone for ages.

Alex came up coughing.

'I could feel ma wey through the wa' partwey,' said Alex. 'It's a fair-sized blockage richt enough, or the rescue team would've been here b' noo.'

'They'll no stop tryin' till they find us,' Robert said to reassure young John. 'It's pairt o' the miners' code, ye ken.'

He caught Alex's eye. They both knew that time was running out and the cold would get them if the rescue team wasn't there soon. They had already done a morning's work without food and all three were chittering.

Alex looked up at the roof of the tunnel where it met the heap of rubble that imprisoned them. The noise of the water drowned out all other sounds but he had expected there to be some sign of rescue activity by now. Not known for his patience, Alex had waited long enough. He made up his mind.

The two men looked into each other's eyes by the light of Robert's lamp. They had so much to say to each other but they couldn't because of the boy. So, everything was conveyed in that look. Robert took his hand firmly and wished him luck.

'Shine yer lamps into the watter ower here, lads. I'm gaun doon tae see if I can mak ma wey through.' With that, Alex took a huge breath then ducked out of sight into the cold, black waters of Broadrigg Number 1.

Robert and John stood together, watching in case Alex returned. He didn't reappear.

'Gie's yer haun, John,' said the older man. They stood in the water, watched as the blackness encroached, their lamps fading fast. Soon it was black as pitch. They had never seen darkness like it. They held onto each other tightly in a darkness coloured by fear.

# Chapter 51

## THE RESCUE ATTEMPT

The first anyone else knew of the roof collapse and the ingress of water was when two empty hutches appeared out of a tunnel without anyone pushing them. A young lad was crushed between two wagons as the runaway hutches bounced off another loaded with coal on its way up the track. His workmate called for help when he pulled him out of the way and men appeared from the bottom of the dook to control the wagons. Miners and lads working near the start of nearby tunnels heard the commotion then ran to see what was happening. A rush of water swept across the rails, washing down the main road to the coal face where a coal cutting machine of the advanced type worked by compressed air was in operation. What seemed like a long period of pandemonium ensued with no one apparently in charge. Some men tried to make their way into the stricken tunnel, their first instincts to help those in need but a torrent of water kept them out. Others wanted to leave the pit altogether, fearful for their own safety above all and, unable to make sense of the situation, feeling that fewer people could achieve more if they had room to manoeuvre. Eventually, however, a chain of command kicked in and order came out of chaos.

The rescue team arrived and others would soon be on their way.

Those first on the scene waded in through the flowing water, now only ankle deep, inspecting the roof as they went. Calls from further into the darkness drew them in. They found two of the lads first, John Wilson and Seamus Murphy, propped up together against a side wall where they had collapsed. Seamus had a wide gash across one shoulder and bruising to his face and abdomen. Blood seeped through his torn trousers, into the stream that lapped round his legs. His uninjured arm was wrapped around John who looked to be in a bad way. John held his arm across his chest. His hand hung at an odd angle with the wrist bone protruding through a meld of blood and tissue. He looked half dead, bloodless. His white, gaunt stare spoke of pain.

A whimper in the darkness took them to John Thomson, lying chest down in the cold stream, propped up on forearms that were skinned and bleeding. 'Ma leg, ma leg,' he whimpered. 'Watch ma leg.'

Further in, they found three more. Davy Potts was kneeling in the water with Jimmy Anderson's head on his lap and John McNab nestled in beside him, a quivering wreck unable to move, covered in cuts and bruises. Davy held Jimmy's head out of the water, talking all the while to John, assuring him that everything would be alright, that the Lord would be there for them, no fear.

Whilst the rescuers who were trained in ambulance examined the injured, others shone torches further down the tunnel. The rock fall that blocked the passageway to the coal face rose up in front of them.

'There's fower mair,' Davy said weakly. 'Ahint the wa'. I heard them shoutin' afore the roof cam in.' He listed their names then explained that the roof had come down in two places, the first with the inrush of water and the second, right there where they could see. He explained how he and the four young lads had been caught up in it as they made their way to safety ahead of the others. Jimmy, unconscious there in his lap, had taken a blow to the head and collapsed after a few paces. It was hard to move him with John McNab in such a state. Seamus had helped dig John Wilson out of the rubble before a slice had caught him on the shoulder.

'We'll get the casualties oot then assess the state o' the roof,' said one man.

'Let me stey an' help ye,' pleaded Davy as men moved in to remove Jimmy. 'I'm fine. I can help.' John clung tighter to the older man and couldn't be prised away.

'Best gang wi' the lad, Davy,' said the man. 'We'll let ye ken whit's up soon as we hae a look, eh?'

As the casualties were seen to, the other members of the rescue team surveyed the blockage carefully. They were soon joined by the pit manager, Mr Brownlee. Pumps were being organised down at the bottom level, he explained, and the doctors were in attendance along at the dook. He was given the facts as described earlier by Davy Potts and, crucially, the news that four men were missing.

'Does it look stable to you?' asked Mr Brownlee, surveying the wall of rubble with an experienced eye.

'Hard tae say, sir. If we plough in an' tak awa' stuff fae the top, mair could come doon ahint it.' The man pointed to the water surging out through the bottom part of the wall and the trickles coming from crevices higher up. 'We dinnae ken whit level the watter is oan the ither side. The pressure could build up an' we'll a' be done for if it comes awa', a' at yince.'

'Well, we'll have tae try. Get your team organised wi' equipment and decide where tae start. But I dinnae want onie mair casualties, mind. Naebody else is tae get hurt. Dae I mak masel clear?' Brownlee went off to check on arrangements elsewhere; to see how the doctors were faring with the injured lads.

By the time he returned, the wall had shifted twice so the men had had to retreat. One had sustained a twisted ankle; another had a cut on his face.

'Onie word on the injured lads, Mr Brownlee?' asked the team leader.

'Aye, but it's not good. The doctors have pronounced Jimmy Anderson dead, I'm afraid. I'll need to go up and speak to his kin. The others will survive, though the lad wi' the broken wrist's in a bad way. Somebody was crushed by a runaway hutch but the doctors wouldn't be drawn on how bad he is just yet.' Brownlee looked over the blockage once more. 'Let's get the ither four oot, back to their faimlies in yin piece if at a' possible. I'll leave ye be the now.'

The rescue team decided that tunnelling through the rubble, just below the roof up on the right was the only way to proceed. A huge slab of shale sat at an angle with smaller pieces filling the roughly eighteen inch space up to the roof. Removing the smaller pieces above would help them assess the stability of the bedrock above the tunnel, letting them estimate the depth of the obstacle in their path. They began by creating a sloping ramp that men could work from. A pile of ropes, sheets of corrugated metal and pit props was assembled in case they were needed. A line of men passed debris back towards the railhead. The way in through the debris was propped up with wooden supports, leaving just enough room for a man to pull himself through. Work proceeded slowly because of the need for regular inspections. Sometimes the rubble shifted in other places and all they could do was retreat until they were sure it had settled down.

As time passed, hope that they would reach the survivors behind the wall started to fade. The opening being created seemed to be taking forever, a case of two steps forward and one step back. Sometimes it wasn't that fast. Some of the rock had come down in flat slabs that were easy to remove but sometimes the slabs sat upright at ninety degrees, blocking their progress like a locked door. Further in, the passage had been made more roomy for that very reason. When Mr Brownlee returned, he urged the rescuers on, taking a shot himself on the frontline. He understood immediately the difficulties of working in the space. It was a claustrophobic and dangerous situation. When he climbed back down the ramp, surveying the obstacle in front of him, he looked despondent.

'We've barely gone twenty feet,' he said, 'and there's no sign of an end to it.' Every man looked in his direction. He would have the final say. Stop or go; life or death for whoever was on the other side, if there were any survivors, of course, after all this time.

Tea and sandwiches were brought in, big heels of bread spread with jam and a layer of cheese for good measure. The rescue team took a break whilst Brownlee went back for another look with the leader of the rescue team. The men watched the inspection intently, willing the search to go on. If they had been caught out like the missing men, they would want their fellow workers to keep trying and never give up; though there was a limit to what was humanly possible. There was a limit to how long a man could live in the cold, black water. It felt cold enough to the rescuers when they stopped work for a rest and a drink of warm tea. They leaned back against the tunnel walls, watching the deliberations going on at the roof. It was hard to be optimistic as the time slipped by.

'We've made it harder by openin' up a sma' space raither than a bigger yin at the start,' Brownlee declared when he came back down the ramp. 'But we'll keep on for another while yet.' He looked around at the men. They were tired but glad. They admired the manager for his decision, a triumph of hope over experience.

A short discussion started up to reallocate the jobs that needed done when an almighty yell got everybody's attention. Half of the men made for the exit, thinking a warning of danger had been sounded. The others stared at the source of the outcry: one of the rescue team who sat on his hunkers, propping up the tunnel wall close to the heap of rubble. His eyes were fixed on the floor where water spilled out at a fast rate from under the debris. Those nearest to him spotted the source of his concern.

'B'Jesus! It's alive!' he shouted, leaping onto his feet and clattering his head against the tunnel roof. A bloody hand crept through the dross towards him, like a dead man emerging from his tomb. Suddenly it flopped right before their eyes, lifeless, unmoving.

Several men got to work, hauling up stones, chucking them away. They shouted for the doctor. Someone got ready with a couple of props, in case support was needed. First of all, an outstretched arm was uncovered then a head and shoulders. As soon as enough of the person had been revealed, two men started to pull him out. There wasn't a second to lose if they were to save him from drowning.

It didn't take long. The lifeless body of Alex Birse was laid out, his grey face to one side. Men shouted his name, willing him to come back to Mary and the twins. What will they do without you, they asked? When Doctor Matheson arrived, he pulled back on the casualty's arms, pushing his elbows down by his head, back and forward as if operating bellows. Water spilled out unimpeded for a second or two. Then the doctor ordered the patient to be turned over and he pushed on his back. More water spilled out. He started on the arms again, watching the man's chest rise and fall with each pull. To the amazement of the onlookers, he held Alex's nose as he breathed powerfully into his lungs, then again and again. He'd read about it, he said when he came up for air. It was what they did long ago but the method had gone out of favour. He returned to pushing the arms back and forward once again. Everyone watched transfixed till Mr Brownlee ordered men back to work on opening up the space by the roof. He shone his torch through the place by the floor from where Alex had emerged. The leader of the rescue team joined him, said it was a miracle. Brownlee said that it meant the other three might be alive. They had to pull out all the stops to get to them in time.

The group of relatives sat crowded into the pit office waiting for news. Each time someone walked past the window, they were up on their feet to see who it was. But as the minutes slipped by, they left it to old Tam Pow to keep them informed. Broadrigg Number 2 had emptied long ago and the shift men had taken over, he explained. A trail of men from Pit Number 1 had emerged intermittently, some wet, some dry, to wend their weary way home to Stoneyrigg. The managers had asked them not to speak to the relatives waiting for news. They didn't want hopes to be raised only to be dashed later and they didn't want rumours to fly. It was better if people heard the truth from the manager and the doctors, and no one disagreed with that.

The sky was leaden. It would soon be dark and a flurry of snow fluttered past the window pane, swirling in the bitter wind. Mr Brownlee appeared out of the grey, snowflakes melting on his hair and eyelashes. The Glasgow man was with him when he stepped into the room.

'Apologies for keepin' ye sic a while,' he began, 'I hope ye understand the difficulties.'

No one said a word. They understood the difficulties very well. They watched and waited.

'We've a few casualties, as ye'll have heard. Ma colleague here'll speak tae ye shortly.' He looked around the room, wondering who they all were exactly, whose relatives were who. 'Is oniebody here for James Anderson?' he asked.

A middle-aged couple indicated with a raise of the hand. The man put an arm round his wife. He looked at her closely as he kissed her shoulder where a lock of dark hair curled onto her hand-knitted shawl. They stood up as one.

'Could ye come wi' me, Mr and Mrs Anderson, please,' he said quietly, holding out his hand to guide them out of the room.

The remaining relatives watched the Andersons till the door closed. Their hearts went out to them. It must be the worst news possible, for the manager to speak to them. They all knew Jimmy, the eldest of a big family who lived in the Back Row next to the wash houses. He was a bit of a tear away, it was said, always one for a lark but he never did anyone any harm.

The Glasgow man explained that some of the men were injured, some worse than others. He would take their relatives to see them shortly. They had been worked on by the doctors then brought up to the surface. They were in a make-shift treatment room by the winding house, he explained. Dr Lindsay had come up with them, was seeing to their injuries. Four men were still missing, trapped behind a rockfall, he explained. The rescue team was hard at work trying to get to them. Mr Brownlee had been personally involved in the search for them. The relatives of the missing men could rest assured that everything possible would be done to bring them out safely.

After the Glasgow man left with the relatives of the injured, Peggy paced the room cradling Maggie in her arms. She took her over to the window where she showed her the snow, whispering and humming softly to her, rocking her back and forward till she settled. She told her that Rob and Sandy would be wondering where their baby sister was but they would all be home together soon. Mary sat with Mrs Purdie and two of her daughters. The girls said little but smiled and nodded when they were asked about themselves. Their mother sat quietly, staring ahead, thinking about her son. Mr Purdie would be along soon, she said, the neighbours would tell him where she was when he came in from Pit Number 3. Old Tam Pow had been joined by his wife to wait for news of their grandson. Their family had grown up and moved away long since. Jamie was all they had left.

When the Glasgow man returned, it was for Mary. He could only tell her that Alex was alive. That was all he knew but she had to hurry and go with him. She cast a glance in Peggy's direction as she hurried out the door. Peggy was pleased for her, gave her a gentle smile. She sat feeding Maggie in the corner by the window where she returned to her vigil, watching the snowflakes fall from the pitch-black sky to land on the window pane – a moment white then gone for ever.

# Chapter 52

## THE TRUE COST OF COAL

When Alex Birse came to, thanks to Doctor Matheson's persistence, he babbled and burbled, gibbering nonsense about Jock the Coalman having to get to the Friday night dance. As he fought to rise up from the wet ground, the reality of where he was and how he had made it through the gap in the wall, started to dawn. Two men held him down whilst the doctor spoke slowly and steadily, telling him to *ca' canny* and that he was no good to himself or anyone else, acting like a bull at a gate. The doctor began asking some personal questions to ascertain his patient's level of recovery and state of mind. Alex just got angry, shouting that he could be *Jesus friggin Christ* for all it mattered, what was important was that there were boys still trapped. Alex asked about the rescue attempt through a fit of coughing. How far had the team penetrated the rubble and what time of day was it? Jamie Pow had been killed in the deluge, buried under another roof collapse close to the coal face, he revealed. But Robert Duncan and John Purdie were still alive when he'd left them. The water was perishing when you were in it for so long, he explained. The trapped men would need to come out soon or the cold would get them.

Mr Brownlee came over when he realised that Alex had regained consciousness. He quizzed him about the passageway through the rubble that had led him to safety. How far had he come and did he think the men could be gotten out that way?

Alex described how open the first part of his escape route had been, maybe the length of two men. Then it had closed up. He'd had to squeeze round some big slabs, lying at an angle. He thought he was done for but had come up in an air pocket, black as pitch with no way of knowing where he was. He had shifted some rubble, moved forward for a bit, retreating back to the gap for some air when his lungs reached bursting point. He had tried again, come up against small stuff, scooping it back with his lead hand to make a way through. He couldn't remember much else, he was sorry.

Mr Brownlee looked down at Alex the survivor, at hands that were torn and bleeding and at his torso, patterned with scrapes and scratches from his journey through the debris. It was incredible what a human being could achieve when they were up against it, he thought to himself, and yet all this man could think about was the fate of his companions, still trapped behind the rubble. Alex started to cough again. He wretched and threw up some more of the water he had swallowed. Then he began to shiver, trembling violently, so he couldn't speak.

Dr Matheson ordered him to be stretchered out to the dook straight away. Had someone fetched more blankets, when he'd asked? They needed to move the patient quickly before he perished.

A shout went up from the top of the ramp. Brownlee went over to find a rescuer being pulled out by the feet. A slab had slipped where they were working – the rescue tunnel was blocked again. They called for more wood and a sheet of iron; no not the big stuff, it wouldn't fit in at the start. Hadn't anyone fetched down the narrower stuff yet? Another man emerged like a rabbit from a hole. He assured everyone that they hadn't far to go. If they could deal with the new obstacle and nothing else shifted, then they only had a couple of feet left, he reckoned. He had seen through to the other side. He was sure of it.

Mr Brownlee watched as more and more rubble was passed down the line. They must be close to breaking through into the underground chamber where Robert Duncan and John Purdie waited, he surmised. The rescue team was getting tired. Several had retreated already, taking the opportunity to get warm and dry when reinforcements had arrived. As pit manager, it was his job to lead and take decisions. As a man, he had to share the risk. He could not live with himself if he didn't and he couldn't work with these men again, if anything untoward happened during the rescue and he wasn't in there with them. He made his way up the ramp then shouted to the men inside the tunnel. As they came out, Brownlee was joined by the team leader. They crawled into the narrow space.

Brownlee and the other man came upon the flooded chamber when the last few blocks of stone were pushed out of the escape tunnel and they made a loud splash on the other side. The men shone their torches into the darkness. Water still trickled down from the broken roof but it was no longer the torrent described by Alex Birse. It echoed and splashed in the eerie blackness, every drop a loud chink like a hammer on a smith's anvil. The light from their caps played on the surface of the water, ripples reflected patterns onto the walls and the roof of the chamber. The second rockfall further in was impossible to make out. The roof dipped down quickly beyond the hole in the shale, vanishing into inky darkness. There was no sign of life.

Brownlee played his light across every nook and cranny then called back for some blankets and two stretchers. He twisted out of the hole in the rubble, scrambled down into the water, steadying himself as he waded over the uneven ground. His companion appeared then climbed in after him. A faint beam of light shone down on them from above.

'Whit dae ye see?' asked a voice. 'Have ye found them yet?'

'Aye, they're here,' came the reply.

Mr Brownlee stepped forward. He prised John Purdie from Robert Duncan's arms then gave him to the man who'd followed him in. Robert stood upright, leaning back against the wall of rubble that imprisoned them. Water lapped around his waist and he held his arms out, as if the boy was still there. He stared into the bright light from Brownlee's lamp with lifeless eyes.

A stretcher was lowered and they strapped John onto it. The men up above hauled him up.

'Wrap him in blankets an' fetch the doctor,' ordered Brownlee.

'Whit aboot Robert Duncan? Is he a'richt?' called a voice.

'We were too late for Robert,' Brownlee called back. 'Too late.' He could hardly say the words. 'But he saved the boy.'

# Chapter 53

## THE END OF CHILDHOOD

Miss Foulkes sat on her tall stool behind her tall desk, waiting for the class to put away their books at the end of another school day. Some of the children put the lids of their desks down carefully and quietly, the way she had taught them. Some closed their desks with a bang or a clatter. The noise grated on her nerves so she screwed up her face to show her displeasure.

'Quietly, children! Quietly!' she shouted at the top of her voice. She was sure that some of them did it deliberately, to annoy her. She would have to sort them out, to get the upper hand. In her opinion, always being in control, alert to dissent, was a necessary part of her employment.

Miss Foulkes didn't particularly like children. They didn't engender the warmth she saw in the gentle Miss Gibson's eyes, who displayed an empathy that made her suitable only for the infant class. A severe exterior and abrupt manner were the best weapons in the armoury of the upper school teacher, proclaimed Miss Foulkes. In that regard she was well equipped.

She wondered if she should select a couple of the boys for belting. Examples of poor work and behaviour could always be found to justify the selection of scape-goats, and the impact on attention and application afterwards was palpable, she always found. She decided against such a course of action at this stage but determined to reinstate her normal disciplinary regime the following week. Recent events at the pit had affected all of the pupils in the school. Even the children whose families were not directly involved in the tragedy had seemed subdued, in sympathy with their friends and neighbours.

The bell rang out in another room. The eyes of the class stared expectantly in her direction as she stared back, waiting long enough to let them know who was in charge. The letter on her desk caught her eye.

'Row by the door, lead on,' she commanded. 'Robert Duncan stay behind.'

The class emptied without a word being said.


'Rob's been kept back,' announced John as they ran down the school steps to join the group of friends, milling about at the school gates.

'Whit's up wi' Rob,' asked Bert of Sandy. The friends crowded round.

'Nothin',' replied Sandy with a shrug. 'He'll catch us up. Come oan, Bert. See's thon ba' for a gemm.'

'Can we gang doon tae the Meadie?' suggested Jim.

'Aye, it hasnae rained for a week,' remarked Dan. 'It'll be fine for a bit kick aboot.'

'Can we come tae?' called the girls, Minn, Sarah, Sadie, Jenny and more besides. They were all there and liked to tag along.

A long line of boys and girls made their way across the road and down the Doctor's Brae. December days were short – they had to make the most of the daylight. They had an hour before it was dark when they would have to be home for their tea. The nights were long enough in the Raws so nobody wanted to be home sooner than was necessary.

A period of snow and sleet at the start of the month had developed into heavy rain that had lasted for days. Everywhere had been saturated and burns had flowed down the roads like tears. That afternoon the sky was clear though, set for another night of frost. There were a few clouds, scudding along on a keen wind but the ground would be firm, good enough for a kick about without getting covered in glaur and feeling the back of your mother's hand when she skelped you for it.

The brae to the Meadie was lined with trees. In a landscape where woodland was scarce, they added colour and texture to a bleak outlook. They weren't the huge kind like the tall chestnuts that stood outside the public hall or the great beech trees that defined the avenue up to the Big House or populated Paddy's Wood, planted a century ago for the laird's pleasure. They were the smaller trees like the rowan that thrived in sheltered nooks, growing beside the fast-flowing burns that ran down the hills further north; and mingling with willow, had been planted by the Red Burn to hold the waters in place, preventing flooding of the flat ground by the mill. The bare branches of winter, stood stark black against the blue sky, defence against the worst of the wind as it whipped across the Moss. Crows sat up in the boughs cawing a loud chorus of displeasure as the children chattered their way down to the Meadie.

Minn looked back up the brae to see if Rob was coming. She hoped he wasn't in trouble and wouldn't be long. There was no sign of him. She had thought about him all summer and, since the accident at the pit, he was rarely out of her mind. She hadn't known what to say to him when he had come back to school. Nobody did. So, they had all said nothing about it and carried on as before; leaving him and Sandy to their own quiet thoughts and memories; leaving the door open to a return to normal life. Sarah saw her sister looking back. She pulled at her arm, laughing to let her know she could read her thoughts. Minn blushed then ran to catch up with the others. It didn't do to wear your heart on your sleeve right enough.

A groan and a gasp from the leading group warned the rest that something was amiss. The stragglers hurried round the bend to the bottom of the hill, peering round the gable end of Spittal Cottage to see what was up. They came to a stop at the bottom of the brae, unable to believe what was right in front of their eyes.

'Whit are they daein?' asked Bert, surveying the scene with his mouth open.

'Whit have they done tae the Meadie?' asked Geordie, ready to bubble.

'Whit are they daein tae the Wood?' asked Dan.

'Whit a mess,' said Sarah.

'They've wasted it,' said Minn.

The Meadie was a quagmire of thick, black mud and rutted tracks. Instead of green grass, pools of water covered the bare, uneven ground. The imprint of large vehicles led past the mill then along to the ford. The tracks crossed to the other side of the burn, where a braided trail snaked across the pasture to the steading at Back o' Moss Farm, standing proud on the drier ground of the river terrace. Stacks of building materials sat side by side with metal girders and wooden pilings. Piles of sand and gravel stood by the water's edge where the river banks had been covered in wild flowers during the summer months. The Wood was all but gone. Only a fringe of Scots pine remained to be felled, taller and stronger than what had already been taken out. Piles of twisted roots lay waiting to be burned.

'It's the road tae the new pit,' said John, 'Ma da' says the pit sinkers have started at Back o' Moss.'

'Looks like they're building a bridge for it,' said Jim. 'I liked the ford.'

'You ay fell in aff the steppin stanes!' laughed John. 'Dae ye mind when we were collectin' the muck fae the kye at the station an' we had tae flee the lang wey roon?'

'It'll no be the same,' said Jenny.

'Would ye look at the colour o' the burn. It's broon wi' muck fae the Meadie,' said Minn. 'A' the mennans'll be deid.'

'Nae mair fitba' here then,' said Bert, his hands firmly in his pockets.

Geordie's lip trembled.

'Mind when we had the fitba' competition an' the big picnic?' said Jim.

'Mind the nicht o' the Gala Day, when ye telt us ghost stories, Jim? An' we hid up in the Wood lookin' for the heidless horseman!' said Dan.

'An' we a' peed oor breeks when thon cry went up, richt oot the fires o' hell thon was,' said Jim, reminding them about the hellish moaning that had everybody running for dear life. As if anybody could forget it.

'I was terrified,' admitted Sarah. 'I thocht the singin' miller would be waitin' for us at the mill tae.'

'Look at the auld mill,' said Sadie. 'It disnae look richt on its ain, bare wa's stickin' oot the ground, naethin but mud a' roon aboot.'

'Aye,' said Sandy. 'It's sad songs the miller'll be singin' the nicht.'

For once, Sandy wasn't joking and nobody was in a

laughing mood in any case. It was a dejected group that made its way round the edge of where the Meadie had been, picking up their feet to avoid the worst of the mud. Nobody spoke as they meandered past the old ruin, and headed for home along the footpath by the burn.

When the noise and bustle of children leaving the classroom had died down, Miss Foulkes studied Rob. His face lacked all expression. He did not look in her direction but stared at the large clock above the mantelpiece behind her desk. As he watched the minute hand lurch forward, he tried to count out the seconds correctly, anticipating each small advancement in time. The teacher picked up the letter that lay on her blotter then read it for a fourth time. She gave a sigh to show her annoyance before folding it once more.

'Wait there, Robert,' she ordered. She left the room and disappeared into the dark corridor by the hall.

The door to Mr Black's study was closed. There were voices coming from inside so Miss Foulkes hesitated from knocking. She didn't want to disturb an important meeting but this was a matter of the utmost importance. As the home teacher of the senior class, it annoyed Miss Foulkes to distraction that Mr Black's salary was twice her own simply because he was male, not to mention the additional allowance he commanded commensurate with the extra responsibilities he carried as headmaster. Miss Foulkes' reasoning told her that she was the equal of any male teacher, including Mr Black. However, a lifetime's conditioning to the contrary, and fifteen years spent at the bottom of the educational hierarchy, had impacted adversely on her nerve, restricting her ability to be assertive and outspoken outside of the classroom. She looked once more at the letter she held in her hand then gave a firm knock before entering.

'Miss Foulkes, do come in,' said the headmaster when she presented herself at the door.

How she hated his condescending manner. She strode into the room as boldly as she could, ready to apologise and explain herself at the same time.

'You may not have met Mrs Duncan. Mrs Duncan, may I introduce Miss Foulkes, your son's teacher. Miss Foulkes, Mrs Duncan.'

As Peggy Duncan stood up, she gave a diffident nod. The teacher did likewise. There was no shake of the hand. This was not a meeting of equals.

'Ye got ma letter then, Miss,' Peggy said, looking at the paper in the teacher's hand.

'Ah, yes, the letter,' Miss Foulkes replied holding it up, her hand shaking a little. It wasn't like her to be lost for words but she forced herself to speak. 'First of all, Mrs Duncan, please accept my condolences on the death of your husband in such tragic circumstances.'

Peggy nodded but couldn't reply. It was easier to keep her late husband out of any discussion. She could maintain some dignity that way. Besides, this was no place for memories and sentimentality.

'Do sit down, Miss Foulkes,' said Mr Black, indicating a chair on his side of the desk. 'I'm glad you've joined our meeting which, as you will have surmised, is about the matters discussed in the letter. As the teacher who knows young Robert best, your opinion will be invaluable, I feel.'

Peggy looked at the two of them: Mr Black in his academic gown who knew nothing of the life she led and Miss Foulkes who cared little for women like her. She waited for the head master to say something which eventually he did.

'So, as we were discussing, Mrs Duncan. It is possible to grant a pupil permission to leave school before the age of fourteen under the provisions of the Education Act, should said pupil have achieved Standard Five.' He stopped, studying the woman opposite.

'An' has ma son achieved Standard Five, Mr Black?' She was distracted by a sharp intake of breath from Miss Foulkes.

'Has he achieved Standard Five?' repeated Miss Foulkes, her voice rather shrill.

Peggy knitted her brows. 'Aye! Weel, has he or has he no?' asked Peggy impatiently, wondering if the woman was doolally.

'Mrs Duncan, Robert achieved Standard Five a long time ago. He is one of the brightest pupils we have here in the school,' explained Mr Black. 'He is well prepared for advancement to the Standard Six Class and I have introduced him to the Classics in order to bring challenge to his curriculum. He has been picking it up with ease.'

Miss Foulkes interjected. 'Can I say that in my fifteen years as a teacher, Mrs Duncan, I have not taught anyone who could match your son in the fields of science and mathematics. He is a very able boy who could do very well in the future, should he remain in education.' Miss Foulkes waited for a response from the mother but there was none.

Peggy stared blankly ahead.

'We understand your circumstances and your difficulties, Mrs Duncan,' continued Mr Black, 'but it would be a further tragedy, on top of the one that has already befallen your family, if your son was to leave school at such a young age. In point of fact, I feel it would be a tragedy if young Robert was not to proceed to a more advanced education at the Academy in Bathgate.'

It was a while before Peggy responded and, when she did, she gave it to them with both barrels.

'First of a', an' wi' the greatest respect tae ye baith, ye havnae the slightest comprehension o' ma circumstances or ma difficulties. Nane at a'. Robert has a young brither an' a sister, new born. Withoot his faither, we hae nae wey o' makin' ends meet. An' ye present me wi' some high falutin idea aboot him steyin oan at this school an' then gaun up tae the big school foreby!'

'Forgive me, Mrs Duncan. I do not mean to patronise you,' replied Mr Black. 'I'm merely asking if there is any way at all that Robert can be allowed to continue with his education?'

Peggy shook her head. 'Naw, there's no. Believe me, there's naebody mair put oot than me aboot hoo things have turned oot.'

'I would be willing,' continued Mr Black thinking carefully about what he was saying, 'to sponsor Robert through his years at the Academy, making provision for the purchase of his books, for example, and perhaps a small allowance for his food and travel.'

'Is it charity yer offerin', Mr Black?'

'Please don't be offended, dear lady. If it makes you feel better, perhaps Robert could see the money in the form of a loan that could be paid back in the future, when he is able to do so.'

'But thon widnae pey the rent or buy coal for the fire or put claes on ma weans' backs and food oan the table. Would it, Mr Black? Young Robert's the breidwinner noo. We've never had need o' the parish an' I'm no aboot tae tak a haun oot noo.' She continued in the same determined vein. 'No thank ye, sir. Yer offer was kindly meant but the answer has tae be no. Oftimes, ye've jist got tae tak the haun ye're dealt in this life, Mr Black, an' mak the best o' it.'

Mr Black nodded. He could see there was no persuading her.

'Robert can leave the school, then, can he?'

'Yes, Mrs Duncan. As of today, he is no longer a pupil at this school.'

Peggy nodded her thanks. 'Yin thing I would ask?'

'Of, course.'

'Dinnae tell him aboot yer offer, if ye dinnae mind. It wouldnae dae him onie guid tae ken whit cannae be.'

'I understand, Mrs Duncan. What we have discussed will not go beyond these four walls.' They stood up.

'Robert is waiting in the classroom. Shall we come along and wish him well?' suggested his teacher.

They walked through the dark corridor of the small school building where they found the boy sitting in the semi-darkness, still staring at the clock.

'Good luck, young man,' said Mr Black. 'Perhaps we'll see you at the Continuation Classes in the future.'

'Good bye, Robert,' said Miss Foulkes. She turned to his mother and shook her hand vigorously. 'Good bye, Mrs Duncan, and best wishes.'

They watched mother and son leave.

'Another flower born to blush unseen upon the desert air, Miss Foulkes.'

'That was a terribly kind offer you made,' she replied, 'offering to sponsor the boy's education like that. I was quite overcome.'

'Such a waste, Miss Foulkes, he said shaking his head.

'One day this country will wake up to the terrible waste of talent. No wonder so many are leaving for the colonies. Such a terrible, terrible waste.'

# Chapter 54

## KEEPING UP APPEARANCES

When Elizabeth returned to the manse from Smiddy Cottage, she went straight into the kitchen and closed the door. It was almost time for the mid-day meal and she had work to do. As Richard was a creature of habit, he required his meal at the appointed hour. He might have visits to make and appointments to keep or he might have to write his sermon that very afternoon, in preparation for the Sunday service.

She stirred the soup that had been left simmering on the range. It was leek and potato, made in the traditional way with a butcher's bone. It hadn't suffered because of her absence, she was glad to see. She uncovered the loaf of bread she had baked that morning and gave it a tap. The hollow sound told her it was baked to perfection. Elizabeth gave a smile, well pleased with the results of her hard work, happy that her baking skills were progressing satisfactorily. The rewards of a job well done were many. She placed the bread on a wooden board and cut several slices. Two were retained for her own consumption; the rest was conveyed to the dining room where the table was set for one. She returned with some cheese and a bowl of apples, a jug of freshly drawn water and a plate of soup.

She rang the bell.

Richard emerged from the study.

'Enjoy your meal, Richard,' she said as she made her way back to the kitchen. 'There's plenty of soup. Let me know if you want a second helping.'

Elizabeth didn't give him the chance to ask where she had gone earlier when she had fled out of the house and she was glad when he didn't pursue the matter. She closed the door then ladled soup into a plate for herself. She ate at the kitchen table facing the window. It was warm from the range and the daylight poured in, even on such a cold, grey day. She glanced from time to time at the recipe book lying open on the table, reminding herself of the recipes she had chosen, organising in her mind what needed to be done. Richard had invited yet another of his colleagues from the Presbytery for an evening meal. It would keep her busy for several hours but a stew was straight forward and there was plenty of leek and potato soup left over. She had chosen rice pudding for afters. It looked easy enough though she hadn't attempted one before: a little nutmeg, sugar, rice, milk and a handful of raisins baked together in the oven.

Elizabeth studied the long back garden as she ate an apple to finish her meal. The ground sloped up towards the boundary wall with Mansefield. It was a rather plain space: just a long swathe of green where the washing was hung out on dry days, one or two shrubs by the back gate onto the lane and a small, square patch of bare ground where she had grown some herbs in the summer. When she finished her meal, she would take a stroll and examine the space for possibilities. Perhaps she could extend the vegetable patch next year, she thought; grow potatoes, onions, and leeks; make sure there was plenty of parsley for cooking and, perhaps, have a greenhouse at the very top by the wall, beyond where the shadow of the house fell. There was nothing to beat the smell and taste of home-grown tomatoes. She remembered the old gardener at her father's last charge: how he would call on her to fetch a bowl, helping her to select the ripe ones for the kitchen. Elizabeth smiled as she recalled his aged blue eyes beneath an old, battered hat; his gnarled hands holding a firm fruit to her nose, entreating her to inhale deeply the beautiful smell of summer.

She would make a plan for a kitchen garden, drawing it out on paper then she would mark out the beds with twine. The old shed in the corner had a few tools, not many but enough for her to get started when the worst of the winter frosts were over in the spring. It was always good to have a plan and something to look forward to, she decided.

She stacked up the dishes for washing then took a tray into the dining room. Richard had already returned to his study, she was relieved to see. It meant she didn't have to engage in polite conversation simply for the sake of it. She was happier when she didn't have to speak to him though a certain amount of dialogue was necessary from time to time. He had been taken aback the first time she had chosen to eat alone in the kitchen like a servant, rather than keep him company. Why should she sit opposite him, in silence, when they had nothing to say to each other that had any meaning? He had expected her to join him and his male guests when they appeared for dinner at his invitation. He'd hoped they would look her over as a potential wife, someone who could cook and clean for them just as she was doing at that moment for him, perhaps consider her as a mate who would keep their bed warm on cold winter nights. She had refused to join him for dinner even then, or especially then. She would not pretend, as he did, that their relations were cordial or that she had any say in bringing these men to the table. She would keep her own company and revel in it. She would look forward to Phee's visits and she would return to the Sabbath School as a teacher, enjoying the acquaintance of the children. She would meet people on her little shopping trips to the Co-operative Store, the Grocer's, and the Dairy, asking after their children and their husbands, and remarking on the changes in the weather. She would bite her lip, hold her head up high, ignoring the stares and the unkind words spoken about her behind her back. She had nothing to be ashamed of, no matter that the gossips thought otherwise.

By the time she had served up the rice pudding, Elizabeth was exhausted. She wanted nothing more than to go to bed. She longed for the coolness of her linen sheets and the darkness of her room at the back of the house. Mr Steele from the presbytery had been very pleasant, complementing her skills in the kitchen to the nth degree. He had been very pleasing to the eye, she had to admit, a relatively youthful presence in a dog collar, with thick dark hair and a bright smile; but she'd been impervious to his charms.

As she served coffee, she fingered the letter in her apron pocket for the hundredth time that day. She had brought it back with her from Smiddy Cottage. It was written in Neil's bold hand, penned before he had left the village. His mother had explained how deeply he had been affected by the circumstances of his arrest and imprisonment on trumped up charges. His later release, when it became clear that he was not the person portrayed by those who had spoken out against him, had catapulted him back into a strange world where no apology of any kind awaited, and he did not care to remain there. He had left the letter with strict instructions to her, his mother, that she was only to hand it over should the young lady in question come calling.

Elizabeth busied herself in the kitchen, clearing up after the lengthy meal for Mr Steele, and making preparations for the next day's breakfast. She lit a lamp then quietly climbed the stairs to her room, leaving Richard and his companion to their heated discussions of matters spiritual and temporal in the parlour, downstairs.

Her room was cold and dark. She placed the lamp on a high chest and the light shone downwards, casting shadows across every corner. She sat on her bed as she removed the letter from her pocket. It was slightly crumpled so she flattened it out with her hands, pressing it down around her knee, examining the handwriting on the envelope: 'To Miss Elizabeth Fraser, The Manse, Blackrigg'. The capital letters were large and well-formed, the others small and compact except for the long confident loop at the end of the last line. She brought it up to her nose, inhaled it, hoping for a sense of him, proof of his presence in the world. She stared at it for a while then took it over to her desk. She opened her notebook, the one where she made drawings of flowering plants and where the best of the dried specimens were kept safe. She placed the letter in the page with the spotted orchid, closed the book carefully then piled a number of heavy tomes on top. She would not read it. Not yet, not here in this house inhabited by her brother who had turned his back on its author, seeing only the clothes that he wore and not the true worth of the man beneath. She would find a time and a place to read the letter. For the moment, all she needed to know was that Neil had already gone away. She had been too late. Only by a day but it might as well have been a hundred years.

# Chapter 55

## THE LETTER

The day of the accident at the pit began a period of snow and frost that would live long in the memory, not because of its long duration for it did not last long, nor for the depth of the snow for it wasn't as deep as it had been in times past. A sadness and a quietness descended as the snow fell, muffling all sound in a respectful hush for the men who had died, for the injured and for their families whose lives would never be the same again. Children were kept off the street and men and women whispered carefully of the tragedies and disappointments of lives cut short. Hope prevailed that Jamie Pow would be found but with the passing days came the realisation that he was lost forever.

The grey skies lasted long enough for funerals to take place and for the men to be buried. Then the clouds parted and the sun shone. The landscape sparkled in the sunshine, clothed in an icy whiteness of spectacular brilliance and village life began again. Children's voices called out, shrill in the windless air. They slid down snow covered slopes on makeshift sleds of metal or wood and skated across frozen pools on the moss. Whirring and clanking, resounding and brash, the wheels of the pithead gear turned back and forth, delivering men in cages back to the coalface and locomotives whistled on the line.

Elizabeth watched her garden through the kitchen window turn from an Arctic paradise into sodden mud as days of rain followed when the temperature rose with a change in the wind. A small stream flowed down the lane washing gravel and soil out of the fields above. Shopping trips in the bright winter sunshine were traded for days indoors, watching the leaden skies deluge the land, downpour after heavy downpour, punctuated by intervals of mere drizzle.

She had been kept busy in the days after the accident, providing tea and sympathy for the many visitors to the manse, and supporting Richard as he delivered words of comfort to those in need. Even those not directly affected by the incident, in a familial sense, seemed to need words of wisdom that reassured them of God's Infinite Love and Mercy. The funeral for Robert Duncan had been particularly difficult, Richard had claimed, the sacrifice of the man in saving the Purdie boy having particular resonance for him as a Christian. His sermons since the tragedy had been intense, emotional affairs. The burden of expectation, apparent in the eyes of his parishioners every Sunday, was indeed a very heavy burden to bear. Eventually, the pressures of work took their toll, and he took to his bed for a rest. He placed a small bell on his bedside table and rang it when he needed something, which was often. Elizabeth ran up and down stairs with soup, tea and toddies in rapid succession, praying that he would be back on his feet soon, for both their sakes.

After the rain comes the sun. In the case of Blackrigg though, it was just a brief respite from the wet: a cold, dry period with the threat of further precipitation never very far away. Elizabeth had looked forward to a decent day for some time: one when she could take a walk up to the shieling with the letter. It was a long time coming. At least the wet period had coincided with Richard's illness when she had been kept busy, though in spite of this Neil was never far from her mind. Richard's continual demands from his sick bed had tested her patience to its limits. So, it was with a huge sigh of relief she greeted him on the first morning of his recovery, when he made the painful journey downstairs to the armchair beside the fire in the parlour. He was heartened by her apparent joy at his recovery, obviously the compassion of a grateful and loving sister, but her announcement that Mrs Tough was going to look after him for the afternoon cast some doubt on this assumption.

Elizabeth took the hill road past the Smiddy. She gave a tentative wave to Mrs Tennant who smiled back from the washing green behind the cottage. As she neared the fork in the road to Allerbank, where the footpath branched off to The Law, she turned to take in the view.

The village was all but lost in the curve of the hill but the burn was visible, its waters still in spate, surging across the flat land beside the railway line, past the pits, and on towards the bridge on the road to Rowanhill. A tapestry of green fields in winter garb merged into the expanse of the wilder moss that spread to the distant horizon. There, the flames and fumes of furnaces and works, far away to the south above the valley of the great River Clyde, discoloured the white sky. The new arrangements at Back o' Moss drew her eye. She caught her breath at the trail of destruction left by the vehicles that had crossed the Meadie and the stony beach by the old mill. In the absence of the Wood, the swollen burn had moved its course. A huge tract of land now lay under water. She closed her scarf around her neck then raised her collar against the cold and the bitter wind of change.

Elizabeth continued past the start of the footpath she would normally have taken to the shieling, hoping for a glimpse of the woods and the arable land to the north. Neil had often wandered there, marvelling at the rookeries, studying life in the hedgerows and on the woodland floor, taking in the view of the Forth and the hills of Fife. She wanted to see the landscape through his eyes, to marvel at the colours of winter, not vivid and vibrant as in summer, but muted and quiet in this long period of sleep when Nature lay in wait for the time when the sun would return, ready to awaken and bloom again in the spring. She lingered by the first stand of Scots Pines, bent and gnarled on the tree line and she listened to the creak of the timber in the wind and the rustle of needles high above her head. Where in this vast world was Neil? Where had he gone and would he ever come back to her?

The ruin on the muir had suffered from the winter storms and frosts. The last of the roof had fallen in, taking a piece of the gable with it. The timber had been removed by scavengers, out rummaging for fuel in the empty, unguarded spaces of the wild. There didn't seem to be anywhere left for swallows to secure their nests and she wondered if the birds would return as Neil had claimed they always would. No matter how they might be drawn by instinct and memory to this special place, it might have changed too much to win them back.

The wind blew hard from the east so she found a sheltered niche on the west side, with a view of Paddy's Wood and Parkgate House far below. The mountains of the north, covered thick with snow, were visible over her shoulder, just a glance away. A buzzard circled high above her on the wind. As she watched the bird intently, she wondered if he knew Grant wasn't there to harm him any longer, and she smiled.

Elizabeth removed the letter from her pocket and opened it.

'*Dearest Beth,*

*If you are reading these words then you have visited my family at last. Perhaps you have enquired of me, knowing that I had left Blackrigg. I am grateful for your interest. Please be assured that I am well, wherever I may be.*

*I do not know my destination but you know something of my hopes for the future. The possibilities are many. We are only limited by our imaginations, Beth.*

*Oh, how I wish that this were true! These last weeks and months have been a dreadful test of my resolve and, yet, the sweetest of my life. Knowing you and the hours we shared, your smile lights up my every waking hour. I see it when I wake each morning and it lulls me to sleep, to dream, at night. I will think of you wherever I go.*

*I cannot live in this place without seeing you, knowing that you do not want to speak to me. I fear that I make you a prisoner in your own home, fearful that we might meet. I cannot have you thinking ill of me. I leave that you may be free and not embarrassed by my presence. Please know that I will always be grateful for your intervention in my predicament. I understand what it must have cost you to speak up on my behalf. But we are nothing without truth, Beth.*

*I leave you with words I once read to you. I hope you understand their meaning and that they give you succour and support in the years to come as they will me.*

*"And this prayer I make,*
*Knowing that Nature never did betray*
*The heart that loved her; tis her privilege,*
*Through all the years of this our life, to lead*
*From joy to joy; for she can so inform*
*The mind that is within us, so impress*
*With quietness and beauty, and so feed*
*With lofty thoughts, that neither evil tongues,*
*Rash judgements, nor the sneers of selfish men,*
*Nor greetings where no kindness is, nor all*
*The dreary intercourse of daily life,*
*Shall e'er prevail against us, or disturb*
*Our cheerful faith that all which we behold*
*Is full of blessings."*

*Goodbye! Dearest, Beth*
*Yours aye,*

*Neil Tennant'*

Elizabeth clasped the letter to her breast as she looked across the wild, empty moorland through tear-filled eyes. The buzzard soared high above her, his call a sorrowful 'peeou', as he circled in the sky.

She whispered quietly, hoping he might hear.

*'"Therefore let the moon shine on thy solitary walk; and let the misty mountain winds be free to blow against thee. If solitude, or fear, or pain, or grief, should be thy portion, with what healing thoughts of tender joy wilt thou remember me?"'*

'Fly high! Fly high!' She watched as the bird circled higher and higher in the sky above her till he was almost out of sight. 'Come back to me, Neil. Please come back.'

Elizabeth sat for a long time. Ice penetrated her body till it felt like a sickness. Eventually, she stood up to shake the chill from her bones, hugging herself, looking for warmth. She pulled her hat down about her ears then took a last look round. The wind blew endlessly across the frozen ground. And the buzzard had gone from the sky.

She left the shieling, that solitary place that meant so much to her and where, in former times, others had departed in sadness and regret for an easier place on lower land. It was a place of the summer, consigned to the memory by people long gone to live in cities and work in factories, or who'd sailed across the ocean to foreign shores, never to return. Her feet crunched across the half dead grass, made hard by the winter frost then she wound her way slowly down the road to her kitchen and her garden at the manse.

# Chapter 56

## THE CLOSE OF THE YEAR

The smell of burning coal from the coke ovens hung in the air and the dim lights from the cottages lit their way. The sky above was clear, inky black, and sprinkled with bright stars. Wrapped up against the frost, Minn and Sarah skipped along the road from Stoneyrigg arm-in-arm. Their father and Meg followed on behind. The Sabbath School Soirée was a much-anticipated event in the calendar and, after so much grief and reflection, it was time to celebrate the happy times and draw a line under the sad. The end of the year was drawing near. Thoughts would soon be turning to the future, with hopes for good health and happiness and prosperity for all.

The Graham sisters had spent an afternoon together, working on the costume that Meg would wear when she married Will Morton in the spring. In the main, weddings were joyful affairs, especially if there wasn't a baby on the way, and the anticipation and planning added greatly to the excitement. Meg had bought a voluminous coat from Jinty Auld, who had claimed it came from a big house in the city. Jinty always sold the best of stuff. The rich, she said, wouldn't wear anything that was out of fashion and regularly threw out clothes they had hardly worn. On her last visit to Stoneyrigg, Meg's face had lit up at the sight of the pale grey material emerging from the pack, telling Jinty she had a sale. Meg had already fashioned a skirt from it. She was reworking the top part into a jacket, neat and fitted at the waist. The lining was a dark silk – Meg had plans for making it into a blouse to match her new suit. It was to have long sleeves and a frill down the front; maybe a bow too, like one she had seen in a picture in the store. Minn and Sarah marvelled at their sister's skill with scissors and needle. She had an eye for design. As soon as she put the strangely shaped pieces together, you could see what she'd had in mind.

Meg had been overcome with joy when her father announced that he'd hired the big room in the public hall for the day of the wedding. There would be a special tea to celebrate the marriage of his eldest daughter, the first to be wed and cause for great rejoicing. Will visited the house often – Meg spent more and more time in his company these days. Their father told Minn and Sarah he couldn't imagine life without Meg in the house but it was high time the couple were wed. They could hardly keep their hands off each other, he said in an unguarded moment. That made the girls blush and they giggled when they caught each other by the eye.

They passed Highland Mary rushing between rows to let Peggy Duncan go to the Soirée with Sandy. Alex was back at work, she explained when Tom asked after him, but he was still in terrible fettle after all that had happened. The twins didn't have the life of *'twa dugs'* because of him, she said, which made Minn sad. She knew what it meant. Mary said that they were lucky Alex had come out of it relatively unscathed, unlike some like Robert Duncan and Jamie Pow of course, or the Wilson lad who had lost his hand and John Thomson who would have a permanent limp on account of his damaged leg. Scant compensation was being paid by the company, she had heard, though they would all have jobs at the end of the day for which they had to be grateful. As Mary hurried off on another mission to help a member of the community, the Grahams watched her go. Minn remembered what everybody in the Rows was saying. Alex Birse had turned to the bottle after the accident. And Alex and strong drink didn't mix, so they said.

Minn and Sarah moved on towards the gaslight that lit up the village ahead. They heard their father and Meg discussing Old Mrs Pow who hadn't been the same since the accident had taken her grandson from her. She had visited the pit every day since the tragedy looking for Jamie, hoping against hope, her knuckles white as she gripped the gate into the yard. She would peer down the road to the pit head, studying the blackened faces of the men as they came out of the winding house at the end of their shift. Meg whispered that it could make a woman go strange in the head to think of her child lying cold and lost, deep under the ground. Mrs Pow wouldn't be able to rest until Jamie came home and, as everybody knew, he never would because that section of the pit had been sealed up for safety reasons, to let them continue working the coal. Minn and Sarah squeezed each other's hand at the thought of it.

Ellen and Jimmy Broadley caught up with them which brought a breath of fresh air to the sombre mood. They were going in the same direction. Geordie took the girls by the hand, giving them his shy smile. Meg remarked about how strong he was looking. It was hard to believe how ill he had been, and Ellen agreed happily. It was a miracle that he was back at school already and doing so well.

When they arrived at the church, they joined friends and neighbours chattering in the street. Greetings and laughter lit up the dark night more than the gaslight ever would. Some held young children who couldn't be left at home whilst others carried plates of home-made pancakes and biscuits for the tea interval. The queue to get into the church hall snaked out of the door, down the lane, and onto Main Street. No one could understand how everybody fitted inside but they always did. It helped that the children were made to sit on the floor, squashed together, or behind the minister on the small stage, ready to sing for everyone's entertainment. Any discomfort would soon be alleviated when it came time for the supper and plates of cakes and sandwiches were passed round. There were always extras so no one minded how many you had as long as nobody else missed out.

When they trooped into the hall, Minn saw Miss Fraser on the other side of the room, talking to Miss Melville. They were Minn's favourite Sabbath School teachers. Her heart gladdened at the sight of them. Miss Melville was always happy and smiling. Sometimes, if you said something quite ordinary, Miss Melville would burst out laughing though you never felt she was making fun of you. It was just how she looked at life. It was funny to watch her trying to keep her face straight during the solemn bits of Mr Fraser's sermons or, sometimes, when he was saying a prayer.

Minn was especially glad to see Miss Fraser back at the Sabbath School. Everybody had missed her. She was gentle and kind and was never ever cross. They said she was pining for Neil Tennant because she loved him with all her heart but he had gone away to seek his fortune. Minn recalled the day of the outing to Wallace's Cave, remembering the fun they'd had when Miss Fraser had told them all about the secret language of flowers, and how she had blushed when Neil had looked into her eyes as he lifted her off the hay cart.

One day, determined Minn, she would grow up to be like Miss Melville and Miss Fraser and she would get to be a teacher at the Sabbath School. She would make nice clothes to wear like her sister, and fall in love with a fine young man who would sweep her off her feet, just like Will had done with Meg or Neil Tennant had done with Miss Fraser. Her young man would stay with her and love her forever. She didn't want to waste her life pining for him like Miss Fraser was doing. It had to be a matter of choosing the right one, she decided.

When the minister stood up to make his speech, everybody laughed loudly when he said that he wouldn't speak for long and he looked a bit piqued. Inevitably, he spent ages talking about the year past, about all the tragedies and departures there had been from this life, and how God was the Light and would deliver them all from the darkness with his Love.

Minn thought hard about what he was saying: about all of the trials and tribulations of this life and about how God was there for you. You could depend on God, as long as you believed. That was the minister's message. She prayed that God could see the goodness in her heart and earnestly promised always to be His humble servant. Sitting behind the minister where everyone in the hall could see her, Minn hoped she looked pure and innocent before God. She concentrated hard; sat up straight when she felt her eyes getting heavy. It wouldn't do to fall asleep in the middle of Mr Fraser's delivery, even if it did seem to go on forever. She found herself surveying the hall, quietly naming in her head everybody who was there. She knew everybody present. That was Blackrigg for you, she thought. Even though new people came to live there every day, it didn't take long for you to put a name to a face.

There were some people who were noticeable by their absence, she realised. Not everybody came to the church so that ruled out a lot of her friends and neighbours, like Jim and John who weren't allowed to come because of Alex Birse, and Sadie who couldn't attend because she was RC. Pansy Morton was there in the corner with the rest of her family who would be leaving the village soon for a new life on another farm, now that Back o' Moss was a coal pit. It was probably just as well that the laird, Mr Melville, hadn't turned up since he was the one responsible for putting the Mortons out of their farm in the first place. The laird hadn't been seen about the village as much as he had been earlier in the year. And that had everybody talking. They remembered the way he had treated the community by refusing to let them go onto estate land so that children could learn to swim. It wasn't lost on folk that Alex Birse wouldn't have survived the pit disaster if he hadn't been able to swim to safety, saving the life of young John Purdie in the process. The laird was betrothed to Miss Imrie now though folk had assumed for long enough that he would marry Rose Matheson. That had people talking as well because it was obvious he was marrying for money. Miss Matheson was studying to be a doctor and everybody said she was better off without him. So, they said.

Minn looked hard but couldn't see Bert then remembered he was at home with the lurgy; and she couldn't see Jenny's mother who was looking after her youngest, poorly with the whooping cough. It was doing the rounds. She spotted Sandy at the very back of the hall and gave him a smile. He was sitting beside his mother who was being very brave, coming out to the Soiree only a short time after her man had died. Rob wasn't there. He wouldn't be back at the Sabbath School, Sandy had said, not now that he was working in the pit just as his father had done before him.

Minn missed Rob. It wasn't the same at the school either, knowing that he wasn't sitting at the back of the class anymore, where he'd had a good view of everybody and could see her busy at her work. She missed that feeling she used to get in the pit of her stomach when she suddenly thought about him, wondering if he was looking at her, right at that very moment. Was he seeing her long black hair tied up in a ribbon and flowing down her back? What was he thinking when he looked at her, hard at work?

At the minister's command, Minn came back to the present as the choir shuffled to its feet. She stood up to sing with the other children: 'The Village Blacksmith', 'Rocked in the Cradle of the Deep', 'Dream of Paradise' and 'When the Ebb Tide Flows.' An encore was called for and 'Hurrah for the Highlands' brought a cheer. There wasn't a dry eye in the house but the audience smiled at the same time. Parents were swollen with pride.

Then it was time for the children to rest before the speeches and the prize giving, as Miss Shanks took to the stage with some of the old favourites, 'The Deil's Awa', 'John Anderson My Jo', 'Loch Lomond', 'Bonnie Wee Thing' and 'Will Ye No Come Back Again?'

More tears, thought Minn. Weren't big folk happy unless they were crying? It was one of life's mysteries that these people who worked deep underground and out in the fields in all weathers, by the sweat of their brow and the power of their hands, could bubble like bairns at the plaintive notes of an old Scotch sang.

Miss Shanks responded to calls for an encore with *'The Braes o' Ballochmyle'* and everyone heard Miss Foulkes comment to Mr Black that, *'as the pupils might say, it would bring a tear to a gless ee.'* The minister tried to mask the utterance with an announcement that it was time for the interval but too late. Even through the commotion, Minn could see that Miss Shanks wasn't pleased. She knew the post mistress would be waiting for Miss Foulkes the next time she came to buy stamps at the post office.

The children had been encouraged to go in for the speech-making competition which every year was hotly contested. Mr Black declined to join the judging panel since he had been approached to assist some of the participants so Mr MacLean, Lady Moffat and Dr Matheson were chosen as judges. They took to the stage looking very serious in their roles.

Maisie Forrest was first up with her speech, 'The New Minister' and the Rev Fraser couldn't hide his pleasure when he realised that the speech was all about him. He was less impressed when Margaret Simpson followed with 'The New Puppy' and it became clear that the girls had collaborated closely, using similar descriptions and epithets such as *'faithful companion'* and *'playful disposition'*. That brought laughter from the floor and had Dr Matheson hiding a smirk behind his hand. Everyone was in stitches when Seoridh Wallace diverted his 'Spartan Life' into a comparison of the ways of the men of Sparta with the Scots, in general, and the men of Stoneyrigg in particular. The Scots, he declared, had similar traits of courage, discipline and endurance but the main difference between them, as far as Seoridh could see, was that the Spartans chose to live the way they did whilst the Scots had absolutely no choice in the matter.

Daisy Gowans was last up, taking to the stage in her usual confident manner. Minn studied her carefully as she made her way down the aisle. She saw Daisy flutter her eyelashes in Andrew Brownlee's direction then toss a blonde pigtail over her shoulder. Yuch, thought Minn, it didn't take Daisy Gowans long to change her affections. Rob Duncan, erstwhile top of the class and presently drawer and filler in Broadrigg Number 1, had been dumped in favour of Andrew, son of the pit manager, and with very good prospects for the future.

Daisy gave a cough of affectation. Silence fell on the audience. She glanced over at the schoolmaster, her mentor, for approval. Mr Black smiled back, giving her a nod of encouragement.

'My talk is entitled, "The Romance of a Piece of Coal", she began, in a voice honed by elocution lessons.

A murmur of approval went round the hall.

'When one thinks of a piece of coal, what image is conjured up in one's mind? A black rock dug out of the ground, perhaps? Or a commodity bought and sold? Is it animal, vegetable or mineral? It is found in great quantity in these parts, under the ground at varying depths in between limestones and shales, so it is most definitely a mineral, commonplace and quite ordinary and not at all romantic. Or so one might think!'

She paused for effect, taking time to look around the hall, catching a few unsuspecting members of the audience unawares.

'Take a piece of this black mineral, this stone, and place it on the fire. That is when one realises that it is not ordinary at all. In fact, it is a most extraordinary substance unlike any other. It gives off heat and light when burned, sometimes fierce, and often with a steady radiance. It brightens any room, bringing warmth and cheer to all. Flames lick the chimney breast, gases escape from within and sparks rise up with the smoke, alive for a moment then gone forever.

The lonely widow, alone in her parlour, is cheered by the brightness and warmth of the coal fire. Her teapot is warming on the stand. Happily, she remembers the past as she sees the passing years in the flickering light. The family gathers around the fireside on a winter's evening. Father reads and mother mends whilst the children play happily on the hearth rug, feeling the warmth of their parents' love in the quiet glow from the coals.'

Daisy looked around her audience. No one had considered a simple piece of coal in such pleasing terms before.

'Should one care to examine a piece of coal carefully, one might find a clue that tells where it comes from and how it has been formed. The Scottish coals are many and varied, formed of differing materials and conditions in the dim and distant past when no man or animal of our present acquaintance roamed this vast earth. Study the surface of these coals and images of forests meet the eye. The imprint of club mosses and horsetails, the Lepidodendron and the Calamites, inform one of the origins of this extraordinary mineral. It is a stone that is almost entirely composed of carbon that was breathed from the air by plants long dead but not entirely gone. The coal is all that remains of the great forests that lived and died on earth aeons ago. When one looks closely at a piece of coal one sees into the past, looking back to the very beginning of time itself! Men of science tell us of the great volcanoes that blew ash and dust out of vents, spilling lava across great marshy deltas and seas. They say that winding streams brought mud and sand from the mountains to cover the remains of the dying forests, thus to preserve them, hidden in the ground until now, when we are compelled to use our imaginations to find them in the Stygian darkness that we might benefit from their bounty.

'For centuries, Man searched for coal where it was easy to find, below the soil and in the sides of small valleys from where it could be removed along adits. Presently coal is harder to find, so shafts many fathoms deep have to be sunk to remove it. Not only that but Man has had to look for it under the wilder tracts of land, home to deer and birds, well used to the harsh weather and the coldest soils. Mosses and bogs, where peat dominates, are not to our minds picturesque but they are sublime, attracting only the hardiest of men and women to live and work there. Against all the odds, they build their tiny cots, low-slung and strong against the wild winds, with long, lonely trackways across the vast frozen wastes to remove the coal. In the early hours of a winter's morning, when we are warm in our beds, the miner is up and about. Peek through the curtains and one will see the shimmer of many small flickering lamps coming from all the airts, going towards the pit where great wheels turn to take the men countless fathoms below ground for their day's work. These are not the pampered people of the sheltered, lowland plains and sunny vistas of southern climes! No, they are skilled and independent colliers, people of an adventurous spirit whose every waking hour is challenged by the power of raw Nature!

'And what does this spirit create? Why it creates ideas and enterprise and industry that are constantly at the forefront of advancement, advancement in engineering and science, harnessing what is best in Man and in Nature, bringing employment to many and fuel to all, for the prosperity of our great country and its people!'

A rapturous applause erupted from the floor. It had been a wonderful tribute to coal and the people who worked it. Minn didn't grudge Daisy her first prize, even though you could tell she'd had a lot of help from Mr Black in the writing of her speech. It had delighted the listeners and made everyone smile and swell with pride. The minister took his chance to capitalise on the emotion of the occasion by saying a prayer about the bountiful gifts of God and that God was our refuge and our strength. He spoke about Love and Hope and Mercy, those small words with big meanings that meant so much to everyone. Then before Minn knew it, the evening was coming to an end. Together, they sang 'The Lord is My Shepherd' and got ready for the best, and the saddest, song of all.

In the traditional way, the children formed a circle in the middle of the hall, the adults surrounding them on the outside. It was a squeeze to get everyone in. Minn hadn't understood the words before but, standing here now in the middle of everyone, she thought she had an inkling. Her father stood behind her with Meg who would soon be married and off to start a new life in Canada in the spring; she saw Miss Melville smiling kindly at her good friend Miss Fraser who looked dreadfully sad, trying hard to put a brave face on it; she heard Ellen Broadley telling Geordie to behave; and she saw Peggy Duncan staring straight ahead, lost in her own thoughts about Robert and Rob and Sandy and Maggie and Lizzie. Minn looked around at the faces. Some were smiling and some were stained by tears. They clasped each other firmly by the hand and sang the verses of the song, not knowing what the future would bring but hoping for the best.

> 'Should auld acquaintance be forgot
> And never brought to mind?
> Should auld acquaintance be forgot
> And auld lang syne!
>
> For auld lang syne my jo,
> For auld lang syne,
> We'll tak a cup o' kindness yet
> For auld lang syne'

\* \* \* \* \*

# The Linlithgowshire County Courant

December 1910    Blackrigg News

ELECTION  Mr Alex Ure, KC, MP, the Lord Advocate (Liberal Party), spoke to a packed schoolroom at the beginning of the month when he declared the forthcoming parliamentary election to be, principally, about whether the peers or the people run the country. Mr Kidd, B.L., candidate for the Unionist Party, also met with voters when he declared his party to be committed to a strong navy; free trade but favouring the colonies through tariff reform that all might benefit from the prosperity to follow; also social reforms but not the methods proposed by the present government; and the extension of democracy to the House of Lords through reform.

Mr Ure was returned as the MP for Linlithgowshire.

ENGAGEMENT       The recently       announced engagement of marriage between Mr David Melville of Rashiepark, younger son of the late Major & Mrs Arnott Melville, and Miss   Catherine   Imrie, only  daughter  of  Mr & Mrs Charles Imrie, Rowanhill   House,   has been met with delight in the local community. The couple have indicated their intention to have a spring wedding.

PUBLIC PARK Mr Imrie of The Coal Company, which employs many in the district, has generously donated a tract of land, locally known as Mansefield, for the use of the villagers. Miss Silver of the School Board and Mr Simpson of the Parish Council praised Mr Imrie for his generosity, thanking him for giving the children of the community a place where exercise and other recreations may be had to the benefit of their health.

SOIREE The annual Soiree of the Sabbath School was held in the kirk hall and was well attended by young and old. In his address, Rev Fraser promised that he would not make a long speech (much laughter) as the evening's entertainment was keenly awaited. He commented that he was very pleased with the attendance during the year by children of all ages and that numbers had increased greatly in the period since he had taken over the charge. The minister praised the sterling work of the teachers in supporting the school. He paid tribute to his sister, Elizabeth, who had joined him in the parish earlier in the year and had been a great blessing to him (applause). He said that the tragic events that had befallen the community in recent weeks had shown what a strong community spirit there was in the village and that its

CONTD strength came from the Lord who had helped them through difficult times and would continue to do so in the months and years ahead when other tragedies would undoubtedly follow. He added that the evening had a particular poignancy as it was the last time that the Morton children would be in attendance since the family were soon to leave the district after three generations spent in Blackrigg, to take up a new tenancy in Lanarkshire. Their dear father and grandfather would always be remembered, said Rev Fraser, for giving the ultimate sacrifice of his life following the evening of the Harvest Home when evil was visited upon the community (applause).    A    programme of singing by the children followed,   accompanied   by Miss Foulkes on the piano. A number of the children gave speeches, prepared by themselves, which entertained and informed the audience on a variety of subjects. Miss Shanks sang a selection of Scotch songs. Readings from the Scriptures and the annual prizegiving took place (see page 9). Mr Ernest Black praised the children whose singing, he said, could melt even the hardest of hearts, whilst Miss Shanks's rendition of The Braes of Ballochmyle would live long in the memory. He also thanked Lady Moffat for taking time from her busy schedule to present the prizes which she also donated.

# Author's Note

The speech given by Daisy Gowans at the Sabbath School Soiree was inspired and informed by an article of the same name, 'The Romance of a Piece of Coal', that appeared in the January 1910 edition of the West Lothian Courier.

The words quoted by Neil and Elizabeth in Chapter 55 come from Wordsworth's 'Lines Composed a Few Miles above Tintern Abbey'.